T

Al

Neas fell back as w............ a second like he'd
lost his footing and both men were about to tumble out
of the truck. Ceallach angled his bike slightly, just in case
- signalling the others not to get in the way. Then Neas
straightened up, but let Osgar go at the same time. Neas
was reaching for his pistol, but even before his hand was
t the holster, he was spinning as if he'd been punched.
Ceallach inched his bike closer to see what was going on.

It was then that he saw what was sticking out of Neas. Thin
wooden shafts, with feathers at the end, embedded in his
shoulder and midriff. Neas had fallen to one side, providing
better look at who'd done this. There, rising from under
some covers, hidden amongst the sacks, was a man.

But not just any man. This one wore a hood and held a
bow in his hand – and Ceallach knew immediately who he
was. The man whose legend had spread across this entire
land over the past couple of years; the man who had
despatched that Frenchman at Nottingham Castle; who'd led
his troops into battle against the might of the Tsar's forces,
armed with only arrows and swords. Some of it was made
up – had to be! Christ, how could one man take down attack
helicopters using that kind of weaponry? To hear people
talk, you'd think he was bullet-proof or something. Rubbish.
But Ceallach felt a twinge of fear when he looked at him,
especially when he saw the man's eyes under that cowl.

THE AFTERBLIGHT CHRONICLES

An Abaddon Books™ Publication
www.abaddonbooks.com
abaddon@rebellion.co.uk

First published in 2010 by Abaddon Books™, Rebellion Intellectual Property
Limited, Riverside House, Osney Mead, Oxford, OX2 0ES, UK

10 9 8 7 6 5 4 3 2 1

Editors: Jenni Hill & Jonathan Oliver
Cover: Mark Harrison
Design: Simon Parr & Luke Preece
Marketing and PR: Keith Richardson
Creative Director and CEO: Jason Kingsley
Chief Technical Officer: Chris Kingsley
The Afterblight Chronicles™ created by Simon Spurrier & Andy Boot

US & Canada ISBN: 978-1-907519-12-3
UK ISBN: 978-1-907519-13-0

Printed in the US

THE AFTERBLIGHT CHRONICLES

ARROWLAND

PAUL KANE

Abaddon
Books

WWW.ABADDONBOOKS.COM

For Richard Carpenter, as much of an inspiration now
as he was back then.

'Then Robin Hood bent a very good bow,
    To shoot, and that he would fain;
The stranger he bent a very good bow,
    To shoot at bold Robin again.

"O hold thy hand, hold thy hand," quoth Robin Hood,
    "To shoot it would be in vain;
For if we should shoot the one at the other,
    The one of us may be slain."'

– *Robin Hood Newly Revived*
(Traditional Ballad)

CHAPTER ONE

THE FIRST SIGN they were in trouble was when a crater the size of a garden pond appeared ahead of them.

There had been very little sound until that moment – then an almighty bang which hurt the ears. This was accompanied by a rocking of the vehicles they were directing up that particular stretch of road.

Mick Jamison, in charge of the lead truck – or, as he called her, 'Stacey' – pulled on the steering wheel to avoid the smoking hole, then glanced in his mirrors to see his companions doing the same. Those using horses and carts, however, had to calm their animals first – not an easy task when none of the animals were used to loud noises. A couple reared, kicking back at the carts and riders.

Mick snatched up his radio, but it hissed static. "Jesus," he said, looking through the windscreen and spotting the tail of another mortar winding its way down to earth. This one struck the side of the road, but had just as much impact. Even with all his years of experience – before and after the nightmare known as The Cull – he struggled to control the tons of metal and cargo.

This hadn't been part of the deal. Actually, there hadn't even *been* a deal. Unlike his jobs before the virus, when he'd been employed by the large haulage companies to transport goods, there was no paperwork for this gig. Back then it had been a nice, relatively safe job – the only danger being from other, less careful drivers on the motorways. People who took chances, nipping in and out of traffic at ridiculous speeds, driving all night without taking stops when they felt tired. But in all his years in the delivery trade, Mick himself had never been in a single accident. He'd certainly never been fired upon.

These were different times.

He'd realised that when the people in his neighbourhood had started dropping in the streets, bleeding from every orifice, coughing their guts up onto the pavement. He'd realised it when he'd reached his girlfriend's house and found her–

That seemed such a long time ago now, years beginning to feel like decades.

If he'd been left in any doubt that things were different, the gangs and cults roaming the streets had soon changed that. At first only disorganised handfuls, then in greater numbers as they'd banded together for a common cause: mayhem and destruction, making the most of the lack of authority figures.

Some had even come from overseas to wreak havoc, like that insane Frenchman they'd heard about – De Falaise. In pre-virus times, he would have been locked up for doing what he did, attempting to take on the mantle of Sheriff of Nottingham. As if that hadn't been bad enough, there had been that Russian, the self-styled Tsar, a year or so later. Mick had lost friends to him and his forces when they invaded Britain, cutting a swathe through towns and villages.

Yes, he had friends – even in these bleak times. *Especially* in these times. Because just as there were those who gathered together to cause chaos, there were others intent on bringing some semblance of normality back to these shores. It was how the markets had started, how he'd become involved in them – stumbling on one particular outfit not far from Wickham. He was impressed that communities had pulled themselves together enough to produce their own food, replacing what had been taken for granted before. Impressed that they were cultivating links with their neighbours, using a barter system now that money was obsolete.

The markets and trading system had been steadily growing, so when Mick got wind of the fact that folk were also delivering these goods, picking up the traded items in the process, he offered his services – and his truck. He'd felt like a bit of a spare part all this time, on the road, hiding out in Stacey's cab and living on whatever he could find in out of the way places, scavenging whatever fuel he could from abandoned vehicles; some days even wishing he'd caught that virus along with the rest of 'em. At least now he could make himself useful, doing the only thing he'd ever really been good at. He was working for – and with – good people; helping to make a difference, perhaps even helping turn things around.

Then came reports of convoys being attacked by armed raiders. These weren't like earlier encounters, small parties chancing their arm in the hopes of coming away with a vanload of fresh beef or eggs; easily driven off by the weapons they carried to protect themselves. No, these guys were well organised and extremely well armed.

Up until now, they'd been lucky. Mick and his mates hadn't come face-to-face with them. He could fool himself into thinking it was just like old times on the open road again. If you ignored the fact that due to the scarcity of diesel, some of the transportation had to be of the old fashioned live variety.

That luck had just run out. On their way up through Corbridge, towards the Scottish border, they'd suddenly become the target of those legendary raiding parties. Mick recalled the pattern: first creating confusion from a distance, an attempt to cut off the route ahead; next cutting off radio communications, probably with some kind of jamming equipment.

Then they would attack.

And if the stories were to be believed, not many of Mick's group would survive.

Another mortar fell to the right of Mick's truck and he grappled with the wheel again, almost tipping the vehicle over – clipping the edge of this new crater but not falling into it. Some of those behind were not as fortunate, or as skilled. One truck, being driven by a guy Mick had known only a few months called Jed Elliott, tipped into the first of the holes head-on. It was now stuck there like some kind of mole burrowing into the ground. Mick thought about stopping, but saw something in his mirrors which made him press down on his accelerator instead.

Jeeps and motorcycles – quite obviously military issue from their colour – had joined the party, skidding down hillocks on either side of the road. A couple of the jeeps had no roofs; mounted on top were huge machine-guns, spitting out bullets as the raiders opened fire. They raked the road ahead of one particular cart, and the two horses pulling it broke free of their reins, running for freedom, leaving both driver and cart at the mercy of the raiders.

If they had any.

Already the lead bikes had caught up with the truck behind Mick's. Riding on the bikes were pairs of raiders, one handling the steering, the other clinging to the back. Both were dressed similarly, though: goggles over their eyes, breathing masks over their mouths, wearing thick, leather gloves and boots. Some kind of dark tartan Mick wasn't familiar with flapped in the breeze, overlaying the combats beneath. And at their hips hung what appeared to be claymores, with rounded guards over the handles.

As he watched, one bike pulled alongside the truck and its passenger fired some kind of hand-held harpoon, like he was hunting a landlocked metal whale. A length of rope unfurled with it and the next thing Mick knew, the raider had leapt from the bike and onto the truck, swinging from its side. The raider launched himself forward, until he came level with the driver's door, then grabbed hold with his free hand before letting go of the rope. Next he produced a handgun and shot out the window. The driver, a woman called Kimberly Johns, looked terrified when the glass shattered, but at least she was still alive. Mick saw her reach over and bring up the rifle she always carried in her cab, but before she could use it the raider had tossed something inside. Within seconds, the cab filled with smoke, and the truck began weaving. That explained the breathing masks. Through the smoke, Mick saw Kim's outline slump against the big wheel, and gradually the truck ground to a halt.

Again, he knew he should stop – but Mick had problems of his own. More bikes catching up, two flanking him, both carrying raiders with similar harpoons. They were going to pull the same stunt on him. "Shit!"

He sped up, but his vehicle wasn't meant for racing. They could outrun and outmanoeuvre him easily. That didn't mean he should just give up, though. There were alternatives to running, and he wasn't going to let them take Stacey without a fight.

Mick lined up one of the bikes in his mirror, making sure it was directly behind him. Then he stamped on the brakes: not enough to tip the truck, but enough to cause the bike to slam hard into the back of his trailer. With a certain amount of satisfaction, he noted the dislodged raiders sprawled across the road, their bike laying a few feet away from them.

Another two bikes joined the remaining one on his tail. Mick accelerated again, but already they were firing their harpoons – up and into the top of his trailer. At least two of them swung over. Mick heard them trying to break into the back – then their footsteps across the top of his truck, heading for his cab.

Unlike Kim, he didn't carry a gun, had never used one in his life and didn't intend to start now. But he was far from unarmed. Even back in his early days, he'd kept his trusty baseball bat – a holiday present from a cousin, now long dead – down the side of the seat. His fingers curled around the handle. Mick didn't know how much use it'd be against bullets or gas canisters, but if even one of those raider bastards stuck their head in here, they'd get one hell of a shock.

Mick flinched when he heard the gunfire, however – waiting for the bullets to pierce Stacey's cab.

Then him.

CEALLACH HELD HIS bike straight, but off to the side of the truck in front of him.

He'd seen what this driver had just done to Ròidh and Machar back there, braking so that they'd run slap bang into the truck. Ceallach glanced across at Garbhan, on the bike running parallel, and Flannagan riding his just a little behind. They'd deposited their kinsmen onto the truck: Neas and Osgar were hanging by their harpoon ropes, while his partner, Torradan, had climbed on top to see if he could take out the driver.

Neas had smashed the lock and Osgar pulled up the back of the truck, which rolled into the trailer's roof. Ceallach watched as the pair peered inside. It was a fine haul today, the back of the truck filled with sacks of potatoes, crates of cabbages, carrots, tomatoes and cucumbers. If an army marched on its stomach, then they would be going far.

Just as *she* had promised.

Towards the back of the truck were more sacks. But as Osgar swung in and approached them, he seemed to stop, cock his head, then stumble backwards. Neas, directly behind him, moved towards his companion – then was catching him as he fell.

Ceallach frowned. What the fuck was happening in there?

Neas fell back as well; it looked for a second like he'd lost his footing and both men were about to tumble out of the truck. Ceallach angled his bike slightly, just in case – signalling the others not to get in the way. Then Neas straightened up, but let Osgar go at the same time. Neas was reaching for his pistol, but even before his hand was at the holster, he was spinning as if he'd been punched. Ceallach inched his bike closer to see what was going on.

It was then that he saw what was sticking out of Neas. Thin wooden shafts, with feathers at the end, embedded in his shoulder and midriff. Neas had fallen to one side, providing a better look at who'd done this. There, rising from under some covers, hidden amongst the sacks, was a man.

But not just any man. This one wore a hood and held a bow in his hand – and Ceallach knew immediately who he was. The man whose legend had spread across this entire island over the past couple of years; the man who had dispatched that Frenchman at Nottingham Castle; who'd led his troops into battle against the might of the Tsar's forces, armed with only arrows and swords. Some of it was made up – had to be! Christ, how could one man take down attack helicopters using that kind of weaponry? To hear people talk, you'd think he was bullet-proof or something. Rubbish. Yet Ceallach felt a twinge of fear when he looked at him, especially when he saw the man's eyes under that cowl. It felt as if he should be ordering a withdrawal before it was too late.

Osgar, who had been wounded in a similar way to Neas, clambered to his feet again, clutching the parts of his body now punctured by The Hooded Man's arrows. It was a clumsy attack by an already defeated opponent, and Hood dodged it easily enough. But then he did something else, something he probably wouldn't have if Osgar had stayed down.

Hood shouldered Osgar, almost giving him a fireman's lift, then he bent slightly before throwing him out of the back of the truck. Just as his aim had been true with the arrows, so it was with this man's body, which struck Garbhan's bike full on, knocking the rider off and dragging the bike itself into Flannagan's path. Ceallach swallowed hard as he saw Flannagan hit the obstacle, the still moving bike tipping up and pitching its rider over the handlebars.

The result, which Ceallach left behind him, was a tangled mess of bodies and machinery. Hood stepped forward, standing on the edge of the truck, taking aim at the final rider and his bike.

Ceallach manoeuvred sideways, avoiding the arrow by centimetres, and drew his pistol to fire a couple of rounds. Hood took cover behind a crate, while more of Ceallach's bullets bounced off the metal of the entrance.

Another close call with an arrow convinced Ceallach to veer off, hopefully out of the Hooded Man's line of fire. Then he accelerated, gesturing wildly to Torradan, who was still on the roof.

"Inside!" shouted Ceallach, but knew the man couldn't hear him through the mask. He pointed his own gun downwards and pretended to fire, hoping Torradan would get the message. The man shook his head in bemusement. Ceallach couldn't blame him – who would have expected there to be a man with a bow and arrow in the back of the truck they were hijacking?

"Shoot!"

Torradan pointed downwards.

"Yes, for fuck's sake! Through the roof!" shouted Ceallach, knowing again his words would be lost. An arrow whipped past the side of Ceallach's head and he struggled to keep balanced. He swore, spitting the words into the mask. But at least it had the desired effect of getting through to Torradan, who now began shooting down at the roof of the truck.

"Now," whispered Ceallach, "let's see if you really are bullet-proof, Hooded Man."

* * *

ROBERT STOKES LOOKED out from the back of the truck.

The biker who'd been firing at him had skirted round the side, trying to get away from the arrows Robert was loosing in his direction. He'd keep for a moment or two, while Robert scanned the horizon, searching vehicles that they'd left behind in their wake. Looking for -

There!

The raiders who were checking the backs of trucks, of carts, were getting just as much of a shock as the two who'd broken into this one. Because there were his Rangers - trained men and women - waiting, hidden, unbeknownst even to the drivers of this convoy, and now jumping up to tackle the armed men.

At the same time, the jeeps that had accompanied the bikers were being set upon by Rangers on horseback - horses that *were* used to the noise - led by one of his best men: Azhar. They were springing their own sneak attack. Mirroring what the bikers had done, the horses were carrying Rangers, who were jumping over onto the jeeps to fight the gunners.

Satisfied his men were handling the situation, Robert risked a peek around the edge of the truck. He spied the remaining biker, making hand gestures to the raider on the roof. Confident the rider was distracted, Robert leaned around and fired off an arrow. His aim was thrown by the movement of the truck, though, and the projectile went wide. But only just.

More frantic hand gesturing followed, then the first shot through the ceiling. Robert retreated just in time to avoid it, pressing himself up against the wall as three more came in quick succession.

He primed his bow and fired upwards. There was little chance of an arrow going through that metal, especially at this range, but thanks to the idiot above him, there were now several small holes in the trailer's roof. Robert's knack with the bow and arrow had always been good, but since he'd stepped out from behind his desk back at Nottingham Castle - to fight the Tsar and The Morningstar cult - it had improved beyond measure. So it was no problem now to guide his arrows through those holes, returning the favour to the man above him.

For a second or two everything was still, and Robert thought he might have incapacitated him. That theory was shattered when more bullets raked the ceiling. Fruit and vegetables exploded in all directions, crates splintered.

He had to leave that confined space, take out the guy on the roof. Thinking quickly, he looked towards the back door. Robert grinned, then shouldered his bow and ran at the open space.

At the last moment, he grabbed one of the harpoon ropes still dangling there, attached to the roof. Robert swung out of the trailer just as another round of bullets were pumped into it. When he reached a certain height, he arched his body around, twisting so that his booted feet slammed against the top edge of the door. The rope taut, Robert pulled himself upright then onto the roof of the truck, crouching on one knee.

When the raider looked across, his jaw fell open. Robert saw that the man's combats were torn at the knee, a wound bleeding there.

A bullet whizzed past Robert, but not from the raider on the roof. His companion on the bike, riding alongside, was providing covering fire. But before Robert could do anything about that, the truck was already veering sideways, causing the raider on the bike to swerve and avoid a collision. Robert made a mental note to thank the driver of the truck when this was all over. Both Robert and the raider on the roof had staggered sideways, but Robert was the one who recovered first, leaping at his enemy before he could raise his pistol.

Robert grabbed his arm, trying to keep the gun down. A shot almost went through Robert's left foot, forcing him to step back a little. It gave the raider a chance to bring the gun up sideways, though Robert still had a firm grip on his wrist.

Robert let go with one hand and punched the man in the stomach. The raider bent, allowing Robert to wrestle the pistol from him. It clattered onto the roof and disappeared over the side.

The raider retaliated by bringing up a fist, which struck Robert's cheek and caused him to reel. Then he drew his claymore, attempting to run his opponent through – but Robert met the blow with the sword he always carried. Metal struck metal, the vibrations going up Robert's arm. The raider wasn't exactly a novice with this weapon, forcing Robert to meet a couple of crafty swipes that almost opened up his throat and belly.

Pushing the raider back, Robert suddenly had the advantage – slashing across the man's blade and kicking out at him at the same time. He was about to deal the winning blow when bullets raked the side of the truck. More heavy duty than the biker's pistol, they could only have come from one of the mounted machine-guns on the jeeps. As Robert was pitched sideways by an erratic swerve from the driver – there'd be no thanks for that one! – he saw that one of the raider jeeps had broken through his Rangers and was attacking.

Another lurch, and Robert found himself going head over heels, losing his sword in the process and slipping over the side of the truck.

He held on to the edge by his fingertips, while the raider above him rose. The man started to laugh. He held his sword aloft, then brought it down where Robert's fingers had been only seconds before. Hanging on by his left hand, Robert replaced this with the right just in time to avoid another sword swipe.

He couldn't do this indefinitely – either he'd end up with no fingers or he'd fall off the truck. Then there was the alternative of being riddled with bullets from the jeep's gun.

But there was nothing he could do. His enemy was giving no ground. Perhaps this was it, perhaps he *was* about to die.

The raider lifted his sword one last time, about to bring it down on Robert's head and cleave his hood in two; destroying both the man and the legend with a single blow.

Then there was another blast of gunfire, but not from the jeep. Not from the biker either, as the bang it made was subtly different. A sound Robert recognised immediately. There was a spark as the bullet stuck the raider's claymore, causing him to relinquish the weapon.

Simultaneously, both Robert and the raider traced the line of fire back to a woman riding a horse. She was just behind the jeep, her dark hair flowing in the wind.

"Mary," breathed Robert, still struggling to hold on to the truck.

She fired again at the raider, the barrel of her dead father's Peacekeeper still smoking from the last shot. Like Robert, she'd been a decent aim even before this past year, but had become even sharper – able to use either hand and either of the two pistols, with equal precision. The raider ducked, but in his confusion stepped too close to the edge. Quick as a flash, Robert reached up and grabbed his ankle, tipping him off balance and pitching him over.

As Robert climbed back up, he saw both the jeep and Mary swerving to avoid the felled raider as he spun over and over on the concrete below.

The gun on the jeep was swivelling in Mary's direction, the raider there fixing to take her out. But before he could do anything, Mary had urged her mount forward, pulling alongside the jeep. She jumped onto it, pistol tucked back in her belt. Robert watched proudly as she gave the gunner a right hook that looked like it would have floored a gorilla, then turned and backhanded the raider who was climbing through from the front of the jeep – so hard, his breathing mask and goggles came off. It gave her time to pull her Peacekeeper out again and 'encourage' them to surrender.

Robert smiled, but it faded fast when he saw the biker from the other side of the truck pull back so he was diagonally opposite the jeep. He had his pistol drawn and he had it trained on Mary.

Snatching up his sword, Robert ran back along the length of the trailer's roof and leapt, grabbing another harpoon rope, swinging round like a pirate in the rigging.

Directing himself at the bike, he drew back the sword and slashed at the rider. The vehicle wobbled as the man attempted to avoid the blade. As the bike straightened again, Robert was swinging back in the other direction. This time he hefted the sword like a javelin and threw it at the front wheel.

It jammed in the spokes and held the wheel fast. The rider was flung from his bike, landing awkwardly on his shoulder.

Robert was dangling from the rope, banging against the side of the truck, but he felt the vehicle slowing. The driver had obviously seen him in his side-mirrors. Mary was forcing the jeep to slow, as well. Soon both had stopped and Robert was able to let go, dropping gracefully to his feet. Finally, he peeled back his hood, revealing his features.

He looked over to see Mary kicking men off the jeep. "That's it, down you go boys." She mouthed a silent 'Are you alright?' to Robert, who nodded.

Overhead there was the sound of chopper blades. Robert looked up to see a Gazelle helicopter coming in to land between them and the Rangers cleaning up further down the road. The familiar figure of Bill hopped out, even before the blades had stopped turning, holding up a hand. He'd been monitoring the situation from above, keeping well enough back that the raiders didn't see him, but close enough to let Azhar and the cavalry know exactly when they were needed. Of course, if he'd had his way he would have brought that brute of an attack helicopter instead; the one that the Tsar's men had left behind. Robert could hear that rough Derbyshire accent in his head right now: "It'd all have been over in seconds if ye'd just let me blow 'em up." But what would that have achieved? These men were no good to anyone dead. Apart from the fact he and his Rangers weren't cold-blooded killers, Robert wanted to question them, find out for sure who'd been behind the raid. Not to mention the many others along the border and inside Scotland itself.

Robert waved back. In fact it had been Bill who'd brought them all here, drawing their attention to the attacks on the trade routes that were interfering with Bill's markets, causing people to go hungry. It smacked just a little bit too much of what De Falaise and his army had been doing in Nottingham all that time ago, reminding Robert too much of those days to simply ignore it.

As Robert watched Bill make his way towards him, carrying that beloved shotgun of his, he suddenly became aware of Mary screaming, "Look out!"

The expression on her face was pure shock, but she was looking past him, over his shoulder. Robert turned swiftly, in time to see a glimpse of the remaining raider from the back of the truck – the one he thought he'd put down – leaping with his sword raised.

As Robert was tensing to avoid the blow, the raider was dropping to his knees, claymore falling from his hand. Behind stood a man holding a baseball bat. Robert looked beyond him to see the cab door of the truck was open.

"That's for what you lot have done to Stacey," said the driver, hitting the raider again just to make sure he stayed down.

Robert nodded a thanks to the man.

There was an engine gunning off to his right. *God, what now?* He looked over to see that the raider who'd been trailing them all this time, who he'd forced off his bike, had got the thing going again. The guy looked half dead, practically slumping over the handlebars, but was able to get the bike upright, gun it, and get it going in spite of the damaged front wheel.

Bill, who had caught up to them, was bringing his cannon of a gun to bear. Robert motioned for him to lower the weapon.

"But he's getting away," complained Bill.

"Let him." Robert's eyes trailed the lone and injured biker as he made his way up the road, attempting to mount the verge. "We need someone to go back and tell whoever's running the show. Tell them what happened here. Tell them they can't get away with what they're doing anymore."

Bill shook his head. Shoot first and ask questions later, that was his philosophy. The amount of arguments they still had about the use of modern weapons... Robert went over and retrieved his sword from where the biker had left it, after plucking it from the wheel. This was the weaponry of the 'future', he'd tried to get Bill to see that. Someday, all the bullets and missiles would run out and this is what they'd be left with: swords, bows, arrows. Robert and his Rangers were just getting a head start.

You only had to look at this convoy to see the way things were going: horses and carts mixed in with the trucks. Of course, not everyone wanted to accept that.

"Bill? Was this your idea?" asked the driver of the truck, slapping the baseball bat into the palm of his hand.

"Aye, Mick," he admitted. "Had to draw them bastards out some way."

"So we were bait?"

Bill looked down for a moment, then back up. "I was keeping an eye on things, making sure ye were all safe."

"You call *that* safe?" Mick pointed down the road at the truck that had ended up in the crater, the Rangers digging its driver out "Explosions were going off all over the place!"

"Look," said Robert, cutting in. "Those raiders would have attacked anyway, whether we were here or not."

"That's right." Mary had joined in now, Peacekeeper still trained on her captives. "You'd probably all be dead right now if it wasn't for us, so maybe a little more gratitude would be nice."

Robert suppressed a grin. When his wife had the bit between her teeth, there was no stopping her. It was one of the many reasons he loved her so much.

The driver, Mick, thought about this for a moment. "I suppose when you put it like that... You still could have warned us you suspected an ambush today. And that bloody Rangers were hiding in our cargo."

"We needed you all to act as naturally as possible," Robert explained.

"Running scared, you mean?"

"To keep them lot on the back foot," Bill told him.

Before the discussion could go any further, Azhar joined them to report – or rather to whisper his report to Bill. The dark-skinned young man didn't say much, and when he did it wasn't to an audience. "Ta, lad."

Robert inclined his head, waiting for the information to be relayed.

"He says the raiders are rounded up – didn't put up much o' a fight. Weren't expectin' this kind of resistance."

"Excellent," said Robert. "And do we have confirmation about who runs their operation? Is it the person we suspected?"

Bill said nothing.

"Then let's find out, shall we?" Mary said. She pushed the barrel of her Peacekeeper into the face of the closest raider, tearing the goggles and breathing mask off. "Who do you work for? C'mon, talk."

The man shook his head. Mary smiled, then grabbed his privates with her free hand, squeezing. "Now, if I don't get a name, I'll just keep twisting until they come off. Understand?"

The raider nodded vigorously.

"So?"

"T-the Widow." the raider gasped. Mary let go and the man breathed a sigh of relief.

"I knew it," said Robert.

"Widow?" asked Mick.

"Someone we'd heard rumours about, but couldn't confirm the existence of until now," Robert said. "She's been gathering troops in Scotland, and by all accounts generally making a nuisance of herself with the local population. That tartan they're wearing must be her personal calling card."

"Seems like it's time the Rangers looked into this Widow character more closely." Mary said.

"Agreed, especially if we're to cultivate better links with the Scottish people, and recruit more local Rangers to help police those territories."

It was something they were already experimenting with in places like Wales, and even down South. Robert realised he was running the risk of being seen as just as much of a dictator as the men he'd fought against in the past, but that was so far from the truth it was funny. All he wanted was to extend the protection he was offering people in and around Nottingham outwards, across the land. He envisaged local Ranger stations being run by locals. It was the only way to stop people like this Widow from rising to power. And it was the only way to keep invading forces out. If they saw a more unified territory that could fight back, they'd definitely think twice before coming here.

It wasn't going to be easy, Robert understood that as well, but then it hadn't been easy getting the Rangers off the ground in the first place. Hadn't been easy rebuilding what they'd lost when the Tsar had almost brought them to their knees over a year ago. But then what worthwhile thing was ever easy?

Robert noticed Bill was frowning, rubbing his chin. "What is it?"

"Hmmm." He was looking at the jeep next to them, then at the bikes that had fallen by the wayside during the attack. Bill bent and picked up one of the raider's pistols.

"Bill?" prompted Robert.

"AGF Serval jeeps, Motorrad motorcycles, Heckler & Koch P8 handguns. And can I see a few MP7 rifles, tucked away in the jeep there?"

"So?" Robert was tempted to add how scary it was that Bill could recognise that kind of weaponry and equipment now; his interest in military aviation having extended further over the past couple of years.

"*So*," said Bill, "they're all German issue, Rob. Don't that strike ye as a bit odd?"

Robert considered Bill's words for a moment. Was this kind of equipment freely available over here? He didn't have a clue. But yes, it did seem strange that it should *all* be German. He didn't know what that meant just yet, or what connection it had with the Widow's people, but he intended to find out.

And where to begin was with the prisoners they'd bagged today. Like Mary, the Rangers had them all by the balls.

They'd just twist until someone started talking.

Germany, thought Robert, as he began to give the orders to round up the Widow's men.

Germany.

CHAPTER TWO

IT HAD WAITED a long time to become the rightful seat of power once more.

Constructed to house the parliament of the German Empire, the Reichstag Building was formerly opened in the late nineteenth century. It existed solely for that purpose until 1933, when a fire – supposedly part of a Communist plot, though some suspect otherwise – ravaged the place. This paved the way for new masters to seize control. After the Second World War, the parliament of the Federal Republic of Germany – or West Germany – decided to meet in the Bundeshaus in Bonn, but it wasn't long before the Reichstag Building was made safe again and partially refurbished in the 1960s.

It would take the reunification of this country, though, before the building was itself fully renovated, at last becoming the meeting place of the modern German parliament, the Bundestag. Then the virus struck.

The parliament itself had been just as helpless as the rest of the world's politicians. Nations blamed other nations back then, arguments raging while the clever few got themselves to safety and hid away. No-one really knew what happened to them, but they'd never been seen again. By the time any kind of plan had been agreed on, it was too late. The virus was killing anyone who didn't have O-Negative blood, and what few safeguards were put in place to try and halt the infection rate proved ineffectual.

Inevitably, the survivors ran amok. Months, years of anarchy followed – of gangs on the streets of all sizes and allegiances, from the small youth groups to the much larger and more organised army-sized variety. Several attempts were made to take over the entire country, of course: those with lofty ideas looking to Russia for their inspiration, and tales of an all-powerful Tsar – now rumoured to be dead, but quickly replaced to prevent a crumbling of the system.

There had even been an attempt by a Frenchman called De Falaise, who had, in the end, travelled to England to try his hand there – with just as much success.

Failed; every one of them.

Until he came along.

Loewe patted back his slicked-down hair, taking in the scene from one of the levels of the huge glass dome that sat atop the Reichstag Building. He'd had any cracked glass replaced a long time ago, so it wouldn't spoil his enjoyment of the 360 degree view of Berlin. Or his enjoyment in watching the troops that he'd amassed outside, along with the many tanks, jeeps, Tiger and NHI NH90 helicopters, Tornado fighter planes, Skorpion minelayers and so on. Not a bad little defensive force from which to move outwards – and upwards.

Not bad, especially for a monumental conman like him.

Loewe began his walk back to the command centre he'd established. "With me!" he snapped, and the two magnificent Alsatians that went everywhere with him dutifully came to heel and trotted alongside. As he walked, Loewe came across various members of his staff, soldiers and military brains alike, nodding to each in turn. All wore the muted grey uniform of his legion, The Army of the New Order: its emblem a variation of the Mursunsydän symbol, using overlapping squares to form a very familiar shape.

God, not even he'd thought he could pull this trick off,

managing to convince those few who still believed in the old doctrines that he was the guiding light of a new force – one which looked simultaneously to the past and the future – when in actuality he didn't give a shit about their dogma. He wasn't a Neo Nazi and never would be. But that didn't mean he couldn't *use* them to get what he wanted. After all, hadn't his whole life been a tissue of lies and deception?

From an early age he'd discovered that you could get more by hiding things than coming right out with the truth.

("Was that you who trailed that mud into the house, Achim?" "No Mütti, I swear. It was the dog." His mother thrashed that animal to within an inch of its life, while it looked at him accusingly.)

In his teens Loewe found that the more he lied, the more women would fall at his feet. He dumped them when he'd had his fun, usually after he'd taken them for their money. That fun soon ended when he was drafted into the armed forces, though he'd pulled a fast one to make sure he was given light duties; the doctor at his medical taken in by his protestations about his bad back. He had to admit he'd learnt a lot during his time in the military, however, like where the real money was. When he eventually left – without permission, naturally – he took a stash of weapons with him and sold them all on the black market. It was enough to fund his escape from Germany, and further operations in Belgium, Switzerland, Hungary and various other countries. His reputation, under an assumed name, as an international thief spread throughout the criminal underworld.

He'd stumbled into the world of terrorism quite by accident, after getting involved with a woman called Letty who had introduced him to the other members of her cell: fighters against the injustices of the world.

"So what do *you* believe in?" he was asked, and he'd told them exactly what they wanted to hear. There was money to be made here, he could smell it. To prove himself, Loewe had to plant a device in the lobby of a certain office building with links to slave labour in the third world. He'd tried to convince them to blackmail the company, but they'd gone ahead and detonated the bomb instead. What a waste. Not of human life, but of an opportunity. And he really hated that.

Once he'd ingratiated himself with the people really pulling the strings, and had got bored with Letty in the bedroom, Loewe planted another device which took out the cell. Then he convinced the organisation that expansion was the key to taking over the entire world, and to do that they'd need money. "For the cause, you understand," Loewe insisted – embarking on his schemes to blackmail other businesses, banks; even holding entire towns and cities to ransom. Sometimes he was paid, other times he wasn't and so had to follow through, or the next time he'd have no leverage. It didn't bother him.

Loewe amassed a small fortune in that time. He would have lived comfortably off the profits of his extortion for the rest of his life had it not been for the small matter of that damned disease. What use was money then? You couldn't buy yourself out of a bullet in the head, not when the monetary system had collapsed. He didn't even count himself lucky that he was immune, just cursed whatever gods were up there for taking away his luxuries.

Once again, he'd had to think fast, and talk even faster. Because he knew the place better than anywhere else, Loewe had returned home. And it was as he observed the situation there that a plan formed in his mind. It was obvious – and should have been all along – who the most organised groups belonged to in his country. They'd been biding their time, waiting for something like this to occur. But they'd also been waiting for a leader to emerge, someone to bring them all together under one flag, and finally under one roof. Someone like General Loewe, military hero – just check his (forged) records – and bringer of terror to the Motherland's enemies.

He told his faithful followers, who'd soaked up his fake promises like sponges, that they should take up residence in the place that once helped Hitler rise to power. It had waited, just as they had, to be put to use again. Not as the home of a democratic parliament, but as *their* home, *their* headquarters from which to plan their next move. Indeed, hadn't Hitler promised there would be a special place for the building in his Welthauptstadt Germania renovation of Berlin after his 'assured' victory in World War II: a key structure in his vision of a World Capital, a reward for services rendered? Now they would make good on that promise.

His growing legions had lapped it up, helping him to take the place from those who were already in residence – hopelessly outmatched amateurs playing at being soldiers. The skirmish had lasted less than five hours.

Now his forces owned not only the building, but most of Berlin. And he was working on the rest of Germany; already they had stretched into Hamburg, Magdeburg, Leipzig and Dresden. He might not be as big as the Tsar yet, but it was a start. As with the terrorism, it was all about expansion, which kept not only his troops occupied but also ensured a comfortable standard of living for him. It might not be about money anymore, but he had people at his beck and call. What's more, he was safe in a world where that word no longer had much meaning for most people. Loewe knew that any number of his men would willingly give their lives for him; were already doing so out there.

He descended the levels with his dogs, hands behind his back, heading towards the main control centre. Striding inside, he noted the maps on walls with dots on them, the table with a miniature landscape built on top: models of tanks, jeeps and soldiers covering it – everything Loewe imagined a command centre *should* look like, in fact. He, of all people, knew how important it was to look the part. Men in uniform were busying themselves, some on radios, others looking at the charts and discussing how their plans to take over the country and beyond were going. Because they weren't a force the size of Russia's, they couldn't just invade a country outright. No, they had to play things a bit more subtly. At the moment his Army of the New Order had its fingers in a lot of pies, covert agents in every country you could think of. But Loewe wasn't doing this simply to take over the world; rather to take out any other opposition before they came looking for *him*. It was all about security again. He'd made himself a target over here, and it was only a matter of time before the Tsar or another warlord came to challenge him. The only thing that had put them off so far was that Loewe talked a good battle, spreading rumours that they were much better armed and equipped then they actually were. That and the fact they were committed fanatics. Nobody would be stupid enough to go after the Nazis unless they absolutely had to, or were completely assured of a victory.

The men all stood to attention when they saw him, but he told them to be at ease. He walked through the area, pretending to be interested, peering at a few maps and nodding. Really, he just wanted to get to his office which was on the other side. It amused him when the men parted to let his dogs through, standing well back so that they wouldn't even brush against the dangerous-looking creatures.

Loewe's spacious office had been furnished to his specifications – lined on one side with books he would never read, while on the other was a well stocked bar. A huge oak table had been positioned near the window, with a reclining leather chair behind and an antique globe of the world not far away, which he would spin whenever he got bored. He had been inside only a few minutes, having just had time to sit down – the dogs taking up positions on either side of the desk – when there was a knock at the door. Loewe spread out papers in front of him and picked one up to study it, before shouting, "Enter!"

It was his Second, young Schaefer, who dealt with the day-to-day running of their New Order. Behind those eyes, shielded by thick-rimmed glasses, was a frighteningly large intellectual capacity. Loewe was more than happy to let the man deal with organisational matters and supervise military operations, just as long as he was kept in the loop every step of the way. Which was what Schaefer was doing here now.

"I was just about to send for you," Loewe lied. "I wanted an update on the situation in–"

"Sir, I come with grave news about–"

"Schaefer!" screamed Loewe, sitting bolt upright in his chair. He may only have been pretending to be their leader – and wasn't really interested in an update on *anything* at the moment – but if there was one thing Loewe couldn't stand it was being interrupted. "Never speak before I have finished, is that understood?"

Schaefer remained silent, until he realised Loewe was waiting for him to give his answer. "Yes, of course, sir. But I bring bad news about one of the campaigns in England."

Loewe raised an eyebrow. *England*: one of their oldest enemies. Well, not Loewe's specifically; he didn't give a shit about the country either way. Nevertheless, his men felt especially passionate about taking control of that isle, which was why they didn't complain – not that they dared anyway – about his use of so many resources over there, when they still had much of Germany to secure. This *was* potentially serious.

"*You* bring bad news?" asked Loewe.

"Er, actually..." Schaefer dragged in a second man, this one not familiar to Loewe. After a while all the uniformed people blurred into one. "Mayer here was the messenger who brought the news." Schafer pushed the other man into the room, closing the door behind them. "Tell the General what you told me," he ordered.

"Sir, I..."

Loewe rose, and his dogs raised their heads. "What is it man? Spit it out, for God's sake!"

Mayer was looking nervously from Loewe to the Alsatians.

"I said *spit it out!*" Loewe snapped. The dogs began to growl.

"I-It's about the Widow's venture."

"The venture we have been *funding*, sir," clarified Schaefer, adjusting his glasses. That word took on a different meaning in this day and age, to the one Loewe had been used to at any rate, but it amounted to the same thing. They'd been supplying the woman with vehicles and equipment in order to cause the maximum amount of trouble. Something had obviously gone very wrong, though, by the look of Mayer. *He's practically shitting himself*, thought Loewe.

"The venture *you* convinced us to fund, Schaefer," Loewe reminded him, then addressed Mayer again. "Go on."

"T-there was an attack yesterday," Mayer informed him.

"The Widow lost a number of men," Schaefer added, "but also, regrettably, several jeeps and motorcycles, not to mention guns, ammunition–"

"*Our* jeeps, motorcycles, guns and ammunition," Loewe reminded him. "Who was responsible for this attack?"

Schaefer prodded Mayer in the back to get him to answer. "Hood," said the man, his voice breaking. "It was Hood, sir."

Hood. Yes, Loewe had heard the tales just like everyone else, about a man who dressed like that famous legend and fought using a bow and arrow. Loewe almost had to admire that conman's audacity; it would be like him donning a toothbrush moustache and insisting they all called him The Führer. But that man had also, it was said, depleted The Tsar's forces – another reason why they hadn't attacked the New Order yet. In any event, if this Hood character was tackling the Widow then reports were correct and he was doing just as they were, spreading out across his own country. It was a dangerous thing, because it meant that at some point their paths would cross. Someone like Hood, who had managed to convince his followers he was on some kind of damned crusade against evil might get the bright idea of coming after them in Germany.

"How did it happen?" Loewe asked through gritted teeth.

"He and his Rangers were lying in wait, hidden in a convoy the Widow's men were raiding."

Loewe slammed his fist down on the desk. It hurt and made him madder than ever. "The silly bitch! We give her all those weapons and she loses them to a bunch of fucking comic book characters." He walked round the front of the desk and his dogs rose again. Loewe tapped his lips for a moment, trying to look thoughtful. He already knew what had to be done. Picking up a large silver letter opener that had been resting on the wood, he touched the tip, testing its sharpness. "Mayer, have you ever heard the saying about messengers who bring bad news?"

"Please sir." Mayer held up his shaking hands.

"You're a member of the Army of the New Order, man! For Heaven's sake act like it!"

Mayer attempted to show a little backbone, but there was still a quiver in his voice when he said, "It wasn't my fault. I was not even there, sir. Please don't–"

"Don't what?"

Mayer looked at Schaefer, then back again at Loewe. "Don't kill me."

Loewe laughed; it was all part of the act. "Oh, I'm not going to kill you. Why would I do that when I wish you to deliver a message to the Widow?"

Mayer let out a relieved breath.

"However, I would like the message to be of a very specific nature. Do you think you can manage that?"

Mayer nodded, almost smiling.

"Good." He clicked his fingers. The Alsatians bared their teeth, and Mayer's eyes widened.

"But you said–"

"I said *I'm* not going to kill you. And I'm not," replied Loewe. He snapped his fingers a second time and the dogs were across the room in seconds, leaping at Mayer. The first jumped up on its back legs, slamming Mayer in the chest with its paws and causing him to stumble backwards. The second took hold of his arm, clamping its teeth around the wrist and shaking it violently. Mayer's scream was loud and piercing.

Loewe watched Schaefer's reaction; it was largely for his benefit that he was doing this. There was no real reason to set the dogs on Mayer. The man was right, it wasn't his fault. If anything, it was Schaefer's, but Loewe needed him. Sadly, for Mayer, if Loewe was to play the part of their General without drawing any kind of suspicion, he had to make it look convincing. Failure should not be tolerated by someone in his position. His men expected this kind of behaviour, so that's what he gave them. Schaefer would be his witness and word would travel fast through the ranks.

The tearing sounds drew Loewe's attention back to Mayer, who had managed to turn but was on his knees. To his credit, and quite the opposite of what Loewe had expected, he was showing signs of being a *true* fighter. This soldier was someone who actually deserved to be in the New Order. Loewe couldn't believe what he was thinking; *he* didn't even believe in the fucking New Order himself! But this was starting to be quite entertaining, and would relieve some of the boredom for a little while.

Schaefer, pulling a face, stepped out of the way as Mayer – now with both dogs attached to him – crawled towards the door. His hand was shaking for an entirely different reason now, as it reached for the handle, then managed to turn it. In a last ditch effort to be free, Mayer flung it open then collapsed in the doorway – both dogs biting and clawing at his body; one ripping off an ear and eating it as blood poured from the wound.

This was good – now there would be more witnesses. As Mayer's screams faded, some of the soldiers from the room beyond came to see what was happening. They gaped at the Alsatians savaging the man's prone body, then up through the open doorway at Loewe.

"I trust you will see that the Widow is sent the remains," he said to Schaefer, loud enough for those watching to hear as well.

Schaefer nodded.

"This Hood problem: I think we need to look into it further," he told his Second.

Another nod.

"I would hate for it to interfere with some of the other projects we're involved with over there," Loewe continued, and almost added 'projects you also initiated, Schaefer', but felt his point had been made. "Perhaps we need to find someone to deal with him." He knew Schaefer understood what he meant and would leave him to it, the example of Mayer spurring him on to succeed. But if he failed would Loewe be able to go through with the punishment, as he'd done when blackmailing his targets back in his 'terrorist' days? He needed Schaefer too much. Maybe another pawn could be sacrificed to keep up the pretence. After all, Schaefer was too damned clever to put himself directly in the firing line: he'd always have a fall guy standing by.

Loewe clicked his fingers and the dogs returned to him immediately, Schaefer mirroring the men from the command centre, standing well out of their way. The dogs' mouths were covered in gore as they took their places flanking Loewe. He gestured for Schaefer to clear the corpse away, then shut the door.

Loewe returned to his seat, tossing down the letter opener and adjusting the position of the chair. As he lay back he thought again of Hood and what he'd done, and hoped the man could be stopped before he really did become a threat.

THE PLANE REMAINED high, circling the area like a carrion crow.

When it finally descended, the small craft came in fast and low, making good use of the fading April light. Like its pilot, it was more at home in the shadows than the glare of daylight.

He'd managed to find a patch of grassland some distance from his chosen goal, near to a place called Creswell Crags. Skilfully, he manipulated the sombrely-painted Cessna into position for a landing. He hardly felt the ground as the wheels touched down and carried him quickly under the trees. The man opened up his door and climbed out, bringing his bow and arrows with him.

The dark material of his stitched clothes and his long black hair, tied back in a ponytail, made him resemble that which he loved so much; his weathered skin completing the picture. It was the reason he had taken that name, the one he went by these days.

Shadow.

He began to camouflage his transportation, bending thin branches and layering foliage over the wings and main body of the plane. Before leaving her, he patted her cooling side. She had served him well during his long trip, admittedly punctuated by stops to replenish her fuel. Fuel supplied by those who'd employed him.

Shadow made his way stealthily through the Crags themselves. When he broke into the rundown visitor centre there, to search for a local map of the area, he noted that one of the caves not far away was named after his quarry – the original version at any rate. According to books he found, under all the cobwebs – ones that hadn't been destroyed by vandals – it had been called this because it was rumoured to have been used as one of his storage holes. But thousands of years before that, it had been used by hunters just like Shadow's own ancestors. There was evidence of stone weapons and tools fashioned from animal teeth.

He dug out a map that showed him his destination was within walking distance. So, quiver on his back, along with a handmade rucksack – knife and hawk axe already at his hip – he set off for the place where his 'mark' had once made his home. Nowadays, of course, the man spent most of his time in the city.

Shadow knew a great many things about him, simply from communing with higher forces, listening to his spirit guides. Even before he had set off, visions had revealed much about the Hooded Man and his forest. Prepared him for the task ahead.

Shadow contemplated the events that had led him here, the bargain he had struck. It had been necessary, like most things in his life. Part of him respected the hunter this Hood was. In another time, another world, they might even have been blood brothers. But, here and now, fate had forced them to cross paths as opposite numbers: Hood the person he must 'deal with' – isn't that how they'd put it? – in order to receive his reward.

Did he feel any guilt? Some, perhaps. Though they looked alike, it was not Hood's people who had murdered his brethren, taken their land and left them a minority in their country. Or was it? Hadn't it been that man's own ancestors who'd crossed the ocean and begun to colonise, begun the war that had lasted so long? His blood was their blood, wasn't it? So how could they *ever* be brothers? Though the natives of this country were worlds apart from those across the Atlantic, they were still cousins. They still had the same ways.

Shadow knew that many of his kind had banded together, forming a United Tribal Nation in order to take back what was theirs from the white man. They judged these post-virus times to be the perfect catalyst; thought the Great Spirit had granted them this opportunity. Shadow had always gone his own way, though, and used his own methods. He felt certain that they would achieve better results than the entire UTN affair.

It was why he was on his way to Sherwood, running at a pace that would see him reach the outskirts within the hour. Even though Hood appeared to have turned his back on it for now, in favour of building his army to police this land, the forest was still his seat of power – and it had waited so long for the rightful heir to come along.

Now Shadow intended to take that power away from the Hooded Man.

It was the only way to defeat him.

It was the only way to win.

HE COULDN'T SLEEP.

The aching in what had once been his hand was keeping him awake again. Not that he slept soundly anyway; the nightmares of the battlefield saw to that. Bohuslav understood it wasn't possible for the hand itself to be aching, because it wasn't there anymore. He understood it was just the nerve endings from the stump of a wrist, extending out into nothingness – perhaps even missing the lost appendage? Was that it; was the wrist, like him, still in mourning? None of which stopped it feeling real. He felt the pain, just as surely as he felt hatred for those who had done this to him.

He was grateful for the fact that the weather was starting to turn slightly warmer. Slightly, as you could never *truly* call it warm during these months. The 'hand' ached more than ever in wintertime, and the winters in Russia were invariably brutal.

Bohuslav pushed himself up on the enormous bed. One of the benefits of his position was occupancy of the Presidential Suite of the Marriott Grand; the only occupied room in the whole hotel. Back before the virus, he would have had the full five star experience. Even today there was a team of staff dedicated to giving him everything he could possibly desire. That included bringing him certain luxuries he craved. Certain 'items': living items. Male or female, it didn't matter which. Not for sex, or anything like that. Bohuslav's desires ran much deeper. It was a way of taking him back to the days before all this, when he would hunt his prey on the streets.

At first they'd just brought them to him, knocking on the door and leaving the meat standing there quivering. Where was the sport in that? He'd soon grown bored when there was no chase, no excitement. Then he'd struck upon the notion of letting them loose in the hotel. If they could escape him, they went free. If not...

None had ever escaped.

He closed his eyes and could imagine the weight of his sickle – once handheld but which now had to be attached to his stump – as it slashed and gutted. A smile played across his face. The memories of all that bloodshed, before – when he had been one of the most wanted serial killers in this country – and after the virus, came back to him all at once. It made him want to grab the sickle right now and slide it in place. Go out hunting and–

Bohuslav sighed. He should really try and rest, because he had responsibilities beyond the ending of individual lives at his... hand. Inherited responsibilities from the man who had once been Tsar, who now rotted away in a distant land – killed by Hood.

It was no use. Bohuslav flicked on his bedside light, powered – like so many things these days – by generator. He padded across the room, yawning. When he reached the door that would take him into the spacious living area, he paused, remembering a meeting here more than a year ago.

Remembering that large, olive-skinned bastard who'd got them into all this, persuading The Tsar to mount an offensive against Robert Stokes. Tanek. The name brought bile to his throat. If De Falaise's former Second had never come here, things would have continued as they were. They would still be at full capacity with their troops and armament – instead of building forces back up again – and would now be thinking about a strategy of moving against other, more important enemies. It was what other countries were now doing, Germany included, from what Bohuslav was hearing.

Hood may have dealt the blow, but Tanek brought them all together. And, while it was true being the new Tsar of Russia did have its benefits, Bohuslav would still prefer to have been more behind the scenes.

Pulling on a robe, he walked over to the bar and poured himself a generous measure of Smirnoff; he preferred this to drugs when his stump was aching. By the second glass, the pain had dulled considerably.

Even after the alcohol, he heard, and felt, the person outside his room before they knocked. The sickle attachment was back in the bedroom, but Bohuslav never answered a door unarmed, even if there were guards out in the hall. He settled for a nearby ice-pick, concealing this behind his back as he looked through the spyhole.

It was a member of his staff called Klopov, but still Bohuslav kept the pick hidden as he opened the door.

Klopov smiled inanely as the new Tsar bid him enter. *It was obviously good news*, thought Bohuslav. If it wasn't, the man might have been more reticent. Bad news ran the risk of enraging him. And very bad news meant the same for the messenger. It was how any military dictator would act.

"Sorry to call at such a late hour," Klopov said.

"Yes, yes," said Bohuslav. "What is it?"

For a second an image of stalking Klopov through the corridors of this hotel flashed through Bohuslav's mind, the pulse at the man's neck exciting him. *No, concentrate. Listen to what he has to say.*

"I thought you'd like to know that he's there."

"Who is where, exactly?"

"The arrow," replied Klopov, then added for good measure.

"The arrow has landed, sir."

Now it was Bohuslav's turn to smile. The first part of his plan had been put into effect. The Native American was on British shores. "Excellent!" If all went well, he would soon be celebrating his revenge, or at least part of it. There would be more to come eventually.

It would be *so* perfect. Bohuslav looked down at his stump for the millionth time since he lost that hand fighting Hood and his men. "Would you care for a drink, Klopov?" He nodded towards the bar.

Klopov smiled again, then nodded.

Bohuslav was happy now, and ordinarily that meant he would leave the messenger be. It had indeed been good news; the *best* news in fact. But as Klopov moved towards the bar, once again the new Tsar's mind was filled with things he'd like to do to him. The way he might wish to celebrate.

The blood. The flesh. The ineffectual pleading of the victim.

Bohuslav smiled and followed him, pick still behind his back, having yet to decide whether the messenger would leave this room alive.

CHAPTER THREE

FROM THE OUTSIDE, it was a spectacular sight.

From the inside, it was even more impressive. Opened in 1999, this stadium marked the end of one millennium and the beginning of another. A fresh new start for everyone, but nobody could have guessed just how radical that new beginning would be.

He'd come here often once upon a time to watch the matches; brought by his Dad – though only after his eldest son, Gareth, had died from leukaemia. It was home to their national rugby union team, after all. He remembered their matches in the Six Nations, mainly their victories – the crowd going wild, that tribal thing of territory against territory. Mimicking his father, he'd cheer on their team. "It's all about that," his Dad repeatedly told him, pointing to the national flags some supporters were waving. Then he'd chorus with the crowd nearest to him: "We are dragons! We are dragons!" He was a poor substitute for Gareth, however, who'd always been Dad's favourite. Still was, to this day.

When they lost Gareth, his Mam and Nan turned all their attention on him, as if they might lose that boy too at any moment. They'd feed him up, putting massive meals in front of him, including cooked breakfasts, sausages and mash or fish and chips for dinners, and all kinds of treats in-between. All while his Dad looked on, the obvious disappointment in his one remaining offspring apparent. It wasn't even as if he had any skills, like Gareth's knack of fixing things. Gareth had been training to be a joiner when he became sick; would have made a good one, as well. Not only that, Gareth also excelled at several subjects in school, especially Maths and History. While he, the younger brother, excelled at nothing, failing all his exams and claiming dole when he left school early. "Nobody'll ever take him on, you know," he'd overheard his father say once to their mother. Straight away, she defended her little darling. "He's just a late bloomer, that's all. One day that boy will show everyone, Ryn, just you see if he doesn't."

He'd been a lot slimmer back then. Obviously, at eighteen stone, nobody could accuse him of being svelte, but compared to now... Actually, he'd lost a bit of weight during The Cull. Thankfully, it hadn't ended like Gareth. They all pulled through. However, they'd also had to evade the men in yellow suits when they came to torch the infected houses and streets. It didn't seem to matter to those bastards whether people were alive or dead!

His family had turned to him, because he'd shown no signs of getting ill at all. Bizarrely, he'd ended up the strongest of the lot. Sure, he was scared to go out, but his Mam and Nan had looked after him all those years, fed him and kept him safe – it was the least he could do in return. So, onto the streets, bringing back what food he could find, as well as other supplies. His Dad accepted the help with notably bad grace, grudgingly accepting the mantle of Alpha male had passed to his youngest. All his life, he'd wanted to make his father proud, wanted to be half the man he was. But now the burly ex-miner had been reduced to this, and was having to rely on him. There was a certain irony to that.

His Mam worried, of course, and she was right to; it was dangerous out there. But he was lucky for a while, managed to get away with foraging. Until that day at the supermarket on the outskirts of the city: one he hadn't hit yet – this was back when there were actually stocks left of food and other essentials. He'd made sure there was no-one inside before entering, actually watched it for several hours before venturing into the storeroom. Halfway through his labours, he'd been interrupted by a gang of youths wielding various makeshift weapons.

"Hey, Porko, if we let you take all that, there'll be nothing left for the rest of us," the leader – a tattooed guy who spat when he talked – had said, making a snorting noise. Whether this was just his normal breathing or he was doing an impression of a pig, there was no way of telling.

"The rest of *the country*," added the pasty-faced girl by his side, sniggering.

"Or the world," another member of the gang chipped in, carrying on the joke even though it wasn't that funny to begin with.

He'd clutched the plastic bags to his chest, the tins inside rattling. "It's for me Mam and me Nan," he'd told them, only adding afterwards, "and me sick Dad."

"Jesus, there are *more* like you?" said the leader, spittle flying from his lips. "Are they *all* your size?"

He shook his head. No, he was the only one prone to putting on weight. And, especially now, the rest of the family were considerably thinner. Hardly surprising when they'd had to share what resources he could scrounge up.

"I bet it's not," said the only other girl, this one dressed in a leather jacket which she'd attempted to do up over her ample chest. In fact she was ample all round, so wasn't really in a position to criticise. It didn't stop her, though. "I bet he's gonna eat it all himself."

He shook his head, but the other members of the gang just laughed. "You're right," said the lad who'd originally made the joke. "He's goin' to scoff the fucking lot."

"No he bloody well isn't," the tattooed leader announced. Then the gang members fanned out. He'd backed up a few paces, but suddenly hit a wall. The gang encircled him, trapping him. He felt like crying, but knew that would do no good. Neither would shouting out for his Mam, nor his Dad – even if they had been nearby, the man couldn't fend off a flea.

"Come on, Porko, show us what you've got," said the boss, holding up a meat cleaver. And as they moved in, he flashed back to all the bullies at school who'd ever called him Porky, or Chubster or Wide Load. Flashed back to his Dad at those rugby matches, to what he was trying to tell his wimp of a second son.

"We are dragons," he whispered. "*I* am a dragon."

"What?" asked the pasty-faced girl, but it was already too late.

Before he realised what he was doing, he'd grabbed the tattooed thug, evading the cleaver blow by inches, and swung his attacker into the wall. The youth's shoulder cracked loudly and he let out a cry. Turning to the joker, he butted him with his stomach, sending the youth backwards into a pile of boxes. The rest of the gang he took down in no time at all. It was as if a switch had been flipped. He even began to enjoy the violence, taking years of abuse out on them. A golf club struck him on the hip but he barely even felt it, pulling his enemy in, throwing him to the floor and then stamping hard on the lad's pelvis.

Looking around, breathing hard, he found there was nobody left but the two girls. The larger one fancied her chances and, it had to be said, she was probably more of a match for him than all the men put together. She tried to kick him in the crotch, but he sidestepped her, then punched her in the face. Bits of cartilage exploded across her cheeks, blood splattering over his own face. The girl sank to her knees and he brought down his fist again, this time hitting her on the top of the head with the base of his fist. There was another crack as the weight of the blow cracked her skull, and she toppled sideways.

The pasty-faced girl stared in disbelief, not able to move as he approached. Christ alone knew what he must have looked like with all that blood covering him. When he reached her, she suddenly decided to escape. Quickly, his hand was out, clamping around her arm.

"Let go! Let me–"

"Shhh," he told her, pressing a finger to her lips. If the other members of the gang had represented all the bullies who'd ever called him names, then this girl, her flesh quivering beneath his touch, represented all those who'd ever spurned him romantically . The Kaiyas and Denises and Aimees and Brennas from his class, who he'd fantasised about but looked at him like he was the scum of the earth; at the same time draping themselves over the boys with model good looks. Well, he'd show them all now, wouldn't he?

The things he made that girl do, before snapping her neck... It was a sort of catharsis.

He eventually picked up the bags and walked back through the streets to his family, not caring now if anyone saw him. In fact a few people did spot him, but didn't come anywhere near. Perhaps it was his appearance, perhaps it was just his demeanour. When he arrived home, his Mam and Nan looked at him funny, but didn't ask about the blood. They were probably afraid to.

"Where have you been?" asked his Dad, then shut up promptly when his son glared at him. He could see it, the fact that he was a dragon. Maybe even *the* Dragon. And maybe his father realised that he himself was no longer one of those creatures. The older man took the food gladly this time, tucking in.

There was even a thank you.

From that day on, there was never any fear about going outside. Anyone stupid enough to tackle him soon regretted it. At the same time, he attracted a gang of his own: those who not only respected the way he handled himself – his size a plus rather than a drawback – but also his allegiance to the flag. Just like in those matches so long ago now. It was every nation for themselves, and they knew if they stuck with him there was a chance of making theirs great again.

It took a lot of time, but eventually that gang became a small army, which in turn became a larger army. Just as his family had done, they all looked to him to take care of them. Which he did at first, then they became big enough and tough enough to begin looking after him again. Why go out on scavenging trips – further and further afield – when you could send bands of your own men to do it? The food was shared equally, *after* he and his family were taken care of. And why fight, when others would fight for you – to *protect* you?

Soon they were much too big to occupy any one building, or even a set of buildings. So, about six or seven months ago he'd struck upon the idea of the Stadium. The place that had inspired him, the place where the Dragons used to meet. The place where this Dragon would rule.

There was just one problem. While he had been gathering his forces, others had been setting up shop in the area. Recruiting the local populace with promises that they would be safeguarded.

Using these lies, a regional division of something called The Rangers had been established. It only took a little digging to discover where they came from and how they'd come about. Some prick masquerading as Robin Hood had managed to convince enough people to follow his lead, to create a peacekeeping force – what could easily be seen from the outside as a personal militia hellbent on taking over Britain.

Well, they wouldn't fucking get Wales; he'd see to that. No matter what it took.

Understandably, as The Dragon was wheeled along the corridor, two of his elite guardsmen pushing what could only be described as a padded sled – complete with feeding troughs filled with food on either side – he was eager to begin today's proceedings. He was about to make an example of these Rangers, make them understand in no uncertain terms that they were not welcome in this country. And the punishment for those born here who'd joined their cause would be severe.

The Dragon sat back and enjoyed the final stages of the ride to his private box – a viewing place his Dad could only dream about, but which now 'belonged' to his son. Inside, he found more guards, each carrying sub-machine guns, with pistols at each hip. They were dressed in green and white uniforms, with the Dragon symbol emblazoned across the chest. A symbol of power and eventual unity, under his command. His Mam had been right all along, he *had* been destined for greatness. It had just taken the death of ninety per cent of the world's population before he saw it.

Also in here were some of the new members of his private harem. Girls brought to the Stadium, some willing, others who'd required more coaxing to enjoy everything his hospitality had to offer. They were wearing a variety of revealing outfits, in silk, satins and lace. The Dragon noted one of the newest, sitting on a velvet couch near the window, wearing a baby-doll nightie. She was looking away from him, her blonde hair cascading over the milky skin of her shoulders, strands falling down between her pert breasts. He licked his lips, then reached for a chicken leg out of the trough and took a bite. He'd settle for sating at least one of his massive appetites for now, because he wanted to get on with the game. Later, he'd turn his attentions towards the women. The one woman in particular who'd caught his eye.

With a waving hand, he motioned for the guards to manoeuvre him closer to the gigantic window. Peering down onto the pitch below, a pitch they'd found overgrown when they arrived and he'd insisted they clean up. There he saw more of his men leading bound figures onto the freshly mown grass. The prisoners were dressed in darker green, hoods down at the back; there were about a dozen or so of them. His guards pushed them into the middle of the grounds at gunpoint.

It had been a decent swoop, he had to admit. Sending his troops into the very heart of the local Ranger's nest, they'd encountered very little resistance. Taken by surprise, swords and arrows were no match for heavily-armed men storming a building. These were the only ones left alive. It was still very much a fledgling operation in this locality, and that told him Hood had a way to go before he was a force to be reckoned with outside his native Nottingham.

What was about to happen today would make him think twice about a foothold here. Either that, or make him mad enough to come here en masse – in which case they'd devastate his numbers and send them packing back off to where they belonged.

"The microphone," he demanded through a mouthful of chicken. "And some doughnuts."

One of the guards passed him the mike. It carried his voice throughout the stadium. Another guard called for more food to be brought, which arrived just as The Dragon began addressing his captives. The young man who brought it was another new face to him, and one that didn't appeal much. Those soapstar good looks reminded him a little too much of the boys from school. He shooed the servant away, noting that the lad held back to watch the proceedings from behind. Oh well, let him. This would serve as a lesson to his own people just as much. You do not cross The Dragon.

"Your attention," The Dragon said, nodding happily at the sound of his amplified voice. The Rangers on the pitch turned and looked up. "That's right, I'm up here," he said, sighing. "Now, I expect you're wondering what you're doing in this place? It's very simple. Your actions have marked you out as not only an enemy of my country, but also of me. I offer you the chance of freedom, though. I am nothing if not a fair man. You are familiar with this nation's favourite sport?"

The Rangers on the pitch did and said nothing.

"Even if you're not, you know the idea is to pass this..." He waited while one of his men produced an oval-shaped ball, "... forward either by carrying or kicking. Then reach the other end of the pitch and score a try without the other team taking it from you. Got all that?" Silence again. "I'll take that as a yes."

His men began to cut the Rangers' bonds, guns still trained on them. Given any opening, these men were sure to retaliate. The Dragon noted that his new blonde odalisque – it was a word he'd 'borrowed' from the Turks, who knew a thing or two about their harems – was watching events unfold below with increasing interest. It was time to move things along so he could become better acquainted with her.

"Be aware that you are playing for high stakes," he told them. "If my men should win and score, then you will lose not only the game, but also your lives." One of his guards motioned for the Rangers and his own men to form a haphazard scrum. There were about the same amount of The Dragon's men facing them, which meant that theoretically they *could* win.

The Dragon nodded for the ball to be tossed into the heap of figures, all of whom immediately began scrabbling for it. They were a blur of reds, whites and greens. Light and dark, limbs out at all angles, they moved like a giant human spider. All were punching and kicking – not exactly within the rules of the game, but then neither was a death sentence if you lost. One of the Rangers suddenly emerged, holding the ball up. When he knew his comrades had seen him, he tucked it under his arm and began to run. Both The Dragon's men and the remaining Rangers started after him, one side to offer support, the others to attack. One guard dived, but missed the Ranger, then spun over and over on the grass. The Dragon pulled a sour face.

The Ranger with the ball could really run, had possibly been some kind of sportsman in his former life. But so had a few of The Dragon's men. They were catching up, and he was looking for one of his mates to take the ball. He spotted another Ranger advancing on his right. The Dragon's fingers dug into the arms of his seat. He needn't have worried, though; his men knew exactly what to do.

Just as the Ranger was about to toss the ball, one of the guards in pursuit pulled out a pistol and fired at the man who would have received it. The bullet blew away most of the Ranger's left kneecap, splattering redness across the grass.

There was an intake of breath from some of the harem watching and The Dragon smiled. He looked across at the new woman, who was fixated on the 'match' and now had her hand to her mouth. God, she was magnificent. Whoever chose her would be rewarded well, he'd see to it. She realised he was watching and glanced at the Dragon out of the corner of her eye. Then she returned her gaze to the pitch, as if what she was witnessing there was preferable.

She'll look at me later, he thought to himself. *I'll* make *her look*.

The Dragon turned his attention back to what was happening below. The Rangers appeared shocked that one of their team had been gunned down, hanging back in case the same should happen to them. Then, suddenly, one Ranger put on a spurt and ran as fast as he could ahead of the pack. He was small and dodged around a couple of the guards to do so. Another one of The Dragon's men pulled out a gun, but another Ranger barged into him, spoiling his aim. The guard turned and elbowed his attacker in the face, knocking him to the ground, but the delay meant the smaller Ranger was racing ahead.

The man running with the ball kicked it across quickly. The smaller Ranger fumbled with it, but managed to get it under control, tucking it under his arm, making a sprint for the end of the pitch. Behind him, four guards were on his tail. He looked over his shoulder to see them drawing their weapons.

He was about to get a bullet in the back, when a couple of his comrades dived on the armed men, tackling them from behind. They all went down and there was the flash of gunfire. The next thing, the Dragon's people were standing again – leaving the bodies of the Rangers on the grass.

He'd told them he was a fair man, and some might say this game was anything but. However, it was his stadium, his game, his rules. The Dragon didn't like to lose.

But it looked like that was about to happen. The small Ranger had his head down, the finishing line in sight. Those Rangers left were sprinting too, catching him up, leaving the Dragon's guards behind.

No: the guards were retreating. They were actually pulling back. Running in the other direction! A couple of the harem women were looking at The Dragon, wondering what was going on – but not his new favourite, she was leaning forward, one hand on the glass. Even the young slave who'd brought his food had moved forward to get a better view.

The Dragon chuckled. Yes, watch and learn.

The smaller Ranger dived with the ball and planted it on the grass, scoring the try that he thought would save them all. His team-mates joined him, still not having put two and two together. They jumped in the air, celebrating. They'd beaten the Dragon's men, they'd–

The explosion wasn't a big one – no mushroom cloud or mortar – but large enough to make sure anyone within a twenty metre radius was caught in it. The harem girls screamed; the servant boy stepped forward again, sucking in a sharp breath. The blonde girl had both hands on the glass, then she turned. The Dragon was holding a radio transmitter in his right hand, thumb still on the trigger that had detonated the device inside the rugby ball. The girl was definitely looking at him now, intently – in fact she couldn't take her eyes off him. *Was* it fear that he saw? Was it repulsion, like the first one, the pasty-faced girl? No, it was something else. Could it be pity; if so, who for? The Rangers or him? There were definitely tears in her eyes. He saw them just before she looked away again.

Why? He'd offered those men their freedom, hadn't he? And he'd delivered. They were free – they couldn't be *more* free. The Dragon looked down on the smouldering crater in the pitch – that would have to be fixed before he played the game again – at the various body parts, and one full torso. He spoke into the microphone, telling the guards to pick one of the two Rangers still alive: a choice between the guy with no kneecap and the one who'd been elbowed in the face. "We need one survivor to send back, to tell Hood about what happened here. Kill the other one."

There, that look again. His latest odalisque was staring at him, her eyes still moist. Now that the match had reached its conclusion, it was time for other distractions. He'd teach her now to look at him in another way. Or Heaven help her.

The Dragon gave the order to be wheeled away, and for the guards to bring the woman. "Just her?" they asked, as often he asked for several at a time to visit with him. The Dragon nodded and she was grabbed by the arm. At first he thought she might resist; there was just a flash of 'fuck you' in those tearful eyes. But she thought better of it, thankfully.

As he was taken away, the Dragon glimpsed the Ranger who'd been knocked to the ground get shot in the head. They'd chosen the man who could barely walk to release, and he approved. The Ranger's wound alone would serve as a warning.

Today had been a good day, he thought to himself. And it was about to get even better.

In his head, he heard those crowds again back when there used to be real matches here. But instead of chorusing with them, he changed his own contribution to:

I am a Dragon! I am *the* Dragon!

HE COULD DO nothing but watch.

Stand and stare as those innocent men were slaughtered by that slug. Gazing down at the devastation, there had been one last act of cruelty to come: a Ranger shot in the head, while his colleague with the shattered kneecap was set free. It was doubtful whether he'd ever walk properly again, though, let alone run as he had been doing when the bullet struck him.

What kind of sadist was this?

He was half tempted to make a move right then and there, but he'd have ended up just as dead as the Rangers in that explosion. Might have been worth it, just to take this so-called Dragon with him.

Dale turned away from the window in time to see one of the women in the slug's private collection get dragged to her feet. She was crying, had been since she saw the killings below. But he saw a strength there also, a determination and resolve. And... something else. Something he couldn't quite put his finger on. Briefly, he caught her eye and the look lingered – far longer than any glances between her and the Dragon. Again, he almost sprang into action, fully aware of what would happen to the girl when those doors shut behind her. When the Dragon got her back to his lair. For some reason the thought of that happening to this one girl in particular turned his stomach.

He looked around at the others on display, all wearing skimpy outfits to tantalise the fat pig. *How is it any different to what you've done in the past?* he asked himself. The way he sometimes thought of women, as disposable, as objects. As meat? Dale shook his head. He might not be the settling down kind, but he was nothing like this. The Dragon forced them to dress this way, to do... things with him. He'd never forced anyone to do anything in his life. So what if he'd never been in love, never had a relationship that wasn't based on sex? It didn't make him the kind of monster he was dealing with here.

It did make him lonely, though, and sad that while people like Robert and Mary were getting hitched, while Mark and Sophie were getting it together, he still had nobody apart from the occasional girl in a village or town he was patrolling, or at a fête like the one they held last Christmas at the castle.

If he wasn't careful, he really would end up like his father: not able to commit to Dale's mum, chasing women left right and centre.

What was the difference between the woman sitting not far away, and those he'd looked at in lad's mags? In those strip clubs he'd frequented? You could tell yourself that they were getting paid, that nobody was holding a gun to their head – like they were, literally, here – but what if that was the only work they could get? *Do you honestly think that they enjoyed it?*

Now really wasn't the time or the place to be thinking about that, but he couldn't get the blonde woman out of his mind. Couldn't stand thinking about the Dragon pawing and molesting her. It wasn't right. Just wasn't–

Rangers have died here today, he reminded himself. Some of them he knew, albeit briefly. Even though he'd taken the name from their flag, that man wasn't representative of this country, any more than The Tsar was representative of Russia's population. Those men down there, who'd been trying to bring peace and stability to the region – they were the *real* heroes of Wales. And it was about time this sick son of a bitch who thought he was in charge was driven out.

That's what Dale was doing here, that was his mission – or part of it – given to him by Jack. The Welsh contingent of the Rangers were well aware of what the Dragon could become, so they'd asked for help. Dale had been sent in undercover to gather information, to find something they could use to take down the Dragon's organisation. He'd only been around a couple of days when they'd attacked the Ranger HQ, decimating their number. He'd heard about it from some of the other servants, but never thought he'd see the survivors of that massacre exterminated in such a sick mockery of what this place was built for.

Again he couldn't help thinking about the girl with blonde hair.

Dale squeezed his eyes shut. Stop the Dragon, you stop the killing, *and* stop what was happening to these women. It was up to Dale. Jack was relying on him. Wouldn't do anything about the attack on the Rangers until he'd heard back from his mole. He wondered if they could even muster a force to take on all the Dragon's people in one go. There were more than they'd imagined, or the Welsh Rangers had suggested. And with Robert's troops spread out now more than ever, the man himself having answered a distress call from Bill up near Scotland, perhaps it really was down to Dale to do something.

This certainly wasn't as cool as Jack had made it sound. "It'll be just like *Mission Impossible*, kid," the large American had promised.

Mission Impossible? Mission bloody unbelievable more like – as in how unbelievably bad his luck was. What exactly would Tom Cruise do now in his position? Off the bad guy, blow up his base and get the girl.

He sighed; that really did only happen in the movies. This was real life and sometimes that stank.

"Hey you," said one of the guards. He touched his chest. "Yes, you. What you still doing here? Clear off back to the kitchens, this isn't a peep show."

Dale nodded. No, it was more like a flesh farm. No doubt these men wanted to be left alone with the harem women for a reason. Only look but don't touch, because they belonged to the Dragon.

No woman – no man, either, for that matter – should belong to someone else. If Robert had taught them anything, it was that. He'd also taught the lesson to De Falaise, The Tsar and countless other thugs who didn't seem to know it already. His men followed him not because they had to, but because they *wanted* to. Because they believed in what he did, in liberty and the right to live a peaceful existence.

Impossible or not, Dale would find a way to bring that to these people again, he had to.

Reluctantly, he left the women behind with the guards.

But still couldn't shake the picture of the one girl who'd gone off with the Dragon from his mind.

CHAPTER FOUR

It was amazing to think how, over the last year especially, this place had become like home to him.

The Reverend Tate even had a place where he would go to pray, a quiet place he'd blessed himself down in the Lower Bailey. He was there now, talking to God; thanking Him for the new day, for keeping his friends safe and asking Him to keep a watchful eye on them. Especially Robert, who never seemed to take a bit of notice whenever Tate told him to be careful. And asking the Lord to look after His humble servant, trying to bring His word to those who were building this new world.

As Tate got up, relying more heavily these days than ever on his stick, he began his slow and steady walk back up towards the castle, and considered the rebuilding they'd done here after The Tsar's attack. That had been such a horrible time.

While Robert and his men had been going through Hell on the battlefield, Tate, Jack, Mark and Sophie had been trying to keep invading forces out of the castle grounds – and failing miserably. If it hadn't been for Dale arriving with more Rangers, this place would look very different. Russian troops would be guarding the walls and the gate instead of Rangers, and they'd probably all have been hunted down and killed. Tate liked to think it was the power of prayer that had helped Robert recover enough to finally defeat the Tsar.

Whichever way you cut it, they owed the Almighty a big one... Two, actually, if you counted that other battle for the castle when they'd put an end to the Sheriff's reign.

But it seemed as though no sooner had they tackled one insane dictator than another cropped up. The Widow in Scotland, for example, or the potential threat of this Dragon character across to the west. In this post-virus world everyone was staking a claim on their own territories – and other people's. The only thing standing in their way was people like Robert and his Rangers.

As Tate hobbled further up, joining the path, he remembered what the castle had looked like earlier the previous year. The gardens torn up, the castle pock-marked – even a hole in one part of the wall where Adele, De Falaise's traitorous daughter, had left her mark.

The attack had left not only the castle and its grounds devastated, but their souls as well. Left them questioning if they were actually doing any good, or just fooling themselves. Luckily, God had shown them the way. Drawn more people to their cause, who wanted to join Robert's police force. Brought folk with even more useful skills, or given them the ability to learn these, enabling them to repair the damage done.

The physical damage, that was. Mentally, it was another matter.

Yet some of his friends and, yes, family – because that's how Tate thought of them now – had thrived in the months after the attack. Mark and Sophie, for example, had finally acted on their feelings for each other. As if on cue, he saw the boy, walking with his new girlfriend. *Boy.* You couldn't really describe him as that these days, he'd grown so tall. Tate could remember the first time he'd met Mark, back when Bill had been running the floating markets. He'd only come up to the holy man's chest then, and he wasn't exactly tall himself. Mark had also filled out somewhat since he'd started his Ranger training, working out whenever he wasn't spending time with Sophie or practising his archery and sword skills. By all accounts, the youngster was turning into a pretty decent Ranger, modelling himself on Robert, of course – still going with him on those private trips to the forest.

Tate raised a hand and both of the young people waved back. They looked so happy. For Mark and Sophie things had actually improved since the Tsar's attack.

The same was also probably true of their older counterparts, Robert and Mary, who were closer than ever. Tate cast his mind back to their wedding the previous summer, a small affair but attended by all those who mattered. Tate had presided over the ceremony, where the old bandstand was, and everyone had clapped when he'd finally said: "I now pronounce you man and wife. Robert, you may kiss the bride." There had been little time for a honeymoon, as a spot of trouble with a new wannabe gang in Chesterfield had required their attention, but both had gone off to tackle the problem together. Tate firmly believed that now they were fighting side by side, they couldn't be happier.

Most residents had been left gloomy and miserable by the events, though – Jack, for one, who even now stewed about Adele and how he'd fallen for her. How he'd betrayed their whereabouts because he thought Adele would harm Mary.

Tate, too, had found it a struggle at times – having lost the place he had once called his home, and finding himself estranged from the person he'd failed so miserably to protect not just once, but twice. Gwen, who'd been the Sheriff's plaything once upon a time, snatched from the village named Hope after her partner Clive had been brutally murdered. Who'd returned to the village after the birth of her son at the castle – Clive Jr, who she still maintained was fathered by his namesake, but as he grew bore more and more of a resemblance to a certain Frenchman they'd all known. Gwen, who'd said she never wanted anything more to do with Tate again. His own fault, assuming he knew what was best for her, sending for her because he'd thought she'd be safer at the castle, then putting her in even more danger. When he'd found out that she'd almost been assaulted by Jace, one of De Falaise's former soldiers, Tate could scarcely forgive himself. So why should Gwen? The castle held many terrifying memories for her, and they all must have come rushing back when that thug–

The man was dead now, killed either by Gwen or someone else, they hadn't been able to determine which. The woman was certainly capable. She'd gone after the Mexican, Major Javier, the man who'd shot Clive, finishing him off during the very first fight for Nottingham Castle. But Tate had a strange feeling she'd had help this time. Gwen had also become even harder, if that was the right word, in the time since all this happened. For the most part she'd hidden herself away in New Hope – turning the place into a veritable fortress, its inhabitants into soldiers.

Tate had only seen her once since the Tsar's men had invaded, a few months ago when they'd held the Winter Festival at the castle – an attempt to put a smile back on the faces, not only of the people who lived here, but also those in the outlying regions. Gwen had come only because some of her own villagers had heard about it. The Festival itself – with live music from Dale – had been a roaring success. But it had been the inroads Tate had made with Gwen that proved the most successful from his point of view.

At first she still hadn't wanted to know. In fact Tate thought, when he approached she might just walk off, turn her back like she had when he'd tried to visit New Hope. But something about that time of year, about Christmas, about peace to all men and forgiveness, must have touched her heart. It was the Lord working His magic again he suspected. No, more than suspected, *believed* completely. For the fact that she'd spoken to him at all must surely have been some kind of miracle.

They'd left it open, with the possibility of talking again at some point; the friendship at least thawing a little. She no longer sounded like she wanted to rip out his throat, anyway. Tate had planned to visit New Hope again soon after and see how the land lay, but up till now things had been so busy at the castle. He'd resolved to definitely go there within the next couple of weeks, though, as spring took hold, because there wouldn't *ever* be a perfect time. He didn't want to waste the opportunity he'd been given back in December. Instead of rebuilding the castle, he had to now rebuild a few bridges.

He'd talk to Robert when he returned, ask for an escort. Once he'd resolved to do it, he found he was actually looking forward to seeing Gwen again. To talking with her, and maybe, just maybe, persuading her to abandon the path of hatred and anger she was currently on.

To return her to the fold of Christ, where she might actually find tranquillity again.

"Jesus H. fucking Christ!"

Gwen ducked back down as the bullet ricocheted off the wall she was hiding behind. The wall she and the other people of New Hope had built for just such a reason – to keep out intruders.

Like the men who'd shown up here today and were attacking her village. She'd sensed there was something wrong, to be honest. Every now and then spotting unusual movement in the woods which flanked New Hope whenever she was on watch; fleeting glimpses of... she couldn't tell what. Gwen had the feeling that someone was watching their little community, but it wasn't like before. Like last year. Back then she'd felt safe, as if they were being watched over, protected. This time she just felt threatened.

These were only feelings, suspicions, so she hadn't mentioned them to the rest of the villagers. She couldn't be sure of anything, couldn't prove anything. But still she had skipped out on the last couple of foraging missions for new weapons, relying instead on Graham Leicester. Once just an ordinary, gentle guy who'd worked in a garden centre, like her Graham had been changed forever by what happened when the Sheriff's men came to call. Now he was more soldier than agriculturalist. Gwen had seen him strip clean a Colt AR-15 machine-gun in minutes, putting the pieces back together like he was doing a jigsaw puzzle. He knew what he was looking for out there, knew just what they needed to defend themselves. The weapons she'd stolen from Robert's castle had given them a head start, but they were always searching for more.

The wall – a huge brick affair, strengthened by sheet metal on the outside – had been young Darryl Wade's idea. Darryl, whose father had been a handyman and had luckily passed on much of his expertise. He'd been helping Clive fix up the school when Javier and his men had–

Gwen had to keep stopping herself from thinking about that day, those painful memories. While it was true at certain times they'd given her strength, now they twisted her guts up in knots. If she didn't have Clive Jr, son of the man she'd loved so much, she didn't know what she might do. What those memories might drive her to. But she did, and that child was the only thing driving her these days.

She'd got her first actual proof that the village was being observed five hours ago, when Graham had returned from his latest foray in her jeep. He'd unexpectedly drawn fire from several locations in the woods. Andy Hobbs, another founding member of Hope, shouted for her to come quickly – which she'd done, leaving Clive Jr in the capable hands of Dr Ken Jeffreys, who'd joined them from a group in Worksop. When she got to the lookout post on the wall, shouldering her M16 rifle as she climbed the ladder next to the gate, she saw why Andy was so concerned.

Flashes of light from the woods, bursts of automatic gunfire which were spraying the jeep Graham and his team were in. The vehicle was barrelling down the country lane, barely big enough to accommodate it, and Gwen watched as Graham leaned out of the side, returning fire. Whoever was shooting at her people was dug in well, using the trees and surrounding woodland for cover. It was only what they did themselves, the countryside concealing them from any passing unwanted attention. Javier had been a one-off; they'd never encountered another wandering army like that here since. It crossed her mind briefly to wonder whether the shooters out there had come specifically for them.

"Unlock the gates!" Andy shouted down, pointing to the wrought iron monstrosities that were also Darryl's brainchild.

"Wait," Gwen said, brushing a strand of auburn hair out of her eyes. "What do you think you're doing?"

"We have to risk it," he replied.

Andy was right of course, she knew that. Graham was one of them, she'd known him almost as long as she'd known... would have known Clive. But there was still that nagging part of her wanting to keep the rest of them – wanting to keep Clive Jr – locked up behind those gates, behind these walls. Risk was a thing she had a problem with when it came to her son's life.

"It's Graham," Andy said, as if that was all he needed to add.

Gwen nodded, allowing the men below to unbolt the gate.

"Get ready," called down Andy. If this was to work they had to open them at just the right time. The jeep had sped up and was now pelting towards the gates, trailing fire behind it. Andy held up his hand; it was shaking. "Ready..." he repeated and she heard the catch in his voice. "*Now!*" he barked and let his hand fall.

The men below swung open the gates, just in time for the jeep to come crashing through the gap. It scraped the side of the opening and, for a second, Gwen feared it might collapse them completely. But Darryl's handiwork was stronger than it looked. Everything held, long enough for the doors to be shut behind the jeep – bullets pinging off the metal. Gwen hoped their enemies didn't have anything that could ram those gates down.

As she got to the bottom of the ladder, Graham was stumbling out of the jeep. He dropped his gun and fell to his knees, the khaki jumper he was wearing stained red at the front. "Oh no," she heard Andy say from behind. "Fetch the doc."

By now several of the residents of New Hope had emerged from their homes to see what was going on. Gwen waved to Darryl, told him to get Jeffreys, and to stay with Clive Jr. Minutes later and the medic was examining the man's wound.

"He's been lucky, it went right through, just missed his lung. But he's bleeding badly. We need to get him to my surgery, as quickly as possible. Here, keep pressure on the wound." Four people picked up Graham, and set off down the road with him. Jeffreys turned to Gwen. "What's the devil's going on? Are we under attack?"

"Yes," Gwen said.

"We're not sure yet," Andy broke in, looking at her.

"Tell that to Graham."

The sound of gunfire was still echoing loudly from outside. And it wasn't long before more lookouts confirmed that there were several shooters at the back wall as well. These too were keeping out of sight, but if anyone stuck their head above the 'parapet' they were setting themselves up as a target. In fact, shooters had been positioned around the whole wall, it seemed – either the same men circling, or quite a number of them in fixed positions.

"We're under siege," Gwen stated after they'd called an emergency meeting in the Red Lion pub. Clive Jr was nearby, happily banging plastic bricks together in a playpen.

"But why?" This came from Karen Shipley, a thirty year old ex-receptionist who'd joined them about six months ago. "I don't understand."

"Do people need a reason anymore?" Darryl answered, and she looked stung by his remark. Everyone knew she had a crush on Darryl – everyone except the young man himself, apparently. "They see something others have built up, and they want to take it, destroy it." He was quite obviously talking about their experience when Javier had rolled into town; Gwen could empathise. It was the kind of thinking she'd used to motivate these people.

"Hold on. Look, we still don't know what we're dealing with here," Andy commented. "How many men, how well armed they are."

"Pretty *well* armed going by the state of that jeep," Jeffreys chipped in, as he took another look at it through the window. "Put it this way, I'm glad it's not my patient." He'd managed to stabilise Graham. New Hope had boasted a small local practise, even before the name change. The doctor's trainee assistant, a young Indian guy called Sat, was keeping an eye on Graham while Jeffreys attended the crisis talks. He'd alert him if anything happened.

"Agreed," said Gwen. "And there's something else." She told them about her suspicions that someone had been watching them for a while now.

"You didn't think to mention this before?" Andy asked.

"What was I supposed to say? I didn't know anything for certain. What good would it have done to worry everyone needlessly? Besides, it's not the first time I've thought people might be keeping an eye on the village."

"What?" This was Jeffreys.

"It's okay, I think they were here to help. It's connected to how I got away from the castle last year." Gwen saw that they didn't understand, and shook her head. "You know what; I'm not even going to try to explain. What's happened has happened. But these people obviously aren't friendlies. And they aren't going away anytime soon."

"How long can we hold out for?" asked Jeffreys.

"Food-wise, a week. Maybe two," Darryl informed them. "It's

ammo we're running short of. Graham brought back a few more supplies, but not nearly enough. If those guys keep pushing and have more than us..."

"They obviously want *something*," Jeffreys said.

Andy sighed. "Yeah: us, dead. And they might just get it, too."

Gwen glanced across at her son, playing without a care in the world. "That's not going to happen." She walked towards the door, then opened it, ignoring protests from the people inside. Gwen strode across the village to the front wall and climbed the ladder. Taking hold of her rifle, she crouched down on the ledge. Gwen stuck her head up over the top, and it was then that bullets raked the wall, causing her to duck again. "All right," she whispered to herself, "if that's the way you want to play it." She swung around and returned fire with the M16, targeting the flashes. "You like that, eh? All right, have some more then." Her teeth were clenched as she fired round after round, until eventually the rifled clicked empty. Still she kept her finger pressed on the trigger, breathing hard.

There was silence outside. The only sound she could hear was the pumping of her heart in her chest. The hand on her shoulder made her jump, and she almost turned the weapon on whoever it was.

"Gwen, that's enough." It was Andy, his expression full of concern.

"No, I–"

He took the rifle from her. "They're camped out. It's a waste of our ammo."

She stared at him, then said quietly, "We can't let them take us, Andy. Not again. We *have* to fight back." Gwen looked down and saw that some of the others had followed her out of the meeting. She saw the worried faces of Darryl, Karen, a half dozen more. Some of them knew what it was like to be invaded, some had no idea – yet.

Andy took hold of her, attempting to rest her head on his shoulder. "It's okay. We won't let that happen." Then it was his turn to tense up.

She pulled away. "What?" Gwen followed his gaze, peering at an angle through the gap in the wall.

"I think you winged one," he said.

He was right. One of the shooters had broken cover, staggering about in the open. He was clutching his leg, rifle falling from his hands.

"We need to get to him, get him inside," Gwen told Andy. If they could question this guy they might get a few answers.

"You can't be serious?" said Andy.

"I am, and I know exactly the way to do it."

For the first time that day, Gwen broke into a smile.

CHAPTER FIVE

SHE HADN'T DONE bad for herself, she had to say. Though, obviously, she'd seen it coming.

And while most little girls' childhood fantasies revolved around living in a castle, it had never been hers. This had been an adult fantasy, something that occurred to her later in life when she realised it actually could be achieved. She'd always been a realist, even from an early age.

What attracted her the most was not the fantasy life of living here, but the fact these surroundings fitted her persona perfectly. A medieval backdrop to match her outlook. Yet she was also a dichotomy, because however much she loved the old fashioned nature of where she now resided, she was still connected to the modern world. The castle had power, it had running water; all right, people who would run and *fetch* her water. It was protected by the weapons of the 20th and 21st century: tanks, jeeps, machine-guns and mounted rocket launchers. Her men might well carry the swords of their ancestors, had changed their names according to the old Celtic ways, but they were also armed to the gills with guns.

It made her laugh to think that if she had been around back in the days when this place had been built – the rock itself had been occupied as far back as the mid-second century – she would have been burned at the stake. Not just because of the modern weaponry – just how would you explain a Weasel 2 light anti-aircraft defence system to a primitive? – but because she studied the ancient arts.

Ancient and modern, it was a curious mix. But one which she found most appealing.

She pondered this again as she sat before her cards. Looking around the faded red walls, then up at the original hammerbeam roof, her gaze settled on the suits of armour flanking the fireplace. Each now held Heckler & Koch MG4 – 5.56 mm light machine-guns at her insistence. There was just something so right about the combination.

But that was her all over, as many had commented in the past.

The past. It wasn't very often she looked back there – preferring instead to look into the future. Now it had crossed her mind, spurred on, no doubt, by the reading she'd just done, and she thought back to how her life had taken this turn.

Maybe she hadn't dreamed about castles and crowns when she was little, because the reality of her situation meant there was no point believing in fairy tales. How could she when she was forced to survive on whatever food her mother could afford, gristly scrag-ends begged from the butchers. And she wouldn't believe in fairy tales ever again after seeing her mother stab her violent and abusive father right in front of her eyes. Her dad had come home stinking of beer and her mother had asked if he had the rent because the landlord had been round again.

"Dinnae bother me, woman," he'd shouted in her face, then turned away. When her maw tried to get him to listen, he'd brought his fist round in an arc and caught her with a back-hander which sent the woman sprawling across the floor. He didn't seem to care that his five year old daughter was in the room, watching. She remembered seeing her mother spit out blood, getting to her hands and knees as her father turned his attentions to the screaming child in the corner. "Shut yer fuckin' trap, or so help me I'll..."

She'd run when she saw her dad approach, scooting past and making for the kitchen. She'd been looking for a cupboard to climb into, when her father grabbed her by the scruff of the neck. "I'll teach yer to run from me, lass!"

"Git away from her," came her mother's voice from behind.

The large man dropped his terrified child and turned. It was then that she saw what her mother had in her right hand. A kitchen knife; meant only to scare him perhaps, to warn him off – stop him from beating them both to a pulp. And if he hadn't tried to wrestle the thing from her grasp, perhaps it wouldn't have slid into his stomach like that. But it was what happened afterwards that really shattered her illusions about fantasies. Her father staggering backwards, clutching his stomach, holding up his red hands and calling her maw a 'fuckin' houk'. Her mother's face contorting, then the knife plunging into him again and again, even when he was on the floor; the years of cruelty at his hands all coming out in those thrusts.

If it hadn't been for that, her mother might have got away with self defence, or at least shown that she was only protecting her baby. As it was, the judge said what she'd done, the amount of wounds inflicted, indicated it was a conscious, perhaps even premeditated, act. Lawyers tried to argue mental instability because of the abuse at the hands of a psychotic drunkard, but the courts hadn't bought it. Her mother died in prison long before the virus came along, managing to hang herself with some bedsheets.

If only I'd been able to see it coming.

It was a dangerous thought that had plagued her throughout her childhood in care, then into her adolescence. One which finally became an obsession. She'd consulted the libraries, though didn't have much joy finding a way to achieve this – and back then there hadn't been an accessible 'net. So she'd turned to someone who might be able to teach her. There was an old fortune teller called Evelyn who operated not too far away from the home they'd stuck her in, making a meagre living from consultations. Whenever she had any spare time she'd visit Evelyn, who welcomed the company because she lived on her own. The old lady taught her much about the different methods of seeing into the future, like the crystal ball, runes and, of course, the cards. But she also told her something else.

"You have a gift, dear," Evelyn would often say. "A real gift. It's only just starting to emerge, as often they do at this time of life, but it's there. And it's strong."

She became the closest thing to a daughter the woman had, though was technically more like a granddaughter. On Evelyn's shelves, in her back room, were row upon row of books on magic and the occult which she'd borrow and read, often without permission or Evelyn's knowledge. When Evelyn passed away at the age of eighty – she'd found her one Sunday, after letting herself in: eyes closed in her favourite armchair – she'd taken some of these books before calling the authorities. For safe keeping, she told herself. Well, Evelyn had no family, so what would happen to them otherwise?

The cow who ran the home eventually discovered them, however, in spite of the fact they'd been hidden away in the back of her wardrobe. She'd thrown out such 'filth' and given her charge a lecture on morals. Angry, and remembering enough to perform one spell in particular, she'd put a curse on the bitch. Who crashed her car about a week later. It might have been coincidence, but she doubted that very much, and it scared her. She'd never in a million years thought the magic would work. It taught her to have a newfound respect for the forces she was dabbling with.

"You have a gift."

She used to look at those girls at school, into the Goth scene, or kids involved in roleplaying games, and think: *You really don't know a thing, do you?*

When she was old enough to leave care and school, she got a job in a local fish and chip shop. For a while she tried to live an ordinary life, mainly because she fell in love with the owner's son. She'd always sworn she'd never get involved with anyone, never let her heart rule her head – never let herself get into the same mess as her mother. But the emotions she felt whenever she saw Alex were impossible to ignore. There was such a connection, such a pull, and they had so much in common. He was strong, but gentle with it, and said that he loved her too. She believed him. He was *so* different to her father: for one thing he never touched a drop of alcohol, and there wasn't a violent bone in his body. It was rare to find someone like that, she knew. So rare, that she'd said yes when Alex proposed.

In spite of everything she'd once said, all she'd once learnt, she didn't even *try* and look into the future this time. She didn't need to, because Evelyn had told her about Alex. Told her that one day that special, perfect man would come along and she'd have everything she ever dreamed of. Someone with whom she'd share a special bond. "Where love's involved, it's difficult to see your own future; it... clouds things, makes them unclear," the old woman had warned, then held up one card in particular. A man sat on a throne, holding a sword: 'The Emperor'. "But I see it. I see it all. He'll come along, your king. You just wait and see, sweetheart. You'll almost be as one, the same. Then it'll be happy ever after."

She should have known better than to believe it, though. Happy ever afters only happened in make-believe. She'd been gutted when she found out Alex was cheating on her after only a year as her husband. Not just with one woman, either, but with several.

"I got bored," was his only defence when she confronted him. It was that night she discovered there were more ways to hurt someone than simply hitting them. "Look, it was a mistake to get hitched. We rushed into it."

"Please, Alex, darlin'." She was tugging at his shirtsleeve – Christ, she could hardly believe that now.

"Lemme go. I-I just don't love yer or fancy yer anymore, all right?"

It was far from all right. About as far as you could get.

"I'm leaving now – and tomorro' I'm getting a divorce."

It was at that point she realised just how similar she was to her mother – and her father, too, ironically. She still had hold of his shirtsleeve, his arm. If she couldn't have Alex, then nobody else would; certainly not those whores he'd been sleeping with. Pulling him round, she dragged him over and shoved his face into the vat of boiling fat. His scream was piercing and she almost stopped what she was doing. But she glimpsed the ring on his finger, felt it brush against hers on the hand she was bending back. He'd worn that every time he'd fucked one of those tarts, the promises meaning nothing.

She'd pushed him even further into the fat, until he went limp and stopped screaming altogether.

It was only afterwards she realised the severity of what she'd done. But there'd been no witnesses. The blinds at the front of the shop had been drawn and it was too late for anyone to be in the clothes store or electrics shop on either side.

That left the question of what to do with the evidence. Then she recalled reading something in one of those occult books about an ancient ritual; about how to take the hurt and pain away, and empower yourself with the spirit of the one who'd done you wrong in the first place. Something to do with ancient tribes. She'd turned her nose up at it when she'd first read it, found it disgusting, but–

The more she thought about it, the more it made sense. A way to dispose of both the evidence, and for a part of Alex to be with her forever. To make her stronger.

And she hadn't eaten all day.

It had taken some building up to, even more determination to continue – to finish as much as she could. But before she knew it she was stripping him, putting the rest of Alex into the fat and turning up the heat. Cooking him until the meat practically slid off. And do you know what, it tasted much better than the gristly scrag-ends she'd survived on as a child.

What little remained she'd disposed of in a secluded spot miles away. But before leaving, she'd packed both lots of clothes and left a note for Alex's father saying that they needed some time away together, to remember what was important in the marriage.

She hadn't returned until after everything went crazy in the world.

The next few years after Alex, she'd spent travelling – Romania, Haiti, China, New Orleans – reconnecting with more than just her dead husband. She'd sought out other people who could help her hone the skills she'd abandoned, and gotten herself into trouble more times than she cared to mention. Not all of her tutors had been as nice as Evelyn, not all of the places they operated in quite so reputable. At one particular underground club, she'd had to fight off three guys who insisted on more than just cash as payment for their knowledge. One would never walk again, another would never see again, and the third would never have children.

The ones she found the most useful, the most adept at the black arts, she beguiled. Sometimes simply with her body, other times helped along with a spell of attraction. She'd marry them, often not legally, then take their power, too. She literally ate men alive, in the end revelling in the nickname some gave her: the Widow. To most that simply meant she'd lost husbands in the past and had a penchant for black, but she couldn't help thinking just how appropriate it was when compared with a certain arachnid.

Had she ever loved any of the men she'd wed, then killed? She'd been fond of some, it had to be said. But loved? She hadn't felt that particular emotion since Alex, hadn't *let* herself because it made you weak. She'd just needed their energy, their abilities, that's all; fashioning herself into something that could survive the coming storm.

She'd known it was on the horizon, even before the first person died of the virus. The Widow had seen it, was prepared for it, knew that she would live through it. Even knew she'd end up here, returning to her homeland and leading an army of men. Knew she'd take the castle once she had enough of them to fight for her, to wipe out those few remaining members of the 52 Infantry Brigade and Royal Regiment of Scotland still protecting Edinburgh Castle. Knew she'd choose her own colours for them to wear, giving them traditional names to further emphasize the marriage of ancient and modern. And knew that she'd be crowned queen of all she surveyed by way of the appropriately-named Stone of Destiny.

She laughed, running a hand through her wild hair.

"Something amusing?"

The voice came from the shadowy archway over to her right, but didn't startle her. She'd been expecting his return, knew her men wouldn't stop him from gaining entrance. Nor should they, because the pair of them had business to discuss.

"Just thinking about destiny," she told him. "Fate. The future."

"You will not *have* a future if you continue to make such mistakes."

"Why don't you come outta there, man? Come out where I can see yer."

There was a second or two's hesitation, but the tall figure did just that, walking cautiously into the hall. His looked wary, as though expecting an attack. This was not a trusting person, but then she'd always known that as well, hadn't she? Even before they'd met.

"Now, what were you sayin' about mistakes?" she asked.

"I think you know already." He wasn't referring to her power; it was pretty easy to guess the topic of conversation. What some might call her recent failure. "I assume you received the message from our mutual friends abroad? The ones who loaned you those little toys to play with."

Toys? Yes, she supposed they were. Just like the men she used. But this was a game on a grander scale than most. "I did. Just didn't want tae make a meal of it."

The man raised an eyebrow. "With your reputation, you surprise me."

The Widow rose from her seat. "Credit me with some... taste," she said. "The man looked like he'd been half eaten already. By animals." There had been no power to gain by devouring *him*. He had no power to give. But this man in front of her, now he was different.

"He had," answered her intruder matter of factly. "There's a difference?"

The warrior in front of her didn't – couldn't – understand. She knew what he must think of her, what most folk out there thought. But they were wrong. They didn't have the first clue what she was all about. "Aye. Want to find out?"

"I'll pass."

The Widow grinned. "So, I presume yer here to follow up?"

The man said nothing, just watched as she came closer. And was he... yes, she caught his eyes roaming over her body. Perhaps she could work her magic on him yet.

"Forget your mind control tricks," he said, as if reading her mind. "They won't work on me."

No, she doubted very much whether they would. His was not a weak mind, and he had purpose. He also had a connection to someone who'd passed over. Someone who had given him a mission to fulfil.

"Why d'ya keep on pretending you're their lackey?" she asked. "Yer nothin' of the kind. You have other motives. Doesn't take someone with my abilities to see that."

"Your 'abilities'?" He gave a throaty chuckle.

She scowled. "Dinnae mock me, I'm warnin' yer."

He laughed and she felt the rage in her rising again. She no longer wished to subdue him the fun way, now she wanted to teach him a lesson. The Widow reached behind her back and brought out a sharp, golden knife with a jewelled hilt.

"It would be the last thing you'd do," said the big man.

She stepped forwards, and he brought a crossbow up, firing off a couple of bolts.

She avoided them easily, having known exactly where he would fire, then continued with her attack. Snarling, he lunged to meet her before she got anywhere near him with the knife. But as he did so, the Widow brought up her other hand, which had been clenched. She opened it and blew the contents in his direction.

Like the seeds of a dandelion, the dust drifted into her opponent's face. He coughed, dropped the crossbow – then froze. The Widow smirked. Relaxing, she walked slowly towards the large man and tutted.

"All that pent up aggression. When was the last time yer released any of it in another way... my Hermit?" She knew the answer to that already; it had been a long time, back before the virus even. Someone no-one else knew about. Someone he'd loved and lost, who'd betrayed him. Someone he'd killed.

She brought up the knife, tracing the tip down the olive-skinned man's cheek – not hard enough to make it bleed, but enough to make her point. Now she was this close, she looked him up and down, just as he had her. Oh, to take him – then take his power. She licked her lips, running her free hand over his chest, over his arms, feeling the bulge of the muscles there. The Widow knew he could feel it too. She'd only prevented him from moving, not *feeling*.

Then lower. She looked him in the eyes, but he didn't blink. He couldn't, even if he'd wanted to. *You can't do it, not yet. You need him*, she told herself. "Look, I understand why you want Hood dead. I know what he did. I know what you've lost at his hands. It's common knowledge, you're going to say. But I know more than yer average bystander. I know about yer promise, Tanek."

His eyebrow twitched, in spite of the paralysis.

"Keep his child safe, isn't that what was asked of yer?" She smiled. "I won't tell. Yer secret's safe with me. Nothing that has happened so far has happened by chance. Everything's in a state of constant balance and flux, Tanek, do you understand? But if you know the outcome of certain events, you can... manipulate that balance. Tweak the future in yer favour. I've given yer a sample of that today. Believe me when I say the sacrifice of those toys, as you call them, was necessary. It's all part of my plan. A plan you and those you claim to serve couldn't possibly hope to understand."

She paused, studying his eyes, trying to work out whether or not her words had sunk in. She'd had this selfsame conversation with Ceallach when he'd returned from the raid, when he'd demanded to know why she hadn't seen the trap Hood had sprung. The Widow could understand how angry he'd been at seeing their men captured, at losing those weapons and vehicles, but it was all for the greater good. Ceallach, had seen that after some gentle persuasion, and a night or two in the Castle Vaults. Tanek would see it as well. He had to, because she needed the weapons those he worked for supplied. Plus she had no wish to anger them, even if she did know what would happen to that nation in the long term.

"Now, I want you tae deliver a message back for me. Tell them they have tae trust what I'm doing. They will get what they want, and so will you. Hood will come here and when he does, we – I – will be ready for him. It has all been foreseen, Tanek."

The Widow removed the knife from Tanek's cheek.

"So, yer have a choice. Leave now, do this for me, and I swear yer'll get what yer want. Hood out of the way and De Falaise's offspring. I think yer know what will happen if you choose otherwise. Do we have an agreement?" The Widow continued to scrutinise his face; she saw the twitch again and smiled. "Good!" She backed off, and when she was far enough away said, "Oh, aye, yer can move now."

Tanek stumbled forwards, shaking his head.

"Take it easy for a minute, the magic's strong."

"Fuck magic. You mean poison."

The Widow sighed. "Believe what yer want."

Some people just didn't have the capacity to think beyond the everyday. Tanek believed in what he could see, in what he could feel – and fight. She couldn't really blame him, but at the same time it soured the idea of taking his power. There were other strengths than the purely physical, and she understood he would never be one of her conquests. That didn't mean she couldn't still use him, of course.

Tanek stooped to pick up his crossbow, raising it again. The Widow didn't even flinch. He was just testing her, to see if she knew his intentions. She did. "Time yer were goin', isn't it," she said. It wasn't a question. "After all, there are others to see."

The larger man's eyes narrowed, then he nodded. "Very well. But we shall see each other again, soon."

"Somehow, I doubt that," the Widow said after him, but she was talking only to his lengthening shadow. She returned to the table, shoving aside a tarot card showing *The Hermit*. She reached instead for the one she'd been seeing time and again throughout her life.

The Widow examined it, and tapped it against her lips. Then she placed it back down.

On it was a picture of a man sat on a throne.

CHAPTER SIX

THE MAN KNOWN as Shadow sat crossed-legged on the ground, gazing ahead and waiting.

This place had tried to repel him from the moment he'd entered. He could feel it. The whole forest was somehow against him. Not only that, but its inhabitants as well. The creatures that called this their home. Birds flapping up in the trees, their song shrill and piercing instead of beautiful. Things scuttling about in the undergrowth: insects, small animals. And the trees themselves had done their best to get him lost, even when light broke, making one part of this place look like another.

Then came the open attack. He'd only just managed to dodge the vicious charge – and as it was he'd been whipped sideways, a sudden pain in his side causing him to wince. He'd glanced down to see blood seeping from a tear in his clothes caused by the animal's antlers.

Rising slowly, he'd found himself facing a large male stag. Shadow stared at it, losing himself momentarily in those black eyes. When he hadn't listened to what the forest was telling him, this creature had been sent to encourage him to leave.

He wasn't about to.

The stag charged again. Shadow dove out of its way, but crouched on his knee this time, ready with his bow – nocking an arrow in seconds. But his aim was off – impossible, his aim was never off! – and the arrow flew wide. Thankfully, when the stag came by for another pass, Shadow was able to draw his hawk axe and deliver a blow to the back of the animal's neck with the blunt side. Crouching next to the felled beast, he placed a hand on its side and felt the rhythm, the pumping of its heart.

He is you and you are him, Shadow said to himself.

His true quarry was linked to this animal somehow in a way he couldn't explain.

Show me, he said to the creature. *Show me this place's true heart.*

It defied him, of course, but the sudden flash Shadow saw in his mind was enough. He'd recognise the location even if it took weeks to find it. Luckily, it didn't. He stumbled upon it by accident, a clearing he doubted whether he'd find if he'd been actively looking for it. And sincerely doubted he would ever leave again if this didn't work.

After stitching up his wound, Shadow set to work, knowing time was growing short. This forest was attempting to expel him, like a body fighting a disease. But he wasn't going to be defeated.

First he built his fire pit. Then he placed wood – logs he chopped with his axe – in the bottom of the hole. By the time he'd completed the pit, it was a good five foot by seven, the sides forming a kind of semi-circle and strengthened by rocks.

Next he chopped more fire wood, ignoring what sounded like screams in his head. Lies, tricks. Telling him this wasn't his to cut, to burn. It belonged to Hood. Only he could use it, granted permission by those who watched over him. Those Shadow was trying to evict, or at the very least subdue, as he had done with the stag. It wasn't theirs at all; it belonged to the universe, to the Great Spirit. He would show them that.

He kept on ignoring the screams as he chopped wood for the framework of the small lodge: facing the fire pit, with an opening at the front. This he covered with hides he'd brought with him, stitched together in the traditional way and weighted down with rocks. Tied inside the lodge were little pouches filled with tobacco as offerings. Using some of the longest logs he'd cut, Shadow built a kind of box about three feet square, which he then built up, filling it with kindling, before building up a dome of rocks – then more wood until the pile was quite high. He had another problem getting the fire to light, the wood refusing to respond to the spark of rock, the kindling unwilling to burn, but finally nature took its course as he knew it would. Soon a roaring fire was going.

It took some time for the rocks in the pit to grow hot enough for his purpose. Shadow removed anything metal from his person. He also made sure he had the bottles of water he'd brought with him, for drinking and for wetting the rocks he'd be using – which would be carried into the lodge using a fork-like tool he'd affixed to the end of a long branch.

He also set up an altar made from dirt found in the hole. On this he placed several items personal to him as offerings, including ashes from previous sweats – through which his mission had been imparted.

Shadow stripped to the waist and began his Spirit Calling ceremony. He started by chanting words known only to him, the lodge preparing him for his journey to another plane of existence. Once there, he would call forth those who watched over *him*, to do battle with the ancients of this place. The prize would be the forest, for he needed to sever the link with Hood before he could defeat the man. Sherwood's favourite son fought with old gods on his side, but then so did Shadow. It was just a question of which were the strongest this day.

To help him on his way, Shadow smoked the pipe he had prepared. While it was in his hands, it represented a conduit through which the universe and the creator's power could flow. It would help him to commune with those he sought.

Shadow felt it flowing through him, felt the rhythms of this place just as surely as he had the stag's heartbeat. He begged the spirits he worshipped to come: to cleanse not only him, but the forest.

They appeared in a miasma of colourful scenes, taking on shapes like the wolf, the bear and the buffalo. The creatures of this forest were pitted against them: led by a representation of the stag, no longer felled – because that was only its physical presence. Here it was strong and majestic, a symbol of the old god's power and dominance. For now. It was a battlefield unlike any other, way beyond anything ordinary humans had ever witnessed. Beyond guns, tanks and helicopters.

Mighty hawks swooped and fought with owls, spinning over and over in the technicoloured clouds. The stag rammed its antlers into the bear, just as it had done with Shadow, only for the wolf to leap on its back and begin tearing chunks out of it. Even the smaller animals, like badgers and foxes, fought – pitting themselves against the creatures of the desert, like the rattlesnake.

Shadow marvelled at the complexity of it, then at the simplicity: a glorious contradiction. The fight seemed to rage for hours but there was no telling the passage of time. The only way Shadow realised it was over was when the bear picked up the stag and held it aloft, delivering it to him.

Shadow gave thanks to the Great Spirit, just before the connection was severed. He managed to crawl out of the lodge – staggering a few yards with a bottle of water he'd hastily grabbed – before collapsing.

But he knew that no harm would come to him now. He was protected by the new keepers of Sherwood. And Hood was soon to find out exactly what it was like to be the prey instead of the predator.

A trap would be set before long, and as Shadow drifted off into unconsciousness, he realised exactly where he would find the bait.

CHAPTER SEVEN

SOMETHING WAS VERY wrong.

It had started with the dreams. It sounded crazy, but he'd accepted that the forest was giving them to him. They hadn't begun until he'd moved to Sherwood. Then he'd moved out of the forest and into the castle to run the Rangers, and the dreams had deserted him for a spell – which had almost cost all their lives. The forest had also – and this sounded even crazier when he thought about it – *healed* him at least a couple of times, even brought him back from the brink of death.

He'd come to realise that he needed to return there every now and again, to recharge. His excuse was the trips he took young Mark on to teach him hunting skills, but wasn't the lad starting to feel the forest, as well? He'd certainly spoken to Robert about strange dreams he'd had while he'd been there.

More and more, though, over the last year especially, Robert had come to understand that he always carried a part of that special place with him wherever he went.

In fact, that was literally true these days, because he'd struck upon the idea of making himself a little reminder of home. His true, spiritual home. In the pouch he wore on his belt were twigs, earth, stones, grass, bark and leaves he'd gathered from Sherwood – and copying him in all things, Mark had insisted on making one as well. When travelling or on a mission, and in times of great stress, he'd find himself clutching the bag unconsciously. It eased his mind. And while he'd been carrying it, the dreams had never deserted him again.

Until now.

It had happened last night while he slept, out under the stars with Mary beside him. He'd refused the offer of staying at a hotel Bill had commandeered for himself and the rest of the Rangers. Instead, Robert and Mary had found a local park and bedded down there; she was more used to sleeping outdoors now since the Christmas surprise he'd given her of a night out in Sherwood. So, falling asleep with the pouch in his hand, it hadn't taken long for the dreams to visit Robert.

His eyes opened and at first he'd thought he was still in the park. But the sheer mass of trees and greenery soon told him otherwise. It had to be the dreamscape, and it had to be Sherwood. He was walking through familiar surroundings, enjoying being back once again, when there was a disturbance in the trees up ahead. At first he thought it was some kind of animal, but when the trees themselves began falling he realised it was something much bigger. Flashes of red appeared between the trunks, then the trees directly in front of him parted.

And he saw a monster.

It looked like a dinosaur, but was nothing so mundane. Robert recognised it from the tales of swords and sorcery he'd read as a kid. It was a dragon, its scaly crimson hide tough and impenetrable. And it was huge: as tall as the trees in Sherwood.

It breathed out fire, cooking the trees, burning the leaves off branches.

But this wasn't the only monster in Sherwood. Another parting of the trees and on Robert's right was a giant black spider, its multitude of eyes bulbous and glassy, regarding him with both hatred and longing. The dragon saw the spider and roared; the arachnid, for its part, made a series of clicking noises and weird shrills. Somehow Robert instinctively knew it was female, and although he was no expert he would have bet his life on the fact that the species was a Black Widow.

These were the opponents he and his men were facing at the moment, or at least that's what they represented. Gaining power, becoming bigger and stronger, they would take over soon unless something was done to stop them. No sooner had he thought this than Robert's Rangers flooded the scene, firing arrows at the two behemoths and swinging their swords. Robert looked on as the Dragon crushed a couple of his Rangers underfoot, while the Widow stopped others in their tracks by spinning a web around them they couldn't break. She then turned on one poor soul and began to eat him, starting with the head. Robert winced at the sight, but didn't – *couldn't* – move.

Faces he recognised now were tackling the threat, such as Dale and Jack on his left, leading the attack against the Dragon; Bill, Azhar and Mary on his right, trying to avoid those webs and deadly mandibles. Mary turned, urging him to join the fight; they couldn't do this without him. Robert tried to move again, but still couldn't.

Then he saw it. Something, some*one* striding out between the two creatures, ignoring them as if they didn't matter. A man, but not quite a man – indistinct and shadowy, his body like fog. He was carrying something above his head. Something with antlers.

The stag. The thing Robert had often become himself in this dreamland. Was that meant to be him there, defeated? Dead even? There was definitely blood dripping from the body, he could see that now. As the man came closer, his features grew clearer. He looked Native American, but Robert didn't have long to take in the sight of him.

Everything happened so quickly. First, the Dragon and the Widow shrank back, reducing in size as something else was revealed behind them – an unclear shape, pushing, or manipulating, them. Next, the shadow man started to increase in size, becoming stronger, more significant. As he did so, the stag he was holding caught fire – perhaps from one of the Dragon's blasts, Robert couldn't tell. The stag burnt fiercely for a second or two before becoming ash which rained down onto the ground.

Robert thought something terrible might happen then. Often the dreams had shown him his own death, in an effort to try and prevent it. But what actually occurred was that everything went black. It was like a TV being put on standby, the picture telescoping away into nothing. At any second Robert thought he might wake up, but he didn't. Nothing happened. He'd lost the connection somehow, the information it was feeding him out of reach.

He awoke not long after, Mary stirring when she heard him.

"What is it?" she asked, half mumbling.

"Nothing," he lied.

She rolled towards him, snuggling up. "Good. Go back to sleep, love."

It was good advice, and he tried. For a long time. He'd finally nodded off before dawn, long enough usually to bring back the dreams. But again there was nothing but darkness.

Over breakfast, back at the hotel provided by the marketeers, Robert was agitated, but refused to discuss it with Mary. She'd come to understand that Sherwood was a special place for him, but still didn't really get *how* special. Nor how much of a role it played in keeping them one step ahead of their enemies. When she looked hurt, Robert had given her hand a squeeze and told her not to worry; he didn't want her thinking he was shutting her out again. But at the same time he wasn't in the mood to talk about what was going on with his dreams.

"So," Bill had asked, "any idea what we're going t'do about this situation?"

They'd questioned the captured raiders and found out more about the Widow. The conclusion they'd drawn was that her men were devoted to the woman, fanatically so in fact. She was power hungry and she was, not to put too fine a point on it, completely insane. The raiders didn't mind telling them about her, in fact they quite relished it, fuelling the rumour that she ate human flesh, that she was into black magic and that she could never die. They were less forthcoming about her defensive capabilities. Loyal, even under pressure, and that didn't include the kind of pressure De Falaise and his goon Tanek put their prisoners under, Robert and Bill had gained nothing from the interrogation sessions, apart from the location of their base: Edinburgh Castle.

That had been when Mary stepped in with the sodium pentothal. Picked up during routine searches of medical facilities for supplies that her and the trainee nurses back home could use, Mary was the only one allowed to administer this drug, and even then only in extreme circumstances. It was surprising how much looser their tongues were then, spilling information about lookout positions dotted around the city, guard changes, patrol patterns.

"This German connection wi' the jeeps, bikes an' guns still bothers me," Bill concluded.

Robert nodded. "This whole thing goes beyond simple raiding parties. We're going to have to stamp on the Widow before she gets out of control."

"What exactly did you have in mind?" said Mary.

What he had in mind was getting inside the castle for a closer look at their operation, perhaps even trying to trace back where the Widow's support came from. If they were facing another invasion then forewarned was forearmed. Essentially a covert and hand-picked strike force, led by himself, would ascertain the level of threat, and eradicate it if necessary. He thought Mary might argue about him going, but she didn't. All she said was that if he went, then she was going too, which was fair enough. As much as he still felt that twinge of dread whenever she wanted to accompany him on a mission, knowing that she could well be killed, maimed or captured, he knew she'd be feeling exactly the same about him. If one of them was going, then both should. Plus which, as he'd observed on many occasions, Mary was one hell of a fighter. She'd saved his skin at least as many times as he'd saved hers – more so probably. If anyone was going to watch his back, Robert wanted – *needed* – Mary.

"Right, when do we leave?" Bill wanted to know.

Robert shook his head. "I want you to stay here."

"What?"

"I can't afford to have all my best people on this. I need you out here, Bill, in case we run into difficulties." Robert wisely withheld the bit about Bill being a loose cannon – often literally with that shotgun of his.

Bill argued a little – "I was the one who bloody well brought ye into all this!" – but in the end he grudgingly accepted the logic of Robert's decision. That was probably a first. *Must be mellowing in his old age*, thought Robert.

"And Bill," he said, "if we do need backup, promise me you won't kit the Rangers out with machine-guns or whatever. No heavy stuff. Let them fight the way they were meant to. The way they were *trained* to."

Bill folded his arms.

"Promise me," Robert insisted.

"Aye, all right," Bill said reluctantly. "But I still think ye're bloody crackers."

Robert grinned. "Nothing new there, then."

Using maps of the castle, Robert had outlined how they were going to play this: entering the city just as they had done when taking Nottingham Castle the first time, only this time they knew exactly which bits to avoid, and they'd be doing it under cover of darkness. He knew his Rangers could move silently, unseen, through the urban forest just as he had once done through Sherwood. When they were close enough, they'd split into three teams of a handful each: one, led by Azhar, making an assault up the rocks on the north side, climbing over the wall at a point just down from the Argyle Battery cannons. The second, led by a female Ranger called Annie Reid, would do the same on the south side, gaining access up and into the grounds near the old Scottish United Services Museum. The third group would take out the guards outside the Gatehouse, replacing them with Rangers dressed in captured raider uniforms, who would then let in the rest of that team. Later they'd regroup within the castle boundaries.

"The good thing is, the Widow doesn't have nearly as many men as either De Falaise or The Tsar at the moment," Robert informed his troops. "With a bit of luck, we should be able to get in there, get the job done, and leave again without anyone having seen us even enter."

Robert and Mary would be leading the frontal assault. "It'll be just like old times," she said to her husband, referring to when she'd walked through the gates of Nottingham Castle to confront the Sheriff.

"Let's hope not," Robert replied. "I don't want to take on her entire army just yet."

Preparations were made and they'd set off on horseback for Scotland's capital in the afternoon, timing it just right so they'd reach the castle itself by nightfall. Everything had gone well, they'd managed to avoid the Widow's people who were watching for signs of intruders in the city, and tethered their mounts once they were close enough to make it on foot. They moved as one through the streets, and even Robert was impressed by the way his people conducted themselves – all those hours of practise had really paid off. He felt proud as they pressed themselves up against walls, checked around corners. They couldn't have been better trained if they'd been on the police force with him all those years ago.

When the time came, they'd branched off: Azhar skirting round one side with his team; Annie taking her group round the other, keeping to the shadows at the base. And near the Esplanade – where many jeeps, tanks and other armoured vehicles were stationed – Robert and Mary held back with the others. Two of their Rangers dressed in the Widow's tartan handled the guards at the Gatehouse. They could have taken them out with arrows, but didn't want to risk that being seen from a distance; guards suddenly keeling over at the same time was sure to raise suspicion. Better to take them out in close quarters then replace them almost immediately. Robert looked on as the Rangers crept silently up towards the Gatehouse, sneaking behind the guards simultaneously, hands over mouths, knocking them out and taking their places.

Once the nod was given, the rest of them moved forwards just as stealthily, finding whatever cover they could in order to reach the arch. "Good work," Robert whispered to his troops now standing guard, as they let them all in through the front door, flanked on either side by statues of Robert the Bruce and William Wallace. Robert couldn't help thinking that Scotland deserved the kind of freedom those men had fought so hard for, not the slavery this Widow obviously had in mind.

Inside, they remained in the shadows, making their way up towards the Portcullis Gate, the second line of the Widow's defence. They waited patiently for the signal that Azhar's team had taken out the guards here from the other side. That came when the lethal-looking gate was raised.

Nicely done, Azhar, thought Robert, waving to the figures up in the building above them.

He motioned for his team to move forwards through the gate, into the castle grounds proper. This place was much larger than their castle, but that meant there were more places to hide between its many buildings: like St Margaret's Chapel, the rounded water Reservoirs, the large War Memorial. No sooner had they entered than they had to conceal themselves when a group of a dozen or so of the Widow's men walked past.

"That was close," Mary said.

He nodded, but Robert found himself frowning at the same time. It was about now that the sense of unease really hit him: his own instinct telling him something was wrong. As good as they were at this kind of operation, this was all a bit too easy.

Robert registered more jeeps outside the New Barracks – which housed the bulk of the Widow's troops – as they moved back and round towards the Royal buildings where he knew the woman herself would be located.

He looked around as they entered the Crown Square, then tugged on Mary's arm. "I think we need to get out of here."

"What is it?"

"This smells like–" He was about to say 'a trap', but by then it was obvious. Lights kicked in from above and they were surrounded by armed guards, swarming from every conceivable nook and cranny. Ranger Madison at the side of Robert raised his bow and felled a couple of the Widow's men, and was shot dead at point blank range for his trouble. Mary's Peacekeepers were out, but Robert put an arm across to stop her from firing. It was no use, they were hopelessly outnumbered and in a confined space. Their only hope was that Annie Reid and her team might come to their aid, but that was soon dashed when Robert heard a voice from one of the open windows above.

"Welcome to our home, Robin," said the woman with the wild hair. "I know what you're thinking, but yer other teams are a little bit tied up right now." The crowds parted to show them the other Ranger groups, including Ahzar's, captured: their hands bound behind their backs. "Who do yer think let you in at the Portcullis Gate?" She laughed, and it echoed around the square. "I knew you fellas were coming even before you did."

It crossed Robert's mind that he could pick her off with just one arrow. Her men wouldn't be able to stop him in time.

"I wouldnae try that," she called down. "It'd just be a waste of an arrow. – and yer life."

Lucky guess, had to be. It was what anyone in this position would be thinking.

"What is it that you want?" said Robert, perhaps hoping to negotiate, but knowing full well this wasn't a woman who could be bargained with.

"Yer come here in the dead of night and ask what *I* want. It seems obvious yer wantin' me. You want to know ma secrets. That's okay, because what I want is you, Hooded Man, so I'd be more than happy tae oblige."

CHAPTER EIGHT

THE MORE HE explored of the place, the more he realised just how dangerous this man's outfit was.

Take Cardiff Arms Park for example, located next door. Dale had managed to sneak a look from up high in the stadium and saw that this had been converted into a giant storage facility. It was filled with all kinds of jeeps, tanks, tracked and multi-role armoured vehicles – the latter with their distinctive eight wheels. They must have widened or knocked down the entrance to get them all in. And more seemed to be arriving every day, enough to take on the rest of Wales, maybe even sometime soon the rest of what had once been Great Britain. Where they were coming from, he had no idea, and he was no closer to finding out.

So here he was, alone and cut off from the outside world: a spy in the Dragon's den. He needed to get to a radio – the Dragon must be keeping in touch with his units that way, same as they did – but he didn't have all that much to report at the moment. Just his observations about how powerful this Welshman was becoming, how the rest of this country would never shift him if they didn't act soon.

He'd never felt so unsure about what to do in all his life. When he was younger he'd always been focused on the music, always known he wanted to be a musician. Surviving after The Cull, on the streets, he'd been confident that he'd get by, travelling with his guitar and fending off anyone who fancied their chances. But right now he just didn't know which way to turn.

It wasn't even so much that he was on his own here, because he'd always felt that way deep down, like he shouldn't really get to close to anyone. That was probably why he could never really connect with the opposite sex. Even after he'd found Robert and his Rangers, joined them, been accepted into their clan, Dale still saw himself as being something apart from that too. A team player, but at the same time a maverick. No, his anxiety was more to do with the fact he was out of his depth, that he wasn't used to all this masquerading. Dale preferred to be upfront, to fight his enemy face to face, not pretend to be something he wasn't in order to figure out a potential weakness.

But it's not the first time you've pretended to be something you're not, is it? He'd done that all the time with the women he'd dated – if you could call one night stands dating. Pretended he'd call them, that things might go further, just to get them into the sack. *This is different, and besides, I've changed.* Or at least he wanted to change, but hadn't quite got it yet.

All this was just to stop him thinking about what to do next. And a distraction so he wouldn't think about–

A radio; he should at the very least check in with Jack, let the man know he was still alive. If Dale knew Jack, he'd be monitoring the frequencies for a call. That man knew the airwaves like the back of his hand, having had an interest in radio since he was a kid – probably the only way he could keep in touch with anyone, cut off in upstate New York.

Cut off, just like Dale was now.

When he was sure he could slip out without being noticed, Dale grabbed a tray and exited the kitchens at the Stadium, praying that another big order wouldn't come in from the Dragon while he was searching. He made his way up one corridor and down another, almost bumping into the man himself, being wheeled along towards a set of double doors.

Dale hung back, but followed for a little while, trailing the Dragon to a set of lifts – actual working lifts! – where he descended with his personal guards. Maybe that was where he took the women from his–

No, you weren't going to think about that, remember? Well, at least if he was heading there, he wouldn't be asking for food again in a hurry. Dale swore under his breath, thinking what the cost might be for buying him some time. It was too high a price. Much too high.

He got on with his task of looking for a radio. It wasn't easy, because he couldn't just stop and ask one of the Dragon's men where it was. Bit of a giveaway for a budding secret agent. On the plus side, only certain key locations inside were lit with proper electric lights; obviously the work of whoever had rigged up the PA system and lifts. If he just carried the tray around with him, none of the guards said a thing because they simply assumed he was on his way back from delivering the Dragon's latest meal, or fetching and carrying for the rest of the troops. In essence, Dale had the run of the place. Now all he had to do was–

There!

One of the Dragon's men was coming out of a well lit room, the door swinging open a crack behind him. Dale spotted a radio on the table inside. There was another guy still in the room, speaking into the mouthpiece. Dale looked left and right. If he took out the operator that was sure to be discovered eventually, and before Dale was ready to get out of this place. Maybe he should just wait for the bloke to leave. But what if he never did? What if the other one came back, and then he had to wait for both of them to vacate the room? Dale was conscious that he'd been absent from the kitchens for a while. People would begin to notice soon, if they hadn't already. He had to do something, or just give up on contacting Jack altogether.

The man inside yawned, stretched and looked as though he was about to get up. Dale smiled. He was in luck, the bloke was about to follow his comrade. But no, instead he rested his head on the table. He was having a fucking nap! There was no way Dale would be able to use the radio with him in there kipping.

Dale had crept further towards the door to watch. It was only now, when a hand came down on his shoulder, that he realised he'd given himself away. A good spy should never be caught snooping in doorways.

He started, almost bringing the tray round and smacking the person in the face – assuming it was the second guard coming back. But Dale held himself in check, as well as holding his breath. It was a good job because when he turned, he saw a face he recognised.

"You're going to get caught sneaking about like that," whispered the girl with the milky skin and blonde hair. The girl he hadn't been able to get out of his mind since the Dragon took her away. Dale's had never been lost for words in his life, but he was now. "Caught or killed." the girl said, her voice betrayed a faint Welsh accent, like she'd been born in this country but had lived further east for a while.

He stepped back, taking her in. She was still dressed in a flimsy outfit; the baby doll replaced by a chemise. Dale suddenly found his voice. "What are *you* doing here?"

"*Not* getting caught," she replied, and he realised that his first assessment of her had been spot on. Back in that VIP box he'd noticed her obvious compassion for those murdered Rangers, but also an inner strength he really admired. It reminded him a little of Sophie, of Mary. "I hope, anyway." The girl pulled him to one side so they couldn't be seen from inside the room.

"Caught doing what?" Dale's curiosity about her had overcome any surprise or awkwardness; now he just wanted to know what she was up to.

"The same as you, I'm guessing. Something we shouldn't be."

She had him there. He definitely shouldn't be sending a radio message out or thinking about whacking one of the Dragon's men to do it. "Okay... Look, just who are you?"

"My name's Sian."

"Dale."

"All right then, Dale, you obviously want to get into that room to use the radio. But you can't with that big lug snoring over there. I want information. We can help each other." Sian skirted around him and made for the door.

Dale grabbed her by the arm. "What are you doing? You can't!"

"Out of the two of us, I reckon I'm the one that can," she said, removing his hand from her arm. She smiled. "Don't worry, I came prepared." She held up her other hand and in it was most of a bottle of whiskey. "Loosens the tongue."

Suddenly Sian was gone, walking into the room and rousing the Dragon's man. He heard the guy ask gruffly what she was doing there, but he didn't catch her reply. The rest of what they were saying was muffled. Although he couldn't see from this angle, Dale knew the guy must be looking at her, his eyes trailing over her body just as the Dragon's had. Just as his own had.

No, not the same, not the same thing at all!

Dale held back as long as he could, but when he heard laughter he edged closer to the door. Sian was explaining to the man that she'd been sent here with a little present for his hard work, that the Dragon had said to enjoy it. Dale wasn't sure whether she was talking about the booze or her. The thought made Dale want to retch. He heard gulping as the man drank and felt grateful he couldn't see what else he was up to. Dale waited as the man drank more, and more. It was only when he heard him telling Sian what he'd like to do to her, his voice slurring badly, that Dale couldn't restrain himself any longer.

The next thing he knew, he was inside the room and had brought the tray he was holding down on the back of the man's head. The operator slumped forward.

"What the hell do you think you're doing?" Sian snapped.

"Giving him a hangover he won't forget in a hurry."

"And what if he remembers? What if—"

"Look, he was about to, you know, try it on." He couldn't believe he'd just said that. This was the woman who'd been dragged off by the Dragon, had done Christ knows what with him, and he was worried about a drunk radio guy getting a bit fresh.

"He was in no condition to try *anything* on! God, if you've screwed things up for me—"

"Screwed things up... what are you talking about?"

Sian let out a weary sigh. "I came in here looking for my Aunt Meghan. We've been together ever since... well, you know. The Dragon's men took her a few weeks ago. She kept me hidden away safe when they found us, I think she thought she could talk her way out of it. But they took her, Dale. They took her so I *let* myself get captured."

"Jesus. I'm really sorry." If anything, that made what Sian had gone through all the more upsetting. "Did you get anything from him?"

Sian shook her head.

"Listen, I'll help you look for her. But first, I really need to send a message out on that radio before his mate comes back."

"Won't be back anytime soon. This one made it very clear we'd be alone for a good while. They just got a message through saying some big foreign guy the Dragon's supposed to be meeting is almost here. His mate's gone off to look after him personally, give him a tour until the Dragon is ready to meet up."

"What big foreign guy?"

"Funny sounding name: Tunic or something."

Dale placed his hands on her arms. "*Tanek?* Was that the name?"

"Might have been."

"Think, Sian. This is important!"

She nodded. "Yeah, I think so.

"Shit!"

"What? I don't understand."

Dale ignored her, flipping switches and attempting to dial up a signal. "Please be out there, Jack," he said.

Now he really did have something to report, but he wished with all his heart he didn't.

HE REALLY WISHED he'd never sent the kid in there.

Jack ground his teeth as he sat in the remains of what was left of the Welsh Ranger headquarters. He and his squad had arrived too late to do anything to help the troops stationed there, and as Jack had looked over the devastation – the bodies of Rangers, men and women alike – his guts tied themselves in knots. It was these people who'd alerted them to the problem in the first place, but they hadn't described anything on this scale. Another wannabe dictator maybe who was still building up his forces, but with nowhere near the capability to do something like *this*. These were trained fighters, damned well trained. He knew because he'd trained some of them himself back at Nottingham Castle.

Now they were dead.

Jack had felt his hands tightening around the staff he always carried as he took in the blood, the glassy eyes, the expressionless faces.

"Sir!" one of his squad had alerted him to the approach of a vehicle. A jeep, travelling at speed on the horizon. He didn't need to order his Rangers to hunker down and find cover, because they were already doing it. If this was a clean-up crew of the Dragon's men, coming to pick off any survivors they'd missed, then they'd chosen the wrong day.

As the jeep came closer, however, it was clear that they had other intentions. The vehicle skidded, doing a handbrake turn as it reached the former HQ. Then two men threw a bundle out of the back... a living bundle, though it was a poor excuse for a human being. In fact the body they tossed out looked in worse shape than some of the corpses surrounding Jack. But he could tell from the hood and dark green garb, it was another one of his Rangers. Where he'd been and what had happened to him, Jack had no idea, but he was guessing it hadn't been pleasant.

As the jeep began to drive off again, Jack broke cover and ordered those behind him to see to their fallen comrade. Jack had a score to settle.

He began to run. Although he wasn't as young as he had been when he'd done the circuits as a professional wrestler, he'd kept himself in good shape with exercise and training. Not to mention actual combat. In the last couple of years he'd been in more scrapes than he ever had in the ring, been in more danger than he had been against Big Bud McCardle or The Terror from Tallahassee. There still wasn't an ounce of fat on Jack 'The Hammer' Finlayson's frame, and it meant that before too long he was catching up with that accelerating jeep. He had also attracted the attention of those in the back. Those within reach of a pretty lethal looking mounted machine-gun.

He saw one of the men pointing, then the other spinning the weapon around before firing. Jack dodged sideways, only just avoiding the bullets which raked the road.

The gunman aimed, but again fired wide – Jack leaping just in time to avoid the deadly stream of lead. Bending, he ran even faster at the vehicle, so fast that his baseball cap flew off. He ignored this, pressing on until he was almost level with the jeep. Before either the gunman or his partner could react, Jack was using his staff to pole-vault into the back. He lost his grip on the wooden stick, but didn't need it now. When the man closest tried to draw his pistol, Jack clipped it out of his hands and grabbed hold of him by the collar.

"Let's see how you like it, pal!" he roared, picking the man up and heaving him from the vehicle. There was an audible crack as one of his legs broke, then he tumbled head over heels. The other man yelped when he saw this, and scrabbled to get away. But a huge hand on his shoulder prevented this, twisting him around so that Jack could take hold of his head with both hands. Then Jack brought it down onto his raised knee. The man toppled backwards, over the side. He must have fallen under the wheels, though, because the whole vehicle rose up in the air momentarily, then fell back down again. When Jack looked behind him, he saw the man's body flattened against the road.

Jack clambered around on the outside of the jeep as it continued to speed up, the lone driver perhaps thinking – bizarrely – that he could escape that way. Jack reached in through the open window and grabbed at the wheel, pulling it towards himself: pulling them off the road and towards a nearby house. The driver attempted to wrestle the wheel back, but there was only one wrestler present. The man just wasn't strong enough and when Jack was satisfied they were on a collision course, he let go and jumped free.

Unlike the two men from the back of the jeep, Jack did know how to fall. So, as he rolled to a halt, he watched with satisfaction as the jeep rammed headlong into the house, pitching the driver through its windscreen.

"*You* have just been Jack Hammered," he uttered in a low tone, but there was none of the usual glibness. This had been revenge, pure and simple, for the Rangers killed back at the base, and for the one they'd dumped by the roadside. Jack only hoped he got a chance to explain how he felt to their boss.

He picked himself up and began his walk back along the road, retrieving his staff and his cap along the way. The man who'd been run over was dead. The other was alive, but badly injured. Jack quizzed him about what had happened at the HQ, and back at the stadium, standing on the damaged leg whenever the man refused to answer. Robert probably wouldn't have approved, but their leader wasn't here. Hadn't seen what these men had done. The injured man told Jack how the Rangers they'd captured had died. "You sick sons of bitches," Jack said. Then he thought about Dale. "Have you seen a young guy back at the stadium? About yay high, good looking? You know if he's still alive?" The man shook his head. "Okay," said Jack, and began walking off.

"Wait, you can't just leave me here," screamed the soldier.

"Our man comes first. Then maybe I'll send someone back for you." Or maybe he would just clean forget. *Things slip your mind sometimes,* Jack said to himself. For now, all he wanted to know was how the fallen Ranger was doing, and if Dale was all right.

His squad were attempting to patch up their colleague, who Jack could now see was suffering from a bullet wound to the leg. "He'll be lucky if it doesn't get infected," a Ranger called Chadwick told him, out of earshot of the patient, "even with antibiotics. And he'll never be able to walk properly again."

All the battles, all the fights he'd been in; nothing compared to this. Slaughtering his Rangers in their home, promising freedom then blowing them up, leaving just one alive but crippled for life. And he'd sent Dale into that maniac's domain. Sure, the kid could handle himself, but Jack still felt as though he'd signed his death warrant. This wasn't the movies. Bad things happened to good people and there were never any guarantees of a happy ending.

So in the time since then he'd sat by the radio. Waiting for a sign that Dale was still alive, that he hadn't simply been shot in the head for the Dragon's amusement. Once or twice he'd heard a crackle of static, but it had only been ghosts whispering down the line.

Then Dale's voice actually came down the line. "Green Three Leader, come in. Green Three, are you out there? Please respond. Jack, answer the radio, will you? Over."

Jack picked up the receiver and spoke. "This is Green Three Leader. Dale, is that you little buddy? Over."

There was another crackle of static, then: "Well it's not bloody Bono, is it. Over." Jack smiled, but could hear the panic in Dale's voice.

"Are you okay? Over."

"Yeah – for now. But I don't have much time. Listen, there's been a development. The Dragon's working with a guy you might have heard of. Big fella, olive skinned. Likes crossbows. Over."

Jack couldn't believe his ears. "Tanek?" The last time Jack had seen that man, it had been as his torture victim, while De Falaise's daughter, Adele, cheered him on. Robert said that he'd escaped after they'd taken down the Tsar in Sherwood, but nobody had seen or heard about him since. Like that proverbial bad penny, he just always seemed to show up – especially when there was something big going down. But what was his connection to the Welsh Dragon? Whatever it turned out to be, this wasn't good news at all. "Do you know what he's doing there, Dale? Over."

"Not yet. But stuff's been arriving all the time I've been here. Weapons, vehicles, most of it kept in Cardiff Arms Park. I think he might be involved in supplying it. Over."

Jack rubbed his chin. That would make sense; first Tanek allied himself with De Falaise, then the Tsar, now the Dragon. Anyone he thought might be able to seize power. *But there must be a third party involved if that pond scum's the go-between,* he reasoned.

"Listen Dale, I want you to get out of there. You've done all you can, now I want you to report back to–"

"What's that? You're breaking up."

"I said get your ass out of there, Dale, and that's an order!" The radio died. Whether it was just a loss of signal, someone had found Dale, or he'd just run out of time, Jack had no way of knowing. But it made him more aware than ever that if something happened to the youth it would be on his head. Jack slammed his fist against the wall, swearing. When one of the Rangers came in, he barked at them that he wanted to be left alone.

After a few minutes, he nodded to himself, then muttered, "Okay, so you're not coming out. Maybe it's about time we came in."

DALE CLICKED THE radio off. He'd heard Jack's orders, but there was no way he was going to pull out just yet.

"Green Three..." Sian said. "You're a Ranger, aren't you? One of Robin Hood's men?"

Back before the virus that would have sounded so stupid, but Sian said it with complete seriousness. Robert's reputation as the new Hooded Man, and that of his Rangers, had spread so far. No-one was laughing at him, least of all his enemies. Dale shrugged, then nodded, feeling slightly embarrassed; what was wrong with him? He wasn't usually this shy about blowing his own trumpet. But with Sian it was different. He wasn't out to impress.

"God, why didn't you say something?"

"Didn't really seem the time or place."

The radio operator moaned. There wasn't much danger of him waking up yet, but it was time they made themselves scarce.

"I think we'd probably better get out of here." Dale said.

Sian nodded, but touched his arm as he made to leave. "Why did you do that just then?"

"What?"

"Cut off... what was his name, Jack? Cut him off when he was ordering you to get out of here."

Once more, Dale felt the blood rushing to his cheeks. He looked down as he answered. "Because I didn't want to leave you here. And you won't leave until you've found your aunty... So..."

Sian looked at him, then, suddenly, kissed him on the cheek. "Thank you, Dale."

He shrugged a final time, feeling as though his cheeks were on fire. Then, as much to hide this as anything else, he nodded towards the door, gesturing for them both to leave.

There was still much to do before either of them could get out of this madhouse.

CHAPTER NINE

THE CAPTIVE'S HEAD rocked to one side with the sheer force of the blow.

"Come on, talk, damn you!" Gwen brought her hand back and hit the man again, almost tipping over the chair he was tied to.

The prisoner – his features pinched, hair closely cropped – spat blood and grinned, teeth stained crimson. Gwen punched him in the side, where her bullet had winged him, and Dr Jeffreys gave a wail of protest.

"You'll pull out the stitches!"

Gwen took no notice, striking the man again. He gritted his teeth, bubbles of red saliva bursting as they escaped his lips.

"I said *talk!*" she screamed into his face. "Who sent you? Who do you work for?"

The man smirked again, even laughed.

Gwen brought her hand back once more, but felt someone grab it. She turned and saw Andy holding her wrist. "Take it easy, Gwen. The guy's obviously not going to play ball."

She looked at Andy, then back at their prisoner. Play ball? This wasn't a game. Gwen pulled her arm away. After all they'd risked to get this dickhead here, she wasn't about to ask nicely. The guy had been shooting at them, for Christ's sake. He'd put her son at risk, why did he deserve any kind of compassion?

The answer was, he didn't – and she proved that by smacking him again, perhaps just to spite Andy. He might be okay with waiting for New Hope to be overrun by armed men, but she wasn't going to just sit here and let it happen.

Andy had been against going out there to fetch the prisoner in the first place. "You're joking," he'd said when he heard Gwen's plan. "You're going to get yourself killed, and then what'll happen to little Clive?"

That hadn't been the smartest thing he'd ever said. Clive Jr was the reason for *everything* she did. It was precisely because of him she'd risk venturing out to get the fallen gunman, even though more of his friends were still in the woods. "It's almost dark, if we use the warren then–"

"What if those nuts have night-vision or whatever? Have you thought of that? Hell, I can't be a part of this madness," Andy had said, holding up his hands and walking off.

"Okay," Gwen had said after him. Thankfully, there had been others willing to go with her. Darryl for instance, who they had to thank for the warren in the first place. When designing the wall, he'd had the foresight to include a back door in case of just such an emergency. The warren was exactly what it sounded like, an underground tunnel which led from the back of New Hope up and out into the woods; the exit covered over with foliage and bracken stuck to the outside of the trapdoor. If Graham had been fit enough, he'd have volunteered as well, if only to pay back the sods who'd shot him, but he was nowhere near. In fact, Jeffreys had reported earlier that his situation was deteriorating, in spite of the drugs they were giving him.

"All the more reason to go and fetch one of them, bring him inside," Gwen told the doctor.

So, she and Darryl had climbed into the warren and made their way up and out into the woods. Rifles primed, they'd crawled along on their bellies as silently as they could to where Gwen judged the man had fallen. She'd posted a watch on him and not one of his friends had come to get him or see how he was. Loyalty obviously wasn't part of their agenda.

Just when they thought they weren't going to find him, Gwen spotted a boot in the undergrowth and tugged on Darryl's arm. He nodded, following as they drew closer to the gunman. Jeffreys had given Gwen a tranquiliser to subdue the guy, but as it turned out he'd lost so much blood that he barely put up a fight. As they started dragging him away, however, bullets splintered the trees surrounding them. The fuckers had been using him as bait. "Quick, move!" Gwen ordered; they didn't have time for messing about. She and Darryl hauled the man back and it was only now he started to cry out, risking giving away their location. Gwen put her hand over his mouth as they pulled him along, racing towards the hole in the ground. They reached it ahead of their pursuers and scrambled back down inside the warren, yanking the trapdoor shut and locking it from inside. They heard boots, but the shooters trampled overhead, running past; oblivious to what was hidden under their feet.

Darryl emerged first at the New Hope end, greeted by the sight of Karen Shipley pointing a pistol at him. As instructed, she'd been keeping it trained on the open black square since they'd entered, just in case they had any unwanted visitors. When she saw Darryl poke his head through, she let out a whoop of joy, hugging and kissing him on the cheek, much to his surprise.

"Oh, thank God!"

Yes, she'd been pleased to see the man she was clearly sweet on. But Karen had also never shot anyone before. Gwen knew the woman might have to if things carried on the way they were going, but felt only a small twinge of sadness about the loss of her innocence. After all, Gwen's had been snatched away a long time ago.

They'd taken the prisoner to Jeffreys who'd patched up the wound and given the man a transfusion. At first no-one had volunteered, but when the doctor pointed out he'd die without one and they'd get nothing from him at all, Darryl once again stepped into the breach. Who'd have thought she'd come to rely on him so much? *He* was the very essence of lost innocence, yet Gwen couldn't have done all this without him. "Hook me up, doc," Darryl had said. "Least we know we're the same group."

Unbelievably, that had been four hours ago, and as the prisoner had recovered steadily, Gwen sat studying him. When she judged he was fit enough to be questioned, she'd taken him at gunpoint – virtually carrying him to the Red Lion – ignoring all of Jeffreys' and Andy's complaints. She was still ignoring them.

"What's happened to you, Gwen?" Andy asked after the last blow.

She gaped at him. "Do I really have to answer that?"

"You're killing him."

"Hopefully not until we get what we want."

"This isn't the way to treat *anyone*. He's still a human being."

"A human being who's been shooting at our home, Andy. Who wants us dead. Those were your words, not mine. Weren't you the one who greeted me holding a rifle when I came back here with Tate? Why was that exactly? Because you thought men like Javier had returned, right?"

Andy said nothing.

"Well, *he's* a man like Javier, like De Falaise. His lot don't understand kindness, Andy. All they understand is this." She held up a fist in front of his face. "And this!" She grabbed her pistol and waved it under his nose. "They see anything else as weakness, do you understand?"

"Oh, I think I'm starting to. Have you ever thought that maybe by doing all this, we attract men like him?"

"You've got it backwards. All we wanted to do here was live in peace and then... Everything changed."

Andy was silent for a moment: "This isn't what Clive would've wanted. He would've–"

Gwen struck Andy with the same hand she'd been using to hit the prisoner. And with just as much force. She hadn't meant to do that. It was the mention of her dead lover's name that provoked her. How dare Andy tell her what Clive would or wouldn't have wanted? Clive was dead, and they would be too if they listened to Andy.

He stepped back, his fingers touching the cheek she'd slapped, which was reddening nicely. Andy said nothing more, just glared at her before storming out of the pub. Gwen looked at the others present – at Jeffreys, at Karen – waiting for them to say something. They didn't, and she knew why. They were scared of her. And were probably right to be.

She turned back to the prisoner. Could she see the faintest glimmer of fear in his eyes? Gwen bent and whispered in his ear: "One way or another, you're talking to me." She raised the pistol, pressing it against his head. "You just have to decide how you want to do this."

"All right," said the man. Gwen was a bit shocked to hear his voice. He had a distinct German accent. *So*, she thought, *at last I know* something *about you. About the people out there.* "I will tell you this. The men out there *will* find a way into your little village, one way or the other." He laughed. "It is for you to decide how *you* want to do this."

Gwen struck him on the cheek with the butt of the pistol. "Who are you people, what do you want?"

He spat out more blood and a tooth, which landed on the carpet not far from her feet. Gwen waited for the answer to her query. "That is very simple. We want your son." He smiled again, a chilling sight. It was Gwen who felt a rush of fear now.

"And I can assure you, we are *not* going to leave without him."

CHAPTER TEN

SHE KNEW THE Rangers were being interrogated, and tortured. Mary could hear the screams throughout the building, throughout the Vaults. What she didn't know was whether one of them was Robert.

Another scream, and Mary – shut away in one of the cells of the French Prisons – curled up on the hard wooden bed, putting her fists to her ears. The thought of Robert undergoing such a horrible ordeal at the hands of someone like Tanek was too much to bear. A mental image of her husband on the rack flashed through her mind; his limbs stretched, the veins at his neck standing proud.

"No! Stop this! Stop it!"

Mary didn't know if anyone could hear her, but nobody came. Another thought crossed her mind. What if it was the Widow herself who was doing the torturing? Was she standing by as Robert's ruined body was whipped or cut to ribbons, enjoying the pain he was going through?

It might not even be *Robert*, said David. She'd been wondering when he would crop up, the voice of her long dead brother, killed by the disease that had liberated her, granting her freedom from the farm where she'd lived as a virtual recluse. The disease that had brought her Robert, the Hooded Man.

And what if it *wasn't* Robert – did it make things any better to know that it might be Azhar being tortured, or Annie Reid, or any of the Rangers they'd come here with? Soldiers, but also friends. She'd laughed with these people, danced alongside them at the summer fête and winter festivals, treated their wounds and their illnesses, been a mother figure to some. At least it wasn't Mark in there, she thought: the boy... the *man* now, who she'd adopted. Who she and Robert had adopted.

I was just trying to look on the positive side, Moo-Moo, said David, using that damned contraction of her name – Mary Louise. She wasn't in real trouble yet, because he wasn't calling her by her full name. *No, it's not you who's in trouble at the moment,* he observed as another scream reverberated throughout the prison.

"Look, that really isn't helping," she told him, and not for the first time she tried willing David away. Mary knew deep down it had to be her own subconscious talking to her, but why did it always have to mimic David?

I keep trying to tell you, it's me, Moo-Moo. Honest. How can I prove it?

"Get me out of here. If it's really you and you're really a ghost, then open up that prison door and get me the hell out. Do something useful for a change."

She regretted the words as soon as she'd said them. Ridiculous, really, because if it was her unconscious mind talking then the only feelings she could hurt were her own. Nevertheless David had helped her plenty of times in the past, rousing her when she was knocked out or half dead..

But that wouldn't be good enough this time. She was already wide awake. How was she supposed to sleep knowing those screams could belong to–

Mary chastised herself; she was going round in circles. "David, if you're really real, and you love me, get that fucking door open."

Language, Moo-Moo.

"Are you going to do it, or aren't you?"

It doesn't work like that. There are rules.

"David!" she insisted, her tone hardening. Was it her imagination or did she hear him sigh?

"David, please." Mary couldn't believe she was begging her own *id* to do something she knew was impossible. But she scrunched up her eyes and prayed anyway.

Mary opened them in surprise when she heard the sound of bolts being drawn back.

"*Yes!* Thanks so much, David I–"

The door opened and there were two of the Widow's men, dressed in that same black and tartan uniform she'd first seen during the raid on that convoy. Her heart sank.

"Yeah, thanks a bunch," she said quietly to herself. David didn't answer. But then what did she expect him to do? He was no more likely to open that door and let Mary out than he was to appear in front of her covered in a sheet and rattling chains.

The men came inside, guns trained on her – otherwise she would have made a break for it. As it was, she struggled with them, not making it easy for them to drag her from the cell and take her wherever she was going. Probably on her way to be tortured like the other Rangers.

They pulled her back up and along corridors she'd been hauled down after they'd been captured, turning her around several times until she didn't know where she was – the sound of screaming still in her ears. Then they opened a final door and shoved her inside, where she landed awkwardly on the floor.

It was dark in this room, lit only by a few candles. Mary got up off her knees, looking over her shoulder to see that the men hadn't gone anywhere. They were covering the doorway to prevent her escape. Was this all part of the torture?

She heard breathing, coming from the other end of the room. "If you're going to do something to me, you'd better get on with it," she snarled. "I'm not a patient woman."

"Now, we both know that isnae true," said a voice she knew, even though she'd only heard it the once.

The Widow appeared in front of her, in a black corset and skin-tight trousers. "Yer can be *very* patient when it suits."

"What would you know about it?" snapped Mary.

The Widow smiled her feral smile, which somehow complimented her face. The backcombed hair she sported accentuated her untamed nature. "More than yer'd think. For example, I know yer waited patiently on that farm, waiting with yer Dad and brother. Waiting in more ways than one. But fer what? I dinnae think you could even tell me."

Mary rose slowly. How could she possibly know that? Must have got it from some of the Rangers. But how many knew that much about her past? Only Robert, and even he didn't know all of it.

"Then yer waited for *him* to come, The Hooded Man. Waited for him tae get over his dead wife and child. Even now yer still worry that he loved them more than he does you, or Mark."

No, couldn't be Robert. He'd never talk about private stuff like that with this trollop. It wasn't his way. God, Mary had enough trouble getting him to open up, getting past that macho bullshit he used as a shield. But there were ways to get information out of people; just look at what she'd done to the Widow's men to get them to talk. What if the Widow had drugged him somehow?

David, whoever, wherever you really are, she said to herself, *I could really use your help right about now.*

"Aye, call on David," said the Widow, circling Mary. "I talk to the dead as well, y'know. They're inside me, all of ma former partners, deceased husbands. They can give yer power, Mary. They have knowledge that we don't. Well, most of us. They know things and, if we're only willing tae listen, they'll tell us. So in that way I suppose we're not that dissimilar, you and I."

Mary screwed up her face. "You're delusional. I'm *nothing* like you!"

The Widow threw her head back and laughed. "Am I? Or perhaps I'm the only sane person left in this world. I see things as they are, or as they *should be*."

"Doubtful."

"Suit yerself. Anyway, where was I? Oh aye, patience. Yer waited for Robert. I don't blame yer, he's very special."

Mary felt herself bristling. "You leave him alone," she warned the Widow.

"Or what?"

"I won't be responsible for what happens," was all Mary could think of. That earned another cackle from the Widow.

"It's a bit late anyway," the Widow said from behind her. Mary spun around. "See, while yer been waiting again, I've been getting' t'know him better. *Much* better. I had to be sure. Certain it was really *him*." The Widow produced what looked like a playing card, its back facing Mary, and stared at it. "Quite a man, isn't he?"

Mary took a step towards the Widow, drawing back her fist at the same time. There was the clack of machine-guns being primed, the guards raising their weapons. But the Widow held up her hand for them to lower their guns.

"Give it yer best shot," the Widow said, grinning.

Mary didn't need to be told twice. She swung her punch, but hit nothing: the space the Widow had occupied only seconds before was now empty. Mary felt someone tapping her on her shoulder and spun back round, lashing out as soon as she saw the Widow again. For a second time she struck nothing, and the Widow was now to the side of her. Mary saved her strength, knowing that even if she tried again to punch the woman, she was too fast for her.

"Finished? Now, can we talk sensibly? Woman tae woman?" The Widow stood in front of Mary. "As I was sayin', that's quite a man yer have there. Or should I say, *had*. I've been waitin' a long time fer someone like him. Someone wi' his strength and power, who will live on forever." Mary frowned at that remark, but let it pass. "Someone wi' the sight, like me."

Now she did feel the need to speak. "What are you talking about? What sight?"

The Widow chuckled. "Yer really don't know him at all. How can yer call yerself his woman, when he keeps so much hidden? When yer choose not to see the blindingly obvious?"

Mary was sick of these mind games. She wanted to know what the Widow was up to. What she wanted with Robert.

"I have special plans for him," the Widow informed her, again seemingly reading her thoughts. "A long time ago I was promised something, Mary. Ma king. Ma Emperor. Thought I'd found him once, too." There was a real sadness to the Widow's voice, and Mary almost felt a little sorry for her. The feeling only lasted a split second, however, when she remembered what the Widow was after. *"What I want is you, Hooded Man."*

"And even when I began to 'see' Robert," the Widow continued, "feel his presence, I still didnae dare hope, Mary. But bein' in the same room as him; now that was different. No denying it then. Our... connection."

Mary laughed. "You and Robert? In your dreams."

"Actually, in *his*. He's seen me, just as I've seen him. He sees a lot of things before they happen. Just like I do."

What was she saying, that Robert was some kind of psychic? All of this was completely ludicrous. "He wouldn't look at you twice. What we share you couldn't possibly understand."

The Widow shook her head. "It's the bond Robert and I share that you cannae understand. You and he were never fated to be together, Mary. That's why when the Frenchman's daughter came along–"

"You shut your filthy mouth."

"That's why he was tempted, if only for a wee while. Yer can't possibly make him happy, don't yer see? Not really. Yer might have some ability, but yer deny it. Don't believe in it. I, on the other hand, embrace it. And Robert can see that."

"I'm not having this conversation with you. You're a lying cow."

"Dinnae take my word for it. Robert..."

The Widow beckoned, and, to Mary's surprise, she saw who had been standing at the back of the room in the darkness. It had been his breathing she'd been able to hear; the man she loved more than life itself. He'd been watching, listening to everything, and never said a thing.

Robert moved forward slowly. His hood was down, and he regarded Mary strangely, like he was seeing her but not really registering her presence. "Tell her," the Widow said. "Tell yer 'wife' how you *really* feel."

He hesitated for a second, then said: "I'm sorry, Mary. What she's said is true. We shouldn't be together. My place is here."

"Robert..." She turned to the Widow. "You fucking witch, what have you done to him?"

"Nothing. Except talked to him, explained things. Got him to see reason. See the link between us and how much stronger we are together than apart. We were never supposed to be enemies."

"I take it back, you're not delusional – you're barking mad. Robert, sweetheart..." Mary came forward, but Robert took a step back.

"Please, Mary, don't make this harder than it already is," he told her. "There are things I've never shared with you, that I didn't think you'd understand. But now I've found someone who does. She's promised to help me get back what I've lost."

Mary shook her head. "Lost? I don't understand."

"His focus. His dreams. His link to forces beyond ours, Mary. A link he'll get back through me. Now, Robert, don't yer have something tae do? We cannae go ahead with our preparations until it's done."

"Preparations?" None of this was making any sense to Mary, and it made even less when Robert reached out and grabbed her left hand. She tried to pull away, but he held on tightly. "Robert, no, you're hurting me." Mary looked into his eyes, but there was no response. This wasn't the man she'd first met at the farm when she'd saved his life, wasn't the man who'd saved her from De Falaise or spent the night with her for the first time after the summer fête a year later, or made those vows in front of Reverend Tate to love and cherish her for the rest of his life. This was someone else, a warped image of her husband created by the Widow. And he was taking back the ring he'd placed on her finger that special day, tugging and pulling so hard she thought he might snap her finger off just to get at it. Mary beat on his chest, but he didn't let go. "Stop it. I said: STOP IT!" She pushed him away, but as she did so the ring came loose and Mary fell back onto the floor.

Robert returned to the Widow, satisfied now that he had what he wanted. He smiled, and it was the same kind of messed-up grin the Widow had plastered all over her face. Feral. As much as Mary hated to admit it, right now they did make the perfect couple. Then, as Mary lay on the floor, Robert took the Widow's left hand and slid the ring onto a finger.

"Not exactly legal, or recognised by the eyes of *yer* God," the Widow told Mary. "But then I never really cared for the law, or for *Him*." She held up the hand with the ring on. "He's mine now, and I'm his." She pulled Robert close, crushing her lips against his.

Mary let out a howl and scrambled to her feet. Before she could get anywhere near them, though, she felt the hands of the guards restraining her.

The Widow broke off the kiss long enough to say, "Take the woman back to her cell," and the guards began manhandling

Mary towards the door. She lashed out, raking one man's face with her nails, but it didn't get her anywhere.

"I'll kill you!"

"This was all preordained," the Widow called after her. "If yer don't believe either of us, ask yer brother. The dead have knowledge that we don't, so ask him."

As Mary was escorted out of the room, the last thing she saw was the Widow all over Robert. She screamed as she was dragged back down the corridor, louder than any of the Rangers had done while they were being tortured.

Ask David? Ask the dead? She didn't need to. Because as she'd fallen backwards onto the floor she'd seen the strange symbol painted on Robert's wrist, snaking up his arm. Talked to him and reasoned with him, her arse! The Widow had done something to Robert. But that fact didn't make it any easier to take. What Mary had waited so long for – Robert's affections – the Widow had managed to secure in hours. And she couldn't get the image of the Widow and Robert out of her mind.

In spite of the fact she hadn't asked for it, David chose that moment to speak up. When she was thrown back into her cell, tears flowing from her eyes, he said in a quiet, serious voice:

I'm really sorry Moo-Moo. But she was telling the truth. She's not controlling him, he's doing all this of his own accord.

"Shut up!"

This was all meant to be, it had to happen this way.

"Shut up! Shut up! Shut up!" she repeated, convinced she was finally going crazy. But in addition to her brother she could also hear the Widow's voice:

The dead have knowledge that we don't. They know things and, if we're only willing tae listen, they'll tell us.

SOMETIMES HE COULD hear what the dead were saying.

One person at any rate. And not directly, but through the people closest to him. It didn't matter what he did, what he'd achieved, he'd always be compared to someone who'd died long before this fucking virus had come along; killed by something else entirely, though still related to the blood. His brother's problem had not been the wrong type, though, it had been an abnormal amount of white blood cells. That's what had done for him, and yet in a way he got to live on forever in the memories of his mother, grandmother and father. His father especially. He'd been the one who'd doted on Gareth, to the point where it might have seemed to the outside world that the man *had* no other child. The golden son, who'd shone so brightly he'd burnt out – leaving the patriarch of the family with no alternative but to grudgingly acknowledge his younger offspring.

A younger offspring who now catered for the man's every need, even though he didn't get so much as a "thanks".

"I don't know why I still bother," he said to his father, who was practically bedridden – or who preferred to stay in bed anyway, being waited on hand and foot.

"You bother because you're a good lad. A good son. You always have been." This was his Mam talking, lowering her romance novel – one of many he had to constantly supply her with. She was next to his father's bed, keeping him company, although it was becoming increasingly obvious that her husband couldn't stand the sight of her these days. The Dragon's Nan wasn't far away; sat in the corner with her knitting, clacking away.

How long had it been since any of them had been outside into the real world? He couldn't remember. Must have been back during those early days when he'd got them safely away from all the fighting, the rioting, the houses being set alight. Got them somewhere safe so he could look after them. Even when they'd moved to the stadium, they'd been transported in the back of an armoured truck. Only his dad had complained, as the Dragon's most trusted aides had hefted him into the lift, taking him to the floor where a home away from home had been constructed. "Mind what you're doing," his father had shouted at the men, still not grateful for the fact that he was being looked after, taken to a place of safety.

His Mam and Nan had been more appreciative, settling well into the routine – "Ooh, look, isn't this nice. At least we can get a decent cup of tea." They hadn't really gone out of the house much even before The Cull, whereas his Dad had at least been able to escape down the pub or to the rugby. The Dragon had thought – mistakenly – that his father might approve of the new venue. "When things calm down a bit, I'll arrange for you to watch some matches," he'd told him. Still stupidly trying to gain his approval, even though the Dragon had shown who was really in charge a long time ago. His Dad had looked at him like he was filth.

Like he wasn't Gareth.

But he still visited them as often as he could, given his hectic schedule. He'd fitted in this quick call after meeting with Tanek, who represented some of the Dragon's associates. "Associates?" his Nan had said, when he explained where he'd been. "Your grandfather fought in the war against their kind, you know." Her knitting needles were going like the clappers. "The Nazis."

"That was a long time ago," the Dragon's mother had said, standing up for her son. "I'm sure our boy knows what he's doing, and what he's getting himself involved in. Don't you?"

His father had huffed at that one.

"You got something to say?" the Dragon asked point blank; he was done pussyfooting around.

"Only that you'd never have seen our Gareth–"

"Fuck him!"

"Now dear, there's no call for–"

"No Mam, *fuck* Gareth. He's not here, I am! I'm the one who looks after you, clothes you, feeds you. Without me where would you be, eh?" He was aware he was breathing hard, his pulse pounding in his ears. "*Of course* I know what I'm doing! Anyway, they're not *really* Nazis," he said, turning on his Nan.

She said nothing, just continued to knit.

"They're a means to an end. Once we have enough weapons and vehicles we can push them out of the picture altogether."

"And they're just going to let you, are they?" His Dad said.

"They won't have any choice."

"Listen to him. They're supplying *you* with stuff and you're talking about taking them on and beating them. They could wipe you out like that, lad." His father snapped his fingers.

The Dragon growled. "We could take them. Just like we did with Hood's men."

"That's going to come back and bite you on the arse, as well."

"How so?"

"They won't be best pleased when they see what you did to their headquarters."

"That was the whole idea. That's why I released one of them. When Hood sees what I've done, he'll think twice about moving against me."

"You're underestimating him."

His mother nodded. "He does sound like a very rough customer to me."

The Dragon sighed.

His Dad continued: "Remember all those stories about what he did. That man pretending to be the Sheriff of Nottingham, the Russian fella? He's someone who's not frightened off so easily."

"And what would you know about military strategy?"

"Please, can we stop arguing?" his mother pleaded. "I hate it when you two don't get along."

Ignoring his wife, the Dragon's father pressed on, "What do I know? Only what I learnt on the rugby pitch, boy."

"Hmmm, you mean the way no-one would tackle a larger opponent, someone who seems stronger, you mean? Someone filled with enough confidence to make people think twice? That's exactly what I'm banking on."

"I think you're out of your tiny mind," his father stated, finally.

"Oh, you do, do you? Well–"

A knock on the door interrupted the dispute and they all looked at each other. Then the Dragon remembered he'd asked for lunch to be brought down. "Enter!"

The woman who came in didn't meet his eye as she wheeled in a trolley carrying a silver soup tureen, bowls and fresh bread on plates. The Dragon gestured for her to serve each of his relatives with the soup, which he saw was tomato. This particular servant was actually not doing such a bad job. He remembered seeing her for the first time, when the men brought her before him as part of a recent haul. She'd been a little too old for his tastes compared with some of the others – that silver-blonde hair a turn off. Though by no means bad looking, she reminded him a little too much of some of the teachers back at school. But he'd decided she was ideal to run about after his family, as some of the younger girls just weren't cut out for that kind of thing. It transpired she'd worked in a nursing home back before the fall of mankind, so he'd set her to work washing his father on a daily basis, changing the sheets on his bed. As much as his Mam wanted to help, she was getting on a bit herself and it was too much for her. Besides, why have servants and do the work yourself?

Meghan, wasn't it? Yes, that was the woman's name. He watched as she set the soup down first beside his Nan, then his Mam, who both thanked her – they didn't get the whole concept of personal slaves – and then on the table beside his father. The older man said nothing, but struggled to sit himself up.

"What are you waiting for?" The Dragon said to Meghan. "Bring a tray across and put it over his knees."

The Dragon's mother nodded, smiling. He knew what she was thinking: *See? A good boy to his Dad after all.*

As Meghan set up the tray, her hands were shaking a little. But it was as she served his Dad's soup that she spilt it on the bed, catching his leg with the hot liquid. The man cried out and Meghan stepped back, hand to her mouth. "I-I'm sorry, I-"

"You stupid bitch!" shouted the Dragon. "Look what you've done!"

She grabbed a cloth and started mopping up the soup.

"Now dear, it was only an accident," said the Dragon's mother, trying to keep the peace.

"I'll have you killed!" the Dragon screamed, and Meghan burst into tears.

"There's no need for that," his Nan told him. She'd never really liked his father. "The lady's been doing a good job."

And the more the Dragon thought about it, the more the idea of his Dad getting a little burnt did appeal. A lesson for arguing with him. Perhaps he had overreacted, initially annoyed that his father had personally witnessed one of his staff cock up. But there was no actual harm done, save for a bit of scalding maybe. His Nan was right: this woman *had* done a good job up to now.

But the Dragon couldn't be seen to be too soft. "Get out," he told Meghan. "Wait in the hall, while I think about suitable disciplinary action."

She left, still in tears, closing the door behind her. The Dragon's father was glaring at him.

"What will you do to her?" his mother asked.

"I haven't decided yet. She'll be punished."

"Like you do to all those other women," his father hissed. "The ones you think we don't know about."

"Ryn!" snapped the Dragon's mother.

The Dragon ignored them both, and called for the guards to come and wheel him out. It always made him feel uncomfortable, the amount of things they knew. How they did know, was anyone's guess; quizzing the guards, quizzing the slaves who saw to them? The Dragon dismissed all this from his mind, as his guards brought him out into the corridor. There was Meghan, as he'd instructed. She was still sobbing. And something about that, the mixture of the crying and the resemblance to some of his old teachers at school, made him wonder if he'd been too hasty in relegating her to simple menial chores. He'd discipline her, yes, as he had never had the chance to do to those teachers who put him down when he was young.

Then, who knows.

"Like you do to all those other women," came his father's voice again, echoing in his mind.

It went without saying, but he could also hear the man suggesting that Gareth would never have done such a thing. He wouldn't need to do things like that to women, because he'd have had his pick – if he'd lived.

Dead, and still speaking to him.

The Dragon decided to take his mind off his problems for a while.

CHAPTER ELEVEN

It HAD TAKEN some time to recover.

The sights that he'd witnessed had exhausted him, both mentally and physically. He was convinced no human had ever witnessed anything like it, so in one way he felt privileged. In another, it made him feel small, inconsequential: a tiny cog in a massive machine. He had his role to play, obviously, and a duty to perform that they couldn't possibly complete in his realm. But in the great scheme of things...

Shadow constantly kept checking that the pouch was still at his hip. Its contents were an important part of pulling this whole thing off. After he'd woken, and after he'd drunk a *lot* of water, he'd gathered the ashes at the place where the forest gods had been subdued. With that taken care of, it was time for the next part of his plan to be put into effect.

That would involve travelling to the Hooded Man's other home. The castle at Nottingham. Entering the city would not be easy, he'd anticipated that. Hood's Rangers patrolled the territory and didn't leave much room for manoeuvre. But there were always

ways into places. Shadow felt brave, he felt lucky, for with such superior forces guiding him how could he possibly fail?

The Rangers were good at concealment, he'd give them that. But he'd sniffed out their presence from a mile away, enabling him to avoid patrols, keep away from the lookout posts and sneak into the city as the sun fell at his back.

He'd studied and memorized maps of the city before leaving for these isles, and it stood him in good stead when it came to negotiating his way to the castle. Once again, Shadow was conscious of the parallels between him and the man who might have been, given different circumstances, a brother in arms. How many times had Hood done this to creep up on an enemy, taking out their defences and leaving the way clear for his Rangers? That wasn't Shadow's intention today. He was just one man, and, in spite of the backup he had on the ethereal plane, he had no army ready to move in once he opened the gates.

What he wanted was not to bring about the downfall of the castle, unlike other visitors in the last few years. He wanted something from it. More specifically, *someone*. It wasn't the Hooded Man himself, because Shadow knew he wasn't here. When he'd severed Hood's link to his beloved forest Shadow had sensed that the man was quite some distance from both Sherwood and Nottingham. But there were others, people important to Hood, still present at the castle.

It was one of these Shadow was stalking.

He leapt across rooftops, he darted through streets, his agility second to none. Not one patrol or guard spotted him and not one alarm was raised. Pretty soon Shadow came upon the outline of the castle walls. Scaling the cliff face was one option, and held the least risk of detection. Then there were the caves at the Brewhouse Yard, although they were sure to be guarded and he would have to incapacitate the Rangers there. Unfortunate, especially if someone happened to stumble upon them while he was still inside.

That left the walls, which again he could see were patrolled regularly, or the main gates at the side. Not an easy decision, but he was running out of time.

As he was waiting, Shadow observed that there was an unusual amount of activity just beyond those gates. Several groupings of Rangers mounting horses, readying themselves to leave the grounds. There must be something going on, some kind of emergency. This was good timing, and good news in two ways. Firstly, there would be fewer Rangers inside, which slashed the chances of him being seen. Secondly, it offered him a way to gain entrance. Quickly, he made his way across the roof he was on, swinging over the edge. He began climbing down, just as the gates were opening and the first batch of Rangers were departing. The noise and confusion of so many horses and their riders leaving the castle at the same time was excellent cover, and Shadow was able to slip through the gates easily. He pressed his back up against the wall while another stream of Rangers flowed through. Shadow became his namesake; entering silently and unseen, keeping to the pockets of blackness where the torches which illuminated the castle grounds didn't extend. As invisible as the wind, he began exploring. It was an interesting experience. Even at night Shadow observed that the castle was a place of safety, a haven for those living under Hood's protection. He was no evil overlord, rather someone trying to bring back balance to a world that had tipped too far over the edge.

Handfuls of Rangers – men and women alike – laughed and joked as they toured the grounds; there were families here, children. Shadow almost envied these people their existence. He had never known a proper home, never felt that he fitted in, not even with his own people. Shadow shook himself. He couldn't let thoughts like this distract him from his task. Making his way silently through the grounds, he discovered a set of steps leading to the castle itself. Then, looking left and right, he entered without making a sound.

MARK SAT STARING at the radio, trying to get his head round everything that he'd been told in the last twenty-four hours. The airwaves had never been so busy, communications not only coming in from Ranger groups on routine assignments, but also from Bill, then Jack. But there was something to be said for that old adage – no news is good news – because everything they'd received had been bad: pure and simple.

First, Bill had informed him that they'd heard nothing from Robert and Mary since they'd taken a team of Rangers to Edinburgh Castle to check out this Widow. What had happened, no-one yet knew, and although Mark still held out some hope they might return it was looking increasingly likely they'd either been captured or–

To take his mind off that, Mark recalled what Jack had said earlier on that day – relaying information about the Dragon from Dale. He'd been sent inside to spy on the man; a mission Mark had actually argued *he* was ready for, but Jack and Robert had vetoed him as usual. Even after everything he'd gone through in the field, Mark knew when they looked at him they still saw that kid with the dirty-blond hair they'd first met when De Falaise invaded England. He'd changed so much since those days. Mark was an adult now, even had a girlfriend – the lovely Sophie – which he had to admit had taken up a lot of his time in recent months. Sooner or later the others were going to have to accept he'd grown up.

Hadn't he shown them he was ready for actual combat? What did Mark have to do to prove he was worthy? Even the dreams he'd been having since starting those trips with Robert into the forest had suggested he should be given more responsibility. He'd learnt to interpret them quite well, the symbols and meanings; afterwards talking to Robert about them, because he knew his adoptive father had them as well. The last one Mark experienced had seen him running through the forest, too close to the ground to be on human legs. His running was awkward, not coordinated – at first, anyway. But Mark found that the further and faster he ran, the stronger those legs became. And then he could see them beneath him, a browny colour with white specks. The legs of a young fawn, but one that was growing faster than usual.

Soon enough, Mark found himself at the lake at Rufford, where he stared down into the water at his reflection. There were antlers there now, budding ones but growing at the same pace as the rest of him. Something was wrong, though; droplets of red in the water, falling from a wound Mark couldn't see. He looked up and saw a grown stag across the water, looking at him. Behind the creature was a man dressed in red, with a sickle for a hand. In one movement, he drew that blade across the stag's throat, allowing a jet of red to shoot out across the lake. Mark tried to scream, but there was someone behind *him*, too. He could see the shadow falling across the lake.

Mark hadn't had time to register anything else, because he'd been woken out of the dream by Robert calling him for breakfast by the campfire. If nothing else, the analogy was clear about growing up. Mark was almost there, and he deserved the right to be treated like a grown man. He should be–

Mark stiffened. There was someone behind him, just like in the dream he'd had all those weeks ago. He pulled off the earphones, rising from the chair at the same time; his heart going like a piston. He let out a sigh of relief when he saw Sophie standing there with a plate, holding a beef sandwich.

She smiled. "Sorry, didn't mean to startle you. Just thought you might like a bite to eat."

Mark smiled back. That sandwich did look good. "No, I'm sorry. Just a little on edge is all. Ta." He leaned over, took the plate gratefully, and gave her a kiss. Taking his face in both her hands, she pressed her lips harder against his. When she pulled away, his smile grew even wider. "What was that for?"

"Do I need a reason?"

Mark laughed. "No, I guess not. And I'm *so* not complaining."

"I just haven't seen much of you today."

Mark pointed to the radio. "Been stuck monitoring in case anything else came in. You heard about what's going on, I suppose?"

Sophie nodded. "I'm worried about Robert and Mary."

"Me too. At least when we were fighting the Sheriff and The Tsar, we were dealing with them one at a time. Now we seem to be split between tackling these Dragon and Widow loonies."

Sophie leaned on the table next to him. "What exactly did Dale say about the Dragon?"

There was a time when Mark would have felt threatened by that question; he'd have jumped to the conclusion that Dale was on Sophie's mind. But way too much water had passed under the bridge for that. He felt secure now about how Sophie felt, knew she only saw Dale as a mate. In fact, he'd got to know Dale a lot better himself over the past year and once that initial jealousy had evaporated, Mark actually found himself liking the guy, too. "You mean what did he say about our mutual friend?"

Sophie nodded again, more sombrely. She remembered fighting Tanek last year as well as he did – it was one of the things that had brought them closer together. "I heard he was acting as some kind of go-between, supplying weapons and vehicles. But didn't Bill also say that the Widow was being supplied with arms from somewhere?"

"He said the jeeps and weapons they took from her raiders were German."

Sophie looked at him seriously. "You don't think there could be a connection, do you?"

"What, Tanek dealing with both the Dragon and the Widow? Working with the Germans?" Mark bit his lip. It was a thought that hadn't occurred to him, but now Sophie had put it in his head, he couldn't shake it. And it terrified him. "God, I hope not."

"Isn't that what he and De Falaise used to do before? Gun-running?"

"Amongst other things." Now the more he thought about it, the more he wanted to fire up that radio and ask Jack and Bill's opinion. Sophie had definitely struck on something. Mark jotted down a note on the pad by the side of the radio as a reminder to broach it when Bill and Jack next checked in. He picked up the sandwich Sophie had brought, considered taking a bite, but found he'd suddenly lost his appetite.

"So what are Jack and Bill going to do?" she asked.

"Jack's requested more Rangers, in addition to those who left this afternoon. They've just been sent. I think he wants to go in and sort the Dragon problem before it gets any worse. Reading between the lines, he also wants to get Dale out of there as quickly as possible."

"Understandable. And Bill?"

Mark shrugged. "Don't think anything's been decided yet. For one thing, if we send any more men up there, we'll hardly have anyone left at the castle. And the last time we did that, it didn't end well."

"So Lord knows what could be happening to Mary and Robert, and we just have to sit here?" Sophie said, folding her arms.

"That's about the size of it. Welcome to my world."

Sophie reached over and stroked his hair, brushing a strand off his forehead. "Your time will come, Mark, you'll see."

Man, he loved this girl – and as he thought it, he rose and kissed her again. She responded in kind, wrapping her arms around him. More than anything in this world, Mark wanted Sophie right then. But it was her that broke off the kiss.

"Not like this, Mark," she said, looking into his eyes, then looking around. She knew what he was thinking, because she was thinking it herself. If they didn't stop now, they never would – and on the table of a radio room was not the most romantic place for your first time. Mark was surprised they'd been able to hold off this long, but he hadn't wanted to rush Sophie. They'd talked about it, sure, and been on the verge several times, but somehow never quite got it together. Mark sensed that tonight they were both ready.

"How about I get someone to take over here?" he suggested. "Then we can find somewhere a bit more private."

Sophie smiled again, then nodded enthusiastically.

Mark kissed her a final time, excited but also petrified. Emotions were coursing through him, and doubts about whether he'd be any good, what Sophie might think of him afterwards... But he knew none of that would matter once they were shut away alone.

It was as he was heading towards the door that he heard it. Sounds of a scuffle outside. Punches being thrown and a cry.

Sophie looked at him. "What was that?"

"I don't know," Mark replied, realising that the chances of him and Sophie being alone right now had just taken a massive dip. "Let's find out."

REVEREND TATE HAD just rounded the corner when he'd spotted the intruder.

Dressed in muted colours, in clothes that looked handmade, the figure almost blended in with his surroundings – making good use of a section of hallway that wasn't as well lit as the rest. Had he stuck to that bit completely, Tate doubted very much whether he would have spotted him at all, but the man had sacrificed this camouflage in order to spy inside a room to his left: the radio room. Tate had heard the reports about Robert and Mary going missing, the Dragon being in league with Tanek. It had made him more vigilant. Usually when things like that started happening, someone, somewhere made an attempt at the castle.

And perhaps this man in front of him was part of the first wave? Tate took in the rest of the fellow. He didn't seem to be armed with any kind of modern weapon, no machine-guns or pistols. Instead there was a bow and quiver at his back, plus what looked to be an axe and knife on his belt. Tate couldn't see the man's face, because of the angle, and also the length of his black hair. Though it was hard to tell, the man's skin tone was slightly darker than his; perhaps some kind of soldier from the Middle East? Tate hesitated, reminded of a moment in his own past...

Now wasn't the time.

But this man definitely spelt trouble. Gripping his stick tighter, he made an effort to get nearer. He wasn't the most practised at this kind of thing – not like Robert or Azhar, say – but he had his moments. Tate could still remember how to sneak up on an enemy in the quietest way possible.

The intruder didn't seem to notice him – he was transfixed by what was being said inside the room. And Tate could now hear voices: Mark and Sophie's. They were discussing the day's events, unaware that everything was being overheard.

Then Tate was behind the intruder. He realised he hadn't thought the rest of this through. Would he just hit the man over the head with his stick, or confront him, try and find out what he was doing here? Or maybe that should come later when they had him locked up?

In any event, he didn't get the chance. The man whirled, ready for him. He'd heard Tate's approach all along, just wanted him to get closer so he wouldn't have to make that much noise incapacitating him. Or maybe he just wanted to see who was stupid enough to think they could take him down. In the instant Tate had time to register what was happening, he finally saw the man's face. The arching eyebrows sheltering intense, dark eyes; the distinctive shape of the nose, cheekbones and mouth. He hadn't seen many of this man's kind, outside of books and documentaries, but he recognised the features immediately and this added to his shock. This trespasser was a Native American.

Tate didn't have any more time to consider this, because as the man turned he also brought round a fist. The punch would have knocked him clean out had the holy man not been quick enough to block it with his forearm. The intruder tried again with his other fist, but Tate blocked that as well. This was one of the things in Tate's favour it seemed; the Native American hadn't been expecting him to fend off the first blow, let alone the second. He'd done as most people had to their cost: underestimated the Reverend, written him off as just an overweight cripple with a stick. That was their first mistake.

They didn't usually get a chance to make a second.

This man did, because he blocked Tate's own swing with the stick – catching it between two hands and attempting to force it out of the Reverend's grasp. But Tate was stronger than he appeared and, with a grunt, held on to the only weapon he ever carried.

The stranger kicked out unexpectedly in a move Tate had never come across before. It caught him unawares and he only just had time to step back and avoid it. As he did so, his opponent drew the axe on his belt. He held it high and swung it, forcing Tate to bring his stick up lengthways. The edge of the axe embedded in the wood, but then the man got in a swift punch to the chin with his free hand – causing Tate to suspect it had been a distraction tactic.

Tate took the blow with practised ease, rolling with it so as not to cause too much damage. The next one came so fast, though, he couldn't help but let out a small cry as the man's fist slammed into his cheek. Tate slid back against the wall, dropping slightly. The Native American yanked his axe out of Tate's stick. Still reeling, Tate transferred the stick to one hand only, and swung it like a club at the intruder – who ducked, coming back up and batting the stick away with his elbow. He then slid it under his arm so that Tate couldn't use it, pulling backwards and at last disarming the holy man.

Tate just had time to see Mark at the doorway, before the stranger swivelled, using the holy man's stick against him; striking him on the side of the head. Everything went black as Tate felt himself slide down the wall.

He vaguely heard the exchange between Mark and the stranger, but couldn't hold on to consciousness any longer.

As he always did in situations like this – when he felt helpless and he'd done everything he possibly could – the Reverend Tate prayed.

SHADOW HAD BEEN aware of the man behind him even before his opponent reached the corner.

Yes, he'd been focused on what the teenage boy and girl were saying, not because the information meant anything to him – Shadow cared nothing about what happened in Wales and Scotland – but because it might hold ramifications for his mission. As soon as he'd heard them mention Robert was missing in action, he'd tuned in. That could affect his plans. How do you lure someone into a trap when they've already been caught by somebody else? This Widow, it seemed, had the Hooded Man in her web, which might potentially mess things up for Shadow.

Nevertheless, he had to press on – trust that forces with more vision than him had things well in hand. That meant handling this situation. Shadow came out from the darkness, let himself be seen – and at the same time saw the overweight man out of the corner of his eye. It would have been comical if it were not for the seriousness of his predicament. This local was hardly worthy of his attention, had it not been for the fact that he needed to complete his task, hopefully without drawing undue attention to himself.

Shadow had to admit, the older man had surprised him. He'd fought admirably. There was more to this stocky individual than met the eye; he'd drawn Shadow into a fracas he had neither the time nor the inclination for. That was what had made him draw his axe, to get this over and done with. His misdirection had finally worked and Shadow had been able to floor his enemy.

It was only as the man slid down the wall and his jacket opened that Shadow saw what he was wearing beneath: the black shirt buttoned up to the top, the dog collar. He'd been fighting with a religious man. All right, not *his* religion, but a religion all the same. It was another surprise from an opponent who had astounded him quite a bit already. The Reverend had fought like a soldier, but stood for the doctrines of peace and goodwill. Shadow was still thinking about this when he heard the boy say from behind:

"Reverend Tate? Hey, get away from him!"

Shadow turned, holstering his axe and looking the boy up and down – not that he hadn't seen him before in the room. It was just that now he was assessing how much of a threat he would be. He'd been wrong about the priest, so didn't intend to make a snap decision this time. The figure in front of him might only be a kid, but could well be highly trained.

"Who are you?" asked the boy.

"That is not important," Shadow told him, stalling for time as he glided forward, leaving the felled clergyman. Shadow saw the boy's eyes flash sideways, about to call out, sound an alarm and cry for help. Shadow couldn't let that happen. He dove at him, pushing the boy back into the radio room.

The boy grabbed Shadow's wrists, taking him backwards in an attempt to throw him over. More a wrestling move than anything, which made Shadow wonder just who had trained him. He was good; but Shadow was better. He resisted, letting the boy hit the ground, but tearing himself away and standing upright.

The girl with the freckles made a move to attack. Turning her lunge back on her, Shadow put an arm around the girl and had his knife at her throat in seconds. It stopped her from struggling, as well as giving the boy on the floor pause for thought. He would not do anything stupid while there was a blade at his woman's throat.

"What do you want?" asked the young man as he started to rise again.

"That is not *your* concern. Which one of you means the most to the Hooded Man?"

"Me," said the girl quickly. "I'm his daughter."

The boy on the ground opened his mouth to contradict her, but Shadow could tell the girl was lying anyway. "Try again."

"It's me," her boyfriend said. "I'm his... son." There had been some hesitation, and it was true that in trying to save the girl he might well say anything. This wasn't Hood's flesh and blood, Shadow sensed that much, yet it *was* his son.

"You will come with me," Shadow said.

The girl was about to scream until Shadow increased the pressure of the blade.

"Don't," he warned her. Then, once he was sure she would keep quiet, he shifted the knife to her side, still keeping the pressure there. He instructed the boy to rip a sleeve from his shirt, and forced the girl to bind him with it at the wrists. With another strip, taken from the bottom of the boy's trousers, she gagged him.

"You won't make it out of here," she promised him. Shadow took no notice. He turned the knife around and brought the hilt down on the back of her head. She slumped to the floor. The boy began to growl something through the gag, and Shadow realised that it wouldn't be nearly enough to shut him up as they exited the castle. So, he did the same to the boy – a glancing blow to the side of the head, rendering him unconscious.

Next he went back out into the corridor and dragged the priest into the room, leaving him and his stick lying next to the girl. Shadow spotted the notebook and pen on the table and scribbled something on the paper, below what had already been written. A note for the Hooded Man when he returned.

Finally, he hefted his unconscious prize onto his shoulder and, checking the corridor, stepped out and closed the door behind. Shadow allowed the pockets of darkness to cover both him and his captive, until they were outside the castle, where it consumed them completely.

CHAPTER TWELVE

HE'D BEEN LOATH to split up again; in a place like this when you did you had to ask yourself whether you'd see the other person alive again. But, as Sian had pointed out, she was meant to be in a certain area, and so was he. If they didn't return, it could raise suspicions.

"I have to get back to the other girls," she told Dale. "You should be in the kitchens."

Reluctantly, he'd agreed. They'd already taken a risk with the radio operator – though they'd poured even more of the booze down his throat, and left him leaning back in the chair. He wouldn't be waking up anytime soon, nor remembering that much when he did. The combination of concussion and whiskey would see to that. He'd probably be reported too when he was discovered, for drinking on the job; put somewhere to dry out... or worse. Dale doubted the Dragon took very kindly to that kind of behaviour.

Splitting up would mean they'd double their chances of finding out something about Sian's Aunty Meghan.

"Can I ask you something?" Dale had said just before they went their separate ways.

"Sure. Anything."

"I have to ask about... you and The Dragon."

"You *really* want to know what happened? What happens when he takes a girl away?"

Dale wasn't sure that he did, but the question was out there anyway. It had been hounding him since Sian had been dragged off, and even more so now that he'd gotten to know her a little. "I couldn't stop thinking about you and that creep."

"I think I got off lightly compared to some. He... he made me dance for him a little; told me what he'd *like* to do to me. But, well, in the end he couldn't."

"What?"

"You know: the *big* couldn't. To tell the truth, I don't think he's actually been with a woman. A girl can just tell these things sometimes."

"And what happened then?"

"Then he sent for the guards to take me away."

"So he's not really got what he wanted from you?"

"With a bit of luck, he never will."

Dale had to be content with that, and hope that while they were trying to find Meghan, Jack was planning something major on the outside. He'd considered taking a quick look around before heading back to the kitchen, but apart from the time factor – it'd already taken quite a while to find the radio room and send the message – he had no idea where the meeting between the Dragon and Tanek was taking place. The only good thing was that at least Dale and Tanek had never met, so he wasn't likely to recognise him as a Ranger, even if he bumped into him accidentally. Convincing himself there wasn't that much more he could do, Dale figured his time was probably better spent helping Sian.

Thankfully, the Dragon didn't have much call for food overnight. It gave Dale some leeway, and after grabbing a couple of hours of restless sleep, he was up and about and looking into the situation with Sian's aunty. And praying the Dragon didn't call on the girl in the meantime.

That morning, he asked around some of the members of staff he'd become friendly with, people who liked to gossip. It was surprising how much actually, seeing as they were supposed to be in fear of their lives. But people were people whatever the situation, and talking about folk behind their backs was still a popular pastime even in this post-apocalyptic age. A middle aged woman called Sally, who did a lot of the cooking for the Dragon and his soldiers, had been of most use. She told him that there was a maid by that name who their boss had drafted into his innermost personnel.

"I'm surprised you haven't seen her yourself," she told him. "She comes to collect food and drink most mealtimes."

"For the Dragon?" asked a puzzled Dale, who did recall seeing a woman wheeling a trolley away from the kitchens from time to time, but hadn't paid much attention to her.

"Don't know and haven't asked. Best way round here."

He'd kept an eye out, around lunchtime especially, but Dale almost missed her because he'd got roped into fixing sandwiches for some of the Dragon's men, back from patrol. As he looked over again, trying not to draw attention to himself, there she was finally – wheeling in an empty trolley to be loaded up. There was definitely a slight resemblance to Sian. The woman had a purple bruise flowering on her right eye.

Dale finished up the sandwich he was working on, then went over on the pretext of lending a hand. He made sure he caught her attention as he was placing the food on the trolley – there looked to be enough for three people there, but that was nothing new with the Dragon. Dale waited until it had all been piled on, then offered to keep the door open as she backed the trolley out.

"I need to speak to you," he whispered when she was close enough.

Meghan glanced away, nervously scanning the room, then said, loud enough for everyone nearby to hear: "Would you mind giving me a hand getting this into the lift?" Dale nodded, flashing what he hoped was a reassuring smile. Following her out into the hallway, he began to say something but she shook her head sharply as two of the Dragon's men walked by. Dale took hold of the other side of the trolley and when they eventually reached the lift, Meghan motioned for him to enter with her. However, so did another of the Dragon's soldiers, squeezing in just before the doors closed. Meghan asked the man what floor he wanted, then pressed the number for them all to descend.

The man got out just a couple of stops before them, but when Dale began speaking, Meghan pressed a finger to his lips. The doors finally opened on their level and Dale helped her out with the trolley.

"Okay, it's safe to talk now."

"Safe?"

"His eyes and ears are everywhere. We should keep walking, I can't be late delivering this stuff."

"To the Dragon?"

Meghan shook her head. "To his family."

"He has *family* here?" This was a new one on Dale, and information he could probably use later, especially if Jack and the other Rangers showed up.

"Mother, father and grandmother. I'm basically their slave."

Figures, thought Dale. The Dragon saw people as his property, so why would his family act any different? It was probably even their fault. "That who gave you the eye? His father?"

Meghan shook her head, and he could feel her hand shaking as she pushed the trolley. "I spilt some soup on his Dad, though. Had to be punished."

Dale couldn't tell whether she actually believed the last bit. Had she been here so long that it felt normal to be beaten for spilling soup? Jesus, look what that fat bastard was doing to these people. For a second Dale wondered if the punishment had involved more than just the punch, but didn't ask; he was afraid to. And more than a little afraid that Sian would be on the receiving end of something similar before too long.

"Look, I'm going to get you out of here. You *and* Sian." Meghan stopped the trolley, a look of complete surprise on her face. "That's right, she's here as well. I'm meeting her in a bit. She came to find you. Don't worry, come with me and–"

"Nobody escapes from here. He kills anyone who tries."

"I don't doubt it, but you have to trust that I'm going to get you both away from this... this..." Dale struggled to find words to describe the place and failed. He'd witnessed more depravity here than all his time on the streets and as a Ranger put together.

"You'll be killed. We all will. He's insane!"

"Look, you have to trust me, Meghan."

"I-I've got to deliver this. If I don't he'll send his men to find me."

That was true, it would arouse more suspicion than ever if the Dragon's family didn't get their grub. "Okay, but I'm coming with you."

"No, you mustn't. It's–"

"Not inside. I'll wait in the corridor. But now I've found you I'm not letting you out of my sight."

Meghan's hands were shaking again, but she nodded. When they arrived at the corridor in question, he let Meghan walk down it alone. There was nobody else around that he could see. Pretty weird in itself, but Dale reasoned that the Dragon probably wanted privacy for his family. He wondered if most of the guards even knew about them. Meghan looked back over at him just once before knocking, and he smiled again to try and reassure her. Then she was inside, and all he could do was wait for her to come out.

He wasn't standing there long, though, when he heard the first of the screams. It was definitely Meghan. Dale raced up the corridor to the room she'd entered. He threw open the door and was already inside before he realised something was wrong. For one thing, the room was in semi-darkness. For another, there was no sign of Meghan or the trolley, let alone the Dragon's family. Just a bank of monitors throwing out the only light. Dale wondered how they were still working, but then the Dragon had all kinds of electrical stuff rigged up. He looked at the monitors more closely, seeing what they were displaying – various parts of the stadium: guards walking up and down corridors; the pitch outside; the entrance; even the lift he'd just been in. It was a damned CCTV system! He'd noticed the cameras all around, of course he had, but he'd made the stupid mistake of thinking they weren't on. Dale hadn't seen one of these in operation since before The Cull. But if the other stuff was working, why shouldn't these be as well? *Stupid, stupid!*

There was the clack of a machine-gun being primed behind him, then another, then a third. Dale froze. A switch was flipped, flooding the room with light. The Dragon was wheeled around in front of him by Meghan.

I don't believe this, thought Dale. She'd led him right into a trap. After Adele deceived them all how could he have been so–

The Dragon suddenly grabbed her arm and threw her violently to the floor, where she knelt crying. Dale could see now that her lip was split and bleeding; those screams had been for real. "Why don't you come further in," he said, that voice making Dale squirm. "Come on, don't be shy. After all, you haven't been during your time here, have you?"

Dale was prodded forwards by what felt like the barrel of a rifle.

"Oh, I've been keeping tabs on you for a while now, all your little excursions. Quite innocent to the casual observer, but you did keep cropping up here, there and everywhere. Sort of like a really crap Jason Bourne." The Dragon laughed. "Except the spy was being spied on himself. I like that, don't you? And then last night... Oh, last night. I didn't catch the show live, of course, because I had other things to attend to, as you probably already know. But thankfully everything was being recorded and I watched it all back today. Made for very interesting viewing. Nice touch trying to frame the radio operator, by the way, but very sloppily executed. Unlike him." The Dragon leaned forward. "What I still don't know is who you are and who you're working for. You see, some of the cameras have pictures, but no sound. Who exactly were you contacting on the radio?"

"Nobody."

The Dragon held up his hand. "Save the bullshit. When I saw those pictures, who do you think I spoke to first, eh?" He pointed to one of the screens behind him. Right next to the one showing the harem's showers – in use right that minute, to Dale's disgust – was Sian in a room, strapped to a chair, head back and unconscious. "But she wouldn't tell me anything either, even under... duress."

"You fucking shit, I'll–"

"Let's be realistic, you'll do nothing." He kicked out at Meghan, who was attempting to stand. "That's why you shouldn't think so badly of this poor cow. Oh, I know exactly who she is now, don't I sweetheart? And I do so believe in family loyalty. That's why she brought you here, although you didn't need much persuading, I have to say. I just showed her what was on that screen, said her precious niece would be cut up into little pieces right in front of her if she didn't do exactly what I said. Actually, be thankful

my tall foreign friend isn't still around because he would have
enjoyed doing that, I think."

I'll bet he would, thought Dale, knowing all too well Tanek's
love of torture.

"The stupid bitch still tried to warn you, though." Another
kick and Meghan was pitched forwards on her hands and knees.
"Unfortunately for you the audio works just fine in the lift and
corridors in this section." He grinned.

Now Dale thought about it, Meghan *had* tried to stop him,
even though it would have put both herself and Sian in danger.

"I'll come with you."

"No, you mustn't."

She'd tried to tell him about the cameras, too: *"He has eyes and
ears everywhere."* Dale had just assumed that she was talking
about his men.

"It's funny, I was warned about a danger from within, but this
still came as a bit of a surprise."

"Warned?" Dale said before he could stop himself.

"My family. Ever since the virus they come out with things...
the strangest things."

"Please! You have to do something!" Meghan said to Dale.
Tears were streaming down her face. "He's crazy. His family are–"

Before she could get another word out, the Dragon had hefted
himself a couple of inches forward, the front wheel of his sled
rolling over the woman's hand. Dale heard the cracking as
the bones broke under that weight, then another scream from
Meghan – much louder than the first. Dale winced. The Dragon
ignored the cries.

"Tell me what I want to know, or this is only the beginning.
I'll make them both suffer. And from what I see already, you're
not a man who'd enjoy that." The Dragon paused, eyeing Dale
up and down. "Or are you? Hmm? Perhaps you enjoy seeing
women get hurt? Perhaps you've hurt a few in the past as well?"
The Dragon rolled off Meghan's hand and she clutched it to her
chest, howling in agony.

Fucking mind games, Dale said to himself. The Dragon didn't
know the first thing about him. Concentrate. Meghan was right,
he had to do something to stop this. But what? There were at
least three men behind him, and so many more outside these

doors. He'd often wondered what the scenario would be if he got caught. Bourne? More like Bond, complete with the psychopathic villain. All the Dragon needed was a cat. It'd be funny if it wasn't so real.

Dale looked over at the screens again, seeing Sian there, helpless. Two damsels in quite a bit of distress, and he couldn't help either. Just then his eyes caught something else on one of the screens. Something everyone in the room seemed to have missed. Movement between the seats out in the stadium itself – brief flashes, tiny but unmistakable. Those hoods, the tips of bows, a quick flash of metal. The Rangers – his friends – were here. If he could just hold on a while longer...

But he'd have to do something to make sure nobody saw the screens just yet.

Dale's mind raced. *Okay, you want mind games, mate. I'll give you mind games.* "I guess that's all you can really do, isn't it?"

"I'm sorry?" said the Dragon.

"Hurt them, get them to perform for you. It's not like you can do anything else with them, you limp-dicked chubster."

The Dragon's face reddened. "What?"

"I bet your men don't even know that, do they? All those women you collect and you can't even get it up when you're alone with them, can you?"

He stared at Dale, fuming. "Shut your mouth."

"Some Dragon. Some leader of men. You're not much of a man at all, really, are you? All you can do is watch, perv over them and wish you were more like some of these guys who fetch and carry for you. Who protect you."

"I said shut the fuck up!"

"I bet it's all recorded somewhere as well, all those times you've made women do things, but haven't been able to satisfy them. Bet the proof's right there for any of your men to see."

"If you don't shut your mouth–"

"What is it, the weight? Or something else? Don't tell me, you have issues with strong women, don't you? Mummy's boy, were we? Is that it? Or maybe even your Dad? Was he the problem? Was he a *real* man, Dragon?"

"I. Said. SHUT UP!" roared the Dragon, leaning forward so far in his sled it was rocking.

"Well come on, if you think you can take me. You don't need these guys to fight your battles as well, do you? Come on, then!"

The Dragon raised himself up and it was at that moment the sled wobbled over, crashing sideways to the floor. Dale used the distraction to drop to the ground, as the men behind opened fire – hitting some of the screens in front, actually doing him a favour by shattering the ones chronicling the Rangers' progress. Dale rolled backwards, taking the guards' legs out from under them. Sending them sprawling in all directions.

He was up first, elbowing one in the face to keep him down and snatching his rifle. The second he shot in the leg; the third he took out with the butt of the rifle. Even if he wasn't as slick as Bourne or Bond, he fought like them: hard and fast, getting rid of the Dragon's men in here, at least.

But not the Dragon himself. As Dale rose, the man was charging towards him – faster than Dale ever would have given him credit for. He'd probably been even quicker in the days before piling on all that meat, but was still quick enough to slam Dale backwards into the wall.

"Not a man, eh? We'll see about that," he grunted as he swatted Dale's gun aside with a flabby arm.

Dale had no room, so when he threw his punch – hard, in the kidneys, which should have crippled his opponent – it simply sank in, having no effect whatsoever. The Dragon might have been overweight, but he knew how to use that to his advantage, crushing Dale against the solid wall, gripping him by the throat.

Dale kicked out, but that had the same effect as the punch. The Dragon squeezed his opponent's windpipe harder. "Who. Sent. You?" he shouted. "Tell me!"

The sound of an explosion came – it was distant, possibly even in the next building. But a second and third followed, and this time they rocked the room they were in. The Dragon looked up at the ceiling as dust fell.

"Y-You really want to know?" gasped Dale. "You'll get to meet them soon. They're here, Dragon... and they're not... very happy about what you did to their HQ... Or their men."

"A Ranger," breathed the biggest of the two men. "I should have known."

Dale grinned again, but soon stopped when the Dragon lifted him up and shoved him hard against the wall, banging his head. Everything went fuzzy for a moment.

The last thing Dale remembered after that was an angry red face, a face that almost did resemble a Dragon in his muddled mind.

Dale fell; fighting for breath and losing his grip on consciousness.

He could still see only red as he lost both battles.

Then the redness turned to black.

CHAPTER THIRTEEN

How EXACTLY HAD he got into this mess?

He was dangling, suspended, above a fire in what had once been the castle's reservoirs.

He thought he'd been so clever, but like always he was really only making all this up as he went along, trying to turn something hopeless into a fighting chance.

Maybe this was his punishment for hurting the woman he loved more than life itself. And, in his defence, the Widow's mumbo jumbo did have an effect on him initially. Some kind of weird hypnosis or mind control. The best way he could describe it was like having a waking dream, where you were doing and saying things you wouldn't normally, but had no control over. He cast his mind back to when they'd first been alone together, back in the Vaults where he'd been chained to the wall. She'd had him stripped naked and he'd assumed there would be some kind of torture involved, especially as he was surrounded by such implements. Maybe it was just his turn, he thought. Both Mark and Jack had suffered at the hands of Tanek – Mark coming away having lost a finger, while Jack's mental scars ran deeper. If they could brave it, then so could he. He'd had to face worse: up against tanks, jeeps, helicopters, armed with only a bow and arrow.

But torture had been the last thing on her mind.

"I do admire a man who's not afraid of being in the raw," the Widow told him as she'd scrutinised his body, approving eyes passing over his taut muscles. "I've been waitin' fer you to come. Expecting yer."

"So you said. Some kind of tip off."

The Widow might have suspected they'd strike sometime, but couldn't have known *exactly* when without some kinds of heads-up.

"Could say that." The Widow laughed. "But no the kind that you'd believe. Not yet, anyway." She'd approached him, and placed a hand on his chest. "Good, strong heartbeat," said the Widow, then ran her hands over his torso. Then her hand moved downwards and she gave an approving and extremely dirty smile.

"Would you like me to cough?" Robert spat.

"Sense of humour. I like that. A perfect man in a lot of ways: fit, strong. Yer know, a lot of men have disappointed me over the years, Robert."

"You do surprise me."

"Something tells me *you* won't disappoint."

He strained against the chains that held his wrists and ankles. "Don't fight it. You and I both know something more powerful than either of us has brought us together. There's something special between us, something we share."

"And what's that?"

She leaned in and breathed: "A kind of magic. 'Course, yours has been weakened, but I can help get it back. Also helps me with what's about to follow." The Widow told him about how it was all in the cards that he'd come and they would one day rule this country, if not the world, together.

"With the help of good old German ingenuity, I suppose," said Robert.

She waved away his comment. "Means to an end. At the moment, our countries need each other. But who knows what's around the corner."

"You do, apparently."

"That's right." The Widow produced a tarot card: a man sitting on a throne, wearing and crown and holding a sword. "This is you, Robert: The Emperor. *My* Emperor. The one I've been looking for my whole life. This is who you will become when we've... joined."

"Are you for real?"

"Aye. An' I knew it was not going to be easy to persuade yer, but I must try."

Then she drew strange markings on the floor and walls around him. Burning odd-smelling incense and candles, leaving them under him so he had no option but to inhale. Robert fought their effects, but it was no use. They made his muscles relax and he hung on the wall like a puppet. She chanted in a language he didn't understand: the words overlapping, tumbling into each other at one point. Robert recalled the Widow lifting his chin, pressing her lips against his, saying something about needing to be sure.

And he remembered the painting she'd done on his body, markings and symbols to complement the words she spoke. He felt drunk by this point, more drunk than he had even on his stag do, just before marrying...

Joanne.

He saw her face, those beautiful eyes, those lips. But it was morphing into someone else. He saw Mary, remembered what had happened, how lost he'd become in the forest when Joanne and his son, Stevie, had died from the A-B virus. How Mary had made him feel human again, her love, her–

Then both faces were replaced with the Widow's, the only person he could see, the only voice he could hear. Over and over, telling him he was hers – that they were destined to be together.

He hadn't even realised he was nodding, until he was doing so. Suddenly it had all made perfect sense, what she was offering him. Though they'd only spent a short time together, those minutes had become hours, days, and somehow he knew this woman better than he ever had Joanne or Mary. So much so that he'd agreed to talk with the latter. The Widow freed him, once she was certain he was under her control, dressing Robert so that he could come with her to meet Mary, to convince *her*.

Even as he'd come forward, walking through that dream haze, speaking words that were his and yet weren't, he'd semi-believed it. Robert told Mary the Widow was going to share her magic, replacing what he'd lost, what had been stolen from him. He believed it all so much he'd taken the ring from Mary's finger.

And then it happened.

Robert recognised that look. He'd been responsible for it once before, when they'd been arguing, drifting apart, when Adele had been on the scene. When there had been doubt in Mary's mind, even though Robert had been faithful throughout. That look, that hurt. He'd sworn there and then he'd never do anything to warrant it ever again.

Memories came back to him of all the time he'd spent with Mary, his wedding day, last Christmas. It hit him like a slap in the face, smashing its way through the fog and clearing his mind.

But now was not the time to strike. Robert was still massively outnumbered and the Widow had armed guards trained on Mary. The only way was to make that harlot think he was still under her control. The fact that she wanted him so badly, that she thought he was some long-promised love, might just work in his favour. So he'd gone along with the kiss, this time responding as the Widow covered his lips with her own – trying hard to ignore Mary's wails and hoping she might understand if, no, *when* they finally got out of this.

Mary had been taken back to her cell, and at least out of harm's way. The Widow had held up the hand on which she now wore Mary's wedding ring. "I'll have tae think about changin' ma name."

Robert had smiled, playing along. The spell was definitely broken, but he couldn't allow this woman to see that. Now, it was simply a question of biding his time until he could incapacitate the Widow. That wasn't going to be easy. Even alone she was a force to be reckoned with.

The question was, how far would he take this performance? Because the Widow was keen to consummate their sham of a marriage. "Come on, lover, I'll show you ma chambers," she'd said, batting her dark eyelashes and pulling on his arm as she dragged him through the halls. There were armed soldiers on every corner, no opportunity for Robert to act. Perhaps he'd stand a better chance when they were alone together in her bedroom.

And what a room that was, located inside the Royal Palace it was certainly fitting for a king and queen. The Widow removed her skin-tight trousers, leaving just her corset and a thong on, then lay back on the four poster bed, beckoning him.

Okay, now what? thought Robert. There was no way he was going to go through with this – even if Mary hadn't been in the equation, the Widow was just too damned... scary. No wonder the men in her past had disappointed her. Now here she was, expecting him to step up to the bat, her perfect man.

The Widow patted the bed beside her. "What yer waiting for? Come here." There was a powerful edge to those words, and if he hadn't been such a strong-willed person, Robert might not have been able to resist. More tricks of the mind, coupled with drug fumes inhaled from those candles and incense sticks. As it was, he moved forward, almost involuntarily, but still in command of his own body. He was walking stiffly, though, finding it hard to conceal his true feelings. By the time he reached the bed, he could see the Widow suspected something was wrong.

To throw her off the scent, he took off his top and sat down on the mattress.

The Widow propped herself up on one elbow, placing a hand on his chest. "That strong heart's racin'."

"With excitement."

She smiled. "Aye. Let me calm yer down a bit." Her hand snaked lower, but before it could reach its destination, Robert grabbed her wrist. Rather than fighting him, the Widow seemed to enjoy it. "I just knew yer liked it rough," she growled. He grabbed her other wrist, pushing her back down against the bed. But she wrapped her legs around Robert, forcing him to straddle her. Obviously her idea of foreplay, but it was more like some of the wrestling moves Jack used.

"Aye, that's it, that's..."

Robert pulled away from her. She gripped him by the shoulders, attempting to draw him down on top of her, but he couldn't help resisting. Almost without warning, the Widow let go of him.

Dammit, she knows, thought Robert.

"There's one link left. She still has a hold on yer, doesn't she?" said the Widow. "Aye. I can see it. I can *feel* it."

Robert said nothing.

"I saw this, as well," the Widow confessed, and now he really knew he was in trouble.

"I-I'm sorry," he offered. And part of him actually was. Because behind those hard eyes of hers, under the exterior – the bravado she put on – there was a woman who just wanted to be loved. Who wanted on some level what he and Mary had, who'd been filled up with nonsense about a perfect man when one didn't exist. And certainly wasn't Robert, could never *be* Robert.

"Aye, well, there's only one thing for it." The Widow looked at Robert like she was expecting an answer, then replied for him. "For me to become yer new Empress, *you* have to kill the former one. Don't worry, there's nothing tae it. I've murdered more exes than yer've fired arrows."

Of course, that woman who just wanted to be loved was also a complete and utter homicidal lunatic. Before he could do anything, she was already calling for the men guarding her chambers – ordering some to fetch Mary, while the rest escorted Robert and the Widow to the Great Hall.

So he had to play along again, part of him relieved that the ordeal of the Widow's bedchambers was over, part of him concerned about what was to come next. It had been necessary for the Widow to believe, he knew that – her blind faith that he was the man from the card, her chosen one, was the only thing seemingly stopping her from focusing. It was a weakness he could exploit, he just wasn't sure how yet.

As they waited in the Hall, though, the Widow impatient to get this over with so he could be totally hers, Robert kept an eye on everything around him: from the positioning of the guards – six on either side of the room, dotted between suits of armour with machine-guns, an eclectic touch – to the space around him and what he could use to initiate an escape; plenty of archways, which would be either a help or hindrance. When Mary was brought in, he attempted to act cool, but what he saw made his heart ache.

She'd obviously been crying, but Mary seemed resigned to what had happened, that Robert belonged to the Widow. Her head was bowed and her body language spoke of a woman who'd given up.

"All right, let's get this over and done wi', shall we?" said the Widow, and produced a knife, which she handed to Robert. *A sacrificial dagger*, thought Robert. Meant to represent the sacrifice not only of Mary, but of their whole relationship.

Yeah, right. That wasn't going to happen.

"Well, go on then," encouraged the Widow, nodding towards Mary. "Yer know what must be done. I cannae do it for yer, Robert."

Yes, he knew exactly what to do. Robert approached Mary, hoping to convey what his plan was. But she wouldn't – couldn't – look him in the eye. *Come on, Mary, look at me.*

"Kill her, Robert. Kill them both," urged the Widow.

Robert paused. Mary raised her head.

"Both?" said Robert.

"Aye, her and the child. The last link. Yer rejected her, now do the same with that creature growing inside her."

Robert's mouth gaped and he stared at Mary; she stared back. Her hands went to her stomach, a look of astonishment on her face. What the hell was the Widow talking about? He could see Mary had no idea either. Something to gauge his reaction, to test whether he was still loyal? Or perhaps to make him rethink what he was planning to do next? But if it were true... If–

"*Do it, man!*" screamed the Widow.

Robert exchanged a look with Mary, all that was needed. "I'm sorry," he said, approaching her with the blade held high.

"I know," she told him.

"Now!" he cried, and twisted – flinging the dagger back towards the Widow. At the same time, Mary brought up both her arms. The guards obviously hadn't been expecting any more resistance after half carrying this defeated woman from her cell, and were taken completely by surprise when she elbowed them both in the stomach. They crumpled up, but Mary didn't wait to draw breath. Grabbing them both by the back of the neck, she knocked their heads together: *hard*.

As the blade was flying towards the Widow, Robert was also diving to attack one of the Widow's men. The man's reaction was slower than Robert's and all it took was a blow across the windpipe to incapacitate him. Robert dragged the soldier around, using him as a human shield as the guard opposite opened fire. The first one took the bullets, his body jerking as they exploded into him. Robert glanced up to see what had happened with the knife.

The Widow had caught it and was turning it around.

"Mary, run!" he shouted, snatching both the guard's claymore and belt-knife before letting him drop. The knife he hurled at the soldier firing in his direction, and this time it did find its mark.

The Widow was rushing forward, preventing any of her men on the opposite side of the room from getting a clean shot at Robert. Mary looked left and right, back towards the door she'd been brought through, then at Robert. "*Run!*" he yelled again, but it was already too late. The Widow had almost reached her, dagger ready to do what Robert couldn't.

He was about to hurl himself at the woman, when he remembered the other guards. He ducked in time to escape the machine-gun fire, rolling over and bringing his sword up into the first. Robert offloaded the impaled man onto the guard directly behind, who was racing towards his companion. Wood splintered around Robert as the guards opposite were now free to train their weapons on him.

Which also meant that the Widow had reached Mary.

Robert rolled again, rising and throwing his claymore at one of the guards like a javelin. He snatched another belt-knife from the closest felled guard and tossed that at another guard diagonally opposite. Ducking sideways, he grabbed one of the suits of armour, pulling that in front of him for protection against yet more machine-gun fire. Bullets sparked off the armour, dislodging the rifle it held, but did at least allow him to move back toward Mary, and the Widow.

To Robert's dismay, those archways were indeed proving a menace, as more guards – attracted by the noise – came dashing in. Pretty soon the whole damned hall would be filled with reinforcements. He had to take out the Widow right now.

Robert ran at her, throwing the empty metal suit – the only weapon he had. As good as his aim was, though, the armour hit nothing, crashing instead across the floor and into the opposite wall. That was because the Widow had already circled around behind Mary and was holding the dagger to her throat.

Weapons were being primed behind him, new soldiers swarming into the Hall. But Robert didn't care. For one thing he was in the direct line of sight of the Widow – any stray bullet might hit her as well, which he knew they couldn't risk – for another, he was more concerned about the golden blade pressed up against Mary's neck, the edge already drawing blood.

"Wait, no!" he begged. "Stop! I'll do anything you want. Just please, please don't kill her." There were tears in his eyes. The Widow looked at him, and froze. Was there still some compassion in her? Something that recognised Mary was the one for him, not her?

"All right," she told Robert. "And you'll agree to *anything* if I let her live?"

He nodded.

"Robert, no!" said Mary.

"There is still a way we can be together. It wasnae what I wanted, though." The Widow ordered her men to restrain Robert. He held up his hands willingly. It was then that both he and Mary were marched out into the open, the light almost blinding him at first. Out, up and round to the reservoir buildings, then in through a door. The Widow had obviously been busy here, the place already set up for its new purpose, away from the prying eyes of most of her army. She only allowed two men inside with her, to help with what would come next, then she bolted the door.

In front of them was what looked like a large funeral pyre. There was also some kind of pulley system that had been rigged up, attached to the walls and ceiling. Robert and Mary exchanged worried glances as they cottoned on to what was going to happen.

With guns on both him and Mary, Robert had no choice. One way or another The Widow was finding a way for him to be her King, to make his strength her own so they could be together forever. Then she went over to a trunk, bringing out several bottles of liquid. She proceeded to coat his skin with this, mixing the solutions generously.

"Cooking oil?"

She didn't reply. There was a distinct air of disappointment in her expression, like he *should* have killed Mary – and his child, if what she'd said was true.

"You and I have lived many lives," she told him. "And we *will* live on forever, whatever happens. We will *be* together."

She nodded at one of the men who took Robert by the arms – wrenching him away from Mary when all he really wanted to do was kiss her, say goodbye to her. In all the scenarios he'd played out in his mind, after all the adventures and dangers he'd faced, he'd never once pictured this one. Being eaten alive by a crazy Scottish woman who thought they were soul mates.

As he was pulled across to the ropes, his hands shoved inside them – then hauled upwards and across – he realised that the Widow had actually done worse to Mary than kill her. Now she would have to witness her husband being cooked alive, only to be devoured afterwards.

On the Widow's orders one of her guards lit the fire, as she began her damned chanting again. Must have been part of whatever process she thought would give her his soul.

He looked over at Mary. She was crying, trying to look away but not managing it. Wanting to capture his face, remember the moment – the last time she'd see him alive.

And, once again, Robert wondered how he'd gotten into this mess.

CHAPTER FOURTEEN

So far, it was mostly going according to plan.

Usually everything turned into such a mess. But not now, not this time. Twice he'd had to suffer defeat at the hands of his enemies. No more. As he drove along the road in the Eagle Armoured Vehicle Tanek thought back to his meetings with the Widow and the Dragon.

Both had gone okay, the latter more so. That Widow was going to be trouble eventually. She'd already *been* trouble as far as he was concerned, with her magic tricks and supposed clairvoyance. More co-operative had been that bloated excuse for a human being, the Dragon. Tanek had radioed in to say he was close to the man's headquarters then, after a tour of the weaponry and vehicles, he'd been escorted to the meet. The Welshman had quite an impressive set up, Tanek had to admit, but funded by the people he himself represented. Tanks, armoured vehicles, guns, all supplied by the Germans.

Both were just playing at being dictators, though. Neither the Widow nor the Dragon had the foresight, nor the clout, to pull something off like De Falaise, who'd swept up the country building an army as he'd gone. Nor did they possess the vision of the first Tsar.

If the Dragon and Widow had pooled their resources and teamed up, however, it might have been a different story.

His thoughts switched to those dreams the Widow had referenced, the promise he'd made to his former leader to watch over his child. Tanek had assumed that was Adele, who'd come out of nowhere and managed to almost cause the downfall of Hood. She'd been shot by Hood's woman, Mary, and had died in Tanek's arms – in spite of his best efforts to save her.

"Take it slow," he'd told her as the bullet finally took its toll.

"No, I must... must tell you... We have to save... He made me promise. My father."

"Promise what?"

"Save–"

"Save who?"

Her grip on his arm had tightened: "His child. My brother. My little brother."

A brother? Could it possibly be? That somewhere out there, another child of De Falaise's existed? Tanek would have bet anything – back when betting actually meant something – that there were lots of little De Falaise bastards out there, providing, of course, that they'd retained his O-Neg blood before the virus hit. If he'd conquered women like he conquered territories, then Tanek would have quite a search on his hands. The kid – if indeed, it was still a kid – could be anywhere.

Tanek had done as he had before, after De Falaise's death: retreated abroad. He figured he stood a better chance of tracking down the Sheriff's child if he scoured Europe first. After all, that had been De Falaise's playground for quite some time. Tanek had even tried searching back in Istanbul where he'd first encountered the Frenchman, but things had changed significantly while he'd been away. So many tin-pot dictators, exactly like the Dragon and the Widow, it was unbelievable. He couldn't move without getting into a fight, or having to prove to the people there exactly who he was; though part of him was very flattered his reputation had spread.

If he hadn't been on a mission he might have stayed and showed them a thing or two, perhaps taking over a couple of their operations and building a force of his own. But he was also aware that it would be nothing compared to the armies already established in places like Germany.

He'd heard the rumours, just as everywhere else seemed to have heard rumours about him. There was some kind of new Reich starting up, not that he was any great fan of the Nazis – the whole Aryan race thing put an olive-skinned guy like him off – but if nothing else they were organised. And this version's belief system was slightly more flexible than the old guard.

That was the impression he got and the confirmation he received when he made contact with the Army of the New Order. He hadn't been able to gain access to the man in charge, but found himself talking to even more sympathetic members. One of whom had given him this gig, based on the tales about him almost taking out Robin Hood; twice! Those stories didn't go into details, thankfully, about how everything had gone to shit both times – just played up the notion that the upstart woodsman had nearly got his comeuppance at Tanek's hands. He hadn't corrected them.

As always, Tanek had been able to use that misplaced trust to his advantage. Yes, he would consent to oversee the distribution of the New Order's property to both the North and the West of what had once been known as the British Isles. Yes, he would make sure they used it wisely, with one eye on trying to eradicate Hood – an extra bonus as far as he was concerned, just so long as he got to do the deed himself. But in return he also required men and equipment to implement one of his own projects.

Because, in the time between leaving England and hooking up with the New Order, Tanek had also heard rumours about a woman De Falaise had once been acquainted with. A woman called Gwen who – for reasons beyond Tanek's comprehension – had appealed to his former leader. Tanek couldn't believe he hadn't worked it out before, the amount of time De Falaise had spent alone with her.

Tanek had lost track of the woman, but it didn't take long to pick up the trail again. He couldn't quite believe she'd been stupid enough to go back to the place where she'd first been kidnapped. Who would do that? Apparently it was because that was where the man she'd loved had been from, the man she –

falsely – believed to be the father of her child. But Tanek felt sure that the son she'd borne belonged to the Frenchman. The timing, everything; it all fitted.

It hadn't taken much effort, with the resources now at Tanek's command, to pinpoint her village. And while he'd been travelling round checking on the Widow and Dragon, his men – sequestered from the New Order – had laid siege to her home. No questions asked, which was the way he liked it.

That was where he was driving to now, across country from Wales. It had taken a good few hours but he hadn't encountered any trouble. Driving the Eagle ensured you fairly safe passage.

In that time, he'd been in contact with the men on the ground – finding out what had happened during the siege. They'd begun a day or so ago, bedding in and using sniper fire to take out anyone coming and out. One jeep in particular returning from some kind of recce had been hit badly, plus a villager who'd fired on them. Ever since then they'd kept the place pinned down tight.

"I'm waiting for the 'but'," Tanek had said to the mercenary in charge, Brauer.

"Sadly, one of our men was captured."

"Tell me that was a joke," he spat down the handset, even though he knew his German comrades very rarely made those.

"I wish I could. But regrettably it is true."

"How did he get captured when your men are surrounding the fucking village?" Tanek snapped. Static was his only reply, which just made him angrier. "Just tell me your men are making progress wearing them down?"

"We will be inside within the next day. I'd stake my life on that."

"Choose your words carefully," Tanek warned him. He had killed people for much less. In fact, he had killed people for pleasure, so the thought of torturing Brauer then ending his life appealed.

"There will be progress before you arrive, Herr Tanek," he was promised. That would have to be good enough for now.

Even with the capture of one German – who knew relatively little in the great scheme of things, save for the reason they were there – Tanek felt oddly optimistic. Everything was pretty much going to his plan, the second phase of which would begin as soon as he reached New Hope.

And there was nothing and nobody to stand in his way this time.

GWEN WAS DETERMINED not to let anyone stand in her way. Not Andy, nor Jeffreys, not even the memory of her dear, sweet Clive. Nobody was going to take her son away from her. If it meant fighting to the death, then she'd do it. The rest of them could go screw themselves.

Ever since the German prisoner had told her what they were after, she'd been like this. His confession that they weren't going to leave without Clive Jr had sent her into overdrive. And, if she'd been hard on their captive before, then that knowledge had pushed her over the edge.

"Tell me!" she'd demanded when she got over the shock, raking his cheek with her nails. "Tell me *why* you want my son!"

When she'd begun to tear into the wound in his side, the one that Jeffreys had spent so long stitching, Gwen had to be pulled away.

"Now that's enough! He's not going to talk," Andy said in her ear as he and the good doctor dragged her away from the man. "You can see he's not going to give you anything more."

"He will when I've finished with him!" But, given a chance to calm down Gwen realised the truth was he probably wouldn't. Not even under the kind of torture she'd love to inflict.

Torture, for Heaven's sakes. Can you hear yourself? This wasn't her, this *really* wasn't her. Yet it was. Nothing in the world was more important to her than her son, and these arseholes had come here specifically to take him. Why, she had no idea – and probably wouldn't find out until it was too late. Until he was gone.

"What the hell's going on?" Darryl had asked, rising from the couch as she'd returned home, slamming the front door behind her. He'd stayed there to keep an eye on Clive Jr, and because he was still quite wobbly after giving the German his blood. She felt a twinge of guilt when she saw how pale he still was, because she'd been ready to drain every last drop of blood from that German in order to uncover the truth. Then again, she knew Darryl would understand – he was probably one of the few who would. He'd only volunteered for the transfusion in the first place so they could ask their captive questions. Clive would have been very proud of the courage and self sacrifice this young man had shown tonight. Gwen vowed to tell him that, when she got the chance. When the time was right.

"No guts, none of them," she grumbled under her breath. "They won't do what's necessary."

"Easy Gwen, sit down."

Ignoring his advice, she paced up and down, explaining what had happened during the interrogation. "I just don't know what to do, Darryl. I won't let them take Clive Jr."

"Course not, none of us will."

"I'm not so sure," she told him, her voice wavering. Before he could ask her what she meant, Clive Jr appeared in the doorway to the living room, wearing his pyjamas and clutching a teddy. He'd been in the other room asleep when Gwen came in. She went to him immediately.

"Oh, I'm so sorry, sweetheart," she cooed, knowing it was her temper that had woken him. "Let's get you back to bed, little man. You need your sleep."

"He's not the only one," Darryl told her. "You look knackered."

"Thanks a lot," she laughed.

"I'm serious," he said, concern etched on his face, and it was then that she realised just how much he cared about her.

Gwen shook her head. "I can't, not with all this going on."

"You're no use to anyone like that, especially him," Darryl said, nodding towards Clive Jr.

He did have a point. How could she fight to the death for her son when she was exhausted? She wouldn't be able to think clearly if she was half asleep. "I'm not even sure I could, even if I tried," she protested, but was already yawning in spite of herself; coming down off the adrenalin high she'd been on during the questioning of the prisoner.

"You'd be surprised. Now go on, take him back to bed and get some rest yourself."

Gwen nodded, holding Clive Jr's hand. She turned back before heading upstairs. "Thanks Darryl. For everything."

He smiled and waved a hand for her to get her head down. Which she did, taking the pistol from the back of her jeans and putting it under the pillow, then curling up with her son. She watched him nod off again, then watched him some more, her own eyes drooping.

She dreamt of *him*. The man who'd once saved her from almost certain death at Nottingham Castle – at the very least rape and who knows what else at the hands of that thug Jace. A Hooded Man, but not the one that everyone knew about. He wore a *red* hood, this one, concealing a face that had been painted to resemble a skull – practically indistinguishable from the rest of his clan, though *she* could tell him apart instantly. She'd called him Skullface once, but now understood what a wildly inappropriate and silly nickname this was; used only because she knew nothing about him, not even his real name. Some would probably have said it was Servitor, because he served the Fallen One, but Gwen wasn't so sure about that. He'd shown her only kindness and compassion, and at no other time since Clive's death had she felt so safe.

In this dreamscape, he came to her again, exactly when she needed him. Gwen reached out and pulled down that crimson cowl, stroking the painted face. The face of a dead man, because hadn't he once died? She didn't know *how* she knew that, but he'd also been reborn in flames. She felt the rough edges of the tattoo on his forehead, etched there with a needle: an inverted pentangle and cross. Her hands went even higher, feeling the bristles of his shaven head, and she wondered what he'd looked like before all this. What he looked like without the painted skull, with his hair grown long. And suddenly her question was answered, because standing there in front of her was a man who looked almost exactly like Clive. It wasn't him, of course, could never *be* him. But the resemblance was uncanny. This man had felt the same kind of pain as her – somehow she knew that as well. He'd lost people he cared about: a lover... no, a wife. And a child.

It was the kind of bond which could only be shared through such a loss.

Gwen felt herself falling into his eyes, pools of sadness coaxing her in. Then suddenly they were holding each other, her arms wrapped around him and vice versa, clinging to each other like a drowning person clings to wreckage in the sea. When their lips met it was with a hunger she'd never felt when she was with Clive. There was an urgency this time, as if at any moment this would be snatched away from her, as it was before. Gwen closed her eyes...

Their mouths parted and his tongue found hers, dancing with it, at first tentatively, then with that same driving need. They were exploring each other's bodies. Gwen's hands ran down his naked back, feeling the strength of him and holding him closer as they continued to kiss: faces locked together until there was no differentiating between them.

Gwen lay back and let him kiss her neck, butterfly kisses which ended at her nipples. She moaned, loudly now, as he took one into his mouth, sucking and biting.

But that sensation was nothing compared to what came next. He was inside her, even though she hadn't felt him slide in. She could feel him there, and it was beyond anything she'd ever experienced before. They kissed again, tongues lapping at each other as he moved backwards and forwards on top of Gwen. The motion increased along with the intensity of feeling. His thrusts were both hard and gentle at the same time, lifting her higher and higher into this feeling. Breaking off the kiss, she was moaning in time with those thrusts. Her hands at his shoulders willing him on.

He kept going until she felt like she was going to explode. It was only at the very point of finishing, when she couldn't hold back any longer, that she opened her eyes. To see something from her worst nightmare:

The Sheriff: De Falaise. Labouring away above her, sweat pouring from his brow, his yellow teeth glinting in the light. A memory from when she'd been held against her will at the castle, used like some kind of sex toy.

Gwen's cry of ecstasy became a scream.

She woke suddenly, just in time to hear a series of explosions breaking the silence outside.

PHASE TWO OF the plan started when Tanek reached the woodland on the outskirts of New Hope.

As he pulled up in the Eagle, he was greeted by Brauer, who saluted him. That made Tanek smile. It was good to be in command of men again, even if it was only a battalion of German troopers for this particular, personal mission. It was the respect he'd earned, the respect he'd commanded when he'd been De Falaise's right-hand man. He'd never felt fully in charge during his time with the Russians – too many people looking over his shoulder, including the Tsar himself. Here he was alone, with a small army who were under orders to obey him, whatever the cost.

The first thing Tanek wanted to know was how they'd allowed one of the men to be taken.

"How did any of the villagers get out in the first place?"

Brauer shook his head. "We have all possible entrances and exits covered, sir."

"Not *all* of them, apparently." But he wasn't going to expend valuable time and manpower searching for them. Tanek needed to step up the siege, force the people inside to give themselves up.

Or give up the child.

Tanek knew that the woman the boy belonged to would never surrender herself – she'd die rather than see him fall into the hands of the Sheriff's former second. But the others might, with the correct motivation. They'd already been shot at from every conceivable position around that damned wall they'd erected – a troublesome obstacle, but a good idea, Tanek had to admit. This prevented them from leaving, in theory. Now it was time to show them that he and his forces would be coming in soon, whether they liked it or not. The only thing that had prevented him from blowing the shit out of them in the first place was that they might accidentally hurt the boy. None of them had the first clue where he was being kept and a stray mortar fired into the village might just hit a building with him inside.

But that didn't mean a barrage against the wall was out of the question.

"Ride with me," he told Brauer, and the man saluted again.

They drove towards the front gates of New Hope, and within seconds the Eagle began to draw fire from a gunman positioned on the wall. The bullets bounced harmlessly off its armoured exterior. Tanek parked the vehicle, sliding out and using it as cover. He ordered Brauer to get out of his side and give him a hand with something he had in the back, under the camouflaged canvas cover.

Brauer barely batted an eye when he saw the huge GMG automatic grenade launcher. Instead, a look of understanding passed across his hard face as he realised why Tanek had asked him along. Resembling a very large M-60, which fired grenades instead of bullets, fed through a belt, this was a devastating piece of kit. The gunmen from the wall continued to fire at them as they set up the mount, Tanek fixing the gun into position. A ricochet sparked off the side of the jeep near his head but he barely even twitched, concentrating on the task in hand.

"Ready?" Tanek asked Brauer, who nodded, holding the grenade belt.

The larger man pivoted the barrel of the GMG and aimed for the wall. The blast almost knocked Brauer backwards, but Tanek remained rooted to the spot. The grenades exploded against the wall, which shook with the impacts.

Tanek shifted position, relying on Brauer to move with him, and fired several more along the length of the wall. *Should get their attention.*

There was no return fire, at least for a few seconds. Then it came again; the bullets, pathetic compared with the GMG's load.

Okay, thought Tanek. *Let's try this.*

Leaving Brauer with the canon, he made his way round the side of the Eagle, picking something up from the backseat as he went. Tanek walked out into the enemy fire, standing there as if daring any of the sentry's bullets to strike him. And indeed they refused: hitting trees, foliage and the dirt track. Then Tanek raised his repeater crossbow, as accurate a weapon as any you could wish for, and fired a number of bolts into the gaps on the top of the wall.

The gunfire stopped. Tanek stood there and grunted with satisfaction.

"People of New...*Hope*," he shouted "You have something we want. A boy belonging to a woman called Gwen. Your leader. You are cut off. Give us what we came here for, or suffer the consequences."

"Do you think they will listen, sir?" asked Brauer.

Tanek didn't reply; he just looked out over the bonnet of his vehicle, up towards the wall. He saw a brief glimpse of auburn hair.

And now he really was tempted to grin.

*   *   *

GWEN HAD WOKEN from the dream feeling flushed and disgusted at the same time, but hadn't had the opportunity to reflect on it because of the explosions.

Several bangs in quick succession, all coming from beyond the wall. From where the Germans were camped out. Clive Jr slept on, oblivious, so she'd retrieved the pistol from under the pillow, hurried downstairs, then asked Darryl to watch her son.

"What is it, what were those noises?" he said as she opened the gun cabinet near the door. Gwen took out a Colt Commando assault rifle, one of the haul she'd originally brought with her from Nottingham Castle.

"Trouble," she replied, locking the cabinet again and tossing him the key.

The first thing she noticed was that it was fully light outside, dawn having broken while she'd slept. Another blast hit as she was running towards the wall – followed by gunfire – and she was joined by more villagers who'd been roused by the noise, including Karen and Dr Jeffreys.

Gwen saw Andy lying on the ground at the base of the wall, not moving; the rifle he had been using was a few feet away. For a moment or two she thought he was dead, and mixed emotions surged through her. How she'd once been great friends with this man, but had found herself at odds with him of late.

She'd be lying if she said she wasn't relieved when she saw him move. Then, as she got closer, Gwen could see what had done this to Andy. Two crossbow bolts, one in the shoulder the other in the chest. She slowed her pace. Only one person she'd ever known used a weapon like that.

Then she heard his voice and it sent a shiver down her spine. He was calling from beyond the wall, telling them it was Gwen's son they'd come here for. She still couldn't understand why, unless after all this time Tanek had decided to believe the bollocks about Clive Jr being De Falaise's child. It was something Tate, Robert, maybe even Mary believed – but a mother knew her own son, in her heart. The boy was Clive's.

Jeffreys was attending to Andy, so she ascended the ladder. Crouching on the ledge of the wall, she risked a peek at her foe. How he'd got his feet under the table with the Germans was anyone's guess, but then mercenaries flocked together, didn't they? It was how De Falaise and Tanek had hooked up in the first place.

Just look at the arrogant sod, standing there like he's indestructible. But like her dream lover, hadn't Tanek come back from the dead once, after the battle for Nottingham Castle? Come back with a fleet of Russian soldiers as his allies. *Working his way around the fucking countries.*

She could see Tanek watching from behind his vehicle, and ducked back out of sight. Gwen wasn't about to give him the satisfaction of knowing she was there. Of knowing she was shit scared about what they were going to do next.

It had been bad enough when she thought the Germans were on their own; now, who knew how many more troops might come? They were just villagers with guns, not that well trained either. Some hadn't even fired a gun before, in spite of her best efforts to prepare them. Some, like Karen, had never taken a life and she couldn't rely on them to begin now.

It was time to start being realistic. In most cases they would have been able to fend off what came down that road. If Javier, the man who'd killed Clive, had trundled up now they could have at least have sent *him* packing. But Tanek was a different kettle of fish. *Face it, you need help,* Gwen told herself.

Tate.

Gwen hated herself for even thinking it, but the Reverend – her old friend who'd left her a prisoner of the Sheriff for so long, who'd put her in danger again when the Tsar had attacked – was probably their only hope.

At the castle there was Robert, and wouldn't he just love to see her begging for their help. But there were also the Rangers. Well trained specialists who'd be able to take those Krauts down without breaking a sweat. With them on the outside, and her lot fighting from within, they might yet stand a chance.

Gwen caught sight of the villagers below. They were looking up, some accusatory – blaming her for bringing this to their doorstep – but most were looking to her for a solution.

There was only one thing she could think of to do.

Gwen got down, motioning for someone else to take her place   on the wall. Hardly worth it, probably, but they still had to make an attempt to defend New Hope.

"Okay," she told the assembled crowd, "here's what we're going to do..."

CHAPTER FIFTEEN

"WAKE UP. OH, please, wake up!"

He heard the muffled words, but didn't want to. They sounded like his mother's cries as she tried to get him up out of bed on a school or college day. "You're going to miss the bus, if you're not careful."

But this wasn't his mother's voice. It sounded familiar, though, like someone else he knew. The same inflections, though maybe a little deeper. Lyrical in tone, almost like music – and if there was one thing he knew about it was that.

Then he saw a face in the darkness.

Sian.

She was in his mind, just as she'd been in his thoughts since he'd first seen her.

"Please, whoever you are, wake up!" The words were sharper now, more acute. More real. He was fighting against the dark, raging against it. Time to get up or he'd miss the bus.

"D-Dale..." he croaked, not caring for the sound it made in his head. He tried to ignore the pain there, and hoped that fat git hadn't damaged his voice permanently when he grabbed hold of his neck. He should have been grateful he was still alive. As it was, he was simply glad he might get a shot at revenge.

Not very Ranger-like thoughts, he told himself. But then, hadn't Robert himself exacted his own revenge – twice – on people who'd hurt the woman he loved?

Love. It was an alien concept to him so he wasn't entirely sure. It was something he always thought he'd feel one day, that he hadn't been able to feel for any other girl he'd ever been with, as much as he'd liked to. He just hadn't been built that way. But the way he felt about Sian... it was either love or something very much like it. Dale knew that when he saw what that slug had done to Sian, he'd do anything he could to save her. That's why he *had* to wake up.

Dale opened his eyes, his vision blurred. And the picture of Sian's face he'd held there now became that of her aunty: Meghan.

"Please... Dale. You have to help her."

Dale moved, and regretted it instantly. He ached all over from the beating the Dragon had given him. From somewhere he heard the sound of gunfire. Meghan looked up and out through the open door. Dale blinked and his focus returned enough to see what the Dragon had done to her hand, which she was holding against her chest as she knelt next to him.

"Please, we have to hurry," she said.

"Where..." Dale croaked again. "Where is he?" There was no sign of the Dragon, just the men Dale had put out of action before the real fight began.

"He left, maybe to see what was happening out there – with your friends?" Meghan winced as her hand shifted position; whatever he'd been through, he was in better shape than her, Dale reminded himself. That hand needed looking at, and soon. But Meghan hadn't finished talking. "Then I saw him on the screen back there, the one Sian had been on." The screen Meghan was talking about had a crack across it, but still showed a picture. The chair Sian had been tied to was now empty. Dale's heart sank.

"Where is she?" he asked.

"He took her," said Meghan.

Dale didn't want to make things worse by saying that Sian had come here to rescue her.

"I was only trying to keep her safe," Meghan told him. "And now look!"

"I think so. Somewhere he'd feel safe, back to where his family are."

"Right," said Dale, picking up the rifle he'd been brandishing when the Dragon came at him. It wasn't a Ranger's weapon but was the only one he had to hand, and he wasn't about to go up against armed men with nothing. He began to make his way outside, but would have toppled over if Meghan hadn't steadied him. What was he thinking? He was in no shape to be taking on the Dragon. He'd get all of them killed.

Dale could hear the sound of gunfire out in the corridor – then another explosion. There was a battle going on and usually Dale would have wanted to be a part of that. Not this time. He let Meghan take the lead, as she knew where the Dragon's family could be found.

They turned a corner and were confronted by two or three of the Dragon's men, who opened fire on them even before they'd had a chance to identify themselves. *Nerves and hair-triggers*, thought Dale as he pulled Meghan back behind the wall for safety, *not a good combination*. These soldiers were seeing their enemies everywhere.

Bullets pinged off the wall and Dale swore. He stuck out the machine-gun and returned fire, but drew even more in return.

He didn't have time for this. For all they knew, the Dragon could have already killed Sian and–

No, she was still alive. She had to be! Dale sprayed another round of bullets in the direction of the Dragon's men, this time chancing a look around the corner as he did.

There were even more now. He checked his magazine; there wasn't much ammo left. Certainly not enough to take on all those guys.

He looked at Meghan's terrified face and couldn't muster any reassurance.

But if he didn't do something, and fast, a young woman that they both cared about would be in really serious trouble.

* * *

THE CASTLE HAD sent all the reinforcements they could, but they were still heavily outnumbered.

However, the fact that one highly trained Ranger was worth at least a dozen of the Dragon's men evened it out somewhat. They also had the element of surprise on their side. Jack deemed the risk necessary. Had done since he'd learned of the connection between the Dragon and Tanek.

If that sadistic son of a bitch was back on the scene, then this outfit needed crippling sooner rather than later. Before another Sheriff or Tsar could come along and take advantage. For all they knew, this Dragon might have the credentials himself – he was certainly psychotic enough. What he'd done to their Welsh HQ, to the survivors he'd then taken back to the Millennium Stadium, was proof enough of that. And although revenge shouldn't have been the motivation for this attack, Jack's mind kept flashing back to those bodies, to the Ranger who'd been dumped on the road by the Dragon's men. The idea that Tanek might also still be around was also too tantalising to pass up.

Jack had a major score to settle with that man. On two occasions, he'd been bested by him – in spite of the rematch *almost* going his way. And that was before the torture he'd put him through.

Still, he'd thought long and hard about this: putting even more Rangers in the line of fire for some kind of personal vendetta wasn't what this police force was all about. But when the men and women had come to him themselves, saying this was the right thing, that they also wanted payback for their comrades who'd died at the Dragon's hands, that had settled it. Each one of them knew what they were letting themselves in for once they put on the Ranger uniform. It hadn't stopped them before, and it certainly wasn't about to deter them now. Far from putting them off or sending a message that the Dragon was not to be messed with, his actions had simply put fire in their bellies.

Then there was the small matter of one of his Rangers being inside. A man he'd personally sent there.

"I'm not one for speeches," Jack had told the collected troops just before they'd headed off. "Robert's the one you want for that. But I do know one thing, whatever happens today you're doing the Rangers proud. Now good luck to all of you, and let's go and kick some butt!"

His people knew exactly what they were doing, which ensured he could rely on them to crush the lookouts on the outskirts of the Dragon's territory without fuss and without their enemies issuing a warning. Jack had watched one particular squad through binoculars from a deserted house, with equal amounts of anticipation and pride. The hooded soldiers slipped through the streets, coming up on the lookouts while the Dragon's men chatted amongst themselves. If the guards had spotted trouble they might have sprung into action, but they were oblivious – and before they could even get off a shot, the group of half a dozen soldiers dropped silently to the ground, taken out by a mixture of arrows and bolas. Jack had allowed himself a slight smile, but there was a bigger test to come.

They'd moved through the city using the buildings, just as Robert had taught them. Nobody from the stadium would have seen their approach, and when they were close enough, teams of Rangers were deployed as planned, surrounding the stadium. There were a handful of Rangers present with scuba diving skills; they were not only well trained fighters, these men and women, but sometimes hobbies from the old days could come in very useful. They used the River Taff to approach the building, after Jack had sourced the equipment from a shop which used to sell tanks and gear before the virus. It would be just like the beginning of *Goldfinger*, he'd told them, but without the dinner jackets underneath their wetsuits.

Any guards they spotted were felled with arrows or bolas, some even with throwing knives if the Rangers were close enough. A team had also been sent out to deal with the problem of the vehicles and weapons stashed at Cardiff Arms Park. As Robert had done during his battle with the Tsar's men, they'd be using chemically-treated arrows to deal with this – the tips carrying a concentrated explosive. At a specified time that team would fire these into the smaller stadium, the result of which would be catastrophic for the Dragon's defences.

A couple of teams had entered via Park Street and Scott Road in a pincer movement. There were emergency doors here – Jack had done his homework – next to the old media access area, which could be used to gain entrance after any guards had been dealt with.

Meanwhile for other groups, including Jack's, the architecture of the stadium itself was a gift: struts and poles for climbing, perfect for arrows with ropes attached to be fired up onto the roof. Jack had to admit, he didn't relish the prospect of such a climb, but he did all right keeping up with some of the younger Rangers. There were absolutely no guards up on top, as Jack had figured – nobody would be stupid enough to camp out there – so the Rangers were able to climb down inside, again using all those metal struts and poles to their advantage. Hanging from the rooftop inside, they could pick off any obvious guards visible out in the open, leaving the way free for the rest of them to abseil down directly from the roof. That one was inspired by *You Only Live Twice*.

Jack and the others watched as a number of the Rangers disappeared under the roof on the opposite side. They waited, and waited. Then the all-clear signal was given; a faint whistle which could be mistaken for birdsong unless you were really listening for it. Jack nodded for them all to begin their run, and looked over the edge at the pitch below. Even with his head for heights this was not something he was looking forward to. "Well, here goes nothin'."

Holding the rope steady – with his staff jammed under his arm – he lowered himself over the edge of the stadium's open metal canopy. Jack pushed himself off, swaying as he dropped. He let out the rope, glancing over at other Rangers doing the same, spotting those who had already climbed up and under now adopting positions between the rows of seats; quietly making their way downwards.

They'd been lucky so far, but that wouldn't last. Sooner or later someone, somewhere, would spot the ropes dangling into the stadium. So they had to move quickly.

Jack heard shouting. Raised voices that didn't belong to his troops.

That was it, they'd been spotted. But the timing couldn't have been better.

Loud bangs sounded from the smaller stadium next door, then explosions as the Rangers' arrows found their marks – blowing up stationary jeeps and motorbikes, tanks and trucks... and ammo.

A chain reaction ensued, the ground and the stadium shaking with the ferocity of it. The distraction bought them some time, but not much. Machine-gun fire came from the left of Jack, and he dropped several metres. The other dangling Rangers, rather than waiting to fall to the pitch, swung into the rows of seats, detaching themselves as soon as they could. Their bows were out seconds later, trained on the source of the machine-gun fire.

Jack did the same, using his momentum to swing across. Bullets missed him by inches and he spotted the gunman. Holding on to the rope with one hand, he let his staff fall from his armpit, catching it with his free hand. He flung it at the Dragon's guard and it hit the man squarely in the chest. The man fell backwards, then flopped forwards over one of the blue plastic seats. Jack swung himself across, letting go when he was over the steps between seats. He landed well enough, but had to duck seconds later because there was more rapid gunfire from another shooter.

A female Ranger Jack recognised as Beth Garrett popped up between the seats and put an arrow in the guy; Jack nodded a thanks and went to retrieve his staff. He knew that inside, his other troopers were fighting their own battles – bow and arrow against hot lead. But Jack's money was on the Rangers.

Heavy weapons fire suddenly drew his attention and he looked across the stadium to see a fixed mounted machine-gun the size of a bloody cannon, spitting out... yes, dammit, those were grenades. A couple exploded near to one of his Rangers and Jack watched, horrified, as the hooded figure flew up into the air along with wrecked seats.

"Hawkings!" he shouted, pointing to the weapon, and was gratified to see that the Ranger in question had already lit one of his chemical arrows. He fired it in the direction of the cannon, and the resultant blast spread across the Dragon's men and set off the grenades they'd been feeding into the weapon.

Jack nodded with satisfaction. "How'd ya like them apples?"

Down below, another skirmish had broken out on the pitch, with Rangers who had made it down that far taking on the guards with their swords. Rolling to duck bullets, they hacked at legs – cutting into shins and thighs. No guard would be getting up after that.

In doorways and from behind the seats, his Rangers continued to hold their own, firing arrow after arrow, some explosive, most not needing to be. A clump of about twenty of the Dragon's men, all armed to the teeth, were taken down in seconds by arrowfire; the fact that they were all together making it easy for his Rangers to wound and incapacitate. Some of the guards were fleeing, retreating back inside the stadium. It wouldn't do them any good, because already the Rangers were spreading throughout this place: down corridors and on stairwells, checking every room and crushing any resistance.

He made his way up towards a door, but as he did so a guard came through it brandishing a pistol. Jack flicked his staff up and knocked the gun out of the man's hand, then whacked him on the temple. There was the sound of boots to the left and right, and Jack dropped immediately, just as the machine-gun fire from two groups of guards on either side opened up. "Chumps," muttered Jack as he rose again and saw the bodies. The Dragon's men had shot each other.

Leaving his forces to carry on their clean-up, Jack slipped inside through the entrance ahead of him.

It was a big place, and it was time to begin his search.

After all, he had more than one person to find.

"WHAT NOW?" ASKED Meghan.

"I'm thinking, I'm thinking," Dale replied. It wasn't easy when you were pinned down and bullets were sparking off the corner next to your head. He looked around frantically for an answer.

Then he saw it. Their way out of there. Dale smiled.

"What?" asked Meghan.

"Here, hold this." He put the gun in her good hand, then ran across the hallway.

"Dale...?" came Meghan's worried voice. It was obvious they hadn't returned fire in a while and she was thinking that perhaps they should. She was right, but not with bullets. Or not *only* with bullets.

Dale finished wrenching the red metal cylinder from the wall, before joining her again. "Okay, you might want to duck," he told her as he relieved her of the machine-gun. She did as she was told and Dale pressed himself up against the wall, closing his eyes. "Fingers crossed."

He set off the fire extinguisher, jamming the mechanism so it sprayed out clouds of white as he flung it around the corner in their direction. When Dale heard the men coughing, he broke cover and fired wildly into the gas. He'd been intending just to hit the men, but one of his bullets hit the canister itself and it went up in the middle of the guards, doing exactly the opposite of what it was meant to – starting a fire instead of putting one out. It sent them sprawling in all directions. The blast also knocked him back against the far wall, reminding him of the injuries the Dragon had only recently inflicted.

But it had been worth it. All the men down in one fell swoop.

No, not all of them. One guard, blackened from the smoke, emerged. His face was blistered, one eye looked as though it was either gone or had skin stretched over it. There was a lump of metal sticking out of his shoulder, but none of this seemed to be bothering him too much. He was more intent on causing harm to the person who'd done this. The man grunted and brought his machine-gun to bear. Dale was still holding his, and depressed the trigger.

It clicked empty.

In spite of the obvious pain he must have been in, the man laughed. It was guttural, deep and throaty, in keeping with his nightmarish appearance. The guard raised his gun and Dale closed his eyes, waiting for the end.

He heard a dull thump rather than the *rat-ta-tat* he'd been expecting. "You've just been Jack Hammered, buddy," said a voice which made him open his eyes immediately.

The guard was on the floor, but there was still no sign of Jack. Then, through the smoke, came the end of the staff that had struck the guard on the head. Jack's face followed, and he adjusted the cap he always wore as he looked down at his handiwork. When he noticed Dale he appeared just as surprised to see him.

"Dale?" said Jack, unable to disguise the delight in his voice. "All that worrying and you're here sitting on your ass."

"You know me. Always slacking."

Jack laughed. "And getting yourself into scrapes. I just had to follow the sound of gunfire."

Dale was having trouble getting up and Jack came over to help, as did Meghan, appearing from around the corner. Jack instinctively began raising his staff, but Dale held up his hand.

"She's with me. Civilian. There are more dotted about this place."

"I see." The large man lowered his weapon, smiling tentatively at her. She smiled back. Dale knew he had a problem with women ever since what had happened with Adele. Dale couldn't really talk – he'd thought badly of Meghan too when it looked like she'd set him up. Then Jack spotted her hand.

"Why, you're hurt as well, little lady." That wasn't Jack being patronising, it was just what he called most women – and there was a certain respectful charm to that, which Meghan appeared unused to.

"The Dragon," said Dale, by way of explanation about her hand.

"We need to get that examined," Jack said, moving closer and placing his hand underneath hers. "We have some Rangers trained in first aid."

"I-I'll be all right," she said shyly.

Jack smiled, then turned and addressed Dale. "I'm guessing he did that number on you, as well."

Dale nodded. "We're on our way to him right now... well, we think. He's got Meghan's niece."

"Okay." Jack handed him the guard's machine-gun in exchange for his exhausted one, then got him to his feet. "So, what are we waiting for?"

As they got moving, Dale asked how their side were doing. "Creamin' em, kid," said Jack. "Tanek still around?"

"Sorry," Dale told him. "He headed off after the meet by the sound of things."

Jack's face fell. Then he turned to Dale and asked, "Listen, this niece we're on our way to save. Are you and her... Y'know?"

Dale didn't say a word, but his expression must have told Jack everything he needed.

"Figures," said the big man, rolling his eyes. "You really have got to get another act, kid."

Dale thought about telling him he had; that this girl was different. But Jack probably wouldn't believe him, and he couldn't blame him for that.

The point was they were on their way to try and save her. Sian. Dale just hoped they were in time.

CHAPTER SIXTEEN

ENOUGH WAS ENOUGH.

He couldn't take any more of this, it was insane! Even though he'd only been up there a short time, the flames very gradually building, Ceallach could smell Hood's flesh beginning to cook. It made his stomach churn.

Not that long ago, he would have gladly cheered at the death of this man. The one responsible for his band of raiders losing that haul with the truck. The one who fired arrows at Ceallach himself as he rode alongside on his motorbike, watching as Hood dispatched most of his companions. Hadn't he himself even ordered Torradan to shoot through the roof of the van and kill Hood? But, when all was said and done, this woodsman had defeated them. Defeated the men Ceallach had ridden with, pretty much single-handedly.

Ceallach had been thrown off his bike during the course of the scrap; or, more accurately, when Hood jammed his sword in the wheel. That had hurt. But, afterwards, when Ceallach had dragged himself back to the vehicle to make his escape, Hood had also been the one who'd allowed him to escape. Ceallach had seen him in the smashed mirrors, preventing that guy with the shotgun from shooting.

The trip back to the castle hadn't been easy. Knowing he was leaving so many of his friends behind, at Hood's mercy, stuck in his craw. But if those captured Rangers were telling the truth then they were at least being treated humanely. Ceallach had heard in the past about Hood's hotel prisons – sounded quite nice actually, better than some of the accommodation here.

And, after he'd returned to tell the Widow what had happened – still hurt and angry that her reputed vision hadn't shown her what would happen – what had she offered in reply?

"Aye, I knew Hood would be waitin'."

Just like that. Which told him one of two things. Either she couldn't see shit, and all the voodoo bollocks they believed about her was just a crock, or she'd let them walk into a trap. Neither option made him warm to her. Why exactly would the Widow knowingly send them into an ambush? She hadn't shared her reasons with him – simply sent Ceallach to the Vaults to be punished for answering back. Re-education, she'd called it. That had hurt more than fucking falling off the bike. Some of the stuff they did to people. He'd thought it was only reserved for their enemies, but apparently not.

Well, he'd been re-educated all right. It had definitely made him think twice, but not about questioning the Widow's motives. More like what the fuck he was still doing here? He'd pretended the experience had done him a favour; the Widow didn't generally try that conversion thing on people like him if they turned against her. Instead she just had you killed. It was less trouble. He played along, all nice like. He knew how to do that from before, when he'd been one of Freddie Banks' guys, pulling bank-jobs and other robberies. You did the work, you took your cut; you smiled, said thanks. That's what he'd done after he'd finished his stint in the Vaults. The Widow usually asked to see you afterwards, to look you in the eye, check out whether you really *were* sorry. And he'd been scared of that, he had to admit, though not as scared as before. See, he was starting to lean more towards the opinion that she was a fake. This Widow could no more see into the future than his testicles were going to sprout wings and fly away, waving a cheery goodbye to his dick.

As it turned out, he hadn't needed to pass the test, because that was when Hood was captured. He'd had mixed feelings about that. On the one hand, he'd wanted to find him and punch him in the face. On the other, it showed that not even this man, the living legend, was immune from the Widow's power. If only those people who'd believed Hood's press over the past couple of years could see him now; naked and helpless as a baby while the heat roasted him.

Ceallach knew what she had in mind next. He'd known ever since they'd called him to help escort these prisoners to the Reservoirs – re-enforcements after something had happened in the Great Hall. What the Widow had planned was something the men always talked about, but no-one could confirm. Something she'd done to men she'd been fond of, but was either bored with or they'd betrayed her. Seems she'd had designs on Hood from what he could make out, even used that mojo of hers on him; the symbols were still painted on his glistening skin. But he'd spurned her, so now she was going to cook him.

Then eat him.

Again, Ceallach felt his stomach lurch. He'd seen some weird shit in his time at Edinburgh Castle, heard tales about so much more. But this wasn't him. Not this. If most of the fellas here knew what was actually going down, they'd feel the same – which was why she'd only allowed a couple to remain, locking the door behind her. Ones she felt sure remained loyal to her. Ceallach had only just undergone re-education so was unlikely to want to go there again in a hurry. The other guard across the way, Artair, really lived up to the name she'd given him; remaining stone-like, unmoved by what was occurring.

Which was more than could be said for Hood's woman. Little wonder, when the Widow had just told them she was up the duff, and now her husband was being treated like a suckling pig on a spit. The Widow was licking her lips at the prospect. Salivating.

This was too much; too much. He'd done some bad things in his time, but a line was being crossed here. Could Ceallach just stand by and watch? He had to do something. Ceallach – no, not Ceallach... that's the name *she* gave you, a Celtic name meaning war or strife; your name is Tommy Neagle, remember? Tommy gritted his teeth, knowing that he was going to regret this, but the time had come to test his theory.

The time had come to see if this bloody madwoman really could see into the future.

He turned his machine-gun on the Widow.

"Let him down," Tommy told her. "Or I'll shoot."

At first he didn't think she'd heard him. She didn't turn or even look. Then, slowly, she shifted her gaze from the fire and Hood, to Tommy. She frowned, perhaps thinking he'd gone insane, unable to see that the only crazy one around here was her. "And what exactly do yer think yer doin', Ceallach?"

"Tommy," he grumbled under his breath. Then, louder: "My name is fuckin' Tommy! Now let him down, for God's sake."

"God?" The Widow didn't move, but he saw beyond her that Hood's wife had begun to look hopeful.

When Tommy looked back at the Widow, she'd moved closer. He raised his machine-gun higher. "Don't move, I'm warnin' yer!"

Then everything seemed to happen at once. The Widow leapt forward again, and Tommy fired. At the same time, Artair turned his gun on Tommy and this was all the distraction Hood's woman needed to strike. She spoilt Artair's aim by grabbing the rifle and twisting, then delivering a punch across the face that any heavyweight boxer would have been proud of. But she hadn't finished yet. With the flat of her hand, she smacked Artair squarely in the face. There was a loud crack as his nasal cartilage not only shattered, but was driven up into the man's brain.

That didn't help Tommy, though. There was no sign of the Widow in front of him, where he'd just fired. She was off to one side, blowing something in his face. He coughed, spluttered; then attempted to move.

He couldn't.

Fuck.

He heard the Widow laughing in his ear. "Time to meet yer God in person, Tommy." She showed him the golden dagger she was about to use, held it under his nose, in fact, to taunt him. Then it was gone, and Tommy felt a sharp, stabbing pain in his side as she slid it into him – the Widow holding his shoulder to stop him falling over. He would have screamed, except for the fact his jaw had locked up completely. And he would have dropped to the ground, but for his knees remaining fixed in position. *Should have called* me *Artair,* he thought, but there was no humour to it. He was dying and he knew that. Tommy felt the blade being removed, and then he saw why.

A blur in front of him, another crazed woman – this time out to save her man from his terrible fate. She grabbed hold of the Widow, then delivered a series of short but effective punches to her face. "Bet you didn't see *that* coming!" shrieked Hood's woman, her words fuelled by hatred. The Widow responded by shaking her head, wiping her nose, and lashing out with the bloodied dagger. The same blood that had saved him when everyone else had died of the virus. Tommy attempted to roll his eyes down to his belt, but Hood's woman wasn't looking. Thankfully, she'd thought of this anyway and turned to face him, unsheathing both his claymore and his belt-knife.

Yes! thought Tommy, now actually rooting for Hood's woman. She was only just in time to block an attack from the Widow, bringing up both weapons she'd taken and crossing them to prevent the dagger from plunging into her chest.

The Widow was still fast, but the unexpected punches had hampered her a little. More evidence, Tommy thought, that she couldn't really predict what was about to happen.

Unless she'd been too close to this whole thing? a voice in his mind said. *Maybe it had clouded her judgement?* It didn't matter now; he wouldn't be around for much longer. But he was holding on to see who would win this grudge match between the two women.

On the face of it, that should have been obvious. The Widow had bested bigger and better opponents. But Hood's woman was fighting with such determination and rage, it made him think twice. She pushed back the Widow's lunge, kicking out with her foot into the Widow's midriff. His former leader crumpled, taking a couple of steps backwards, but soon straightened again. Hood's woman swept the claymore around in an arc and the Widow only narrowly avoided having her head separated from her body.

The Widow's response was to kick up and sideways, knocking the sword from the woman's hand, sending it spinning across the room. That left them with just the knives. Both women hunkered down, trying to anticipate what the other would do. The Widow still looked sluggish from the blows to the face, otherwise Tommy knew she would have been on Hood's woman in seconds, and her enemy wouldn't have stood a chance. As it was when they clashed, it was Hood's lady who had the distinct advantage, her knife slashes fast and furious while the Widow seemed to be having trouble avoiding them.

Tommy watched as the Widow began to mumble something in that unknown language she'd been using before. But whatever spell she'd been trying to muster either didn't work or she didn't get time to finish it, because Hood's woman brought down the knife – forcing the Widow to grab her wrist with her free hand to stop it from entering her shoulder. Hood's woman had to do the same with the Widow's wrist to avoid getting stabbed in the ribs, and the pair staggered around like this for a few moments, each looking for an opening.

It was the Widow who was losing ground, though, having to find her footing again and again as Hood's woman heaved her back. On the very last push, the Widow used her opponent's momentum against her and dragged her around full circle before flinging her to the ground. She struck the floor hard and Tommy looked on in dismay as his knife flew out of the woman's hand, clattering across the stone. The Widow followed this up with a swift kick across the jaw which sent the woman's head whipping sideways and saw her flat on her back. The Widow laughed.

"I was goin' tae let you watch what came next, but I suppose the time's come for doin' what Robert couldn't. Killing you and that little maggot inside yer. Cuttin' all links to ma intended."
It was then that Tommy realised how completely mental the Widow was. She was still talking as if she was going to marry Hood or something, when in actual fact she was intending to devour him. The Widow held the dagger high, ready to bring it right down into the woman's stomach.

Tommy was aware that his vision was fading as his body went numb. He'd hung on for as long as he could, but it seemed that the woman's fate was sealed. Just like his. It would have been nice to have seen his death avenged, even if

Hood's woman hadn't known she was doing it. But everything was growing black, in spite of the fact he couldn't close his eyes.

Then something happened that made him fight for every second he had left. The Widow was just about to strike when a pair of legs appeared, wrapping themselves around her shoulders and neck. Using all the effort he could muster, Tommy looked up slightly to see that Hood had swung over using the rope and grabbed the Widow, locking her tight there between his legs.

Again, the Widow seemed shocked – and before she could think about bringing the dagger up and into Hood's leg, he was straining on the ropes and pulling her backwards. Tommy was amazed at the resolve he was showing – perhaps there was something to the legend after all, if he could pull victory from the jaws of death like this. Or just sheer bloody-mindedness? The muscles in the man's taut body were bulging, thighs pressing against the sides of the Widow's head, causing her obvious pain. But he was also pulling against the ropes, his biceps fighting against the Widow's insistence to stay still.

With a last concerted effort, gritting his teeth, Hood pulled the Widow backwards, so that her feet came off the floor a few centimetres. Turning, she realised too late what was about to happen and again began chanting in that strange language, as if that was going to save her.

It wasn't. And Tommy watched, with a certain degree of satisfaction, as the woman was pulled onto the pyre. It seemed only fitting for a witch to be killed that way. Hood used whatever strength remained to pull his legs and feet up out of the way of the flames as they caught the Widow's body, drowning her in a fiery sea.

Tommy was aware of banging at the door. They didn't have long before the rest of the Widow's men would be inside. But Hood's woman was already getting to her feet, limping across to the rope that held the man she loved suspended above the fire.

He didn't see her get the man down or what happened next, because Tommy's life was pretty much at an end. But as his vision went completely and his heart stopped, he celebrated this small victory at least. The Widow, the woman who'd killed him, had been defeated.

But Tommy also knew that this was far from the end of Hood and his woman's problems.

As THE VEHICLES had pulled up, the driver of the largest nervously gripped the wheel.

This had been a stupid, stupid idea and was bound to fail. How on earth had he let himself get talked into it? Because, he remembered, the people inside there had put their lives on the line for such as him. He owed them. They all did. So it was the least they could do to try and free them.

But Jesus, was this the wrong way to go about it. They'd never get away with it. They'd been lucky that they'd managed to get past the check-points so far, although a couple had needed taking out when they got too nosey. That, to his mind, didn't give them much time before their subterfuge was discovered. Weren't check-points supposed to check *in* every now and again? What happened when they didn't? Was a radio screw-up blamed, or did it mean another ambush awaited *them*? At one of the security checks someone had mentioned radioing in, but then a guard had said that the Widow was engaged in urgent business and wouldn't want to be disturbed. That gave him some hope, at least, that they might make it to the castle.

And they had enough captured uniforms and vehicles to make the Widow's men think twice about firing in case they really were on the level; though reason also told him that they knew these had been stolen a few days ago, so might be expecting such a trick. After all, Hood and his team had gone in there and never come out again. If *they* could be taken...

Matt Jamison could hear Bill's voice even now, knew what he would say in reply to that. "Show some bloody backbone!" Well he was here, wasn't he? When they'd been told of what had happened, about the Widow taking Robert's group prisoner, he and his friends had volunteered to make up the numbers.

"I just heard from Nottingham Castle. Some kind of big push goin' on in Wales," Bill had explained, "so we won't be getting any re-enforcements. But I've decided to mount some kind o' rescue anyway, with the few Rangers we already have."

"It's suicide," one of the traders had said and Bill had flown at the man.

"They'd do the same for me, for ye. They've put their lives on the line more times than I've trodden in cow dung. So if ye think I'm just going to wait around here playin' with mysen, think again."

Bill was right, of course. Whether or not Matt agreed with how they'd gone about scuppering that raid – he still said they should have warned the drivers – the Rangers had come to help at Bill's request. They'd also saved lives that day, and who knows how many others by taking those raiders into custody. Even now, they were being guarded in makeshift prisons by other volunteers from the trader community, most of whom now pledged their support for Bill.

Just like Matt had done.

It was then that Bill had told them about his scheme. In a way, Matt shouldn't have been that surprised. The Rangers were known for their brass balls when it came to things like this – God in Heaven, how Robert and Mary could have gone to Edinburgh in the first place like that was beyond him. Asking to be killed, all of them. But they'd felt the need to do more digging, perhaps even take out the Widow quickly and quietly. That plan had failed, so what made Bill think this one would fare any better? Those men at the castle were much better armed and greater in number. Bill was asking Matt and his trader friends to go up against that when most of them hadn't seen any combat in their lives.

Again, Bill's probable answer echoed in Matt's head: "Then it's about time, in't it?" They were living in a different world these days, had been for a while. A new and dangerous world, one which Robert and his men were trying to enforce and police – as impossible as that might seem. That's what they'd been attempting to do up here, and *that's* why Matt had agreed to all this, he reminded himself. Now he was beginning to regret his decision.

Matt had gulped when he saw all the vehicles on the grassland either side of the Esplanade; enough to win a small war, he reckoned – though Bill assured him Robert and co. had faced worse. He was waiting for things to kick off at any moment, as there was no way they could continue getting away with this. For one thing wasn't this damned Widow supposed to know everything that was happening in advance? A stupid rumour, but one that had started somewhere. Indeed, even as he thought it, Matt saw the Rangers in the jeeps up ahead being flagged down – those riding bikes pulling up also. They were dressed in the Widow's tartan, had the same attire as those people telling them to halt, but they'd surely be marked at any time as impostors. Matt watched anxiously as one Ranger pointed down the convoy line; clearly trying to convey what a great catch they'd made and how full all the vehicles were with foodstuffs. If nothing else the Widow and her lot were greedy beggars and might let them in purely because of what they could be carrying.

There was also the distinct possibility that the people in charge at the Gatehouse were going to want to search the vehicles – which is what they looked like they were about to do. Matt spotted raiders heading down towards those armoured vehicles he'd seen, perhaps getting ready to go out on a routine patrol but maybe also in anticipation of something else occurring? If their enemies chose to attack from both sides, then Matt and his friends would be caught in the crossfire to end all crossfires. And where the devil was Bill? Not here in the trenches, that was for sure. "Don't ye worry," he'd told them, "I won't let ye get caught with ye britches down."

Matt gripped the wheel even harder as the Widow's men traipsed down the line of vehicles. If Bill had thought they could just waltz in here, he was dreaming. But then he saw something else.

Men, crawling underneath the vehicles in the convoy – Rangers who'd climbed out of the backs of carts and the other vehicles, making their way beneath to reach the Gatehouse unseen; pausing if any of the raiders walked by.

· As one of the guards passed by, Matt gave him an uneasy smile and salute. The man paused and, for a moment, Matt thought he was going to ask something. He didn't – just continued up along to the tail end of his truck. Matt watched him in the rear view banging on the side of the truck. "Open her up!" he called down to Matt.

"Well, Stacey," he told his truck as he prepared to get out, fingers curling around the handle of the baseball bat he kept down the side of the seat. "This is it."

From somewhere there was the sound of a helicopter. Matt looked sideways and saw something black coming in fast and low: a beast of a thing that meant business. It was armed to the teeth with missiles, and – as it got closer – what looked like machine-guns.

It took just one of those missiles to cause complete and utter pandemonium. Detaching from the helicopter, the projectile whistled into the banks of armoured vehicles to the right of Matt and the convoy. He watched, mouth gaping, as a couple of jeeps flew up into the air with an explosion loud enough to almost deafen him.

Matt saw the guard at the back of his truck fling himself to the ground as the helicopter flew over them, so close he could have jumped up onto Stacey's cab and hitched a ride. As it passed by, Matt caught a glimpse of the painting on the side door – it was a cartoon shotgun which had just gone off, the sound effect 'Blam!' written next to the red and yellow explosion.

"Bill," Matt said to himself as the chopper came about on the other side of the convoy. It fired another missile into the vehicles there, taking out a good chunk of the assembled jeeps, tanks and bikes. It was all the distraction the Rangers near the front of the convoy needed. With practiced skill, they reached into their jeeps for bows and arrows; those riding bikes pulling out bolas which they flung at the Gatehouse, causing whatever was inside them to explode on contact.

At the same time, those Rangers who'd been crawling under the convoy sprang up to pick off the guards defending the entrance. Arrows were fired over the walls, and seconds later Rangers were scrambling up them and over onto the other side like ants into a hill. Matt could do nothing but watch and marvel at the efficiency of their attack. More exploding bolas and projectiles struck the Gate and suddenly it was open, free for the Ranger-manned jeeps to enter.

There was no way Matt was getting inside there with his truck, however. But Bill had thought of that, too, it seemed. Because as soon as his men had cleared the Esplanade and Gatehouse, another – smaller, targeted – missile hit the entrance and expanded the opening. Matt winced at the damage, but knew the history of the place wouldn't have crossed Bill's mind. The tourist days were over for this castle and it was time to worm out the woman who'd caused so much havoc in the region, no matter what the cost.

Matt put Stacey into gear and began to move forward. Carrying his payload into the castle, up towards the Portcullis Gate.

"Shot!" Bill said in his rough, Derbyshire accent.

What he'd just done to the Gatehouse was regrettable, especially to students of history, but he'd needed to create an opening for Matt and his truck to get inside. The Widow's people would have no such qualms about doing the same, just as the Tsar's folk hadn't with their own castle back home. The Widow had picked this spot because it was easy to defend, and the gate there was *part* of that defence. Which was why it needed to be obliterated. Thoughts of rebuilding would come afterwards, *if* they won – right now all Bill could think about was taking this place back from the thieves and murderers who'd made it their home, returning the castle to its true inheritors: the locals who'd had to put up with the Widow's shenanigans for too long. Scottish people like those traders who'd chosen to fight with the Rangers today.

From his position, Bill could see his men making their way up towards the Portcullis Gates, in jeeps, on bikes and on foot, but he could also see the amount of guards on the other side, in the main part of the castle grounds. Roused by the explosions and machine-gun fire, they were flitting about: especially near the building Bill knew to be the New Barracks; arming and generally gearing themselves up to repel boarders.

There was no way of telling from up here where Robert, Mary or the other Rangers might be – *if* they were even still alive. That would be the job of those on the ground to ascertain. There were some good Rangers down there, all of whom had been trained to the best of their abilities. But, in Bill's opinion, you couldn't beat some top of the range firepower on your side. He knew what Robert would say, and if he'd been around he would have prevented Bill from using the Black Shark at all – which he'd lovingly restored after the battle Robert fought with the Tsar's men; including re-arming her with spares from other wrecked Black Sharks that had been taken down that day, plus making quite a number of important modifications himself. But Robert *wasn't* here. He'd gone and got himself and his team captured, so it was up to Bill to try and sort this muddle out. He hadn't been able to obtain any more men or weapons from Nottingham because Jack had bloody well requisitioned all they could spare – and Bill fully intended to have words with the big, dumb lummox later about that. So what else was he supposed to do? They needed a way of taking out some of those heavily armoured vehicles down there, and this was the only option he could think of.

The fact that he'd been dying to try this baby out in combat since he'd fixed her up was neither here nor there.

"That's my girl," he said, nudging the one-seater craft to one side. She handled like a dream, even better than his old Sioux or Gazelle, and she definitely packed more of a bite. In all honesty, Bill reckoned he could probably take on the whole of the Widow's mob single-handed, decimating the castle and everyone there if it weren't for the fact his friends were somewhere inside.

He opened up the cannon on a group of the Widow's men, his targeting system so precise he could put the wind up them without having to kill. The vehicles were another matter, and fair game as far as he was concerned, so he loosed another couple of missiles into what was rapidly becoming a military vehicles' graveyard, twisted metal resembling bones jutting up from the ground.

Something was moving to his left, and Bill manoeuvred round to see a Gepard anti-aircraft tank emerging from the smoke, massive twin guns being raised in his direction. Those Germans who'd supplied all this kit had obviously thrown in a few lessons for the Widow's men. The brute trundling over the green, up and onto the Esplanade itself, was the first thing he'd seen which could give him a run for his money. Both 90 calibre guns spat out their payload at once, armour-piercing rounds which could tear through the Black Shark's torso like paper. Bill pulled back on the control stick sharply; perhaps a little too sharply because the Black Shark protested somewhat.

"Bear with me, girl," he said to the chopper, then angled her round. The fire from the Gepard was still reaching into the sky. Fortunately the men aiming the guns were lacking in practise, and Bill had done nothing *but*, even if he had saved most of the live ammo salvaged for just such a occasion. He fired an anti-tank missile and grinned as the laser-guided projectile found its target, allowing Bill plenty of time to get clear of the blast zone. The Gepard opened up like one of those old bangers in a black and white slapstick movie.

Coming about, Bill flew over the top of the castle once more, noticing that a Ranger jeep was about to ram the Portcullis Gate, the driver inside throwing himself clear at the last moment. The vehicle slammed into the gridded obstacle, knocking through it before grinding to a standstill. The other vehicles behind drew up, Rangers climbing out of jeeps or from bikes, while Matt's truck – too wide to get any further – was opened at the back.

A mass of men – traders and Rangers, men and women – leapt from the trailer, rushing forward through the Portcullis. They'd meet the guards heading in their direction any moment, so Bill decided to even the odds a little. He sprayed a covering fire of bullets in front of the Widow's forces, enough to make them pause. Some even fired up at the helicopter, but hit nothing. Then his troops were there, on the ground and tackling the soldiers. They may have outnumbered his lot, but Bill was proud to see the guards falling first and fast, spinning round to reveal arrows in shoulders or thighs. And yes, there was Matt himself, having climbed out of the cab of his truck. He was putting his baseball bat to good use, whacking opponents as they came round one of the corners near the Portcullis Gate.

More had taken up positions along the wall, to shoot at his people from above. Bill wasn't having that, and so spun the chopper around, splattering them with gunfire and causing the guards to fall back from the walls. But it was as he did so that he felt something strike the side of the Black Shark to his right. Bill craned his head to see the old cannons from the Argyle battery had been pulled around and raised up so that they could fire at the chopper. The mixture of old and new weaponry obviously extended beyond those Claymores they fought with.

Two more fired at him, one hitting the tail end of the Black Shark. "Why you little–" began Bill, but before he could say any more, he was being fired on from the left as well, similar defences aiming at him, each one firing heavy cannonballs at speed. Bill attempted to dodge them, but he'd flown in too close, assuming, wrongly, that those old relics didn't work anymore. They worked just fine, though, as he'd found out to his cost. His control panel was lighting up like a Christmas tree, emergency alarms going off in his cockpit. "Damn and blast it," he said, narrowly avoiding another blast from a cannon which would have downed the Black Shark there and then if it had hit.

Bill searched for a place to put her down, and quick – only now spotting smoke coming from one of the reservoir buildings and wondering what it was. But he didn't have time to dwell on that. The square next to the palace appeared to be the only open-plan area nearby to attempt an emergency landing. He dipped the nose, hopping over the War Memorial and almost catching the back end of his helicopter on the roof. His landing was rough, to say the least; only some of his gear responding when he flipped the switch.

"Easy," he said, tapping the roof of the helicopter from the inside after he'd set her down, calming the thing like it was some kind of pet. He didn't have much time to check on the damage, because he was already being fired on by the Widow's men. Bill risked using his cannon: the aim was totally shot but he hoped he could scare the gunmen enough so he could effect an escape. He pressed the trigger, but only one round went off, hitting the building in front of him and causing dust to spark up from the stonework.

It would have to do, so he grabbed his shotgun, opened the cockpit and dived out. Rolling, he balanced on one knee and let off both barrels into the group of approaching soldiers. It scattered them, but a couple still came at him on the left. They fired and some of the gunshot sparked off the pilot's helmet he was wearing. "Judas Priest!" he shouted. With no time to reload, Bill turned his gun around and hit one on the side of the head, sending him toppling. The other he grabbed by the collar and pulled him in close, one punch settling it. He snatched up their machine-guns in both hands and sprayed the other guards with bullets, left and right.

Then he ran across the yard, looking for a way inside, using the wall of a building for cover. "Might as well start searchin' while I'm 'ere," he said to no-one in particular.

And, with that, he ducked inside the building that would take him to the Castle Vaults.

CHAPTER SEVENTEEN

"You, um, need to know something before we go in," said Meghan.

They'd almost reached the part of the stadium where she delivered food. Dale hoped so, because he was sick of chasing this particular Dragon. It was nowhere near the place he'd gone with her the first time, but then he guessed the Dragon hadn't wanted the ambush to take place anywhere close to his family. Probably hadn't wanted any of them seeing what he liked to look at on those screens, either. *I'll bet he kept that very quiet*, he thought, *unless they're all as twisted as him, of course.*

"What is it?" asked Dale as they made their way down along yet another corridor, nearly at the end of their journey.

"I-It's his family."

"What about them?"

"They're, well, it's hard to explain but–"

Jack shushed them both as they came to the corner. "Guards," he said, pointing.

That meant the Dragon *had* to be inside that room. Even with everything that was going on, with his empire crashing down around his ears that creep could still command some kind of respect – still command his men. There were a couple of the Welshman's guards outside, and Jack motioned for Dale to take out the one to the right of the door. "But quietly. We don't want to tip off whoever's inside," he told Dale. "You up to it?" he whispered, scrutinizing the young man.

Dale stood a little straighter, hiding the discomfort he was in. "When have I ever refused an invitation to party?"

Jack grinned. "So let's dance, kid."

The trick was to incapacitate the guards before they could get off a shot or a warning cry. Jack rounded the corner first, jabbing a guard with his staff. Dale followed close behind, using the butt of his machine-gun first to double over the second guard, then strike his temple to put him on the ground. When the man started to get up, Dale delivered a blow to the back of the neck for good measure. He looked across at how Jack was getting on: the bigger man was in the process of disarming his opponent. The machine-gun clattered to the ground, a little too noisily, and from Jack's expression Dale could see the element of surprise had already been lost.

The guard then foolishly attempted to grab Jack around the neck; foolish not only because of the sheer size of the man, but also because of his former profession. Jack bent and threw the guard over his head, then gave the man an almighty kick, which not only knocked him into the door, it knocked it *down*.

Jack was inside first, but his reward for being so eager was a smack in the face from a waiting guard. Dale stepped in and felt the barrel of a pistol against his temple. "Drop it," he was told, so he let the machine-gun fall to the ground. These were two of the Dragon's most trusted guards; they had to be considering the secrets he kept in that room.

As Jack was rising, a machine pistol trained on him, he was relieved of his staff. And now he saw what Dale was looking at, too.

The room was laid out almost like a bedsit; a living room area with chairs and a bed. There were people sitting in the chairs and one lying in the bed, Dale could see, but there was something wrong with them. They were much thinner than they should have been, in spite of all the food Meghan must have delivered.

In fact they were malnourished, these people: with stick-like arms that hung down – although one was attempting to knit. The Dragon's grandmother, Dale supposed. The figure in bed was sitting up, leaning back against the pillows. Not because he'd just woken, Dale reasoned, but because he must have been injured at some point.

His mind wouldn't let him see it at first, *couldn't* let him see what in front of him. Because the truth was too hideous to contemplate. That someone could do this, even after everything else he'd witnessed at the Dragon's hands, was too much. It threatened to bend Dale's mind, just as something must surely have bent the Dragon's long ago.

"Dale... they're..." This was Jack, obviously having as much trouble processing the information as him. "They're all–"

"Dead," finished Dale. Because they were. All three of them. Oh, they'd been dressed up to look as though they were still alive, positioned as if they were. Not only was the gran knitting, but the mother had a magazine on her lap open at some celebrity gossip that had long since failed to have any meaning. The father was just staring out in an accusatory way at anything that happened to be in front of him, including Jack and Dale. That is, he would have been staring if he'd still had eyes. All of the corpses were in a distinct state of decay, the flesh rotted from their bones, eyes long since gone to jelly, leaving empty black sockets behind. Dale wondered how they all still had hair, but then noticed the artificiality of it, especially the tight curls of the mother and gran. Wigs taken from some kind of hairdressers or fancy dress shop.

Thankfully, there wasn't the usual stench associated with death – and Dale knew this all too well, from his time walking the streets post-Cull. Instead the air smelt quite sweet, the result of large amounts of air-freshener being pumped into the atmosphere, no doubt.

Dale turned as much and as slowly as he could and saw Meghan being ushered in by one of the recovering guards from the doorway. "You brought *them* food?" he asked.

She nodded. "I had to, and change their clothes. I did everything for them." Tears were in her eyes again and Dale shuddered at what she must have gone through as their personal slave.

"And don't think we didn't appreciate it, dear," came a voice from the back of the room. It was female, and appeared to be coming from the mother.

"That's right," said another feminine voice, this time sounding much frailer: the grandmother. "We don't know what we would have done without you."

Dale frowned, searching for the source. He didn't have to look far. There, at the back of the room, now stepping out from behind a partition was the Dragon. He was half dragging, half holding up Sian, the girl's head drooping as it had been on the screen back in the other room. Probably drugged, Dale suspected, or just worn down by her interrogation.

Dale took a step forwards when he saw her, forgetting about the gun until it was cocked. "Let her go!" he shouted.

"He really should, shouldn't he," said the mother, and now Dale could see the Dragon's lips moving, throwing his voice across the room so that it appeared to be coming from the corpse. Christ, how long had he been having conversations with his dead relatives? "But she's such a sweet young thing. The only girlfriend he's ever brought back to meet us."

"I wonder why." This voice was gruffer, a thick Welsh accent. The Dragon's father.

"Now, don't you two start again," said the mother.

All the voices sounded real. Genuine imitations of the voices of his family Dale was willing to bet; honed after years of hearing them.

"I really like this one," the Dragon said in his own voice, and for a second Dale didn't even recognise it. This was the first time he'd spoken since they'd discovered his little secret.

Dale tried to look to the side, at the guard, but the barrel of the gun was pressed harder into his temple. "Look, can't you see what's happening here? The kind of man you're protecting?"

"Your boss is a Grade A fruitcake," Jack added.

"I am *not* a—" the Dragon began, then smiled. "You're only jealous, all of you."

"Of what?" Dale spluttered.

"My family survived. I'm guessing most of yours didn't."

"They're not exactly looking too healthy for people who are supposed to be alive," Dale argued.

"What's he talking about, sweetheart?" asked the mother.

"I feel as fit as a fiddle," the Dragon now said in the grandmother's voice. "Never felt better."

"Don't know what he needs a girlfriend for anyway," the father piped up. "It's not like he'd be able to do anything with her."

"Ryn!" snapped the mother.

"Well, look at him. Even if he wasn't such a pansy, he's the size of a bloody house."

"This is crackers," said Dale, stating the obvious. "Let her go right now, you sick fuck or–"

"Hey, boy, don't you talk to our Owain like that! Little prick."

The Dragon looked sideways, at the dead body that had once been his father. "Dad?"

"Well... You're still my son. Might not be anything like Gareth, but you're still my flesh and..." The Dragon paused in his imitation, some small part of his brain realising the significance of what he was saying.

If they had exactly the same blood, then his father would still be alive. Or had the man died after whatever had befallen him post-virus? Dale wondered. Whatever the case, the Dragon had stopped; had realised this fact. It was probably also the most touching moment he'd ever shared with his father, and it wasn't even real. Dale might have felt sorry for him, if he hadn't caused so much death and destruction. If he didn't still have Sian in a vice-like grip.

"It's time to end this," Jack said. "Right *now!*"

Dale moved quickly, ignoring the pain he was feeling, ducking and elbowing the guard who had the gun on him in one, swift movement. The pistol went off, deafening him, but he couldn't allow that to stop him, too much was at stake. Dale grabbed the guard's gun arm, pulling it down and forcing the man to depress the trigger again, to shoot himself in his foot. Dale barely heard the muffled howl of agony. He looked over to see Jack wrestling with his own guard, having already disarmed him – now all it took was a head butt which saw the man sinking to his knees. "The girl," Dale just about made out from Jack's lips, while the larger man concentrated on the guard holding Meghan. The guard pushed her to the floor, readying himself for Jack's second attack of the day.

As Dale moved forwards, though, the Dragon pulled Sian into a headlock, threatening to twist it off if he came any closer. "Let her go," Dale repeated.

"No! She's mine."

There were two gunshots in quick succession, and Dale – wrongly – assumed they were the result of Jack's tussle with the final guard. But then he noticed the two bullet holes in the Dragon's chest. Dale traced the bullets' trajectory back and was surprised to see Meghan holding the first guard's pistol, the one that had been pressed against his own temple. She was on her knees, her wounded hand hanging by her side, but the other was outstretched, still holding the smoking gun.

Dale often thought back to that day, and wondered if Meghan had just been really lucky not to hit Sian, or if the size of the Dragon had helped with her aim; after all, there was so much more of him than her niece. Meghan didn't know either, and she'd never fired a gun in her life before, as she'd explained afterwards. But something had just made her pick it up and shoot. Something that was guiding her hand. An instinct that had tried to keep Sian safe long before the Dragon came along.

Sian dropped from the Dragon's grasp as he tottered backwards. Dale went across to her, keeping his eye on the big man as he went. The Dragon was looking down at the holes, the blood. His eyes were wide as he dipped his fingers inside, not daring to believe he'd been hit.

"I can't," he said. "I'm..."

"Oh Owain, let us have a look at that. I'm sure it'll be all right if we put some antiseptic on it and a plaster," he managed in his mother's voice – though Dale noticed the tremble of fear.

Then Owain said one thing in his father's tones: "Prat."

Dale began pulling Sian away from the scene. The Dragon clutched at his wounds, and his hands came away scarlet. He rubbed his face with them, closing his eyes.

Dale shuddered as the Dragon opened them again, looking more like his namesake than ever. "I... I am..." he said, then stumbled forwards. He held on to the back of his father's bed for support. Dale watched him reach down, lifting the pillow.

"Do you remember, Dad? When you brought me here?" The Dragon's voice was weakening as he brought out the object he'd hidden there. "D-Do you remember those rugby games?"

"Jesus," said Dale. "Jack, Meghan, we have to get out of here!" They looked at him, puzzled, so he thumbed back towards the Dragon – now holding a rugby ball. "It's a bomb!"

That did the trick, and Jack helped Meghan up, pulling her out through the door. Dale followed closely behind with Sian, struggling to hold her up but knowing they only had a few moments left. His ears had finally stopped ringing and he clearly heard the last words to come from inside the room.

"Do you remember what we said, what you taught me? Say it with me now. We are Dragons. Come on..." He sounded like he was half crying; but to Dale, right at the end, it also sounded like there was more than one voice. "We are Dragons. I. AM. A. DRAGO–"

The blast from the doorway blew them halfway up the corridor, but the walls protected them from much of the explosion. It had to have killed the Dragon, though, even if his gunshot wounds hadn't – not to mention the other men who'd chosen to guard him. Everyone else in there had been dead a long time ago.

As the smoke cleared, Jack and Meghan rose, and Dale picked Sian up. She was starting to stir a little, thankfully, even tried to smile when she opened her eyes and saw him. He smiled back, brushing hair out of her eyes.

"Come on," Jack said, "that's enough of all that." But then he realised he was still holding onto Meghan, and let go. He coughed. "We'd better check what's happening in the rest of this place. It ain't over yet, kid."

But, compared with what they'd just gone through – what he, Sian and Meghan had been *going* through for a while – how could the battles raging upstairs be any worse?

THINGS WERE ABOUT to get much worse.

Robert thought that as Mary freed him from the ropes at his wrists. Oh, his legs were scorched in places, but it could have been so much worse. And they'd had some good fortune: take the guy who'd confronted the Widow, who was now standing like a statue, quite clearly dead from the knife wound she'd inflicted on him. Robert felt sure he recognised him, had seen the man somewhere, but couldn't place him Why had he done it? They'd probably never know, but they *had* been lucky. That luck, though, was about to run out. Apart from the veritable army about to knock down the door, Robert still had his wife – his *real* wife – to face. And apologise to. "Mary, listen–"

"Later," she told him.

"But..."

She placed a finger to his lips, helping to hold him up at the same time. "I know what you were doing," Mary told him. "Buying us time. Trying to fool her. You weren't the only one acting back there, you know. Oh, I didn't want to listen at first, but then someone close forced me to."

He was about to ask what she meant when she kissed him, long and hard on the lips. It was as she was doing so that the first of the explosions went off. "Did the earth move for you?" she asked.

"Always."

They kissed again, the explosions and gunfire outside a million miles away. But when they broke off, Robert frowned. "Can you smell–"

"Burning!" Mary screamed, pushing Robert away. Coming at them was a flaming figure, risen from the bonfire like some kind of phoenix. The Widow rushed at them, flailing her hands, still wielding the sacrificial dagger that meant so much to her. For a moment Robert thought that the words she'd been uttering as he dragged her back onto the flames might have worked; that instead of burning her alive, they'd somehow made her more powerful. But if it was black magic keeping her alive, it didn't last for long. She dropped to the ground after failing in her attempt to either share the fire with the couple, or stab them.

As she fell she let go of the dagger and Mary promptly kicked it away, out of reach. The flames went out unusually quickly, leaving her body blackened and crisp. Still the Widow struggled to rise, getting up on her hands and knees. Robert thought then how much she resembled the thing he'd seen in his dream: the spider that was her namesake.

She toppled over onto her back, her breathing shallow. Only her eyes and her teeth now shone white. Though it was clearly agony for her to do so, the Widow gestured for Robert to come closer. He remained where he was, and she whispered something inaudible.

Robert took a step nearer.

"Robert, *no!*"

"She's trying to speak," he told Mary.

"All right, just be careful. She's dangerous."

There was a laugh from the Widow at this, which hurt her even more judging from the moan she let out afterwards. Robert leaned in, close enough to hear but not near enough to be grabbed if she decided to pull a stunt.

"W-Won't hurt yer..." breathed the Widow. "Just wanted to tell yer, we will meet agin...Robert, ma Hooded Man. I'll see yer agin..."

Robert shook his head. It was highly doubtful, but then hadn't he seen De Falaise and The Tsar again after their deaths? After he'd *taken* their lives?

"It's... it's fitting..." she told him. "What I deserved... but it is not the end...You'll get yer magic back, Robert... This I promise... And we... we *will* see each other again." She reached up now, too quickly for him to pull back. She grabbed his arm, pulling him closer. Mary made a move, but he held up his other hand.

The Widow smiled, eyes closing. "Tae bad." she whispered, It could have been... somethin' quite special." Then she collapsed back to the ground.

Robert looked at the thing in his hand: a blackened card, but he could still make out the picture of *The Emperor* on its surface. He shook his head.

Mary said nothing. She just crouched down on the other side of the Widow, wrapped her fingers in the edge of her top and pulled off the golden ring on the third finger of the woman's left hand. "Mine, I believe."

They'd been so caught up in the Widow's final moments that they hadn't noticed the escalating gunfire and explosions outside. But the banging on the door continued nonetheless, those loyal to the Widow still trying to get in.

Robert barely had time to stand when the door finally caved and in rushed several raiders. Mary helped him to his feet, not knowing what either of them could do. But then they saw the guards were lowering their weapons. "Robert? Mary?"

He squinted, trying to see beyond the goggles and masks. One pulled off his headgear to reveal a face he recognised. "Saxton!" It was one of their Rangers.

The others came inside and Robert saw there were more dressed like the Widow's men, but bringing up the rear and shouting for them to let him past was a voice he recognised all too well. "Come on, move aside. Let the dog see the..." Bill paused when he saw Robert. "Well, I didn't really want to see *that* much!" he exclaimed, nodding at his friend's nakedness. Mary stood in front of her husband, at least until she could find something to cover him with.

"Bill, you came for us," said Robert, giving him a weary smile.

"Aye lad, in the Black Shark. Didn't ye hear me?" Bill laughed but then caught the chastising glare Robert was giving him. "Ahem, but look who I found in the Widow's dungeons," the ex-farmer said, changing the subject. He stepped back to reveal Azhar, Annie Reid and some of the other Rangers from Robert's original strike force.

Robert's smile widened. "What's happening outside now?"

"The battle's still going on, but we're holding our own, with the help of the traders I brought with us. Won't take long to settle now we're all back together again. It's the Widow we're really after, mind. Fix her and you fix the probl-" Bill suddenly stopped, as if only now seeing the blackened thing between them on the ground. "What's that?"

"Consider the problem fixed," Mary told him, putting her wedding ring back on now that it had cooled.

CHAPTER EIGHTEEN

SHE'D BEEN ON the move for hours. Her legs ached, her feet had blisters, but she marched on. She didn't need the torch anymore, because the sun had started to rise. *Nearly there*, she kept telling herself. *Reach the outskirts and you'll be spotted. They'll take you to the castle and you can explain everything. You can do your bit.*

Walking through the woodland at night had been the hardest part – all those strange sounds and movements in the undergrowth. After finding the dirt track leading to the main road, it was just a matter of following the map to the city. It reminded her a little of the walks her parents would insist on taking when she was younger, out every weekend into the country, boots and backpacks on, striding out over hill and dale. If nothing else, that had prepared her for a hike like this. And she'd kept herself relatively fit during her adult years, going to the gym three nights a week, keeping her alcohol consumption down. *Yeah, only because you never used to go out anywhere at the weekend; even the walks with your folks were better than the marathon weepie sessions with a chick flick and a box of Kleenex.*

Approaching thirty and still a virgin, stuck in a dead-end job as a receptionist with a boss she hated, fancying male employees but never having the courage to ask any of them out. Karen Shipley, hopeless romantic with no-one to lavish her affections on. It had taken most of the population of the planet being wiped out before she stood even the remotest chance with a guy.

Karen hadn't really wept for anyone during those early stages of the virus, because she didn't have anyone she loved as such – her parents having died in a car accident long before that. Perhaps they'd been the lucky ones? Neville from Human Resources didn't count because he was creepy, and she'd only snogged him under the mistletoe that Christmas because she had given in to the booze at the office party. It had taken her so long to stop him from trailing her around the place that she was almost grateful for the virus... No, that was terrible. Poor Neville. Poor *everyone*. She didn't like to think the only reason it had happened was so she could actually get herself a man.

Yet it was looking like that might be a happy by-product. The one ray of sunshine in this whole, stinking mess. It wasn't her fault the virus killed all those people who didn't have O-Neg blood like hers. The more she thought about it, the more it made a kind of sense; it was the duty of those left behind to hook up and try and repopulate the planet, wasn't it? Karen knew exactly who she wanted to start her own particular repopulation with, as well.

She'd known from the minute she set foot in the village, after being picked up by a scout party from New Hope. Karen had convinced them she had skills they'd find useful – typing counted, right? By the time they discovered she didn't have any specialisms to offer, she'd already made herself indispensable fetching and carrying, working hard on whatever needed to be done. Like the wall and the tunnel, for example; both his ideas. The man she planned to marry someday: Darryl.

Karen had spotted him as the jeep drew up, younger than her definitely, but extremely hot – especially with his shirt round his waist like that, sweat covering his muscles. He'd noticed the jeep arriving, breaking off from his labours working on the first few sections of the wall, and trotted across to greet the new arrivals. As usual, she'd made a complete arse of herself and tripped over her words. But she'd smiled at him and he'd thrown her one of his

casual smiles back. The kind of smile she'd walk a million miles –
not just this piddling distance – for.

That's why you're doing this, she reminded herself every time she
felt her feet hurting, or her legs aching. *For Darryl. Because he'd
volunteered again to do this, but you wouldn't let him. And to keep
him safe. To fetch help, making sure those German people didn't get
to him and kill him.*

It had been Gwen who'd come up with the notion, who'd wanted
to go herself – trusting only Darryl to look after her son, Clive Jr.
Karen didn't care much for the bond between Gwen and Darryl, but
they had known each other a long time. Plus which, Karen didn't
see her as too much of a threat because she was always banging on
about that dead father of her child, the guy who'd founded Hope
and got himself killed for his trouble. Gwen wanted to slip out again
using the tunnel, this time to fetch help from Nottingham Castle
even though there was some kind of stupid feud going on between
her and the new Robin Hood. "They'll help once I've explained,"
Gwen had assured everyone. "It's what they do. It's *all* they do." But
Darryl had played the hero again, putting himself forward.

"You can't, Gwen. We need you here," Darryl had said. "*I* need
you."

Karen winced inwardly at that one, but chose to read it as he
needed her leadership skills. Dammit, even after the hug when he
climbed back up through that hole, he still didn't seem to get it.
Which was why when Darryl said that he was going instead, Karen
had piped up, volunteering herself.

He'd looked at her oddly, then, like he was seeing her for the first
time. "You?"

"Yes," she said. "Why not? I'm a lot more resourceful than I look,
matey. I'm quick and used to walking long distances, have been
since I was a kid." The fact she hadn't walked more than a couple of
miles in one go during the past ten years was irrelevant.

Darryl smiled, but wasn't there a tinge of concern there too? Did
he realise, just a little bit, that she was doing it for *him*? Yes, Karen
thought that he did. "If you're sure, then?"

Karen nodded emphatically. "But when I get back, I'll expect
another hug," she told him. Probably the boldest thing she'd said
or done in her life; even bolder than Neville, and she'd been drunk
then.

Darryl had smiled again, a little awkwardly, but she'd take it. He'd also exchanged glances with Gwen, probably to see whether she was okay with Karen taking this on. Gwen had looked concerned as well, but shrugged. "If you're sure that's what you want. Thanks, Karen."

So she'd set off, armed with a pistol, carrying a map and torch. Gwen had issued orders and instructions, especially about not being seen as she emerged from the tunnel on the other side of the wall. Karen had nodded, not really taking any of it in; she was too busy watching Darryl in the crowd of people who'd come to see her off. "But most of all, hurry," Gwen said. "We don't know how much longer we can hold them off now Tanek's here. Not to mention the fact that Graham and Andy aren't getting any better." Andy had been badly injured by Tanek's crossbows on the last attack, and now resided with Graham in the surgery. Both were growing weaker by the hour. Karen had nodded, taking at least that much in.

"Hurry. Got it."

She'd left amidst the 'thank yous' and 'good lucks', a bit disappointed that Darryl hadn't come across personally to say goodbye. But she knew he'd see her in a different light if she pulled this off. All she had to do was bring back help and *she'd* be the hero of the hour. Then she'd get that hug and more besides.

Karen had listened at the trap-door for a good while before opening it, and then only a crack. Once she was certain nobody was about, she'd come up through it and covered the door back over again. Keeping low, she'd moved what she thought had been stealthily. She'd had one scary moment when it looked as if a German soldier had spotted her, but she'd carried on away from the area – away from New Hope – undetected; unscathed. And she *had* hurried, to begin with. But her lack of fitness soon began to tell on her.

Nevertheless, she'd trudged on to the main road – then followed it along, keenly aware of what might be coming along it from either direction at any given time. Thankfully tanks and armoured jeeps were quite easy to spot and hide from. Hardly surprising it was on the last leg of the journey that she'd flagged, having to stop every few yards at one point because she was out of breath.

It was then, as she'd stumbled along one of the smaller roads on the way to Nottingham, that she'd been seen. She hadn't spotted anyone herself – but then, that was what these Rangers were good at, concealing themselves, being urban chameleons. All of a sudden she was confronted by three of Hood's people, all pointing bows and arrows at her.

"Lose the gun," one told her, and she'd cautiously taken her pistol out of her jeans, tossing it on the floor.

"I need to see Robert," she'd told the Ranger who'd spoken. "Or Reverend Tate. It's about New Hope – the place is under siege."

The Rangers exchanged glances and one detached a walkie-talkie from his belt to radio in. The next thing she knew she was being marched up into the city. When she'd complained about how far she'd tramped already, arrangements had been made for a horse to be brought. Karen had never ridden before and it was a strange experience to do it for the first time through the empty streets of Nottingham. The ride seemed to take ages, and just when she thought they'd never get there, she was led up one final street and the castle was in front of them.

She'd never visited it before, having opted to remain at home the time that Winter Festival had been going on here, probably because Darryl had stayed behind, too. Karen had no idea whether this was the norm, but there didn't appear to be that many Rangers in evidence as she was taken through the gates. She was greeted by a portly man she hadn't seen before, walking with a stick. But she knew immediately who he was from his dog collar. The man who used to live at New Hope, but who Gwen threw out because of his actions. The holy man who'd left her at the castle during De Falaise's reign; who'd coaxed her back and almost got her killed during the Tsar's invasion.

"Welcome, my child," said the bald fellow. "Welcome to Nottingham Castle. I'm Reverend Tate."

Karen was helped down off the horse and shook his hand. "Karen Shipley, I'm from New Hope."

"So I gather. The men here mentioned something about a siege?"

"Germans are shooting up the place. Gwen told me to tell you Tanek is with them."

"Tanek? She's certain?"

"There are injured people, too. Look, I need to see him. Robin... Robert... whatever he prefers to call himself."

The Reverend sighed, then rubbed his chin.

"Is he here?"

There was another pause. "He *is*, just got back after we managed to get hold of him. But you couldn't have picked a worse moment."

It was then that Karen noticed the bruises on the holy man's chin and cheek; he'd recently been in a fight, and looked like he'd come off worse. Still, Karen had a mission. "*Please*, I need to see him."

Tate nodded and took her up the long path towards the castle. They ascended a set of steps, the Reverend appearing to have trouble with them. Karen took his arm and he thanked her. He led her inside the castle itself through a set of double doors, then up some more stairs and along a corridor. She could hear raised voices even before they reached the room Tate was zeroing in on.

"...even if you do go," Karen heard someone say, a woman's voice.

"You read the note." This was a man's voice. "He wants *me*, Mary. Alone."

Tate knocked on the door, which was ajar, then pushed on it when he heard: "Who is it?" The woman – Mary, Karen assumed – was speaking again.

Tate entered first, leaving Karen waiting in the doorway of the small room. "Someone to see Robert."

Karen could see the pair now, the woman with her dark hair tied back; the man in his trademark greens, that famous hood hanging down at his back. His face was stubbled, as if he'd been away from home for a while. "Can't it wait?" This was Mary once more, looking past Tate. Directly at Karen.

"I'm afraid not."

Robert came forward. His movements were slow, as if he'd been injured. But he had a bow in his hand and looked like he was either packing, or getting ready to go out again. "Reverend, you of all people should know this isn't the time for–"

"This lady, Karen Shipley," Tate interrupted and moved aside so that Robert could see her, "has come from New Hope."

"You'll forgive me, but that place is the last thing on my mind right now," snapped Robert. "I've just rushed back here after being held prisoner and nearly roasted alive, because my son's missing. Kidnapped. His girlfriend's frantic, blaming herself for not doing more to prevent it. The man who took him says he wants me to come alone to Sherwood. I don't know whether Mark's alive or dead, and you're asking me to listen to someone Gwen's sent?"

Tate was silent, then said: "Yes, I really think you need to hear what she's got to say."

Karen came forward, not waiting for the answer. She was sorry for what had happened here but *they* needed help too – if not from the Hooded Man himself, then at least from his Rangers.

"Please, Mr Hood," Karen began, "our village has been surrounded. Armed soldiers, Germans. They came a couple of days ago."

"So how did you get out?"

"It wasn't easy. I don't know how much longer the other people there can hold on."

"Thought that place was like Fort Knox now?" Robert said.

"These men are professionals. If they want in, they'll *get* in." Karen was beginning to see what Gwen meant about Hood. He wasn't the easiest of people to talk to, but she had caught him at a spectacularly bad moment. "People are injured, they're dying."

"Dying? I've just come back from a battle to take Edinburgh Castle from a cannibalistic witch woman, a battle that some of my Rangers lost. I've heard my other troops in Wales have suffered casualties, as well, trying to remove another crazed dictator from power. We only just made it back alive, and now you're asking me to help a village that pretty much turned its back on *us*?"

Karen wasn't around when the bulk of this bad feeling had built up, so she couldn't comment. Instead she said the only thing she could. "I understand what you're going through with your son, and I really do hope you get him back safely. But Gwen has a son, too. A son these people want to get their hands on for some reason."

Robert frowned, then looked at Tate.

"Tanek is with them, Robert," said the Reverend. "There's definitely a link between the Germans there and what's been happening in Wales and Scotland."

Karen could see Hood was still thinking about it, the mention of Tanek enough to stop his rant. Then he waved his hand. "I don't have time for this. I need to get to Sherwood. Mark's been missing for over a day now as it is."

"Even if you can't come yourself, could you at least spare some of your Rangers? Then we might stand a–"

"Look around you! Most of my men are still in the North and the West. The castle's practically defenceless, and you want me to send more of them away with you?"

"Robert," chastised Mary.

"I'm sorry, but Gwen and her lot have made their own beds as far as I'm concerned. She's repeatedly ignored our warnings about what would happen if she carried on arming herself to the teeth, poaching people from other communities just because they're useful to her. She's also point blank refused any protection from us in the past. Gwen likes to do things her way, and look where it's got her!" Robert turned to Karen. "I don't care for or condone the way you people operate. Like attracts like, Miss Shipley."

"Please, you *have* to help us."

Robert pointed a finger at her. "Give me one good reason why I should."

There was silence for a moment, then Karen said: "Compassion."

He looked into her eyes, then hung his head.

"If you won't send anyone else, then I'm going anyway," said Tate. "I've let Gwen down twice in the past before. I will not do so again."

"That," said Robert, "is your choice. I'm going to try and save my son."

Tate took Karen's arm this time. "Come on. Robert, I pray for you and that you will bring Mark safely back home. I'm only sorry I couldn't stop the man who took him."

As the Reverend was walking out of the room with Karen, she heard Robert call after them. "Take a dozen Rangers with you, but bring them back in one piece." Tate smiled at her, as if knowing the man would do that all along.

Karen felt less reassured, though. A crippled Reverend and a handful of men. What good would they be against the German troops and that giant they called Tanek? She was almost embarrassed to be returning with them.

"Don't worry," Tate had said as they'd made their way back out of the castle. "It's going to be alright this time. I'm going to make up for everything."

Karen hoped to God that the holy man was right.

CHAPTER NINETEEN

ROBERT RODE LOW on his horse, trying not to think about the events that had forced him here.

But he couldn't help it. That had always been his trouble, dwelling on things. His mind harking back to the past. In his early days at Sherwood, it had been the life he'd led with his former wife and son. Now it was the more recent events of the last couple of days, and hours.

After Bill had shown up at Edinburgh Castle, freeing the other members of his captured team – rectifying Robert's first, but not his only, major mistake of late – the resistance had soon been quashed. Once word spread through the Widow's men about her death, it hadn't taken that long. Even the depleted number of Rangers on their side had been enough in the face of these thieves and comparatively untrained yobs. Bill had already destroyed most of their heavy armaments in his initial run with the Black Shark, and though Robert had to openly disapprove of these actions – having denounced modern weaponry in all its forms – there was still a part of him that was glad they didn't have to tackle these with bows and arrows after what he'd already gone through.

The victory had been hard won, but satisfying, leaving the way clear for the local Rangers to set up their own HQ at the castle in the future. Securing a way of life for the Scottish people which didn't involve bowing down to that mad woman. They'd once said no-one could ever take away their freedom, but hadn't banked on one of their own trying it. At least now the bare bones of a free Scotland – protected by a Scottish contingent of Rangers – looked more likely.

Then, when most of the fighting was over, the message had come in about Mark. That someone had broken into the castle the previous evening and taken him, leaving a handwritten note by the radio which read:

Hooded Man. You will come to the forest alone if you ever want to see him alive again. Send anyone else and I will kill him. I will wait for you there.

It had been signed simply 'S'.

Tate had described the intruder as being Native American, which didn't give Robert much to go on. But the very fact the holy man had been bested by him spoke volumes. Though at first glance Tate might look like he was a helpless old cripple, he could actually handle himself extremely well in a fight.

The fact that Mark hadn't been able to take the man, either, further emphasised that his kidnapper was a professional. Mark had been coming up in the ranks over the last twelve months. He was no longer the boy Robert had first met at that ad-hoc market three years ago; he was a fully grown man – in spite of how he might be treated sometimes by them – and had been training with the Rangers for a long time. He'd handled himself excellently during the Tsar's invasion and had even started to have those same prophetic dreams Robert enjoyed, especially during their frequent visits to the forest he was heading towards today. He was becoming everything Robert had anticipated he would. But then he'd heard this, and it took him right back to that day when De Falaise had taken the boy. To when that bastard Tanek had cut Mark's finger off.

Over the time since, Mark had become every bit as much a son to Robert as Stevie once was, and would always be. In fact he liked to think Stevie might have grown up to be something like Mark. Obviously if the virus hadn't happened then Stevie would have gone on to aspire to being something other than being a Ranger; but that was another life, an alternate Stevie, living happily in an alternate universe. The important thing was that Mark was his own man, and he'd *chosen* to follow in Robert's footsteps. In fact, Robert liked to think that Mark might well take over this whole operation one day. But he couldn't do that if he was dead. Robert needed Mark, probably as much as his son needed him right now.

But as much as Mark was now his son, Robert couldn't help thinking about the Widow's revelation – that Mary was pregnant with his baby. They'd yet to confirm or deny it, but Robert had the weirdest feeling it was true. As did Mary, going by her words when they'd found out about Mark. "You might have another child," she'd said – not to suggest that Mark wasn't theirs, because he was, no matter what. But Robert knew that she'd said this to remind him the Widow was right; that they *might* be having a baby together. And that if Robert got himself killed she'd be bringing it up alone. The Widow could just have been playing another mind game, granted, but there wasn't time to find out one way or another.

Ultimately, as weakened and wounded as he was, Mary knew Robert had to do as the message said. She hadn't said anything more as he'd prepared to leave, other than pointing out the obvious, that it was a set up. She was just worried about him; they'd almost lost each other up in Edinburgh, and hadn't even had time to draw breath before the next crisis. Then the woman had arrived from New Hope.

Robert had such conflicting opinions about that place. The last time he'd seen Gwen properly, to talk to, not simply across the way at the Winter Festival, she'd made it quite plain what she thought about him. He might as well have been to blame for leaving the woman there at the Castle while De Falaise had his way with her, in spite of the fact he hadn't even known her at the time. Robert's forces weren't anywhere near organised or strong enough to tackle the Sheriff when Gwen was taken, but when

Mark and those other villages had been taken and threatened with execution he'd been forced to act. The simple fact was he hadn't been able to do anything about Gwen's situation, as rough as it had been for her, just like he couldn't do much for the people of New Hope now. His Rangers were scattered all over the country; even letting Tate take half a dozen with him was leaving the Castle open to serious trouble. But he'd done it anyway, because of what that Shipley woman said. Because of what the Rangers *should* stand for: the compassion she'd spoken about.

Would Gwen show the same if Nottingham Castle came under attack and needed a return favour? Robert seriously doubted it. But then, didn't Tate say they should always turn the other cheek?

All this and more was racing through Robert's mind as he himself raced towards his former home – the one he'd retreated to after the Cull, been talked out of by Tate, and remained estranged from to this day.

When he came to the outskirts, he decided to leave his horse tethered there, rather than risk coming in through the more obvious entrance: up through the Visitors' Centre and into the forest that way. It was asking to walk into some kind of ambush. Robert instead entered the forest the way he had when he'd first come here: through Rufford. Although he was acutely aware of the loss of his connection to this place he still had tracking skills he could rely on, and his enemy had left a trail even a blind man could follow. But as Robert crept through the forest, he sensed something else was wrong. It was connected with the fact that he was no longer receiving the dreams, no longer in tune with this place. He'd lost 'the magic' as the Widow had said. It was at this point Robert almost fell into the most rudimentary of traps: a concealed hole underneath him. He felt the ground slip away, just quickly enough to grab the side of the pit, scrabbling up and back onto terra firma. God, that hurt! It was a sign that his enemy had left the trail on purpose. And also proved his opposite number had the upper hand. Back in the old days, when Robert had lived here, *he* would have been the one setting the traps, Today, he knew he was walking right into one.

Picking himself up, Robert stumbled further into the forest that had once felt so familiar, and now felt so alien. He didn't have far to go before he saw a figure tied to a tree, slumped against the trunk as if drugged. Or beaten. And as Robert crept closer, he saw that yes, it was Mark, head lolling; a red welt on his temple. He had no idea whether the lad was still alive or not, just knew he had to find out. Find the man responsible.

Robert crawled along, using the woodland as cover, just like he always used to do. The only problem was he didn't feel at all confident this time. Felt that somehow the grass and trees just weren't on his side anymore. That it was revealing snatches of him where once it had hidden his presence completely. Robert might as well have a neon sign above his head telling anyone on the vicinity that he had arrived.

Undaunted, he pressed on. He had to reach Mark, free him, ascertain what injuries he had sustained. Robert was almost at the tree when he heard a rustling to his right.

"Dad, look out!" This was Mark shouting – at least he was still alive. Robert rose and brought his bow and arrow to bear.

Standing directly opposite him was a man. Dressed in black, he was dark-skinned, with dark hair to match his attire. He looked more like a shadow than a man. As Tate had described him, he was Native American in appearance, had a backpack over his shoulder – which contained his quiver – with an axe and knife at his belt. He had his own bow drawn, primed and aimed at Robert. For a second or two both men stood their ground, fingertips pulling back on their twines. The bows shook slightly with the pressure of each man holding the shot.

Both Robert and this newcomer had one eye closed, leaving the other open to judge the distance to their respective targets. But with that one eye they were also judging their opponent. What he might do, when he might release the projectile he was holding back.

It was Robert who released his arrow first, sending it flying towards what should have been the stranger's head. The man moved out of the way, though, allowing Robert's arrow to embed itself in the tree just behind him.

"Impressive," came the response, even as the stranger was firing himself.

Robert saw the arrow coming and dived out of the way, feeling the wind it carried with it brushing his ear. The other man's arrow thudded into an oak several metres behind, causing Robert to flinch. Already both bows were primed again and ready to fire.

"What do you want?" he asked, more to stall than anything, although he was genuinely curious.

There was no reply, except for the release of another arrow, again flying directly towards Robert. He flopped to the ground in order to avoid it, the missile whipping over his hood and sailing off into the woodland beyond. Robert's answer to this was to fire from the ground, the arrow targeted at the Native American's head. He let go of the string and it shot off towards the stranger at incredible speed. But, again, the stranger was quicker; sidestepping this shot with ease and allowing it to disappear off into the forest.

The pair exchanged a couple more shots like this, pulling arrows from quivers and letting them loose, as Robert managed to get to his feet. Then they wound up where they'd first began; staring each other down. Both men with bows primed and aimed at the other.

Time this was ended, thought Robert, searching for a sign the Native American was going to fire. When he found it, he released his own arrow.

Both pieces of wood and metal twirled in the distance between the men, heading directly for each other. They met almost head on, but it was the stranger's that had the advantage while Robert's suddenly flew way off course. The stranger's projectile struck Robert's left shoulder, lifting him up off his feet and back into one of the oaks he'd once considered his only true friends. Then the arrow carried on through that shoulder and into the wood behind, pinning Robert there.

"Dad!" screamed Mark, struggling to free himself from his bonds with no success.

Robert dropped his weapon, writhing in agony. It was now that he knew exactly what had happened – somehow this man in front of him had *stolen* his advantage. Taken away the protection the forest once afforded him, leaving him virtually defenceless against this new threat.

"How?" shouted Robert. "How have you done this?"

He could tell by the look on the Native American's face that he understood the question. But he didn't tell him. Just walked over with a satisfied smile on his face – so slight it would have been missed by the average person – and stood in front of his impaled prey.

Robert reached down for his sword, but the stranger grabbed his wrist, pulling the length of metal out of its sheath and flinging it away. There was a part of Robert that wondered if it was because of his exhaustion, the burns he'd suffered at the Widow's hands. But he'd endured more in a shorter period before – and it wasn't just the fact that he was getting older, either. This man had taken something from him, of that Robert was certain. Not just the dreams, but the almost superhuman strength he apparently drew from this place. If he'd faced the Tsar's men at this point and fallen in battle, there was no way he'd be getting back up to finish what he'd started. If the stranger chose to end this now, then Robert – the Hooded Man – would be dead. No two ways about it.

But that wasn't his intent. It *never had been* his intent. The stranger examined the arrow, nodding. "Clean wound, straight through. You'll live."

"D-Do what you want with me," Robert said, breath coming in sharp gasps. "But let my boy go."

The stranger regarded him with those dark eyes, sheltered by even darker eyebrows. "That was always my intent. This was never about him."

It was then that Robert realised what this man had in mind all along. Like him, he was a hunter. Mark had been the bait, obviously, but this stranger had never wanted to kill either Robert or his son. Especially not the latter.

"Then what's this about?" asked Robert.

"That is not for me to tell, but rest assured, I will free your son now I have you. There is nothing he can do to stop me, anyway."

"Stop you from what? Who are you working with: Tanek? The Germans?" Robert's questions went unanswered once more.

"It is time," said the stranger, then he took something out of a pouch at his belt. He emptied the contents – which looked like tobacco – into the palm of one hand, then grabbed Robert's chin with the other. *Not again*, he thought. *I'm not being drugged again!*

"This will help the journey pass more quickly," the stranger told him, forcing the weed into his mouth. Robert spat the first lot back into the stranger's face, but he just squeezed harder on his cheeks, forcing more into Robert's mouth, clamping his mouth shut. Though he didn't chew, Robert felt some of it slide down his throat. Not only that, the weird concoction was dissolving on his tongue. In his own way, this stranger was just as much a magician as the Widow.

No, have to fight it, Have to–

But already the stuff was having an effect. The stranger's face looked to be melting, the whole scene falling away in front of Robert. He tried to look over at Mark, but couldn't focus.

"Sleep now," he heard the stranger say.

That seemed like such a good idea. He was exhausted and it *had* been a gruelling couple of days. Yes, some sleep would do him the world of good.

Robert felt his eyelids closing, then there was blackness.

But there was also the total absence of dreams.

CHAPTER TWENTY

S<small>HE'D BEEN GONE</small> for hours now. And while they all knew the trip to Nottingham was quite a trek, things were growing desperate at New Hope.

Not only were people sick of the periodic attacks on the walls, which had started when Tanek arrived – scared that at any moment, the Germans would just come crashing inside – their friends were dying. Graham and Andy weren't doing well at all, in spite of Jennings' best efforts. Apparently one of the bolts Andy caught had caused internal injuries that the doctor couldn't do much about. "We need to get him somewhere we can operate. Otherwise I don't think he's going to make it."

Gwen had gone to see Andy, at his request, and they'd talked: about the old days, about what had happened to New Hope, about the direction she was taking. "Y-You have to promise me," Andy said, "that you'll turn away from this course you're on."

"I don't know what you're talking about," she'd told him, avoiding his eyes.

"There's so much hatred inside you now, Gwen. This..." Andy winced, gasping in pain. "This isn't what Clive would have wanted for you."

She'd said nothing. What she'd wanted to do was get up and leave when he started talking like that, but she owed him her time. Owed him the opportunity to get whatever this problem was that he had with her off his chest. Regardless of how things were with them now, Andy had done a lot for New Hope. He'd been there with her and Clive right from the beginning, just like Darryl, just like Graham. And this might be the last chance he'd get to say his piece.

He'd reached out for her hand and she'd let him take it. "You promise me, Gwen. Don't let it eat you up inside. I'm worried about you."

"You don't need to be. I'm fine."

"No, you're not," Andy insisted. "You–"

"Listen, should go and see what's happening out there. You get some rest." Gwen removed her hand and let Andy's flop back down on the bed. "Look after him," she told Sat, the doctor's assistant, as she left. She looked back just once to see Andy staring at her. He didn't believe for one minute she was all right, but she didn't know what to do to convince him. More than ever, she felt guilty for striking him when they were interrogating the prisoner. And, in a way, Andy had been right; they'd gotten nothing more out of the man, even after she'd gone back again.

During the last session overnight, she'd dismissed the guards keeping an eye on him and got down to business. "Just you and me now," she'd told the soldier. "I know who your boss is; he's just outside."

The man had laughed. "You know nothing." That earned him a punch in the face which broke his nose. He hadn't been laughing then.

"Me and him go back quite a way, did you know that?" Gwen said. "There's not much love lost between us."

"Go to Hell, *hure*!"

"You first, fucker!" She'd kicked him hard in the side where his injuries were and smiled as he'd howled in pain.

They'd gone on like this for about an hour, until Gwen was satisfied she'd get no new information. In the end she'd wound up kicking the chair over, placing her foot on his windpipe and threatening to crush it just to try and get some answers. "*Why* does he want my son?" she'd spat into the German's face. He'd remained silent, either not willing to say or because he didn't know.

Gwen left the room, calling the guards back in and giving them specific orders not to fetch Jeffreys when they saw the state of the prisoner. "We might still be able to use him if push comes to shove, but it won't matter what condition he's in. He's alive, that's good enough."

Was there a part of her that connected Andy's words with her actions? No, she felt them entirely justified. She was protecting her village, protecting her son at all costs.

When she looked into the faces of those villagers, however, she didn't think that they felt the same. Yes, they wanted to keep this place safe, but she wasn't convinced they wouldn't just fling Clive Jr over the wall to save *themselves*. She'd thought about telling them: "I know Tanek. He'll kill you all anyway, then, just for fun. The only thing keeping you alive right now in fact is that he wants my son and daren't risk storming in and harming him." But they wouldn't have listened. She'd need to keep a close eye on them, especially when it all hit the fan. Darryl was still the only one she trusted to keep watch over her child, and she was pleased to see he'd almost fully recovered from giving his blood to the German.

Gwen had been on her way from seeing Andy when she heard her name being called. "Come quickly," came the cry, and when Gwen reached the part of the wall it had originated from, she got a sinking feeling in the pit of her stomach. It was the section directly overlooking the opening of their tunnel's hidden trap door. The man who'd called her across – Henry Collins, a middle-aged ex-veterinarian who helped look after their livestock – was crouching, holding his rifle and jabbing his finger in the direction of that secret entrance. Gwen climbed the ladder to join him, not liking the stern look on his face.

"What is it?"

"See for yourself," he told her, taking off his glasses and rubbing his forehead with the back of his hand.

Gwen peeked out through the gap, and spotted it instantly. A group of German soldiers at the opening. They'd uncovered the camouflage Karen had replaced and were pointing down at the door. One was running some kind of wire from it.

"They're getting ready to blow it," Gwen said.

Henry nodded. "Bingo. And guess where they're going once they have."

Gwen didn't need to, she already knew. Up the tunnel and into this damned compound. How had they found out about the door in the first place? Must have been Karen, the stupid idiot! Someone must have seen her, even though she'd told her to be careful. Or maybe the Germans had just stumbled on it by accident? Gwen hoped that was the case, because if anyone had seen Karen then it meant she'd either been followed, or killed, or both. In spite of herself, the first thing Gwen found herself thinking was not about Karen's death, but that they shouldn't rely on any help from the castle now.

More important even than that, their enemies were about to step the siege up a notch. If the people of New Hope weren't going to give them what they wanted, their enemies had just discovered a way to come inside and get it for themselves.

TANEK WAS HAPPY.

For the first time in a long while, he was really, truly happy. And he was *never* happy. It didn't happen. There was always something that came along to balls things up. Not this time. Luck was on their side for a change.

Even before they'd made arrangements to begin the next phase of this campaign, they'd been given an unexpected break. Determined to get to the bottom of how his man was snatched, Tanek had ordered a thorough – but covert – search of the perimeter. It was then that they'd discovered the trap door. It hadn't been concealed properly, and was almost definitely the way they'd snuck in and out. Tanek knew that it could have been used to go and fetch help, which was why he had to move now. They'd forced his hand. But they'd also given him the perfect way to gain entrance.

And while the villagers were dealing with German soldiers coming up through that tunnel into New Hope, Tanek and his team would concentrate on breaking in through the front door, sealing this locality's fate. Once they were inside, they'd see just how fast the woman and her child were given up.

That moment had now come, his men preparing to blow the lid on that secret door. Tanek felt satisfied this was going to end well.

But more than anything else, he was looking forward to seeing De Falaise's woman again.

They still had unfinished business.

GWEN HAD POSTED at least three people on the tunnel door in the village grounds. Like Karen before them, they had orders to shoot whatever came through that didn't look like one of theirs . The only person out there was Karen, and no reports of her return had been made, more's the pity. Even if she had come back alone, then she wouldn't be able to get past the Germans to crawl through the tunnel.

"Chances are it'll be unfriendlies," she warned. "Don't give them the chance to fire on you first."

In the meantime, Gwen had gathered the rest of the villagers and handed out weapons to anyone who wasn't yet armed. Whether they'd have enough firepower was another matter, but they'd bloody well try to fight those bastards off. Gwen would, at any rate – she still wasn't sure about some of her fellow villagers. Would they turn their guns on her to hand over Clive Jr? Would she have to shoot the very people she'd been trying to look after all these months? People she'd lived alongside, fought alongside?

She'd find out soon enough, because the word came down from Henry that the hatch door had been breached and men were climbing inside the tunnel. Gwen made sure Darryl was *extremely* well armed – a rifle, a shotgun and two pistols – and told him to stand guard over both her house and Clive Jr, while she waited out in the street. It was the longest wait she'd ever had; even those hours back at the castle when she'd been De Falaise's prisoner hadn't been as bad as this.

Gwen shook her head; even though such thoughts made her angry, made her want to put a bullet in every one of those men invading her home, it also distracted her at a time when she needed to be focused. She gripped her Colt Commando rifle, holding it across her chest like some kind of shield.

Even though they were expecting something to happen, the loud bang still came as a shock. But what happened next, none of them could have predicted. The door to the tunnel on this side was blown clean off its hinges, but what came out of the tunnel wasn't men. At least not at first. Grenades were tossed up, causing the villagers defending it to move back. They began coughing as multi-coloured smoke – some of it yellow, some orange, some blue – got into their lungs.

"No, stay where you are!" shouted Gwen, running towards it. But that was easier said than done when they could hardly breathe.

The next thing they knew, German soldiers were inside. Nobody saw them climb up through the hole, they just appeared wearing gasmasks, striding through the smog, rifles held high and zeroing in on the villagers surrounding the trapdoor. Several shots were fired and men and women fell straight away. One woman, Carol Fawkes, was shot point blank in the face.

Gwen opened fire on the advancing soldiers. They were spreading out, some heading to the nearest cottages and taking up covering positions – or maybe searching them? – others crouching in order to pick off those up on the wall defending the village. Henry was one of the first to buy it, standing and firing on the men but being riddled with bullets from an automatic rifle for his efforts.

Gwen barely batted an eye; she didn't have time. The soldiers were getting closer and closer to her house – to Darryl and to Clive Jr. Hefting the rifle up to her shoulder, Gwen aimed at one of the soldiers and got him directly between the eyes. She'd become so much better with a gun than when she first used one to kill Major Javier, the man who'd slaughtered her beloved Clive.

She turned, shooting another German who was coming up on her left. Then she fired at a group on her right, breathing hard – relishing the feel of the rifle as it pumped out bullet after bullet. A smattering of machine-gun fire forced her to pull back behind the wall of a house, but she immediately bobbed her head back round the corner, firing again.

The screams of villagers filled the air, but some were taking her lead, realising that if they didn't fight, they'd die. Two or three had taken cover behind a notice board. The wood splintered as German troops fired at them, but they ducked and returned that fire, causing the soldiers to try and find shelter now. One didn't make it; shot in the legs as he ran.

Gwen grinned, targeting the fallen man and putting a bullet in his chest to make sure he was out of the picture.

"Fall back!" she heard someone shout, and for a moment Gwen thought it might be the Germans. No such luck, it was another team of villagers, being driven into doorways by an advancing squad of enemy soldiers. They just kept on coming out of that hole. Gwen needed to put a stop to it. She moved up, sliding along the wall of the house she'd been using for protection. Then she ran across, making the most of the thinning smoke cover. She could see the tunnel entrance, and put several bullets in a German using his elbow to climb out. Gunfire raked the ground ahead of her and she dived out of the way, rolling and coming up shooting. She clicked empty and sprinted towards the bench just ahead of her, leaping over and ducking behind it as more bullets followed in her wake.

Ejecting the magazine, she grabbed another from her pocket, slapping it in place. Then she got up and rested on the back of the seat, firing off in the direction those bullets had come from, shouting in triumph when she saw one German soldier fall to the ground.

Just when she thought they might stand a chance, there was an explosion at the front wall.

Jesus, Gwen thought. *What now?*

She wished she hadn't asked when she looked over and saw the gates bowed inwards, then flung wide as Tanek's armoured vehicle smashed through.

"Shit!"

Villagers fired at the jeep, but their bullets just zinged off. One man was caught in the vehicle's path and turned just as it was upon him; he fell under the wheels and was crushed. His head popping like an overripe melon.

More German troops entered behind the armoured car, picking their targets, not wasting a round. How did she ever think they could stand a chance against professional fighters like these?

Then there he was, climbing out of the jeep. He was even bigger than she remembered, but that dour face, that olive skin was the same. He'd only been out a few seconds and he'd already put two crossbow bolts into someone. Tanek was coming for her son, but she was damned if she was going to let that happen.

Gwen came out from behind the bench, heading back in the direction she'd just come from: heading Tanek off at the pass before he could reach–

"Shit!"

The giant was striding across, busting in door after door and killing whoever resisted. He was checking every house for Clive Jr, and he didn't have many to go. A villager she recognised as Sam Coulson came up behind Tanek, rifle raised. Gwen held her breath, watching as Sam was about to pull the trigger, but Tanek had already sensed his presence and was spinning, so quickly Sam didn't have time to fire off his round. The weapon was knocked clean out of his hands and Tanek grabbed him by the throat, lifting Sam into the air as though he weighed nothing. If Gwen had been closer – and if there hadn't been so much noise – she probably would have heard the cracking of the bones in Sam's neck as Tanek squeezed. Sam's eyes bulged, his tongue flopping out as he dropped to the ground, legs giving out beneath him.

Tanek looked around, hardly flinching as bullets ricocheted off the building behind. It was then that he saw her. His eyes narrowed and he pointed, as if to say 'I'm coming for you.' Gwen had to admit, she was scared. Probably the first time she had been since the castle. But not just for herself – for her son. Because she could see now that De Falaise's old second in command was on a mission, and he wasn't about to let *anyone* get in his way. Without looking, he held his crossbow out to the side and shot another villager – a young woman this time – twice. One bolt between her breasts and another in her temple.

So much death. Too much, thought Gwen. But this wasn't over yet.

She was distracted by the fact that Jeffreys was being dragged out of the doctor's surgery. He was pleading with the soldier who had hold of him.

"Where is the boy?" asked the German.

Jeffreys said nothing, so the soldier shot him in the shoulder. Jeffreys screamed and clasped his hand to the wound. The soldier put the gun to Jeffreys' head. "The boy!"

Jeffreys glanced over to where Gwen was standing, and she gave a small shake of the head, pleading with him not to do it. But she could already see in his eyes he'd made the decision. He pointed at Gwen's house. "In there. Please don't–" His final words were silenced by the *blam!* of the pistol as it blew his brains out.

Gwen felt nothing at his death, the betrayal still stinging. She couldn't even consider what she might have done in his position; could only think about the fact her son's location had been given away. The German was already motioning towards Tanek.

"No!" shouted Gwen, training her rifle on the soldier who'd just killed Jeffreys. She opened fire, the bullets smacking into his body, so many he was lifted off his feet to land several metres away. Perhaps she thought that by killing him she could somehow turn back time; erase what had just happened.

But *nothing* could do that and, as Tanek began to head towards her home, Gwen ran. She was halted by a rain of bullets from a semi-circle of soldiers who appeared out of nowhere. Gwen fired into them, but such was the intensity of the return fire that she had to duck back behind a wall. If she fell here then Clive Jr was as good as Tanek's.

Gwen peered round the corner and let off a few more rounds. Then she was empty. There were no more magazines left, so she dropped the rifle and took out her pistol, cocking it. Gwen also reached down for the knife she kept strapped to her ankle.

She came out, making every shot with the pistol count, taking out four soldiers with the first volley. Gwen threw herself down and slashed at another soldier's calves with her knife, causing him to drop to one knee. Then she plunged the knife in his ribs several times in quick succession. He toppled over onto his face, twitching.

Gwen rose with one eye still on Tanek, who was about to enter her house.

"Gwen! Watch out!" she heard, and then she was being pushed out of the way, falling to the ground where she landed awkwardly on her shoulder. She looked up as bullets hit her rescuer. It was Andy, who'd staggered out of the doctor's perhaps in the vain hope he might be able to help Jeffreys. Instead he'd taken about a dozen bullets for her. He turned towards her, an expression of disbelief on his face.

"Andy!" she cried. But it was too late. He was beyond hearing her.

Firing off a few rounds in the direction of the German machine-guns, she didn't waste the opportunity he'd given her. She raced after Tanek, just as someone came crashing through the living room window of her house. The body was covered in shattered glass, and rolled a few times before stopping. It was Darryl.

"No... Christ in Heaven, no!" she wailed.

Tanek emerged from her place, carrying a crying Clive Jr – holding him by the scruff of his T-shirt and brandishing the crossbow as if daring anyone to take the child from him.

"*No!*" she screamed and ran forward. Then, suddenly, she was aware of the fact that she wasn't moving anymore. Her leg had given out and there was a white hot pain spreading through her thigh. Looking down, she saw the bolt there, embedded deep. She began to crawl, holding up her pistol with a shaky hand but not daring to fire in case she hit her son. Gwen was a good shot, but not *that* good, especially in this condition. Then another bolt slammed into her shoulder, causing her to drop the gun altogether.

As the pain from this kicked in, machine-gun fire continued unabated all around, and she realised that no one was going to ride in and save the day. Not Robert and his Rangers, not anybody. He'd probably left her to it just to spite her, that's if Karen had even made it to the castle.

"If only De Falaise could see you now," Tanek shouted over the noise.

"L-Leave my son alone, you bastard!"

"Sorry, I made a promise."

What promise? Gwen didn't understand what all this was about. Wasn't really interested – all she wanted was her son back. She would give anything for that.

Tanek raised his crossbow once again, aiming at her heart..
"And now your role in the story ends."

It was at that moment Clive Jr began to wriggle and kick out. Tanek pressed the trigger, and the bolt went off target, but still hit Gwen just below the ribs. She sucked in air through her teeth as it thudded in.

At the same time there was a hissing sound. More smoke bombs had been thrown into New Hope, but they didn't originate from the hole. And it didn't appear to be the Germans who'd set them off. They looked at each other, mystified, as red smoke filled the area. Tanek looked over, frowning.

Gwen squinted, catching glimpses of figures in the smoke, moving through the German troops. Taking them down with the kind of skill her villagers would never possess. Professional fighters, even more professional than the Germans. Gwen grimaced from the pain, but started to feel a glimmer of hope, especially when she saw a hood. *Karen had made it after all!* And it looked like she'd brought back company.

There was only one thing wrong. Where were the arrows? Where were the bolas those men favoured? She saw a flash of metal. Yes, swords: they used swords instead of conventional weaponry. But, when one of the hooded figures appeared beside a German soldier, bringing down his blade across the man's wrists and severing his hands, Gwen knew this wasn't Robert and his men. Blood pumped from the soldier's wrists as he raised them, looking uncomprehendingly at the stumps. He didn't have to suffer for long, though, because the hooded figure twirled and cut off his head in one quick, clean stroke. It was as the blade lowered that Gwen saw it wasn't a broadsword he was holding, but a machete.

And the colour of the hood had nothing to do with the red smoke that plumed around the figure, because the material was red to begin with. *Morningstar Servitors!*

Tanek obviously recognised this, he'd spent long enough working with them when they'd allied themselves with the Tsar. They'd thought the Russian was their chosen leader on earth or something, but had abandoned him soon after the fight for the castle.

Here and there, Gwen saw snatches of what was happening out in the crimson smog: a German soldier firing into the mist, but hitting nothing, only for a machete blade to appear in the centre of his chest; another German firing a pistol off to one side, arm outstretched, and then the next moment a blade coming out of nowhere, hacking his arm off at the elbow. It was a similar story everywhere you looked: a leg here, a hand there. The Servitors – and yes, there were definitely more than one – were everywhere and nowhere at once. Finally, Gwen saw one German staggering through the smoke, his rifle held close, eyes darting left and right – when a hooded figure materialized behind him and planted his machete deep into the man's head, practically slicing it in two.

It was clear the Germans didn't know quite what had hit them, and they were rapidly losing the battle. Tanek fired off a couple of bolts at the approaching hooded men, but in spite of his accurate aim they didn't end up anywhere near the targets. As they moved forwards, holding their machetes in one hand, they removed their cowls with the others, revealing those skull faces Gwen knew so well. Tanek fired again, but found he was out of bolts. In order to change the magazine, he had to drop Clive Jr. Her son began crying even louder as he was dumped unceremoniously on the ground. Tanek reloaded quickly, firing off a couple of bolts – hitting nothing, once more. But when he reached down to retrieve the child, Clive Jr had disappeared. Gwen hadn't seen him vanish, either; perhaps he'd got up and toddled off into the smoke?

Whatever the case, Tanek had other matters to deal with. The Servitors were closing in and no matter where he fired, Tanek didn't seem to be able to land a hit. It was like he was firing into the fog itself.

Slinging the weapon over his shoulder, he brought out his knife and prepared for hand-to-hand. The Servitors rushed him as one, machete blades swishing. Tanek avoided the first of the blows, grabbing one Servitor – not so insubstantial now – and throwing him into three of his brethren, who tumbled to the ground like bowling skittles. But one of the machetes caught Tanek a glancing blow across the forearm and he roared.

Gwen attempted to move, to crawl forward and search for her son, but her whole body cried out in agony. She tried to call his name, but doubted whether he could hear her. "C-Clive sweetheart, where are you? It's...it's Mummy."

She gritted her teeth, severely hampered by her wounds but desperate to find her son. Suddenly, in front of her, was a set of feet. Gwen looked slowly up, and there he was, hood removed.

It was the man who'd saved her once from the castle, only this time he wasn't wearing his skull make-up. He was here again to save her. And he was holding Clive Jr in his arms, safely returned to her. Gwen couldn't help herself, she began to cry. "T-Thank you," she whispered. She didn't know what else to say, there weren't the words to express how she felt. Gwen held up a trembling hand to take her child. But the man she'd once known only as Skullface cocked his head, frowning. It was then that she saw it: the tears tracking down his face, the humanity she'd sensed in him before. Yet still he held on to her child...

The smoke was clearing a little, and though the circle of Servitors remained, there was no sign of Tanek. There was, however, another development. At first Gwen thought more Servitor reinforcements had arrived, but these people in Hoods were on horseback, and they were armed with bows and arrows. Karen was with them, riding with a shocked-looking Reverend Tate, who immediately ordered the Rangers to fire at the Servitors. Arrows struck several in arms and legs before they could find cover. "No, wait!" Gwen wanted to shout, but didn't have the voice anymore. It came out as a croak.

Tate had dismounted and was leading a team across the square. A couple of the Rangers had engaged the Servitors in swordplay, taking advantage of the fact they were fresh from fighting the Germans. The Reverend was limping towards Gwen and her saviour, and calling for the man to release his hostages. Gwen wanted to explain, to tell him he'd got it all wrong, but even if she did have the strength Tate probably wouldn't have believed her. The man who'd come to her aid looked from Gwen to the Reverend, and he finally let Clive Jr down to be with his mother.

Then he ran, calling for the other Morningstars to retreat as well. Tate attempted to stop him, swinging his stick, but the man easily dodged it. Within moments he and the other robed figures were gone.

Though it was agony to do so, Gwen put her free arm around Clive Jr, growing weaker by the minute. That final bolt had done something to her, torn something vital inside, she realised, and part of her wondered if that was why the Servitor was crying? She couldn't help looking at the bodies of the fallen all around, clearly visible now the smoke was gone, and thinking that soon she would be joining them. Gwen cried again, this time not because she'd been reunited with her son, but because she'd have to say goodbye to him shortly.

As Tate came over – concern etched on his face and calling for medical assistance – she also wondered if Clive Jr would have been better off with the man who'd *really* saved them? It was clearly what the Servitor himself had been considering right at the end.

But one thing comforted her as she lay there, bleeding out from her wounds.

At least she knew her boy wasn't with that bastard Tanek.

TANEK WONDERED WHAT exactly had happened.

One minute everything had been going brilliantly, according to plan. The villagers were being worn down, they had pretty much been removed as any kind of real threat. The woman Gwen was on her knees in front of him, where she belonged, and De Falaise's child was his for the taking.

Then... *they'd* arrived, out of nowhere. The Morningstars. Tanek simply couldn't get his head around it. He'd not seen a single one of those freaks since the battle at Nottingham Castle; they'd fucked off and left the rest of them to it, abandoning the Tsar to die at Hood's hands. Now this. Why had they stepped in? What was their argument with him? Or the Germans for that matter?

It just didn't make sense.

But Tanek believed in the evidence of his own eyes. Back there, with those Servitors all around him, their machete blades cutting him in at least half a dozen places, he hadn't questioned the fact that they were there; that they were attacking for no reason. He'd fled, ensuring his own survival. If he lived, then there was always another chance to capture the boy. A good job he had too, because he'd only narrowly avoided a run in with some Rangers on horseback, riding in like the fucking cavalry. It was definitely time to beat a hasty retreat, put some distance between him and the Morningstars, *and* the Rangers. Once he might have actually stayed and slugged it out with both, despite the superior numbers, but Tanek was on to a good thing with the Germans. And he'd figure out another way to get to De Falaise's child at some point.

His way had been blocked to the jeep so he'd had to escape on foot, losing himself in the woodland area that surrounded the village. Tanek kept looking over his shoulder as he went, nursing the cuts on his arms and torso, trying to stem the bleeding because it would leave a trail.

Tanek didn't like being the hunted, didn't even think of himself that way now. He wasn't some vulnerable prey, and even if they caught up with him they'd wish they hadn't and—

There, in the trees: a noise. Tanek stopped, bringing the knife up and shrugging his crossbow off his shoulder.

There was definitely someone... Yes, movement. *There!* Tanek fired a bolt, then set off in the opposite direction. There was a rustling from behind, the sound of someone coming after him. Just one or several? He couldn't tell. Tanek was a good distance from New Hope, so they really must have been determined, to follow him this far. But who was it, the cultists or the Rangers? Maybe he should just make a stand, get this over with, use the cover the woods afforded him to turn the tables on his—

The ground suddenly fell away, and Tanek found himself tumbling. Down into a deep hole that had been concealed, just like the secret exit and entrance to New Hope. Whoever had created that must have made this one, he thought as he hit the bottom, hard. It wasn't the Morningstars' style to do something like this.

It was more like Hood's.

Tanek shook his head, attempted to get up, but found he couldn't. He touched the base of his skull and his fingers came away wet. He didn't have long before he blacked out.

A lone figure appeared at the edge of the pit he'd fallen into. Tanek made to raise his crossbow but realised both that weapon and his knife must have slipped out of his grasp during the fall. It didn't matter, he couldn't focus properly on the man anyway. What he could see, though, was that he wasn't wearing red or green. He was wearing black, from head to toe. In fact, as Tanek gazed up, it looked to him very much like a shadow was standing there.

"Hello, Mr Tanek," said. He had a very distinctive accent. "I have been waiting for you."

Tanek attempted to reply, but found his grasp on language was about as good as his grasp on his weapons.

And now he was falling again, into another deep pit.

Filled with darkness.

Filled with shadows.

CHAPTER TWENTY-ONE

"CAN'T THIS THING go any faster?"

Jack's driver – a Ranger called Doherty – shook his head. He was already coaxing all the speed he could out of the jeep, one of the few German vehicles that had survived their attack on the Dragon's power base. Jack gritted his teeth, and slammed his fist on the dashboard. "Damn!"

"I'm sure he'll be okay, sir," Doherty told him.

Jack appreciated the sentiment, but there was no way of knowing. Nobody could see the future, except that mad bat up in Scotland that Robert, Bill and Mary had just seen off, if the rumours about her were correct. There wasn't much to choose between her and the Welshman by the sounds of things. Just thinking about that man's secrets sent a shiver down Jack's spine. In all their years of doing this, standing up to people like the Sheriff and the Tsar, Jack had never come across somebody as deranged as the Dragon. Someone so unbalanced he thought his family was still alive even though they were just a collection of bones. There were so many horror movie references he could have made – the Dragon gave

Norman Bates a run for his money for starters – but seeing that in real life... It just proved that fact was stranger than celluloid.

Thankfully, they'd seen the last of him, and the rest of the operation had just been an exercise in clearing up. With a decent amount of Rangers to hand, it hadn't taken them long to seize control. And because the Dragon had deprived the Welsh Rangers of their HQ, it seemed only fitting that they should take over the Millennium Stadium now instead.

"Think of the training you could do on that pitch," Dale had said, after commenting that he'd loved to have played there when it was still used as a concert venue. Dale had been a marvel throughout; not only during his undercover work, but also afterwards, offering to stay and help with the setting up of the new Ranger base. How much of that was to do with Sian, Jack couldn't say – or indeed whether they'd be seeing Dale back at their own HQ in Nottingham again anytime soon – but the lad deserved a break. Why shouldn't he spend it with that pretty gal? Jack reckoned she'd been through just as much, so maybe they could make each other happy.

"You know, I think Meghan's taken quite a shine to you as well," Dale told him.

"Hey now–"

"All I'm saying is think about it, mate. She's really nice." And Jack did have to admit he had a point. In fact she'd even come down to the entrance to see Jack off.

"I hope things work out okay," she told him, then kissed him on the cheek. "I don't know how I can ever thank you and Dale for what you've done."

Jack had felt his face reddening, just as it had once done when he'd helped rescue Adele from the Morningstars. It was those kinds of memories which held him back, forced him to keep Meghan at a distance. Not that he was saying she was a traitor or anything; she was far from that. But Jack still had trust issues and they weren't going away anytime soon. "It was all in the line of duty, ma'am," he told her, "nothing more."

But he'd spent the first few miles of travel regretting that cool response. Hoping maybe someday he'd get to put that right. Perhaps get to know Meghan better, become friends, then – No, he wasn't about to jump in again. His poor heart couldn't take another battering like the last one. But Jack was lonely, he had been for some time.

Not that any of this was a priority at the moment; just something to take his mind off his real concern of the day. It was funny; all that fighting, everything that had happened with the Dragon, and the disappearance of just one boy could send him into a tailspin. But then Mark was a very special young man.

They'd always had a connection, Jack and Mark. He remembered their first meeting, when Jack and Robert had fought because the Hooded Man had mistaken him for an intruder in Sherwood. It had been Mark who'd recognised him as The Hammer, a former professional wrestler who the boy had followed on the circuits. Robert had taken Mark's word when he vouched that Jack was one of the good guys, and a good fighter to have on board. Jack had returned the favour by teaching Mark, training him whenever Robert wasn't able, taking him under his wing and showing him all his own moves, plus a few more besides. Mark was family, like Sian was to Meghan. Jack had always thought of himself as an uncle to the boy. Which was why when he'd heard about the kidnapping, he'd told Mary he was on his way back to the castle ASAP.

"Bill's already been told," she explained over the radio, "and he's coming back here. Jack, we need you."

"I'm already there, little lady."

Except he wasn't. It was taking forever in this piece of shit, designed more for protection than speed. It wasn't just the fact that Mark was missing, although that was bad enough. Robert had gone in after him, alone; heading to Sherwood like the note said. Who the Sam Hill was 'S'?

"I'm coming with you," Dale had said when he heard, but Jack had shaken his head.

"You're still getting over being pummelled by the Dragon. No, you stay here and do what you said you were going to do: look after Sian and get things in motion for setting up the base."

"But–"

"You're more use to me here, Dale," he'd insisted, then clapped the lad on the shoulder. "Please." Jack had put him through enough already, sending him on this mission, he didn't want to be worrying about him all over again. They'd hugged and Dale had told him to look after himself. He could tell the kid was worried about Robert and Mark, just as much as he was. Now that they'd got over their difference of opinion about Sophie, those two had become quite good pals.

The radio crackled into life and Jack looked at Doherty. *You know what they say about the best laid plans, Jackie-boy.* He picked up the receiver and identified himself. It was Mary again, calling from the castle, but he was having trouble hearing her.

"Say again. Over."

"Found... I repeat... Mark... unharmed...."

"Sounded like you said Mark's been found? Over."

"Affirmative."

"*Wahooo!*" Jack removed his cap and slapped it on his thigh. If he'd been out in the open he might have thrown it into the air. But he was celebrating too soon.

"...missing now..."

"Didn't catch that, Mary. Could you repeat? Over."

"I said..." And he could hear the tears in her voice. "Robert's missing... same... took him... Over." Although he hadn't heard it all, Jack got the picture.

That wiped the smile off his face. They'd been given one member of their family back, only to lose another. Mark had been the lure all along, it seemed, and Robert had been the real target. But what did this 'S' want with their leader? While it was true he had a lot of enemies at home and abroad, why now, and why take him rather than kill him? Jack wasn't sure he wanted to know the answer to that. There was a distinct possibility that whoever this kidnapper was, or whoever he worked for, wanted to have a little fun with Robert before finishing him off. A slow death. Jack said nothing about this to Mary, but knowing her as he did, she'd probably already thought of it.

"Took him? Took him where?" asked Jack. "Do we have any leads? Over."

There was silence at the other end, static at his. Then Mary said: "Maybe. Over."

Maybe was better than nothing. She wouldn't be drawn on the rest, preferring to wait until Jack was home so she could report in person. It was probably wise – this frequency might well be monitored by third parties.

When he hung up the radio, Jack looked out at the open country roads stretching before them, and then across at Doherty.

"Hey man, can't this thing go any faster?" he repeated.

CHAPTER TWENTY-TWO

IT WAS THE smell that roused him.

This place stank of sweat, even though it was so cold. But there was another aroma he was also quite familiar with; the coppery stench of blood. Plus one that was harder to pin down, distinct and sharp.

Death. That was it. This place smelt of death.

Robert had smelled that many times before in battle. It was rank and he couldn't stand it in his nostrils for long without opening his eyes. Unsurprisingly, it took a few moments for his eyes to adjust. And in that time, he felt the ache in his shoulder where the arrow had passed right through. Blinking, he reached up to touch the wound. It had been stitched. The stranger had obviously wanted Robert in one piece before delivering him God knows where. Robert also felt as though he'd slept for decades, drugged obviously, but the result was he at least felt rested.

He shivered. Robert had been stripped down to just his vest and combats, he realised. He blinked a few more times then heard the noise, the sound of people all around – not saying anything, in fact remaining as quiet as they possibly could, but giving themselves away with their breathing.

He put a hand beneath him, feeling concrete. Where in Christ's name was he?

The first thing he saw were people, surrounding him. Lots of people. Some dressed in uniform, some in little more than rags. They were staring at him, and all had that same tired and resigned expression on their faces. The hard lives they'd lived were reflected in every downturned mouth, every crease of the brow. These people were pissed off, Robert just didn't know why.

If it was with Robert, he was in trouble. Kidnapped and dumped here to be pulled to pieces by an angry mob. He couldn't hope to fight off a fifth of them, especially without his weapons, which – yep – he checked again and confirmed he definitely didn't have.

And why was it so bloody cold? Even the harshest spring in England was never this chilly.

There was a groan from behind, and Robert was suddenly aware of someone else on the floor with him. Someone not that far away. He looked around, though the effort of doing so hurt considerably.

The other man was face down on the ground, also just waking up. Robert couldn't see his face yet, but could see a bandage on the back of his head, cuts on arms that, like Robert's wounds, had also been stitched. *Our Native American friend's been busy,* he thought. *Glad it's not just me that he's been dicking around with. Why should I have had all the fun and games?*

It did beg the question: what did he have in common with this other prisoner, and could he use that to his advantage? Shadow had nobbled both of them and brought them to this place; that demanded a little payback, didn't it? If nothing else, Robert might have someone to stand alongside as the mob closed in on him and–

The man on the floor put and elbow underneath himself and raised his head. Robert's face fell. He'd seen that on two occasions in the past – when he and Bill had flown into the middle of the fight for Nottingham Castle, and then at Sherwood a little over a year later. This was one of the most dangerous people on the planet, and that was saying something these days. Robert would rather face a dozen Widows than this man.

"Tanek," he said.

Responding to his name, the giant shook his head and opened his eyes. "Hood," he snarled – not even bothering to look at anything else, not the crowds surrounding them, nor the armed guards now dotted here and there. Armed, Robert noted, with AK-47s; meant to keep the people in line, but also maybe to stop him and Tanek from escaping.

When Robert looked back at the large man, he found he was already up and ready to charge at him. Robert rose too, only just avoiding Tanek's assault – but made the same mistake a lot of people had in the past. Assuming that because Tanek was of gargantuan proportions he wasn't that fast or nimble. When Tanek swung round, striking Robert on the back with his laced fists, it felt like a battering ram hitting him. Robert was sent hurtling across the pit. He fell and rolled, wincing when the ground caught his injured shoulder.

But, as woozy as he was, Robert staggered to his feet. He couldn't afford to be lax with this big ape after him. And, sure enough, Tanek was lunging towards him again. This time Robert pretended to duck one way, only to slide the other, bringing his fists down between the bigger man's shoulder-blades. It actually hurt his hands, the man was so solid, but it did unbalance Tanek enough to send him tumbling head over heels. Robert looked around: the crowd was going wild. They weren't here to attack, they were here to watch him and Tanek fight. There was even a cordon, almost totally obscured by the throngs of people. Keeping them back and the contenders in.

Tanek was on his feet once more. "I'm going to kill you!" he shouted, rushing towards Robert.

"You and whose army? Oh, that's right – you tried that *twice* already."

It had the desired effect of aggravating Tanek, making his next move clumsy, easier to avoid. Robert rolled under the punch his opponent threw, barging into Tanek sideways and almost pitching him over; the giant's momentum nearly doing the rest. It was the only way he'd be able to keep avoiding Tanek, but he couldn't keep this exertion up for long. Already the giant was lunging back round again, delivering a kick that practically flipped Robert over in midair. He landed on his front, winded for the second time in as many minutes.

The crowd was cheering with delight, and Robert felt Tanek standing over him, about to deliver a killing blow. Though it took just about all the strength he could muster, Robert shuffled backwards and just out of reach as Tanek's fist came down. Instead of grinding Robert's head into the dirt, the giant punched the floor and growled with pain. Robert scrabbled back further away from the man he'd just angered even more.

Tanek was about to leap on him again when a sharp banging from above interrupted. It reminded Robert of those old courtroom dramas when the judge would strike the bench with his gavel.

"Enough!" came a voice. Robert recognised the accent, and sadly recognised the voice, too. He looked up for the source of this command, spotting a ledge with a railing. Part of what had once been an overhanging office, stripped bare to provide a viewing platform.

It was then that Robert matched the voice to the face, and the face to the name. "Bohuslav. This day's getting better and better." Standing there was the new Tsar of Russia, crowned after Robert had killed his former master. Bohuslav was dressed in what looked like a red velvet uniform with yellow piping – replacing the previous Tsar's leather – and a cape flowing behind. In place of the hand that Dale had taken from him was Bohuslav's favourite weapon, the sickle, but he was also holding a heavy metal hammer with which he'd struck the edge of the rail. All in all, he looked like a living embodiment of the Russian flag.

Robert glanced over at the man who'd been about to kill him and saw that Tanek was equally surprised to see their captor.

"Do not kill each other so quickly. I have gone to great pains to arrange this. I want to savour it," Bohuslav said with a wide grin.

Great pains, thought Robert. *Ah, now I understand.* He could see the Native American on that viewing platform as well. He was looking on with interest, arms folded. A satisfied Bohuslav turned to one side now, though, nodding to one of his personal guards, who gave the man in black a bag. His payment for services rendered. Robert wondered what was inside; thirty pieces of silver would get you nowhere nowadays. Had to be something else, something–

"I will kill you!" This was Tanek, now addressing Bohuslav, who turned back to face them.

"Not before you've killed Hood, surely? You just said that is what you intend." His broken English was exactly how Robert remembered it. The last time he'd clapped eyes on this nutter it had been when his Rangers had defeated the Tsar's not inconsiderable forces, led by Bohuslav. He'd taken advantage of Robert's weakened state and if it hadn't been for Dale coming to the rescue... Robert had assumed the man had been killed by the wounds that lad inflicted, but obviously not. And the new Tsar wanted revenge, not so much on the person who'd mutilated him, but on the man responsible for the Rangers in the first place. The man who'd also killed his lord and master.

When Tanek said nothing, Bohuslav laughed. "So, kill him, and we will talk about what happens after that. On the other hand, Hood might kill you. He has just as much of an axe to grind." The new Tsar nodded to a guard below, who tossed a weapon into the area of combat: a large, double-edged axe. "If I remember rightly you, Tanek, favoured the pollaxe the last time you were here. Yes, Hood, Tanek has an advantage over you. He has fought in this place once before." And with that, a staff with a lethal-looking voulge on the end – or pole cleaver as they were sometimes known – landed near Tanek's feet. He looked down at it, then up again at Bohuslav.

The Tsar banged his hammer on the rail again, before tucking it into his belt. "Go on, pick up your weapons. If you do not, then your opponent might gain the advantage."

It was a ploy to get them to fight. Robert was about to say something to Tanek when the bigger man grabbed his pollaxe and tested its weight.

Okay... thought Robert, snatching up his axe, *a ploy that obviously worked.* A large net and a round shield were also thrown into the ring, but they were for whoever picked them up first.

Tanek made it to the shield, so Robert had to settle for the net, winding the thick rope around his hand and wrist. Just in time, because Tanek made a swift lunge with the pollaxe, which Robert snagged in the netting, attempting to swing the larger man round. Tanek held his ground, however, raising the weapon and almost taking the netting with it. Robert held on, feeling himself being lifted along with the mesh. But he used this to his advantage, swinging forward on it and bringing his axe around in an arc to try and hit Tanek. The giant was forced to lower the axe, and in doing so both of them wound up on the floor.

"Tanek," said Robert, catching his breath. "Tanek, listen to me. He's playing us both off against–"

The big man was up and swinging the axe at him again. Robert sighed, ducked, then rose to block the next swing. The wood of both his own handle and the axe handle juddered with the strain, but Tanek was just too strong when it came down to it. Robert had to defect the blow sideways or risk being struck full in the face by the business end, which would have cleaved his skull in two.

"Tanek, dammit, listen to me! You know he'll kill whoever's left when–" Robert had to step sideways to dodge yet another attack, but this time he clambered onto Tanek's back, kicking as he used it as a springboard. The larger man lost his footing and ended up on the ground, while Robert landed awkwardly and turned. "He'll just kill whoever wins," Robert finished.

"He will not get the chance," Tanek said, sneering. Then he righted himself and came at Robert once again. He lunged with the axe, but then twisted and brought round his shield, using that as a weapon instead. Robert barely had time to lean back, but he managed it, falling over in an effort to prevent the edge of the shield connecting with his windpipe. It would have either slashed his throat open, or at the very least cut off his oxygen supply.

Damn and blast, that Tanek's stubborn, thought Robert. "Unless we work together, it'll–" Robert rolled to the right, missing another stroke with the axe. He couldn't believe this; it wouldn't be his first choice to try and work with one of his greatest enemies either, but Tanek was too obsessed by the idea of killing him and Bohuslav to see clearly. To see how they could win. There was only one way Robert could convince him, that he could see.

That was to beat him.

Robert hunkered down, trying to ignore how his body was protesting and waiting for the next strike from Tanek. When it came, he rather clumsily swung his weapon – but hit the wood of the handle nonetheless and splintered it. Then he cast the net, but instead of tangling up Tanek's weapon, he laid it on the ground, so that Tanek would step into it, the force of his momentum ensuring he could do little else. Then, Robert put the end of the net he was holding over his good shoulder and tugged as hard as he could. Tanek wobbled, but didn't fall – so much for that plan – so instead Robert ran around the big man, tangling him up. Tanek's struggles to free himself pulled the section he was standing on out from under him. It was then a case of batting the axe out of Tanek's grasp as it poked up through the net. This left Tanek with just a shield that was bound up with him and couldn't be shifted.

Robert saw there was a newfound respect for his fighting abilities in Tanek's eyes. With shaky hands lifted his weapon aloft, blocking out the cheers of the crowd. "The only way we're going to do this is *together*," Robert said, close enough that only they could hear. "Remember that."

He brought the axe down, but veered off at the final moment, cutting through the netting to free Tanek. As far as the onlookers – and indeed Bohuslav himself – were concerned it simply looked like he'd missed, but what he'd done was not lost on the olive-skinned giant. Again, Robert could see in his eyes that an understanding had finally been reached.

Which was why he was surprised when the big man got up, leaving his shield on the floor and grabbing the pollaxe, lashing out again with it seconds later. Robert blocked him with his own axe, but this time he could feel there was no real tension. Tanek grunted, as they drew closer together in a struggle with the weapons. "I will settle with you later," he promised Robert, then suddenly turned his back, and thrust his axe into the nearest guard.

Robert himself jabbed the blunt end of his axe into another guard's stomach, bringing it up and knocking the man backwards, taking him down without serious injury. He refused to do as Tanek had and just kill the armed men surrounding them. That was the difference between them, and always would be.

There was gunfire as the remaining guards attempted to get the 'gladiators' to move back into position. To fight each other again, not them. Robert ducked and rolled, lashing out with the handle of the axe to knock a rifle out of a guard's hand. Then he whacked another over the head with the flat of the metal. Twirling, he saw a gunman draw a bead on him and fire, so he raised the axe, holding his breath as the bullets pinged off the metal. "No, you idiots!" Bohuslav screamed from above. "I want them alive. If they will not kill each other, then *I* will have the satisfaction of ending both their lives!" He ordered one of his personal troopers to gun down the pit guard who'd fired on Robert. At least that would work in their favour, thought Robert; the others wouldn't dare shoot to kill now.

More gunfire, this time from behind. Tanek with the first guard's rifle, spraying bullets into the air, sending the crowd into a panic. It provided necessary cover, but then he shot at more guards on the lower level; bullets hitting chests, heads and stomach.

"No! *Wound* them, Tanek. Just–"

Another blast told Robert the giant wouldn't listen. Life meant very little to Tanek and it was too late to try and change him. For a second Robert wondered what would happen if it came down to him and the giant? If he couldn't take him alive? Would he himself do as he'd done to De Falaise, to the Tsar? Kill to rid the world of another monster? And wasn't there more than a hint of good old-fashioned revenge, as well? Didn't he want retribution for all the things Tanek had done to them. To Mark and Jack in particular?

Another smattering of machine-gun fire, now targeted at the viewing platform. Robert looked up to see the Native American withdrawing; obviously thought this wasn't his fight. But Robert needed something from him; wanted back what the man had taken.

He looked around and saw Tanek's discarded shield on the ground. He slipped it along one arm until it covered his shoulder, then made a play for the platform, ducking beneath the cordon. Robert pushed through both the guards and the crowd.

"Hood!" roared Tanek. "Leave him!"

Robert cast the axe aside and began to climb towards the ledge. It was a struggle, his muscles and shoulder on fire, but he had to get up there and follow the man in black. It was more important right now than anything else, even getting his hands on Bohuslav.

Bohuslav's guards were now leaning over the rail, firing at Robert. He pulled his arm across, letting the bullets bounce off the shield. They sparked around him and he wondered how much more the metal could take. In the lull of changing magazines, he urged himself upwards. The threat of being shot at again was a distinct incentive.

Just as one guard was about to open fire, Robert put on a final spurt and grabbed the barrel of his rifle, pulling him over the ledge. Another man turned and aimed at Robert's head, but was slashed across the back of the neck by Bohuslav. The fact that he wanted to kill his captive personally was still warping the Tsar's judgement, and for that Robert was grateful.

"Hood!" he heard Tanek shout up again, and risked a look over his shoulder. He saw the giant making his way through the panicking throng.

Robert pulled the shield down to his forearm and struck an oncoming guard full in the face, sending him crashing onto his back. There were now only a couple left – and Bohuslav. Robert bent when one of the remaining guards attempted to restrain him, lifting the man and pitching him over onto the ground before kicking him across the face. The final one he dispatched by bringing up the shield again and catching him under the chin.

There was a swishing sound and Robert leaned to his right as Bohuslav's sickle came down. He had to duck, because the blade slashed sideways to try and catch him across the face. "I was intending to savour this, but I should just get it over with," Bohuslav told him. "Now, where did we leave things last time? Ah yes, I was about to end your life." The mad Russian lashed out again and Robert brought up the shield to block him. He had no intentions of letting it get to that stage this time.

"Hood! He's mine!" came Tanek's distinctive rumble from beneath them. It said a lot for what Tanek thought of Bohuslav's chances against him.

Robert brought up the shield again, deflecting another blow. "You can have him," Robert answered, then pushed forward, taking Bohuslav to the very edge of the rail.

"No... Wait..." said Bohuslav, but Robert shoved again; harder this time, tipping the man over.

Bohuslav managed to grab one of the bars, his cape flowing behind him. Robert placed his boot on Bohuslav's fingers. "You two deserve each other," he told the man, then removed his foot. "Happy landings!"

Leaving Bohuslav to fall, Robert, headed off through the doorway of what had once been the office, in search of the Native American.

It led out into a corridor and, if the open area of the fighting pit hadn't been enough of a clue, Robert now realised he was in some kind of abandoned warehouse. Checking doors left and right, holding the shield up in case there were more guards with guns inside, he ventured up the corridor, following the trail of the man who'd brought him here. The man in black had a head start, that was true, but Robert had to hope he'd just carried on in a straight line, since his tracking abilities were all over the place at the moment. For all the Native American knew, Robert was still downstairs occupied, so with a bit of luck he hadn't tried to hide his trail too much.

And suddenly there he was: up ahead, a shadow amongst the shadows. Like the professional he was, the Native American *felt* Robert behind him, casting a quick glance over his shoulder, then focusing on the route ahead. There was a bend coming up, which the Native American negotiated quickly.

Damn, I'm going to lose him, thought Robert, speeding up.

When he rounded the corner, he found the man in black had waited. The first blow struck Robert across the chin; a warning. "Do not follow me."

"Like Hell. You have something that belongs to me."

The man grimaced, then came at Robert again; this time with a knife suddenly in hand, slashing furiously. Robert could do nothing but use the shield to fend off the attack. The blows were raining down so hard, though, they knocked the battered metal from his arm. "My quarrel is not with you," the kidnapper told him.

"You should have thought of that before," Robert replied, grabbing the Native American's arm, bringing it down on his knee and forcing the weapon out of the man's grasp.

The response was a fighting move Robert hadn't come across before; sort of a cross between wrestling and kung fu. It took Robert's legs out from under him, coupling that with a swift elbow to the stomach. "I will not say this again. Do not follow me."

Robert was getting ready to rise again, so the man in black gave him a kick to keep him down.

"Hey, you," Robert heard a voice. "I think we've got unfinished business." A fist slammed into the Native American's face; hard. It knocked him back against the corridor's wall. Robert couldn't see who'd delivered it at first, but then a hooded figure stepped out, following up his first move with a roundhouse kick. "I owe you this!"

The figure pulled down his cowl and it was Mark, his son, last seen tied to a tree, his head covered in dried blood. Robert didn't question this. Instead, he got up, and while the man in black was still disoriented, Robert snatched his bag he'd been carrying – the one the Tsar's guards had given him. Mark had his bow and arrow out already and was covering the Native American at close range, the tip of the arrow pointing directly at the man's head. "So much as a twitch," warned Mark, jabbing the weapon even closer. "Go on, try me."

Robert smiled; the boy had come on in leaps and bounds since his training began and, despite the circumstances they were in, he was proud. "Now, let's see what this was all about." Robert opened the bag and looked inside. He looked up, puzzled. Then he took out the single object inside: a stone.

"This is what you sold us out for?"

"I don't expect you to understand. You do not even understand your *own* heritage."

"I understand enough. What did you do, out there in the forest? How do we put things back to... to normal?"

It seemed a strange thing to say and Mark glanced at him, but they both knew what he meant. It wasn't exactly normal to dream about things that were going to happen, to have a connection with nature that gave you strength and staying power, but it was *their* normal. If Robert himself had been a superhero, then this man had found his weakness. He looked again at the stone he was holding. "Is this it? Is this the way to put things right again? Destroy this?" Robert made as if to drop it on the floor.

"No!" shouted the Native American, holding out his hand. Mark drew back his bow even further. "No... please don't do that."

That got his attention anyway, thought Robert. "Okay, so tell us, or I really will break your precious stone."

Shadow sighed, slumping back against the wall. He reached down to his belt and Mark readied the bow and arrow. Shadow held up one hand to show that he was only reaching for another small pouch.

"Easy, mate. Nice and slow. We've both seen what you keep inside those things. I don't fancy another nap."

"You asked for the way. This is it," explained the man. He threw the pouch to Robert, who looked inside.

"Looks like ash. What is this?"

"You must take it back to your forest. Release it there and the spirits, your gods, will be freed." When they both frowned, he continued: "It must mix with the essence of your spiritual home. Now, hand me back what *you* have taken."

"How do we know this will wor–" Robert didn't finish the sentence because gunfire filled the corridor. Russian soldiers were approaching. Everyone ducked, and Robert tossed the stone over to the man in black to free his hands, then shoved the pouch of ashes in his pocket. Mark shifted his aim to fire on the Russians, which left their enemy free to nock his own bow, after tucking away his prize.

At first, Robert thought the man might actually fire at them. Instead, he let off a couple of accurately aimed arrows towards the guards. Robert nodded to him and the Native American nodded back. But then he was off, running towards the Russians and leaping over the tops of several. Mark was about to fire an arrow after him when Robert placed his hand on the boy's shoulder. "Let him go. We have other problems."

They certainly did, as a succession of bullets raked the walls. Rounding the corner, Mark pressed himself up against the pock-marked plaster and let off some arrows in the direction of the men. Robert had already grabbed the shield to protect himself from the barrage and joined him. "Now what?" asked Mark.

"Fall back," Robert told him. They backed up the corridor until they reached one of the rooms Robert had checked on his way. "Inside. Cover us."

Hiding behind the doorframe, Mark continued to pull arrow after arrow from his quiver. Robert called for Mark, pointing to the window. His son loosed a few more arrows to buy them some time, then followed Robert as he ran at the window, using the shield to break the glass and then plummeting towards the ground.

Robert hit the concrete below badly, but it would have been much worse were it not for the shield and the thick snow covering the street. Tiny shards of glass followed, sprinkling Robert as he watched Mark bend and take the strain on his much younger knees, dropping perfectly beside him. They were somewhere round the side of the warehouse, in a deserted alley. Deserted, that was, apart from what looked like frozen statues lying on the ground. The slowly decomposing dead, who thawed in warmer weather, then refroze when the snow returned.

"Come on," Mark said, helping him up and looking above him to where the Russian soldiers were now taking up firing positions at the window. "Time we weren't here."

Robert couldn't agree more, but as they rounded the corner of the building they were stopped dead in their tracks. Assembled at the front of the warehouse was a vast collection of jeeps, tanks and other armoured vehicles; not to mention dozens of soldiers with rifles. And they were all trained in Robert and Mark's direction.

The air filled with the clack of those weapons being primed, as Robert saw the new Tsar stumble through the main doors of the warehouse. What had happened to Tanek, he had no clue.

Bohuslav grinned slyly when he saw the scene.

"What are you waiting for? Execute them!"

CHAPTER TWENTY-THREE

THE FIGHT HAD been a vicious one, but it had been he who'd been victorious.

He'd often wondered in the time since their last meeting – in the time since their *first* meeting as a matter of fact – who would be the eventual winner. Both of them were sadistic bastards, quick to kill by whatever methods were available. But also, if time allowed, keen to savour the act of extinguishing life itself.

That hadn't been an option today, but Bohuslav didn't care. He'd tried to do this the slow way, to make Tanek and Hood perform a little before their deaths. But now it was over for at least one of them, he felt good. And he felt all the better for having got it over and done with quickly.

When Hood pushed him over that ledge, he'd thought that was the end of it. Grasping onto the rail, that bastard had practically kicked him off into the lion's den. Luckily, Bohuslav knew how to fall – and *who* to fall *on*, making use of a couple of guards and civilians below. He'd walked away relatively unscathed, but that had just been the start of it.

Tanek had been rushing towards him by the time he found his feet again. Bohuslav had just about managed to dodge the first attack, stumbling over the bodies he'd fallen on. As he rose, Bohuslav wielded his hammer, aiming specifically for the big lug's fingers. Tanek had let out a cry as they opened in pain, his axe flying out of his grasp. With his good hand, Tanek grabbed the length of the hammer and tugged, pulling Bohuslav in for a head butt. It was a glancing blow which opened up a cut over his right eye, disorientating him long enough for Tanek to yank the hammer from his clutches.

Tanek swung it, but Bohuslav ducked; slashing at Tanek with his sickle while he was down there. Most of these attacks missed their mark, but one opened a wound on Tanek's side. The giant snarled, bringing down the hammer on Bohuslav's shoulder in a blow that almost dislocated it. Bohuslav lashed out with the sickle again, slicing open Tanek's forearm and forcing him to drop the weapon. The larger man dived on him and they rolled over and over, the floor relatively empty now that the crowds had thinned. People were racing for the exit now that the majority of guards were either dead or wounded.

When they came to a stop, in the middle of the fighting pit, Bohuslav found that he was the one on top. Before he could embed his sickle in Tanek's flesh, though, the giant had thrown him off, flinging the Tsar onto his back.

As Tanek was getting to his feet, Bohuslav was already crawling around the rear. He slashed at the tendons at the back of the big man's ankles, severing one and cutting almost all the way through the other. Tanek dropped onto his knees, but still whirled, trying to grab Bohuslav.

The Tsar was reaching for something as well: he'd discovered the axe Hood had abandoned. Getting to his feet, he ran at Tanek with the weapon. The big man grabbed it just below the blade, squeezing the wood. Bohuslav could feel the power in that hand still, even after he'd struck it with the hammer. Tanek was threatening to break the handle in his grip, or at least snatch it away from Bohuslav. It was time to finish things.

"I *will* kill you," Tanek said.

Bohuslav jerked sideways suddenly, causing the end to snap off, but he'd put enough weight behind the move that the wooden shaft carried on moving... into Tanek's chest, rammed through a good few inches. The big man opened his eyes wide, looking down at the wood. "Just... just like the Sheriff..." he said, a slight smile playing on his lips. Lips that were growing redder by the second. "No... I must live... the promise... the–"

Then he fell and Bohuslav stood over him, watching as he breathed his last. To make sure, he bent and cut the man's throat open from one side to the other. "Goodbye Tanek." he spat. Then he began hobbling towards the door, leaving the body of the giant behind.

Bohuslav made it to the main entrance, the last person to leave. He used his sickle like a hook to drag himself through. Imagine his surprise when he saw what was happening outside. He'd assumed Hood had already fled, that he'd have to send out a search party to bring the escapee back: one dead, one to go. But here was the man himself, in pretty bad shape by the looks of things, being helped by one of his lot; a lone man sent in to free him. Ridiculous, the arrogance of those Rangers!

What made the picture perfect, however, was the forces already summoned to tackle him – a guard must have sounded the alarm. Even Bohuslav was impressed with the speed with which his men had assembled, the sheer amount of vehicles and soldiers that had gathered.

Looking across at Hood and smiling, he gave the order to kill them.

It was only then that Bohuslav noticed the men were not wearing the grey uniforms of his own army. Yes, they were similar – *very* similar in fact, but there were subtle differences. For one thing the symbol worn on the shoulders of their uniform was different. A symbol from history, the same yet new and updated – overlapping squares now marking out the shape. A shape that had struck terror into millions during the 1930s and 40s. And the vehicles, they weren't of Russian origin either. Not the standard issue they'd used against Hood back in England, nor those he'd been building up again since. Bohuslav had become quite an expert in scavenged military gear, and he knew which army had once used these vehicles. Which country.

The deciding factor had been when their commander had ordered for the troops to turn on *him*: turning their guns away from Hood and his Ranger, towards the Tsar.

"Wait," said Bohuslav, holding up his hands. "Wait a second–"

The commander shouted for them to open fire.

Bohuslav barely had time to breathe out, "God forgive me," before the soldiers pulled their triggers.

ROBERT AND MARK'S mouths fell open.

They'd thought this was it. That death had finally caught up with them. Staring down the barrels of so many guns and cannons, how could they possibly cheat death again this time? Robert felt more sorry for Mark than for himself; the boy had never really had time to become a man, to become the great Ranger Robert knew he would someday. Now all that was about to end.

To make matters worse, Bohuslav had somehow got away from Tanek and had come to watch. Had ordered their deaths, in fact; obviously too tired and pissed off to want to do it slowly anymore.

Robert held his breath as Bohuslav told his men to execute them. Then let it out, amazed, as all the guns were trained in the Tsar's direction.

It was only now, with the luxury of not having those guns facing them, that Robert took in what was really happening. Who those forces actually belonged to. Both he and Mark looked on as another order was given to kill Bohuslav.

Robert couldn't watch beyond the first salvo of bullets, keeping Bohuslav upright long after he should have dropped to the ground. The gunfire seemed to go on forever, until finally the last bang sounded. Mark touched his arm and Robert jumped, the loud cracks still ringing in his ears. He looked but couldn't see Bohuslav – just a red smear against the whiteness of the snow: all that was left after the automatic weapons had done their worst. Robert shivered again, but it had nothing to do with the snow all around.

The German soldiers turned back in their direction. What had happened with Bohuslav had been merely a stay of execution, it seemed. There was no bargaining with the Germans, either. Actually, it made things worse, because he and Mark had just been given a preview of what would happen to them.

As Robert steeled himself, he felt something touch his arm. He assumed it was Mark again, but when he turned his head he saw it was a rope dangling from above, which must have just dropped. "What..." began Robert, looking up, but there was no time for questions. Mark grabbed him, then shoved his foot into a loop at the bottom before winding his hand around the rope already lifting them. Robert grabbed on himself so Mark didn't have to carry him. He followed the line of the rope up towards a shape above – something dark in the sky; something huge. A helicopter.

The Germans were about to fire, and probably still would have blown them to pieces – had the Russian forces not turned up at that point. Too late to save their Tsar, they nevertheless engaged the Germans on the ground level, their own jeeps and tanks approaching through the streets, soldiers with more AK-47s opening fire. Now the Germans had more on their plate than a couple of escaping men on a rope. One vehicle exploded as Robert and Mark were pulled up and away from the scene – they had no idea whose side it had belonged to. While the rope was being wound back into the helicopter, the battle below raged on, and looked like it was going to for some time.

Next thing they knew, the pair of them were at the back door of the chopper, being helped in by familiar faces. Jack was there, taking his hand off the winch lever to grab Robert's own hand, while Sophie clapped her arms around Mark, planting a huge kiss on his lips.

And there, in front of Robert, was Mary. She smiled and ran to him. The helicopter lurched and he and Mary fell against one side. Robert grabbed onto some netting. He heard a garbled apology called from the front of the craft. "Hold on, I'm tryin' to pull 'er out of range of those bigger guns below, before they drag us into their fun and games."

"Bill?" shouted Robert. "Where in Heaven's name did you find *this*?"

He heard a chuckle, then the reply: "Like it? Thought I'd upscale a little. Amazing what those locals up North had kickin' round at their flyin' museum. They let me borrow their Chinook for a while. Whoops. "

They lurched again, this time to the other side, but Robert held Mary close. "And how did you know where to find me?"

"That was Mark," she told him. "Said he thought he remembered overhearing something about Moscow and the Tsar when he was kidnapped. Wouldn't tell us the rest. Insisted on going in alone, that he was the only one who could find you." Robert studied Mark's face, and knew full well that nothing had been overheard. For one thing the Native American wouldn't have been that careless. But Robert fully intended to get the truth out of Mark later on.

For a third time the helicopter lurched, but now they heard a noise from the open back, a whooshing sound as a missile flew past. Bill had lost it. Robert thanked God it wasn't a heat-seeker.

Next came machine-gun fire, but it was too close to be coming from the ground.

"Look!" Sophie was pointing at two aircraft, jet fighters with crosses on the side: formerly of the Luftwaffe. They were flying in as low as the chopper, on their trail while the rest of the Germans were otherwise engaged.

"Tornadoes," Jack called across to Robert, frowning.

"Blast," Robert said. "Just when I thought we might be out of the woods." That phrase, that sentence, connected with him and he suddenly had an idea. He took out the ash the Native American had given him, and then he shouted for Mark to hand him the pouch on his own belt. The pouch, like Robert's, which contained foliage and twigs from Sherwood. Well, if he couldn't get to the forest... Mark handed it to him and Robert quickly mixed the contents.

"What are you doing?" asked Mary, but he didn't reply. He was too busy willing this to work, praying that, although they weren't in Sherwood, this mobile link might be enough.

"What kind of weapons have you got back there?" asked Robert.

Jack looked at him sideways. "Nothing that can stop those, chief." But he went to fetch Robert's usual selection: bolas, arrows – some chemically tipped, Robert was pleased to see – a bow and his sword.

"Robert," Mary began, starting to look worried. "What are you going to do?"

"What I have to," he said, strangely starting to feel better as he hooked Mark's pouch onto his belt.

"Whatever it is you might need this." Jack tossed across his hooded top. "Your uniform."

Robert put it on, then found Mary clutching at the material on his arm. "Robert, listen to me. There's something you need to know before you do anything stupid. The Widow was right, Robert." She touched her stomach as she whispered the words. "Do you hear me? The Widow was right."

Robert paused, smiled, then kissed her on the top of the head. That was all the more reason to do this, to keep them safe. "I'll be back," he assured her, strapping on his weapons. He was feeling more invigorated by the second, the aches and wounds of the past few days fading – might have been the adrenalin of what he was about to do; might have been something else. Robert wasn't about to analyse it.

"Let me come with you," Mark said, but Robert held up his hand.

"You've already risked enough today. I've got this," he told his son, glad that Sophie was pulling him back, and that Mary was not trying to do the same to him. Robert took hold of the line from the winch, opening up the loop and slipping it around his waist. Then he pulled up his hood.

And he was gone, racing towards the open end of the Chinook. He heard the cries as he jumped, the length of rope slackening as he dropped.

Robert swung out, falling towards the first of the nearing fighters. When he was close enough, just metres away, he reached for his bow. Before he could do anything, there was another smattering of machine-gun fire. And suddenly he was dropping much faster than before.

Looking over his shoulder, he saw the line had been shot through. He was no longer attached to the chopper. Gritting his teeth, Robert threw back his shoulders and angled himself towards the first jet.

Robert slammed into the plane, just behind the cockpit, rolling over onto the join between the right wing and the trunk of the craft. He'd had just moments to register the shocked look of the pilot as he tumbled past. Robert hadn't been prepared for just how fast the wind would be coming at him, though, and he gripped the edge of the wing as the pilot attempted to shake him.

When the plane righted itself, Robert slid across and onto the main body of the craft again, so that the pilot couldn't see him. The man could only turn his head so far and as he didn't try to bank again, he probably assumed he'd shaken the hooded lunatic. The pilot began firing at the Chinook once more. Robert had to act. He began crawling along the spine of the plane inch by inch, until he reached the cockpit. Then he drew his broadsword and, pulling it back as far as he could – the wind almost taking it from his hand – he rammed it through the glass and into the pilot. The plane took an immediate dive, and Robert found himself sliding over the edge – hanging on only by the sword's handle, embedded in both the cockpit and slumping pilot.

He looked down to see the other Tornado below, rising swiftly. Robert waited until he could judge the angle, then dropped. As he fell, the first plane dipped suddenly, then banked. Robert barely looked; he was too busy pulling the bow from his shoulder, nocking one of the arrows with the chemical payload and preparing to fire at the second Tornado. He had a split second to do this, so his aim had to be dead on. Ignoring everything around him, he targeted one of the missiles the plane was carrying.

The wind suddenly took him sideways, and his aim was spoilt – the arrow going wide. Robert continued to fall, passing the Tornado now on his way down. He could see the pilot smirking, then opening fire himself, but Robert pitched himself forward, torpedoing downwards and underneath the jet.

Flipping himself around and onto his back, coasting on the breeze, he drew another arrow and fired upwards. This time it struck its target, the chemicals heating up the missile in seconds, igniting this, and the plane carrying it, seconds later.

As Robert continued to fall, down and down, his only compensation was that he was leaving the Tornado as a burning wreck to fall from the sky. He continued to fall, letting his bow go as he closed his eyes. There was no way back to the helicopter, the rope well out of reach.

He resigned himself to the fact that this really was his final act, but he'd kept all those he loved safe from the missiles and guns. He'd done the task that he set out to when he first left the forest. The Rangers would be in good hands with Mark, who'd shown his leadership qualities on this mission.

The one regret he did have was that he could never tell Mary again how much he loved her, how much finding her had meant. Would never feel her in his arms again. And would never get to see his child be born, or grow.

Robert felt himself still falling – there couldn't be more sky left, surely, he was going so fast.

Then he hit something. Not the ground, which he was rapidly hurtling towards. But something soft. Some*one*.

He opened his eyes again to see Jack swinging on the rope, his cap long gone. The length of it was still dropping, so the wrestler had hitched a ride and gone down with it. Now the larger man was matching Robert's descent, and had closed in on him thanks to Bill's skilful flying. As he swung again, this time Jack reached out and grabbed Robert by the hood of his top. He heard the big man yell as he took the strain; Robert doubted there was another person alive who was strong enough to do that.

Robert turned and again took hold of the rope, gripping it tightly as the winch lever was pulled by someone up in the chopper. They stopped in mid-descent, then were suddenly being winched back up towards the helicopter.

He'd been given *yet another* chance. His life extended, watched over by whatever spirits the Native American had been talking about.

But he also knew that his luck really would run out one day.

And as Robert was pulled back up to the Chinook, looking forward to holding Mary again – something he hoped to do so many more times – he couldn't help dwelling on that thought.

Wondering if when that day came, he might not be wishing that Jack had simply let him fall.

CHAPTER TWENTY-FOUR

LOEWE WAS FUMING.

It hadn't been a good week. Usually, he couldn't care less about what happened out there in the real world; he was safe and sound in the Army of the New Order's headquarters. But the setbacks his organisation had suffered this week had a knock-on effect, threatened what he had established in Germany. As a leader of these men – even if he was only a fake leader – it was his responsibility to take action, to punish those responsible for losing all those vehicles and equipment in Scotland and Wales to Hood's men. As a person whose lifestyle was in jeopardy, he was frightened. And when Loewe was frightened, he got mad.

"On top of all that," he bellowed at young Schaefer, "you okay'd a mission to Russia, which has practically sparked a war."

"I thought it necessary to retrieve the man responsible."

"Tanek. A man *you* hired, let us not forget. Did you succeed?"

Schaefer was silent.

"We lost tanks, jeeps, countless men – and *two* aircraft in the process!"

"Hood was–"

Loewe skirted the edge of his desk, fists clenching and unclenching. The Alsatians rose as well, snarling. "Hood! Fucking Hood! I'm sick to death of hearing about him! This whole thing has been a catalogue of disasters from start to finish." He wagged a finger at Schaefer. "And I'm holding you responsible." This time he had to, Loewe had no choice. It had been Schaefer's idea to supply both the Widow and the Dragon with arms, his idea to have it overseen by that olive-skinned idiot.

"The Russians are in disarray themselves, sir, now that the Tsar is dead."

That was something at least, but it also meant they might be after revenge; might want to carry on this war until both their sides had nothing left. And besides, it didn't make up for the humiliation. Someone still had to pay. Loewe's reputation as a ball breaker was at stake. As much as he relied on the bespectacled man in front of him, it was going to have to be *his* head that Loewe took.

"I'm sorry it has come to this," he told Schaefer. "Guards!" Two members of the New Order were inside the room immediately, and Schaefer looked worriedly over his shoulder at them. He knew what was coming next, knew that the men were here not only to stop him from getting away but to witness what came next. He'd seen it happen with Mayer not that long ago. A trickle of sweat ran down his forehead, dripping onto the left lens of his glasses. Any moment now Schaefer would be on his knees, begging Loewe not to set the dogs on him. Any moment he would–

Schaefer began to laugh.

Loewe's brow furrowed; that was not the reaction he'd expected. He'd seen men cry, whine, shit themselves in this position. Never laugh. *His mind must be gone*, thought Loewe. *All the more reason to put this sorry excuse for a human being out of his misery.*

"You're sorry. *You're* sorry?" Schaefer was shaking his head, the laughter still pouring out. The Alsatians' growls were getting louder; Loewe would let them off the leash in a moment. The young man wouldn't be laughing then. "You complete and utter moron," said Schaefer. "You haven't got a clue what's going on, have you?"

"How dare you talk to me that way!" Loewe said. Now he was livid. "Oh, you've asked for this." Loewe clicked his fingers for the dogs to attack.

Nothing happened.

Loewe clicked his fingers again. The dogs continued to growl but remained where they were, flanking the desk. "Get him! What are you waiting for?"

Schaefer laughed harder now, so hard he had to take off his glasses and rub his eyes because they were watering. "You haven't got a clue because you can't see further than your office, than all this." Loewe was clicking his fingers frantically, but the dogs were still ignoring him. Schaefer whistled sharply, and at last they sprang into action; not leaping to attack, but coming to heel. The young man replaced his glasses. "Who do you think oversaw their training, Loewe? Who has overseen *everything* around here?" He touched a hand to his chest. "Because you're good at the talking, but not so great at the strategies, are you?"

Loewe licked his lips, realising he was on thin ice but knowing there were still two guards in the room who could shoot the dogs if necessary. Schaefer's little back up plan hadn't succeeded quite yet. "Like the strategies you fucked up this week?"

"I'll give you that one. Things haven't gone exactly to plan. But there's always the future, hopefully. One, sadly, that you will never witness."

"Men!" Loewe roared. "Shoot him, right now!" The guards, like the dogs, did nothing. Now Loewe began to worry, to grow even more frightened.

"You see, I know who you really are, *General*. I have done for a while. And now the men know as well; I've told them. Your loyalty is not to the cause. It is to yourself, pretender."

Loewe opened his mouth, the mouth that he could rely on nine times out of ten to talk him out of a scrape. This must have been the tenth time, though, because nothing emerged.

"The New Order was never meant to be yours." Schaefer took a step forward and the dogs followed. "My choice of liaison wasn't an accident, either. Poor Tanek once knew my cousin, Henrik. He was part of De Falaise's army. Hood killed him."

Loewe found his voice again, sensing an opportunity to turn this against the young upstart. "So, this was about revenge?"

Schaefer shook his head again. "No. Family is important to me, but so is my country. Hood represented... *still* represents a threat. But enough of this chit chat. Let's get on with things, shall we?"

Loewe backed up against the desk, holding a hand in front of him. "Listen, please... Guards! Men!" he called beyond his office, to the control room, into the HQ itself, but nobody came. Schaefer was in charge here. The *real* conman. "Please, we can talk about this. Work it out and–"

Schaefer gave two sharp whistles and the dogs leaped forward, one springing up to go for Loewe's throat while the other sank its teeth into his privates. He felt pain like he'd never experienced before. As he lay back on the desk, the Alsatians' teeth were everywhere, ripping chunks out of his arms, legs, hands and feet in a feeding frenzy. He tried to reach up for help, but the dogs were weighing him down. All those times he'd given the order for them to attack, he'd never once considered what it might be like on the receiving end... until now.

"What is it they say?" he vaguely heard Schaefer comment, through ears that were being ripped to shreds, but realised now quite how insane he was. "Cry havoc and let slip the dogs of war, General!" There was laughter again, before his young Second concluded with: "Well, I would love to stay and watch these final moments, but I have places to be. I would like to say it has been a pleasure, but that wouldn't be true at all. So instead I will simply say, *auf wiedersehen.*"

Loewe didn't hear any more, only felt a few more seconds of torture before passing out. His last thoughts were of his very first lie, about the dog he'd blamed for trailing mud into the house.

"Was that you who trailed that mud into the house, Achim?"
"No Mütti, I swear."

Remembered its whine as his mother had thrashed it.

And he thought about how, in the end, that dog – through its brethren – had finally got its own revenge.

Finally had its day.

First a wedding, now a funeral.

Not just for one person, but many. The Reverend Tate had presided over the internment of all those dead at New Hope, even the Germans, who were buried out in the woodland. The villagers who'd been killed during their brave offensive had found their ultimate resting place in the graveyard, with Tate leading the prayers for them. It had been a touching and poignant day, the service attended by those still left alive, as well as many from Nottingham Castle – including Mary and, yes, Robert had even shown his face, though he seemed embarrassed and ashamed to be there.

Probably because of what he'd said to Karen Shipley, even though he'd relented and sent Rangers to assist. She'd been there on the day also, pushing a recovering Darryl in a wheelchair to pay their respects. Doctor Jeffreys' assistant Sat had been able to stem the bleeding from his wounds after the battle, until they could get him back to the castle for proper medical care – along with Graham Leicester – but could do nothing for Andy. Nor for Gwen, ultimately.

It was her grave Tate was standing over today, mourning the loss of this courageous woman who'd died after Tanek had shot her. She'd died cradling her beloved son, Clive Jr, who Tate had saved from a Morningstar Servitor himself. The cult had gone to ground again after being defeated here by the Rangers – those taken captive during the fight having already committed suicide, as was their way. He had to admit, it had been a shock to see them there as well as the Germans, and Tate had reported the fact to Robert immediately upon his return from Russia; while the rest of the surviving German prisoners – including a very battered captive they'd discovered in the Red Lion – were being locked up in Nottingham's hotel jails. The Reverend doubted they'd see the evil cultists or Germans again anytime soon, but just in case Robert had allowed a contingent of Rangers to remain in New Hope to make sure.

"I'd like to stay as well," the Reverend had informed him. "These people need my guidance, Robert. They've lost their way a little."

Robert had agreed, but was sad to see Tate leaving again, especially when he was so settled now at the castle. However, he also recognised the fact that the holy man had been there at the village's birth, that he'd been best friends with the man who founded it. Perhaps it was time to take the place back to that original vision, under the Rangers' protection. Tate also owed Gwen – buried beside that man, the person she'd loved with all her heart – because he'd been too late once more. And this time it had cost her dearly.

As for Clive Jr, Darryl and Karen had offered to bring up the child. "It's what Gwen would have wanted," Darryl told him. Tate had a feeling Karen was only helping out to get closer to the man she quite clearly adored, but then maybe that wasn't a bad thing. In time, perhaps they'd become the family that Clive, Gwen and Clive Jr should have been. And while Tate was on the scene, he'd make sure that not only were the villagers brought back into the flock, but also that Gwen's son was taught right from wrong according to The Good Book.

Tate wiped a tear from his eye, saying the words he'd said every day for a month now. "I'm sorry, Gwen. So sorry."

As he turned away and began his walk down the path of the graveyard, Tate paused and looked back over his shoulder. Was it his imagination, or had he felt a presence? Just for a second seen a glimpse of a figure. Someone on the periphery of the graveyard itself? Someone who might also have come to pay their respects, but hadn't ventured inside for whatever reason?

Tate shook his head. Just his imagination, he told himself.

That was all.

THE TREES HID him from view as he sped through the forest.

He was alone today, but then he needed to be. He would spend time with Mark here soon enough, spend time with Mary elsewhere, but first Robert needed to reconnect with Sherwood. Needed to feel the grass beneath his feet, hear the birdsong; needed to fly.

All was well back at the castle, and reports were coming in that the establishment of both the Welsh and Scottish arms of the Rangers was going very well. Dale had asked to remain as liaison in Cardiff, ostensibly to help with that regional chapter's growth, but reading between the lines he'd fallen for this girl Jack had told them about. It also appeared to be catching, because the big man himself had talked quite a bit about the girl's aunty, Meghan. Robert hadn't met her yet, but there was talk of the woman coming to visit Nottingham. Hopefully she would help Jack get over the heartache he'd experienced with Adele.

Tate was the only one sad at the moment, because of the way things had gone at New Hope – about not being able to save Gwen. But, helping to piece that community back together was at least taking his mind off things.

And their enemies, including the Morningstars, Germans and the Russians seemed to be out of the picture for now, thankfully ; either lying low or fighting each other. What would happen in the long term, though, was anyone's guess.

He'd been thinking about that a lot recently: the future. Thinking about what Mark would become. The young man had told Robert when they were alone that he'd seen the Tsar in a dream, back when they'd been camping out in Sherwood, before the Native American did his thing. "I just *knew* where I'd find you," Mark said. "Don't ask me to explain, because I can't. And definitely not to anyone but you. That's one of the reasons I couldn't tell the others. Plus I wanted to return the favour by saving *you* this time."

Robert also wondered what his new daughter or son might be like, whether they'd have the same kind of insights eventually. He supposed he'd find out in time.

Robert's legs pumped harder. With his hood up he was like a green blur streaking through the forest. It was as if he was getting to know it again, everything fresh and new – and that was re-energising him. He should have felt old, worn out, but instead right now he felt so young.

He'd found evidence of the man in black's presence in Sherwood, primarily the sweat lodge he'd constructed and used to tame the forest somehow. Robert had released the contents of the pouch here, a formality but one which he knew he had to go through for things to get back to normal. For the magic – the dreams – to return. They hadn't so far, but he figured that was only because they were granting him a desperately needed respite. He'd been through so much over the past few weeks and he was far from ready for any more emergencies.

It was strange, but he still felt the Native American here today as he was running. Felt like he might be behind the next tree about to spring out, or watching from a distance. Robert scrutinised every single patch of blackness as the day was waning, in case it might be him. No, the Native American had his own agenda. Something to do with what the Tsar had given him.

Just a stone, Robert told himself, but he didn't believe that for a minute – and he also wondered whether there were more where it had come from.

As if to prove him wrong, the shadows ahead lengthened and he saw movement behind one of the oaks. Robert stopped, his bow primed in seconds, ready for another duel if necessary.

But it hadn't been *the* Shadow. Robert eased back on the tension when he saw his old friend. The creature he'd left alive all that time ago, now walking through the forest towards him. Not scared at all, not worried Robert was going to hunt or kill it. Because the stag *was* him. He'd seen that so many times in those dreams.

It was wounded, or had been – red stains on the back of its neck. Robert was only guessing, but perhaps the animal had been trying to defend Sherwood against its intruder, in lieu of him being around.

They regarded each other, just as they'd done that first time – an understanding passing between them. They were guardians of worlds: both real and imagined. They were the stuff of legend, just like this place.

The stuff of song, of words and of deeds. They had always been here and always would be.

And really, their story was only just beginning.

THE END

Paul Kane has been writing professionally for almost fifteen years. His genre journalism has appeared in such magazines as *The Dark Side, Death Ray, Fangoria, SFX, Dreamwatch* and *Rue Morgue*, and his first non-fiction book was the critically acclaimed *The Hellraiser Films and Their Legacy*. His award-winning short fiction has appeared in magazines and anthologies on both sides of the Atlantic, and has been collected in *Alone (In the Dark), Touching the Flame, FunnyBones* and *Peripheral Visions*. His novella *Signs of Life* reached the shortlist of the British Fantasy Awards 2006, *The Lazarus Condition* was introduced by Mick Garris, creator of *Masters of Horror*, and *RED* featured artwork from Dave (*The Graveyard Book*) McKean. As Special Publications Editor of the British Fantasy Society he worked with authors like Brian Aldiss, Ramsey Campbell, Muriel Gray, Robert Silverberg and many more, plus he is the co-editor of *Hellbound Hearts* for Pocket Books (Simon and Schuster), an anthology of original stories inspired by Clive Barker's novella. In 2008 his zombie story 'Dead Time' was turned into an episode of the Lionsgate/NBC TV series *Fear Itself*, adapted by Steve Niles (*30 Days of Night*) and directed by Darren Lynn Bousman (*SAW II-IV*). He also scripted the short film *The Opportunity* which premiered at Cannes in 2009. Paul's previous books for Abaddon's Afterblight Chronicles – *Arrowhead* and *Broken Arrow* – detail the adventures of a post apocalyptic version of Robin Hood, and his other novels include *Of Darkness and Light* (with cover art from the award-winning Vincent Chong) and *The Gemini Factor* (with an introduction from Peter Atkins, screenwriter of *Hellraiser II-IV* and *Wishmaster*). His website, which has featured guest writers such as Stephen King, James Herbert and Neil Gaiman, can be found at www.shadow-writer.co.uk He currently lives in Derbyshire, UK, with his wife – the author Marie O'Regan – his family, and a black cat called Mina.

ACKNOWLEDGEMENTS

Thanks again, first and foremost, to editor extraordinaire Jonathan Oliver for his faith not only in the idea, but in this trilogy of Hood reworkings. Thanks to Jason Kingsley for being equally behind the books, and many thanks to Jenni Hill for her insightful edits on this one. My thanks also to Mark Harrison, who once more brought my protagonist to life in a stunning cover, quite possibly the best of the three. A heartfelt thank you to Richard Carpenter for his kind words and encouragement, not to mention his stamp of approval. A huge shout out to Trevor Preston for his tireless checking of military and weapons details, and for answering all my crazy questions. Thanks to Joe Daley at Seraphim, who invited us to the set of *Clive Barker's Book of Blood* in Edinburgh which sowed the seeds for the Widow. And thanks to my Welsh pals – you know who you are – the old homestead is once again yours, fellas. Thank you to David Bradley and the gang at *SFX*, not only for such a great mag, but also for inviting me to be a guest at their first Weekender. I thoroughly enjoyed myself chatting to fans of the *Arrowhead* books – and it helped immensely in the writing of this one. Thanks to my support mechanism of friends and family, who've kept me going through the writing of all the Hood adventures. And last, but never least, I want to thank my darling wife Marie, who helps me so much – not just workwise, but in life generally. We've shared this journey through the forest together, and for that I'll always be grateful. Love ya, sweetheart.